"Juliette Fay [...] [...]y researched nov [...] [...]ully drawn female characters. Billie and Charlotte will capture readers' hearts in this powerful story of female friendship, strength, and ultimately love."
    —Jillian Cantor, *USA Today* bestselling author of *Beautiful Little Fools*

"*The Harvey Girls* may be Juliette Fay's best historical novel to date, full of unforgettable women, juicy conflict, and fascinating facts about an under-explored chapter in the history of the American West. A must-read."
    —Greer Macallister, bestselling author of *The Thirteenth Husband* and *The Arctic Fury*

"A heartwarming, satisfying read centering on two well-drawn characters from opposite sides of the track. Compulsively readable and immersive, Fay writes another winner!"
    —Heather Webb, *USA Today* bestselling author of *Queens of London*

"Fay's enjoyable . . . tale of friendship, love, and tribulations, set mostly in the breathtaking Grand Canyon area, is an intriguing look into the world of the Harvey Girls, with a well-developed plot and characters that bring the era to life."
    —*Library Journal*, starred review

"This is historical fiction at its best; Juliette Fay has truly created magic on the page."
    —Kristin Harmel, *New York Times* bestselling author of *The Paris Daughter*, on *City of Flickering Light*

"Perfectly encapsulates the social mores and pressures of the early twentieth century . . . don't miss this page turner!"
    —Sara Gruen, #1 *New York Times* bestselling author of *Water for Elephants*, on *The Tumbling Turner Sisters*

Also by Juliette Fay

Shelter Me
Deep Down True
The Shortest Way Home
The Tumbling Turner Sisters
City of Flickering Light
Catch Us When We Fall
The Half of It

The Harvey Girls

Juliette Fay

G

GALLERY BOOKS

NEW YORK   AMSTERDAM/ANTWERP   LONDON
TORONTO   SYDNEY/MELBOURNE   NEW DELHI

G

Gallery Books
An Imprint of Simon & Schuster, LLC
1230 Avenue of the Americas
New York, NY 10020

This book is a work of fiction. Any references to historical events, real people, or real places are used fictitiously. Other names, characters, places, and events are products of the author's imagination, and any resemblance to actual events or places or persons, living or dead, is entirely coincidental.

First Gallery Books trade paperback edition August 2025

GALLERY BOOKS and colophon are registered trademarks of Simon & Schuster, LLC

Simon & Schuster strongly believes in freedom of expression and stands against censorship in all its forms. For more information, visit BooksBelong.com.

For information about special discounts for bulk purchases, please contact Simon & Schuster Special Sales at 1-866-506-1949 or business@simonandschuster.com.

The Simon & Schuster Speakers Bureau can bring authors to your live event. For more information or to book an event, contact the Simon & Schuster Speakers Bureau at 1-866-248-3049 or visit our website at www.simonspeakers.com.

Interior design by Erika R. Genova

Manufactured in the United States of America

1 3 5 7 9 10 8 6 4 2

Library of Congress Cataloging-in-Publication Data is available.

ISBN 978-1-6680-9506-5
ISBN 978-1-6680-9507-2 (ebook)

For those who've had to flee in fear or been driven from their homelands, which, by way of our ancestors, is all of us;

For those who feed us: the farmers, grocery clerks, cooks, bakers, baristas, delivery drivers, food bank workers, and servers;

And for the waitresses, past, present, and future.

"Wild buffalo fed the early traveler to the west, and for that, they put his head on a nickel. Well, Fred Harvey took up where the buffalo left off. For what he has done for the traveler, one of his waitress's pictures (with an armload of delicious ham and eggs) should be placed on both sides of every dime. He has kept the West in food—and wives."

—Will Rogers, entertainer, cowboy, newspaper columnist, and social commentator (1879–1935)

Prologue

In 1853, a seventeen-year-old named Fred Harvey emigrated from London to New York City with only a few dollars in his pocket. He got a job as a pot walloper (dishwasher) at a popular restaurant, where he rose up the ranks to line cook and nurtured a lifelong passion for fine dining.

By the age of thirty he was working as a traveling railroad agent, but he never gave up the dream of owning his own restaurant. At the time, steam engines stopped every hundred miles or so to refuel with coal and water. Rustic food stands cropped up at these stations to serve hungry passengers. At best, the offerings were simple; at worst, they resulted in death by food poisoning.

Fred was certain that if he could provide high-quality food at these stops, both he and the railroad would prosper. He approached the Atchison, Topeka and Santa Fe Railway, which had stops from Kansas throughout the Southwest, and in 1876, Fred opened his first restaurant at the Topeka, Kansas, depot. The reception was so enthusiastic that many more Harvey Houses, as they were called, soon followed. In fact, the slogan of the ATSF became "Meals by Fred Harvey." Thus began the first hospitality empire in America.

Fred's success was achieved through razor-sharp business acumen and an unwavering demand for quality. His restaurants had white tablecloths, fine silver, excellent food, and arguably the best coffee in the nation. He was remarkably unafraid to try new business methods. This was never more evident than when he hired an all-female waitstaff.

At the time, women's options for respectable employment were limited to jobs such as being a nurse, secretary, or teacher. Domestic or factory work was for the lower classes. Restaurant service was considered only a few rungs up the ladder from prostitution. Fred Harvey's problem, however, was that his male waiters tended to get drunk and into fights.

He solved this problem—for himself and for approximately one hundred thousand women who would become not waitresses but "Harvey Girls"—by instituting puritanical rules. They wore uniforms that were about as alluring as a nun's habit, lived in dorms with strict curfews, and were prohibited from dating other Harvey employees. They had to comport themselves with utmost propriety at all times or risk immediate termination.

The irony is that in return for complying with all these rules, they received unprecedented freedom. Harvey Girls were better paid than women in almost any other profession and could spend that money during generous vacation time, during which they were allowed to ride the trains and stay at other Harvey Houses at no cost. Former Harvey Girls often reported that it was a remarkable education, not only in how to do things well and with care, but also in how to take control of their own destinies.

Many also found love. Until well into the 1900s, the Southwest was populated predominantly by men—ranchers, farmers, prospectors, railroad workers. As the saying went, there were "no ladies west of Dodge City, and no women west of Albuquerque." Local men were all too happy with the influx of females into their communities.

It's estimated that about half of all Harvey Girls chose to remain in the Southwest after their service ended, many marrying and raising families there. Thousands of baby boys from these matches were named Fred or Harvey.

Such an honor was understandable. The man not only fed the Southwest and taught it manners . . . he was also indirectly responsible for populating it.

Part 1
1926

One

Charlotte felt the woman's scrutiny like heat from a flame too close to her skin. She forced herself not to flinch away from it; flinching, she'd learned, only invited more trouble.

"And you've never waitressed before?" Miss Steele said lightly, as if to counterpoise the obvious fact that she was making far more important assessments. Charlotte could practically see the cogs turning behind the woman's benevolent facade.

"No, I . . . well, I worked at a milliner's shop, and I served people. But not food."

A hat shop. Even now it was hard to believe. That was not the life he'd described, the life he'd promised. But becoming a shopgirl was the least of it. Promises had fallen like autumn leaves on the Boston Common, hadn't they?

"That's just fine. We prefer girls without prior experience. They tend to have fewer bad habits to correct."

"Bad habits?" Charlotte was certain that if she'd had any—which she doubted—they'd been trained out of her at the highly esteemed Winsor School for Girls. "A Sound Mind in a Sound Body" was their motto, and she'd taken it very much to heart. Until lately.

"Like serving a beverage without a tray, or wearing an apron with a spot on it," Miss Steele explained. "Or smiling a little too long at a customer."

"Flirting."

"Exactly."

Miss Steele was the head of personnel for Fred Harvey, and she wore the confidence of her position plainly but without condescension. Charlotte had never heard of a woman achieving so high an appointment in such a large company and assumed that Miss Steele was a member of the extended Harvey family. Either that or she knew things they preferred to remain private.

"Keep your friends close and your enemies closer," her father often said when he'd returned from a particularly trying day at his shipping company. She'd been living the "enemies closer" part of that adage for far too long now.

"I don't flirt." This seemed important to say. In the last two years, Charlotte had become a keen observer of what to say—and, more crucially, what *not* to say—at any given moment.

"I'm glad to hear that." Miss Steele studied her face, particularly her right eye. She glanced down at Charlotte's left hand, the one that had, until an hour ago, worn a gold band. "You're not married?"

"No."

Sometimes you had to fib. That was important, too. Charlotte fought the urge to touch the tender skin under her eye. She had waited a week for the swelling to go down and the car-tire black to fade to jaundice yellow.

"And there's nothing keeping you from traveling far from home?"

"Oh, no. Not at all." Charlotte almost laughed. *Quite the opposite.*

Miss Steele pursed her lips and looked out the window. The office was on the second floor of Union Station in Kansas City, Missouri, and a cold March rain speckled the panes, obscuring the train yard and the city beyond. Charlotte curled her toes in her best black patent leather pumps with the champagne-colored bows. Well, the bows were gone now; one had come off, and she couldn't go around with one bow, so she'd torn the other from its spot and tucked it away. For what purpose she couldn't say. A reminder of better times, perhaps, or the abysmal depth of her own stubborn foolishness.

The woman leveled a meaningful gaze. "Miss Turner, I feel I must ask about your eye. You seem to have received a blow of some kind."

I was reaching for a book on a high shelf at the library, and it just leapt out at me! She'd say it with a self-deprecating chuckle.

But sometimes you had to tell the truth, which Miss Steele seemed to intuit anyway.

"Yes," Charlotte said. "And if you give me a job, the bruise will fade. If you don't, it will simply be renewed."

———

Billie had heard that the famous Fred Harvey food was the best in the West, but the biscuit tasted like a mouthful of flour straight from the sack.

"Now, eat that," said her mother. The remnants of Lorna Mac-Tavish's Scottish brogue came out when she was tired or worried. Today she was both. "We can't have you fainting away up there. You're looking awfully peely-wally."

"You have it." Billie pushed the plate down the lunch counter in Union Station. "Or save it for the ride back."

"We'll be splitting it, if you don't pull yourself together."

Billie blinked the tears back from her pale lashes. "I don't want to go," she whispered.

"Och, dinna fash, now," murmured Lorna to her eldest child. "There's a whole big world out there! I never got to see it, but now you will."

"Who'll help with the kids and the washing? Who'll get dinner on when the mending's due for the Suttons?" Billie fingered tears out of the hollows under her eyes. "Not Malcolm."

"Your father works hard, and don't call him by his given name, cheeky," Lorna scoffed. "You want to go and haul bricks for ten hours and then fetch dinner for nine squalling bairns?"

"Maw, I don't want to leave them. I . . . I don't want to leave you."

She had seen her mother cry only once, after her toddling sister Sorcha had fallen into the great wash barrel and drowned. Lorna smiled hard, but the tears trickled down her face nonetheless. She put her knobby hand on Billie's, the fingers softer than rough work should've allowed. "You'll have your chance to see new places and have an adventure! You'll earn good money, and then you'll come back to me, and we'll all be together."

"Don't make me go . . . "

A sob broke out of the woman's chest. "If I had any choice in the matter, lass, you'd never leave my side."

———

Billie waited in one of the chairs outside the personnel office as her mother had instructed. The letter inviting her for an interview was clutched in her hand along with a clipping of the advertisement they'd answered.

Wanted, young women, 18–30 years of age, of good moral character, attractive and intelligent, as waitresses in Harvey Eating Houses on the Santa Fe Railway in the West. Wages $25 per month with room and board. Liberal tips customary. Experience not necessary. Write Fred Harvey, Union Station, Kansas City, Missouri.

She didn't know why her mother had insisted she have the ad but could only guess that Lorna MacTavish had seen more than her fair share of offers reneged, and those words indicated a contract of sorts. Billie would supply the good moral character, intelligence, and fair looks Fred Harvey required; now he had to hold up his end.

That business about being eighteen . . . well . . . her maw always said she was born fully grown. Wise beyond her years and—at five feet, ten inches—taller than most of the men she knew: her father and his friends from the brick factory, her younger brothers, and even the other boys at school. Of course, it had been several years since she'd stopped attending school so she could help her mother with her washing and mending business. Maybe those schoolboys had grown.

Billie's mother had bobbed her long blond hair to make her look more grown-up. "It's the fashion now," Lorna had said. "All the flippers wear it."

"Flappers," Billie had corrected her. She still missed her braids.

But sitting on that hard wooden chair in the seemingly endless hallway outside Fred Harvey's office, there was nothing she missed more than her mother.

"This one, all we did is feed her," Lorna would say with a hint of pride when someone complimented her on her daughter's hard work, pleasant demeanor, kindness to the younger children, or even that silky straight blond hair. As if Lorna's love and guidance all those years had been unnecessary, and Billie would've turned out well all the same. But Billie knew plenty of girls whose mothers were too angry or worn out from hard luck to give any such kind attention to their older children, focused as they were on just keeping the younger ones alive. Most of those girls had gone hard and mean, and Billie had to assume she would have, too.

It was on her mother's insistence that Billie read the paper every day. "It's your education!" Lorna would say. "The world is a damn sight bigger than this speck of sod."

Billie herself had seen the advertisement for Harvey Girls, as they were called, and remarked on it as they took a few minutes to eat their lunch of hard bread and a bit of cheese one day. Lorna had seized upon the idea immediately. "It's a fortune they're offering, and you'll see the country! I wish they took tired old ladies, but I'm three years past the deadline." The fact that at fifteen Billie was three years below the deadline was scoffed away.

The money was, in fact, a fortune. Twenty-five dollars a month! Her father made forty dollars, and her mother about fifteen from taking in other people's sweaty, dirty, sometimes even bloody clothes. With room and board included, Billie could send virtually all of that vast sum home. It would mean her younger siblings could continue with school, her father could fix his broken-down truck, and her mother . . . her mother might be able to get just a little bit of a rest from time to time.

Billie didn't want the job.

But she knew she had to get it.

A woman with blunt-cut brown hair and a matronly but fashionable blue serge dress opened the door. "Wilamena MacTavish?" she said. Her eyes widened as Billie rose from the seat to her full height. Billie quickly slouched down just a bit, so as not to look so ungainly.

She followed the woman into the office, and to Billie's surprise, she sat down behind a large mahogany desk. "I'm Miss Steele," she began.

"Oh. I . . . I thought . . . ," stammered Billie.

"Yes?"

"Aren't I supposed to talk to Fred Harvey?"

The woman smiled, and Billie could tell she was biting the inside of her lip to keep from laughing. Billie slunk a little lower in her chair.

"Oh dear, I'm sorry," said Miss Steele. "It's been a long day, and I suppose I've got a little bit of the giggles. Does that ever happen to you when you're tired? You get the giggles?"

"Oh yes," Billie said solemnly. "Certainly."

"Let me explain. Fred Harvey started the company many years ago, back in 1876. He passed away in 1901, and his sons took over the business."

"But that was twenty-five years ago!"

"Yes."

"So why do all the railroad advertisements say 'Meals by Fred Harvey' if he's not still doing the cooking?"

Miss Steele was biting her lip again. She coughed into her hand several times. "Mr. Harvey never actually prepared the meals himself, dear. It was his company, and he hired people as chefs, butchers, pastry men . . . "

"Are you saying he never cooked a meal even *once*?"

Miss Steele smiled indulgently. Billie knew that sort of grin—hadn't she smiled like that a thousand times when her younger sisters and brothers misunderstood something? She felt her cheeks flush for shame.

"He was no stranger to the kitchens in his many restaurants," said Miss Steele. "In fact there are those who might say he took an excessive interest in how every last thing was prepared and presented, right down to the butter pats." She clasped her hands and set them on the vast expanse of dark wood. "Now, shall we commence the interview?"

Miss Steele wanted to know about her life, where she'd grown up, how long she'd gone to school. Lorna had warned Billie that she'd have to lie and say she was older, with more schooling than she actually had. Fifteen with a sixth-grade education would not get her that job. They had practiced, and Billie felt she had sufficiently presented herself as qualified.

But Miss Steele was not laughing anymore, nor even smiling. "You seem a little young to me. Perhaps you might apply again in a year or so."

Billie's heart soared. She didn't have to go! She could apply again in a year, and a year was a long, long time.

But then she thought of her mother waiting downstairs with only one return train ticket in her hand. They barely had enough money for that. How could Billie ever tell her they needed another?

"Miss Steele . . . " Billie unclenched her hands from her lap and laid them gently on the desk between them, willing them not to tremble.

"Yes, Miss MacTavish?"

"Can I just say . . . thank you. Thank you very kindly for giving me the chance to come here and talk with you. And that I'd be proud . . . so very proud . . . to be a Harvey Girl. It would be a . . . a crowning achievement." (She'd read that phrase in the newspaper once and puzzled over it. When did anyone get a crown for achieving anything? You were lucky to get a handshake.)

Miss Steele's scrutiny, dark eyes taking in the newly cut hair and cheeks that had only lately lost their roundness, seemed to last an hour, though it was likely only a moment.

"You're well-spoken. You say you're a high school graduate?"

"Oh, yes." A thought occurred to Billie, and she added quickly, "I would've brought my diploma, excepting it was setting on the piano for all to see when a strong breeze blew it straight out the window." She shook her head mournfully. "We never could find it. Must have ended up in an owl's nest."

She'd never told so many lies in all her life! They no more had a piano than they had Charles Lindbergh sitting in his monoplane behind the clothesline.

Miss Steele's face went quizzical for a moment, and Billie was certain she'd lost the job.

"All right," said Miss Steele. "We'll give you a try. You're to report here tomorrow morning at seven thirty sharp. Does that suit you?"

"Oh, yes! Thank you, Miss Steele! I'll be ready and waiting."

She certainly hadn't lied about waiting. She told her mother the news just in time for Lorna to catch the last train back to Table Rock, Nebraska. They barely had a moment to say their good-byes.

"Now work hard, and they'll all love you," Lorna murmured into Billie's tearstained cheek as she clutched her daughter one last time. "And stay as good as you are."

"Maw . . . ," Billie whispered. "Think of me."

"I'll be doing nothing else till I see you again, darling girl." Before the catch in her throat turned to sobs, Lorna kissed her first-born child and closest friend, pressed the half-eaten biscuit into her hand, and strode quickly toward the tracks.

Before she'd gone, she had scouted out the perfect well-lit spot for her daughter to await the dawn: between the ticket windows and the all-night Fred Harvey lunch counter. Billie sank down onto the wooden bench, pulled her wool cap low over her brow, and had herself a long, silent cry.

———————————

Charlotte chose the darkest, most untraveled corner of the cavernous train station and sat with her monogrammed suitcase tucked under the bench behind her crossed ankles. The suitcase was fairly well battered—Simeon had seen to that. He had a tendency to throw it when he was railing against oligarchy in its many serpentine forms, and the robber barons with their heels on the working man's neck, etc., etc. She could recite it all like a many-versed poem, *The Rime of the Ancient Mariner*, perhaps, which Simeon had taught to her freshman English class at Wellesley College.

A little thing like a gold-embossed monogram could set him off. She'd taken to hiding the suitcase in various places, which had gotten harder once they'd moved from their two-room flat when they first arrived in St. Louis, to the one-room, fifth-floor walk-up. It was there that she'd developed a fear of heights from regularly being pushed up against the window and threatened with a quick descent to the street far below.

When his presumed speedy advancement from cub reporter to city desk at the *St. Louis Post-Dispatch* failed to materialize, they'd taken an even smaller room at a boardinghouse, at which point it had been all but impossible to hide the suitcase, his second-favorite target.

Simeon Lister had impressed all the Wellesley College girls with the breadth and depth of his knowledge of English literature, his love of poetry, his ability to capture minds—and more than a few hearts—with his passion for words. He was not wellborn or overly handsome, but oh, how he could talk.

He could also listen. Unlike boys their own age, he asked about their lives, interests, and hopes for the future. His gentle questioning and appearance of deep interest could unearth long-buried secrets. This uncanny talent for exposing closet-dwelling skeletons combined with his growing disdain for teaching "the overfed, husband-hunting, vapid spawn of the bourgeoisie" led him to quit academia and pursue a career in journalism, where he planned to expose the depraved machinations of the rich.

He had been raised in a fairly comfortable middle-class family in Worcester—a family he'd rejected as "dull and incurious" as he strove for higher education. As a successful college instructor, Simeon likely would have risen through the academic ranks, but his own hubris had derailed him. He'd thought getting work as a newspaper reporter for an educated man like him would be easy. He'd been wrong.

The move to Missouri was Charlotte's fault, of course. They'd had to settle far enough from her family to make a statement about the permanence of her commitment to him, he'd said. She learned only later, when cheap bootleg gin had made him loose-lipped, that he'd applied to every major news outlet in the country—including his beloved *Boston Globe*—but only the *St. Louis Post-Dispatch* had responded.

Could he find her now, with his hound's nose for sniffing out apparently random details that soon braided themselves into a fact trail? She had used a false surname, that of a brave college classmate who'd been badly burned in a fire and lived with many more scars than Charlotte now bore. She kept her first name because she was afraid of rousing suspicion if she forgot to answer to a new one. Besides, as Simeon loved to sneer, "There are countless Charlottes."

She had told no one of her plan to become a waitress, of all things. Not even her brother, Oliver, the sole family member who still occasionally wrote to her after she'd run off like that, sullying the exalted Crowninshield name with elopement.

She had taken nothing but her latest wages from the milliner's shop—most of which had gone toward the train ticket from St. Louis to Kansas City—and the suitcase with her clothing and what few mementos hadn't been tossed out various windows by Simeon over the last two years. She had been scrupulous in her secrecy, even waiting to arrive in this unknown city to pawn her wedding ring. He would never find her in the vast and barren frontier lands. With his persistent disgust at her privileged upbringing, he wouldn't think to look west, and wouldn't expect her to last more than a week if he did.

She was safe—or would be soon enough. Safer than she'd been in years, despite being a woman alone in a public train station, at an hour favored by criminals and miscreants.

A battered suitcase was nothing to invite the interest of thieves, she reminded herself as the night passed. But no matter how many times it had sailed across a room, that monogram had a way of shining like a beacon.

Two

By six in the morning, Charlotte had spent a nickel of her diminishing funds on a cup of tea at the twenty-four-hour Fred Harvey lunch counter. She'd sipped it slowly as she waited for the wagon-wheel-sized clock to make its plodding way toward seven thirty. She had dozed throughout the night, eyes flicking open at the sound of any approach, as she'd learned to do when Simeon was out. Best to feign sleep but be ready to cover her head and softer spots when he came in.

There was a young girl slumped on a bench across the vast lobby of the station. She had slowly tipped into the corner of the high wooden back and crumpled like a used napkin, with what looked like half a biscuit clutched in her hand, and lips slightly parted as if she'd recently been sucking her thumb.

The sleep of the untroubled, Charlotte thought. Her mother often blithely referred to her own night's rest in these terms, as if the woman hadn't a care in the world. Oh, but she cared. Many, many things bothered Beatrice Crowninshield, and when she wasn't busy insisting that her life was one endless series of scones with clotted cream, she was detailing all the aspects of the world that weren't quite right. Starting with Charlotte.

Brown eyes with a sort of melancholy behind them. "A sparkling eye is the first thing one notices," Beatrice would say, glowing as if she'd swallowed a lit lantern. But how did one actually go about making one's own eyes sparkle? Charlotte had practiced in the mirror in her dressing room countless times until she'd given up altogether.

She was petite with an admirably narrow waist . . . but with shoulders on the large side for her frame, and her mother worried they might turn mannish as she aged. Her skin was pale yet "lacked a normal propensity to blush."

Beatrice knew the value of a blush and had put her own pink cheeks to good use. Her father had escaped the Welsh mining town of his birth by going to sea, rising from cabin boy to captain at the Crown shipping yards. In his later years, he'd come to be a great favorite of the company owner, Wallace Crowninshield, who, against the better judgment of his wife (a Cabot, no less) and most of Boston society, had allowed his son, Casper, to marry the lovely, wealthy, but unpedigreed Beatrice.

"She's got a lot of making up to do," Charlotte's brother, Oliver, would often whisper when their mother had a twist in her knickers about some small thing or another—the whiteness of her table linens, for instance, or the length of a dodo feather on one of her many hats.

The sleep of the untroubled. Charlotte wondered if she'd ever be able to sink that deep into slumber again.

Billie woke herself with a little snorting laugh. She'd been dreaming of her brother Angus, only a year younger than she was. He was driving their father's truck in circles around the open field behind the brickyard, and she'd been hanging out the window, arms in the air, fingers spread wide so the wind rushed through them, screaming for the sheer joy of it.

"Miss?" A man's voice sifted down through the dust motes shimmering in a ray of sunlight flooding in from a high window. She blinked against the brightness, trying to make the speaker's silhouette come into focus. "Miss, are you . . . ah . . . Charlotte Turner?"

"No, I told you *I'm* Charlotte Turner." This voice was softer, more refined, but somehow more commanding. "She must be the other girl."

"Ah, right. Wilamena? Wilamena MacTavish?"

Billie struggled to sit upright. "Yes," she croaked, then coughed to clear her throat. "That's me, Billie MacTavish." She raised a hand to brush the newly unbraidable hair out of her face and nearly smashed a biscuit into her cheek.

Oh, yes, Maw's biscuit. The memory of Maw's teary face as she'd tucked it into her hand floated before her, and it was all she could do to keep herself from bawling all over again.

"You won't need that," said the man. He wore a stiff cap of some kind. "Toss that out, and we'll get you a fresh one." He introduced himself with a name Billie immediately forgot as she brushed the crumbling roll into a nearby wastebasket, set her woolen hat straight on her head, and gathered up the threadbare tapestry bag that held her other set of clothes, two sets of drawers, a comb, and her sister Peigi's pencil drawing of their house with little cameo insets of each family member. An artist, was Peigi. Billie had vowed to buy her a real charcoal pencil and sketch pad with her wages.

The man led them to the lunch counter and waved over a Harvey Girl. Billie had heard of the famous Harvey Girls, of course, even before she'd seen the employment ad in the paper. But since they only worked on the Santa Fe Railway, which did not run through any part of Nebraska—not to mention that yesterday had been her first train ride ever in her whole life—she'd never seen one in person before.

The young woman wore an unfashionably long black dress that came almost to her ankles, with sleeves that puffed at the shoulders and reached her wrists. Over this was a crisp white apron, V-necked and wide at the shoulders, narrowing to a white sash at the waist, then cascading almost to the hem of the black dress, creating an hourglass effect. The only adornment was a little black bow tie at the neck.

"They're going into training in Topeka," the man told the Harvey Girl. "Give them whatever they want." He handed Billie and the other woman squares of stiff paper with the words ISSUED BY THE ATCHISON TOPEKA & SANTA FE RAILWAY SYSTEM printed across the top, and ONE-WAY ECONOMY TO TOPEKA below it. "Don't worry," he said with a chuckle as Billie studied the ticket. "If it doesn't work out, we'll give you another to come right back."

"Oh, it'll work out," Billie murmured.

The other woman only looked at him with those serious, almost sad brown eyes of hers as if to say, *Well, I'm certainly not coming back.*

Billie ordered a couple of eggs scrambled, a biscuit, fried potatoes, milk, and one of those big steaks the Harvey Houses were known for.

"How would you like it done?" asked the Harvey Girl.

"Done?"

"Rare, medium rare . . . "

Billie blinked up at her. *Just cook it,* she wanted to say.

"I'd suggest medium," said the other woman. "Not bloody, not dry."

"Oh, yes! That sounds just right."

"Tea with milk, please," the woman told the Harvey Girl. "And a poached egg with toast."

Billie could feel the blood simmer in her cheeks. She'd been greedy. But she'd also been hungry! So hungry it hurt, and she'd never been to a restaurant before, much less given leave to order anything she wanted. Who knew when she'd get the chance again?

"I'm Charlotte L—" The woman tightened her lips suddenly. "Turner." Perhaps she had a stutter, like Billie's brother Ian.

"Very pleased to meet you, Charlotte LaTurner," said Billie brightly, so the other woman would think she hadn't noticed. "I'm Billie MacTavish of Table Rock, Nebraska." She'd practiced that with her mother, too. She'd grown up knowing everyone in Table Rock, so introducing herself to strangers was a new skill. Lorna, of course, had come all the way across the ocean, introducing herself wherever she went, Billie reckoned. She was that worldly.

"Actually, it's simply Turner," said Charlotte smoothly, without a hint of impediment or explanation.

"Ah." Billie nodded as if she understood this turn of events. "And you're not too hungry, are you? Bellyache?"

"I'm just fine, thank you."

The food arrived quickly, a thick slab of rich-smelling meat that lay tantalizingly in its own juices. Eggs and potatoes forgotten—and for that matter, the whole rest of creation!—Billie tucked into her first restaurant steak, the most giant piece she'd ever laid eyes on. It should've been tough, a slice that thick, but having not lain in salt for weeks on end, each mouthful was tender with tendrils of flavor the likes of which she'd never tasted before. By God, it was a feast!

Charlotte Turner ate her food in small bites, fingers delicate on her fork or single slice of toast. When Billie had nearly laid waste to her steak, Charlotte said, "I believe it's time to go."

"Already?"

Charlotte nudged the tickets into Billie's view. "We take the eight fifteen, and it's nearly eight o'clock now."

"Oh, but . . . " It wasn't that she was still hungry. In fact, now that she had stopped to take a breath, her stomach felt like she'd eaten a whole bucket of oats. But those lovely eggs and crispy fried potatoes . . .

"There'll be more when we get there," said Charlotte wearily. "It's a restaurant. We'll be utterly surrounded by food."

Utterly surrounded by food. What would that even look like? And yes, they'd be serving it, but would they be allowed to eat it? Her father was surrounded by bricks every day, but he couldn't take any home to repair his own ramshackle house.

Charlotte dabbed her lips with her napkin and dropped it daintily by her plate, then fished a nickel out of the little pochette bag that swung from her wrist and set it by her teacup. Billie imitated the napkin routine, although she was sure Charlotte could tell she'd never used such an awfully white cloth napkin before. She was dumbfounded as to how to handle the nickel situation.

"It's all right," Charlotte murmured. "Mine can be from both of us."

"I'll pay you back," Billie insisted.

Charlotte smiled wanly. "Of course." But it didn't seem to Billie as if she said it with much conviction.

They headed for the platform where the Navajo Number Nine huffed steam and awaited their boarding. Charlotte handed her suitcase to the porter and said simply, "Topeka," and the man knew just what to do. He looked at Billie's ancient bag, the one her maw had brought with her from Scotland all those years ago, and Billie said, "I'll keep it with me, if that's all right."

The porter smiled kindly. "It's your bag, ain't it?"

Billie followed Charlotte down the aisle. With its velveteen seats and gleaming wood window frames, it was a far grander train than she'd taken from Table Rock.

"Do you prefer the window?" Charlotte asked.

"Oh, um, which do you like?"

"It couldn't matter less to me." An unspoken thought seemed to play across those sad eyes. "In fact, I plan to sleep the sleep of the untroubled."

Billie chose the window seat and stared out at the enormous train yard, which quickly slipped from view as the Navajo Number Nine made its way to the outskirts of Kansas City. Her mother was right; the world was so much bigger than she'd ever suspected! Children played by the dusty tracks and waved up at them as they passed. Billie waved back, smiling, and turned to see if Charlotte saw them, too.

The woman was fast asleep, arms crossed against her bosom, head tipped back. Her lips were slack, slightly parted, with the corners turned up just a fraction, as if, though she could not see the children, she were smiling at them nonetheless.

Three

The ride was a little under two hours from Kansas City to Topeka, and in that time, fine snow crystals had begun to swirl frantically across the brittle fields, collecting like granular white pebbles in the crevices of the train car windowsills, only to escape when a strong gust hit them sideways. Though it was nearly April, winter still had its teeth in the desiccated landscape.

"Windy," the younger girl whispered, her earlier enthusiasm for train travel apparently having diminished considerably since having her nose practically pressed against the glass as they'd pulled out of Kansas City.

"I suppose we should be glad we haven't signed on as street sweepers," said Charlotte, stretching to rouse herself from the deepest sleep she'd enjoyed in months.

"Might be a walk to get to the restaurant," Billie murmured. "I hope it's not too far."

Charlotte stared at the girl a moment. Did she not understand any aspect of what she'd undertaken? Clearly she was young—Charlotte wondered if she had inflated her age a tad—but now she was beginning to think the girl might have some mental deficiency, as well.

"The restaurant is *at the depot*," she said slowly, hoping to keep the condescension she felt from revealing itself too clearly, though she considered that the girl might not pick up on it anyway. "It's specifically for railway passengers, so it's actually right there, where they get off. The walk is likely about twenty feet from the train door."

Billie's cheeks went geranium. "I don't . . . I haven't . . . "

"No, of course not," said Charlotte quickly. "Harvey Houses are only found on the Santa Fe Railway, and if one hasn't traveled on the Santa Fe, how would one know?"

"How did *you* know?"

"Well, I suppose I'd heard about it from others. Girls I knew in college who—"

"In college?" Billie's eyes were wide with surprise shaded with suspicion. "You're a college girl?"

"Well, not anymore, I . . . I . . . " Good Lord, how had she let that slip? And she'd sworn to stick to the story she'd so carefully devised while waiting for the most recent shiner to fade.

"Graduated?"

"No, I never did, actually." She quickly switched to her practiced response. "My parents died in a car crash several years ago, and the money ran out, so I needed a job. And there was a young man who wanted to marry me, but I didn't share his enthusiasm. He was heartbroken, and I felt very bad about it, so I thought it best for both of us if I went far away, and we could both make a fresh start."

"But you went to college."

"I did."

"What did you study?"

Charlotte was taken aback. Most of the girls she knew would've pressed her for details about the romance. Why would anyone care about what she had studied? Was this question meant to trip her up? She had to gather her wits for a moment.

"It was a liberal arts education. I studied everything." There. That would do it.

"The American Revolution?"

"Yes, of course." She'd been raised in Boston. Schools taught the war for independence as if the British might return any day, and children needed to be prepared to take up muskets if called upon.

Billie smiled. "I can recite 'Paul Revere's Ride.'"

"Lovely. Perhaps a customer will request a rendition with his steak."

The girl's face fell.

"Oh dear. Don't take it so hard. I was just teasing." Simeon's sense of humor, so charmingly outlandish when they'd first started meeting outside of school her sophomore year, had turned toward sarcasm as misfortune had embittered him. Or possibly he'd always been sarcastic, but he only began using it as a weapon against her after they'd married. Apparently the tendency had worn off on her.

Billie's head turned toward the window, and Charlotte thought she might be good and truly offended, but it was only the outskirts of Topeka that had caught her eye. "Oh," she said. "This is a big city, too."

Topeka, thought Charlotte. *Good Lord.*

The depot was two stories of red brick, and long—Billie guessed there were at least twenty of those large arched windows along the span of the second floor. *That's a lot of brick*, she thought. More than Table Rock Brick and Tile could've produced in a week. A wooden porch roof jutted out over the station platform, sheltering the benches on which travelers sat awaiting the train. A newsstand was built right into the depot next to the main entrance of the lobby.

As they descended from the train onto the platform, a young man all in white—brimless cap, shirt, pants, and knee-length apron wrapped around narrow hips—came from the side of the building. He was gangly in that way boys often were when their bones had stopped growing but their flesh was still playing catch-up, like Maw's gravy before it thickened, all flavor but no heft. The broad knobs of his shoulders curled against the cold as he banged a mallet against what looked like an enormous metal dinner plate that hung from a rope he grasped.

"Diners this way!" he called out. "Lunch now being served!"

Billie clutched her bag to her chest as the passengers pressed past her into the station, others stamping their feet in the cold until they could board. She waited for Charlotte to be given her suitcase, despite the fact that the woman had been rude to her. "Your betters are no better," Maw often said, "but best not to get on the wrong side of them."

Besides, a wave of homesickness had suddenly hit her in this foreign place bustling with people, all of whom clearly knew their direction and their business, while Billie had no idea of either. Where was she to go? Who was she to ask? She found herself futilely searching the faces of the people who scurried by for some sign of familiarity. Yesterday morning she knew every last person within five miles of her. Now she was nearly drowning in a sea of strangers.

Her chest tightening in panic, she made herself focus on the young man banging the metal plate, how his knuckles had gone bloodless from the cold. *Needs mittens*, she thought, and half considered offering the loan of her own, as if he were her brother Duncan, who was always flying out of the house careless to the cold or wet, the wee eejit.

She glanced up and saw that the young man had caught her staring at his nearly white knuckles. He blinked once or twice as if trying to divine her purpose. Startled, she raised her mittened hand to indicate she was only thinking about how cold his must be, nothing more. But he took it as a greeting (though an odd one from a complete stranger) and gave a small, pleasant, mildly confused wave back.

Charlotte had her suitcase now and nodded at Billie to come along. "Let's make the best of it, shall we?"

Inside the station, there was a large waiting room with wide, arched doorways on either side. Charlotte heard the hum of voices and gentle clacking of cutlery on china drifting toward them from the right and headed toward it, with Billie at her heels like a lost puppy.

"May I seat you?" asked a woman in her thirties, Charlotte guessed. One curling thread of silver escaped from otherwise straight black hair pulled back at the nape of her neck. She had crow's-feet, or the beginning of them.

Crow's-toes, thought Charlotte, and at twenty-two she wondered if she, too, would soon have tiny creases at her eyes and across her forehead. It fell on her like a brick from a crumbling building how thoroughly she had wasted her youth on such a one as Simeon Lister. Gladly given away the privileges of her birthright to be beaten and berated. To be "loved" until she was nothing.

Billie mumbled something at the woman.

"Pardon me? You're what?"

"The new Harvey Girls," Billie said, as if it were some sort of jail sentence. Maybe she wasn't as simple as Charlotte had thought. The girl knew a prison when she saw it.

"About time," the woman muttered. "We've a need for you, that's a fact. Now just stand back there beside the coffee urns and watch. I'll get to you directly, once they're all safely back on the train."

The coffee station stood between the lunchroom—a wandering U-shaped counter with swivel chairs attached to the floor by thick metal poles—and the larger dining room, with its white linen table-cloths and crystal glasses. The urns themselves must have held endless gallons of coffee, the lids towering around the height of Billie's head.

The Harvey Girls moved rapidly without appearing to jog, skimming along the gleaming wood floors like low-flying aproned birds. They smiled brightly but never seemed to raise their voices as they attended to even the most garrulous of customers.

"Why, look at this! What a lovely sandwich, but see here, is this the roast beef? Because I feel certain I ordered roast beef, and this appears . . . does it? . . . so it does, it seems to be corned beef. Now my memory isn't what it once was, and I supposed it could be my very own fault, but I wonder if you could just check the order on this, and if I ordered corned and not roast, why then, I'll just live with my mistake, won't I?"

The Harvey Girl smiled, nodding as if this were the most scintillating conversation of her young life. "Let's not worry about what you ordered and get you what you wanted. I'll be right back with a roast beef sandwich for you."

"Oh, now, I don't mean to be any trouble."

"No trouble at all!" The girl whisked away the plate and sailed toward a door behind the urns before another word could be spoken.

Charlotte's already low spirits plummeted. She'd been born with a sharp tongue (her mother never tired of reminding her) and her years with Simeon had only sharpened it. He'd encouraged her energetic, if not entirely ladylike, use of an exclamation in service of a point he agreed with. He'd actually admitted to her during that very first meeting in the library to review a paper she was writing that he sensed a kindred fiery nature in her that he very much appreciated.

Fiery. She had been, and certainly those instincts were still there. But in recent years, as he'd become more inflamed, it had been left to her to cool his temper. She wondered now if she could stand to listen to the blathering complaints of customers without the fear of a flying fist to deter her from snapping back.

She glanced at Billie. The girl's eyes were wide with some combination of fascination and anxiety as she watched the billiard game of Harvey Girls bouncing from one counter to the next like cue balls. "How will we ever learn it all?" she murmured.

"How did you learn 'Paul Revere's Ride'?" Charlotte hoped it sounded encouraging.

"With a lot of mistakes," the girl said ruefully.

———————

Thirty minutes later, when the gong had sounded and train customers had risen virtually in unison and made their way back to the platform, the Harvey Girl with the silver thread in her hair returned to them. "Let's get you upstairs and into some uniforms," she said.

"We're to start today?" asked Charlotte.

"Oh yes, right away. We need to get you up to speed before the next train arrives in . . ." she glanced at a large clock with a white face and black roman numerals affixed to the back wall, "about forty-five minutes."

She took them down a hallway beside the kitchen and up a narrow flight of stairs. "I'm Frances, the head waitress. The dormitory is up here. You two are friends?"

Charlotte and Billie glanced at each other blankly. "We've only just met," said Charlotte, "but I suppose we've become friendly." Billie's face, readable as a signpost, said she wasn't entirely sure about that, but Frances either didn't see the look or chose to ignore it.

"Good! You'll room together."

As they walked down the dormitory hallway, Frances pointed out the bathroom, sewing room, and parlor, and opened the door to a small room with two iron-framed twin beds and a small armoire that had seen better days. It had two drawers below and a narrow rack for clothing on hangers above.

Charlotte and Billie were told to unpack while Frances sized them up for uniforms and headed down the hallway to the linens room. In moments, she had returned with two sets of vastly different lengths—one short and one long. She laid one on each bed and said, "Now get yourselves dressed, come down to the lunchroom, and we'll get your career as Harvey Girls off to a roaring good start!"

Four

Billie wasn't sure which was more uncomfortable—the stiff black dress itself or changing into it in front of someone who was no relation to her and hadn't even known her for a full twenty-four hours. She had shared a room with her four sisters at home, of course, and they ran about in their underthings, but they were little girls, and they were *her* little girls. This Charlotte was a full-grown woman. And a stranger.

For her part, Charlotte seemed to take it all in stride, simply turning her back and slipping off her coat. She wore a nice—though somewhat faded—green drop-waist dress with a square neckline and long tie knotted below her ample bosoms. That came off just as quickly, and Billie spun around so she wouldn't see the woman's brassiere and drawers.

Billie was tempted to put the long black dress on over her own, then wiggle the other dress out from under it, but that seemed silly. She had nothing particularly worth looking at, with a camisole covering her small breasts, and drawers that went down her narrow thighs.

"I'm too thin," she had occasionally whined to her mother. "I look like a soup spoon on a hunger strike." She hoped one day to have a soft womanly body like her mother's, to which her mother would laugh and say, "Nine bairns'll soften you up, but good! Soften your insides, too!" It had become a private understanding between them that whenever Lorna sneezed, Billie would run and get her a new set of drawers.

There was an oval mirror on the wall by the door, and Charlotte stood back to survey herself in the dress and massive pinafore apron. "Good Lord," she muttered, then moved in close to squint at her hair, as if she were searching for something she hoped she wouldn't find. She turned to look at Billie and let out a humorless laugh. "I'm not sure if we're off to work or the convent."

Billie stiffened. "I'm Catholic," she said, drawing herself to her full height, "so it could be either for me."

The other woman's eyebrows went up. "No offense was meant."

"Then none taken," said Billie, but she kept her chin high nonetheless.

––––––––––––––––––

Down in the lunchroom, Frances introduced them to the other Harvey Girls, who all seemed friendly despite frantically preparing the restaurant for the next onslaught due to arrive in twenty minutes. A girl named Alice was standing at the coffee station with one of the spigots open, letting the dark liquid drain into an old bucket.

"We don't serve coffee more than two hours old," explained Frances. "It's the standard." It wasn't any standard that Charlotte had heard of, even in the finer restaurants in Boston. The Crowninshields themselves drank coffee that had been brewed in the morning by a kitchen maid and was reheated throughout the day. True, the early coffee always tasted best, but for an enterprise attempting to make a profit, it seemed like a strange waste of time and money.

"I'll start you two on beverages. You know the cup code?" They both shook their heads. Frances turned to the lunch counter and took a cup and saucer from the ones being quickly dealt out at each place setting by a girl named Edie as she made her way down the snaking counter.

"It's simple: cup right side up in the saucer—coffee." She turned the cup upside down. "Hot tea." Then she set the upside-down cup on the table tipped against the saucer. "Iced tea." Upside-down and flat on the counter was milk. "Now you do it." She slid the cup to Billie.

Billie set the cup upright in the saucer. "Coffee?"

Frances glanced up at that big, black-rimmed clock on the wall. "Don't ask. Is it coffee, or isn't it?"

"Yes, I . . . I believe it is." Billie turned the cup over. "Iced tea."

"No." Frances slid the cup and saucer to Charlotte. "Let's see if you were watching."

Charlotte had, in fact, been watching quite closely and committed the information to memory just as she had for any one of a thousand quizzes, tests, and exams she'd taken over the years. A teacher almost always wanted simply for you to listen and parrot back her answers, and Charlotte had had more practice than ninety-nine girls in a hundred. Of course, she hadn't retained a lot of it— the pluperfect French and Pythagorean theorem—but she had always known what she needed to know for the test. Simeon had been the only teacher who'd wanted to be surprised by a girl's answer.

"Coffee, tea, iced, milk," she said as she flipped the cup into the various configurations.

Billie's face fell, and Charlotte immediately felt guilty. She'd never been one to lord it over the slower, less confident girls. It was just another example of how she'd deteriorated, this flaunting of her intelligence.

"Correct," said Frances quickly, glancing once again at the clock. "Carlotta, you're in charge of asking customers for their drink orders. Bobbie, you're to fill a coffee pitcher and follow after her, pouring coffee *in upright cups only.* Understand?"

Billie nodded, eyes cast down in shame.

"Yes?" said Frances pointedly.

"Yes, I understand."

For the next ten minutes, they helped Edie bring out the dainty little glass cups of fruit and set them at each place along the counter. Where did they find strawberries in March, for goodness' sake? Charlotte didn't have time to wonder. Suddenly a gong began to sound out on the train platform.

"Stations, please, ladies!" Frances called out, and everyone seemed to know where to go.

Where do I start? wondered Charlotte, but then she saw Billie at her elbow. "Go get one of those pitchers and fill it like she said, and then follow along behind me." Billie's eyes flashed in the briefest moment of anger at the bossy tone. "We'll work together, all right?" added Charlotte, forcing a smile. The girl's pique subsided, and she went to get the coffee.

Thirty minutes. That's all the Harvey Girls had in which to ask several hundred customers for their orders, relay them to the kitchen, attend to beverage requests, serve the food, ensure that every diner was happy with their generously portioned meal (plus extra ketchup over here, and a clean knife to replace the one that dropped on the floor over there, and the fourth glass of water across the room), lunch dishes cleared the moment the patron was finished but not a moment before, dessert presented with more coffee or tea, the bill paid, and everyone happily out the door. Thirty short minutes, and it only worked if every last one of them was on their toes, working in perfect concert with the others, as tightly choreographed as a Russian ballet.

———————

Billie watched Charlotte approach the first customer, a smile more like a grimace on her naturally serious features. "Would you like coffee, tea, iced tea, or milk?" she asked as her hand hovered over his cup. The customer squinted at her, as if trying to make sense of the too-wide smile and the too-high tone.

"I'll just have water," he said.

"Oh, well then." Her smile deflated. She glanced around. "I'm sure the water girl will be right along."

Water girl? thought Billie. There had never been any mention of a water girl. "I'll get that for you," she said, and hurried back to a small table where she'd seen pitchers. She poured the water and gave the customer a little smile. "Just let me know if you need any more later."

He grinned up at her. "Thank you kindly, Miss."

Charlotte was a couple of customers down the counter by now, so Billie rushed to the next person. Cup right side up in the saucer. Coffee.

She tipped the coffee jug over the cup and watched as it sluiced in one side and sailed high over the rim on the other, splashing several drops of hot liquid onto the woman's brown leather clutch purse that she'd laid by her plate.

"Ohhh!" shrieked the woman. "My purse! It's ruined! My favorite purse! And you nearly burned my hand!"

"I'm so sorry!" Billie panted with fright. "I'm so terribly sorry!" With a pitcher in each hand she swung around to find a place to set them so she could clean up the spill. There was a little table behind her, and her trembling hands landed the coffeepot all right, but the metal water pitcher went clean over the side, splashing water onto the floor. She stared at the pitcher rattling on the floor and thought she might faint with panic over what to do next.

"No need to worry, ma'am." It was Charlotte's voice behind her. "We'll get that cleaned right up, and your purse should be fine."

"No it's *not* fine! It's splattered with coffee! And she nearly burned me!"

"The purse is brown leather. Here, I'm wiping it off, you can't even see it. And she didn't burn you, she just scared you." Charlotte's tone, even more than her words, sent a prickle down Billie's neck as she bent to retrieve the water pitcher. She jumped up and spun around quickly.

"It's all my fault, Miss," she said. "I'm so sorry. You must have been scared near witless with all that coffee flying about."

"Of course I was!"

"And this purse—so pretty! How'd you come by it?"

The woman gazed down at the purse, which, after Charlotte's quick wipe, had begun to dry. The spots were barely visible. "It was a gift from my sister."

"My, she must love you."

A soft, sad smile whispered across the woman's face. "She lives in Spokane now, and we don't get to see each other but every five years or so."

Faraway family. Billie could feel her throat tighten. "Bet she misses you."

"I miss her, too. I think I'll go over to the newsstand and buy a postcard to send her."

"Oh, she'll love it!"

The woman smiled and patted Billie's hand. "You're a sweet child."

"You sure you're okay?"

"Yes, I'm fine. Just fine."

As she moved to the next upright coffee cup, something caught the corner of Billie's eye.

It was Frances scowling at her.

———

When the last train passenger had scurried out the door, and only the locals were left to eat their meals at a more leisurely pace, Frances called Charlotte and Billie over. They followed her to a corner of the kitchen out of sight of the lunchroom and were soon met by a large man whose overworked suit buttons looked as if they might leap to their death at any moment.

"This is Mr. Gilstead, the Topeka Harvey House manager."

"Very happy to meet you both," he said.

"I wouldn't get too happy about it," said Frances. "I'm not sure which one of them I'd like to fire more. This one"—she nodded her chin at Billie—"poured coffee all over a customer. And this one"—she hitched a thumb at Charlotte—"tried to improve the situation by telling the customer she was fine and not to complain so much."

"I didn't actually say—"

"See what I mean?" Frances said to Gilstead. "A quibbler."

"We can't have that."

"No, we can't."

Mr. Gilstead nodded. "I'll call Miss Steele."

Frances frowned at them for a moment. "We could use the help."

"We are short-staffed, it's true."

"This one's mind is as sharp as her tongue, and the other's good with the tough customers. Had that coffee lady buying postcards instead of complaining inside of a quick minute."

"They'll stay, then."

"For now. But I'll keep my eye on them. I won't brook incompetence."

Frances walked back into the lunchroom with Mr. Gilstead lumbering after her like a trained bear. Billie let out the breath she'd been holding and crumpled against the wall.

"Whatever is the matter?" said Charlotte.

"We just about got fired!"

"We most certainly did not," Charlotte scoffed. "They never had any intention whatsoever of firing us."

"But she *said*—"

"It was a false threat. She was just letting us know who's really in charge, and it certainly doesn't seem to be that Gilstead fellow. If there was firing to be done, she would have done it." If living with a bully had taught Charlotte anything, it was how to tell bluster from danger.

"She's right about that," came a voice from behind the pot rack. A moment later a young man appeared, the one they had seen calling for diners across the train platform. At close range, there was a tiny constellation of gravy spattered across his white shirt.

He gazed at Billie for an extra minute and raised his hand. Billie's face went hot, and she looked away. Charlotte frowned in confusion.

He crossed his arms and went on. "Frances cows the other girls, but only because she takes it so serious."

"Takes what so serious?" asked Billie.

"Lunch." He shrugged and smiled at the absurdity of it.

Billie grinned. Charlotte shook her head, but she felt a little less annoyed about the ridiculous dressing down she'd been given. The young man introduced himself as Leif Gunnarsson. He'd only begun working at the restaurant a few months before, as it turned out, but it was long enough to get the lay of the land.

"They're tough on you because they want to weed out the ones who won't make it out on the line. Topeka's a railroad town. Half the people who live here work for the Santa Fe, and the other half are the barbers and butchers and boardinghouse keepers we all go to. They don't make a fuss if a girl drops a plate or gets an order wrong. Out on the line—especially at the big houses like the Alvarado in Albuquerque or El Tovar at the Grand Canyon—you can't have a lemon wedge out of place."

"So we can expect to be hectored and threatened," said Charlotte, "but as long as we learn what's required and don't fall apart, they'll keep us."

Leif nodded. "That's the size of it."

"Oh, thank goodness," Billie breathed.

He studied the girl for a moment, then looked at Charlotte.

"We need the jobs," she said, and headed back to the lunchroom.

The trains came and went all afternoon and into the evening. If the Harvey Girls weren't serving customers, they were polishing silver till it seemed lit from within, folding napkins to stand perfectly at attention at each place setting, or wiping down every imaginable surface over and over until Charlotte began to wonder if they'd wipe the varnish right off the wood.

After several hours, Charlotte's back began to hurt—she'd never done so much manual labor in all her life! Billie, however, seemed to chug along like a freight train. The girl lifted tray-loads of dirty dishes as if they weighed as little as the hats Charlotte used to sell. She also tended to run into things, but with a little smile or self-deprecating comment, she seemed to be able to put people at ease. Charlotte wished she had both the girl's strength and temperament.

Finally at nine o'clock, after the last train had come through for the evening, and every station had been cleaned one last time and prepared for the morning shift, the women trudged upstairs.

"Change into your nightgowns and come and sit in the sewing room with us, so we can get to know you!" said one of the other girls.

Charlotte didn't want to get to know anyone, especially not some gaggle of uneducated farm girls. She wanted only to make it through the month of training so she could be sent out on the line, with any luck to one of the Harvey Houses in California or Texas. The farther away from St. Louis, the better. Besides, she'd never been so physically exhausted in all her life.

"Aren't you sweet," said Billie, smiling a little too brightly, "but I'm about to fall asleep in my shoes!"

The girl let out a laugh. "Ah, you've never had a day as long as this one, have you? Don't worry, you'll soon get used to it."

Charlotte hitched herself behind the wagon of Billie's excuse and followed her back to their room. As soon as the door closed behind them, Billie sank down onto her bed, put her hands to her face, and began to sob. The freight train had suddenly become a fragile flower.

Charlotte had never seen a girl weep so profusely with so little provocation, not even Lucretia Lodge, who was forever making excuses about her delicate nature. At least Lucretia had the decency to secret herself away in the dorm linen closet when she felt it coming on, red-rimmed eyes the only indication of her weak constitution. Charlotte found it mildly pitiable. Crowninshields didn't have weak constitutions, nor did they cry. Ever.

This girl didn't seem to understand the social imperative of emotional control or, at the very least, secrecy. She certainly wasn't dashing for the linen closet. Charlotte decided to give the wretched thing a moment alone to collect herself. Besides, she seemed strangely sensitive about changing her clothes in another's presence, which Charlotte had grown accustomed to from her days of sharing a dorm room. Didn't these lower-class girls always have scads of siblings? Surely someone like Billie had never had a bedroom to herself.

Feeling charitable, Charlotte gathered up her nightgown and headed for the bathroom to change her clothes, brush her teeth, and splash some water on her face. When she returned, Billie had changed as well. But she was still crying.

Good Lord. She makes Lucretia Lodge seem positively stoic.

In the few moving pictures Charlotte had seen, emotional women were often comforted by other women. The husband had gone off to war, or absconded with the rent money, or some such nonsense, and a friend or sister would clutch the poor weeping wife to her breast and croon words of sympathy.

Well, there certainly would be no clutching or crooning on Charlotte's part, but perhaps a bit of chin-up-old-bean might make the girl settle down and go to sleep.

Charlotte sighed and sat down on her own bed. "It's been a long, tiring day," she said. "Best to get some rest."

Billie's hands came from her damp, red face, and she glared at Charlotte. "I'm not *tired*," she hissed. "This was a regular workday for me. Twelve hours with hardly a minute to fart. The problem with you is you think you're too good for it, and you're dead wrong!"

"And the problem with you is you think you're not good *enough* for it, and *you're* wrong. It's waitressing, for goodness' sake, one step up from a saloon girl!"

"Keep to yourself, is all I want."

"And you shall have it!"

Charlotte yanked the chain on the wall lamp with a snap, pulled up her covers, and faced the wall. The sniveling giant baby had seen the last of her pity!

On the other side of the room, the bedsprings creaked and then went silent. But the sounds of muffled sobbing continued unabated.

Five

The retching was so violent it practically made the walls shudder.

Half-asleep, Billie rolled into a sitting position on the side of her bed, remembering only then that it wouldn't be one of her sisters or brothers, to whom she was ready to run with a wet rag and the old tin bucket. It was . . . someone else. A stranger hurling the contents of her stomach—and possibly a few of her smaller organs, from the sound of it—in some unknown room in this rabbit's warren of a building.

"Stop . . . ," Charlotte murmured in her sleep and tucked her knees up over her own stomach. One arm snaked quickly across her chest while the other went up over her head. "Please . . . "

Billie rolled her eyes. Miss Smarty-Pants had probably never had to deal with a vomiting sibling. High-society college girls had maids for that sort of thing, she supposed. Maybe the maids even did the puking for them. She chuckled at the thought. "It all comes out the same in the privy," her father would say.

The retching started up anew, and Billie wondered if the poor thing might need help. After all, who would help you in a place like this with no family? Silently she took her mother's green cardigan sweater from the armoire and tugged it on over her nightgown, unlatched the door, and slipped into the hallway.

Locating the retcher was not hard. She was in the bathroom, her cheek resting on the toilet seat, a clump of damp black hair stuck across her sweaty neck like a velvet choker. "Sorry for waking you," croaked Alice (or possibly Edie).

"I was almost awake anyway," said Billie.

"Farmer's daughter?"

"No, a father and two brothers to get out the door for the early shift at the brick factory, three brothers and sisters to get ready for school, and three little ones who rise at dawn for no reason at all!"

The girl smiled wanly but then suddenly pushed up onto her knees, her stomach convulsing inward, the muscles on her neck bulging as she heaved into the commode. Billie held her hair away from the bowl with one hand and pulled toilet paper off the roll with the other. When the girl finished and sank back down again, Billie handed her the paper for her mouth.

"I'm embarrassed—" said Billie.

"*You're* embarrassed," the girl muttered. "Think how *I* feel."

"I can't remember your name."

"Elsie." (Not Edie *or* Alice!)

"I'm Billie."

"I know."

"You do?" Billie's heart sank.

"No, not really. I was just teasing."

"That's pretty quick thinking for a girl with her head in the pot!"

"It's all that Harvey training," Elsie muttered. "If the devil himself sat down at the counter, you'd be expected to smile and get him a nice plate of brimstone." She groaned and got up on her knees again.

They went on like this for a bit, chatting in between bouts of upchucking. The sun began to creep above the bottom of the windowsill, bathing them in its fiery light, and Elsie said, "I think I'm about done."

"I'll tell Frances you won't be down."

Elsie slowly got up onto her knees again, hanging on to the edge of the deep claw-foot tub to hoist herself to a standing position "Maybe for the lunch shift . . ."

"Yer bum's oot the windae," muttered Billie, taking Elsie by the elbow to keep her steady.

"I'm sorry, my bum is where, exactly?"

Billie chuckled. "Out the window. Something my father says. It's a Scottish way of saying you're talking nonsense."

"Well, regardless of the location of my bum, I'm starting to feel a little better."

"You just about coughed up a toe. Besides, you don't want to be passing this along. Imagine a trainload of heaving passengers—they'd have to hose out the cars at the next stop."

"I suppose you're right. I just hate to let the others down. More work for them."

"I'm starting to get the hang of it—I can help more." It wasn't a lie, exactly, more of a fib. She'd been allowed to fetch desserts, but not to take meal orders, which were expected to be committed to memory. This was hard enough when there was only one or two in a party and they didn't ask for anything unusual, like a baked potato instead of mashed.

That Charlotte, though. Billie was sure her roommate could memorize the *Encyclopaedia Britannica*, volumes A–L, without breaking a sweat. She was also familiar with the menu items in a way that was frankly infuriating. Blue Point oysters—who ever heard of that? And for the love of all that's holy, who would actually want to *eat* such a slimy, bad-smelling mess?

By six a.m., all eight girls on shift were to be dressed and eating breakfast at a long oak table at the back of the kitchen. The first train would arrive at seven, and they had to be poised and ready to greet and feed.

This morning, of course, there were only seven girls.

"Charlotte!" barked Frances, the head waitress, and Charlotte felt her neck muscles go taut. "You'll fill in for Elsie. And I'll remind you that every last customer should be treated as if they were the king of England on a royal tour."

Charlotte nodded curtly but muttered under her breath, "No doubt Topeka, Kansas, would be his first stop."

Breakfast was easy—the menu was limited to generally accepted morning foods like poached eggs, hotcakes, or Grape-Nuts cereal. Of course, there was the occasional strange substitution—one gentleman with the pallor of old snow ordered hotcakes with bacon, "but I don't like bacon, so I'll have buckwheat cakes instead."

"I'm sorry," said Charlotte, brushing a wisp of hair from her temple and wondering where Billie was with the coffee, "buckwheat cakes instead of hotcakes?"

"No, I like them both."

"Buckwheat cakes and bacon?"

"No, both, I said *both*." Annoyance rose in his voice. "Buckwheat *and* hot."

"Hot . . . ?"

"Cakes!"

"Right away, sir." Charlotte turned on her heel and strode toward the kitchen to place the order so he wouldn't catch her eye roll. *Cakes with a side of cakes,* she thought. *No wonder you look as bloodless as a blanket.*

She glanced up just in time to see Mr. Gilstead arch a woolly eyebrow. "Difficulties?" he murmured as she passed him.

"None whatsoever," she said, voice coated in dusting sugar.

It was the showgirls at lunchtime that nearly did her in.

They click-clacked in from the train platform on their kitten heel pumps, about ten of them. The men in the room sat up a little straighter, gazes lingered a little longer. Mr. Gilstead offered the women various seats in ones and twos along the winding lunch counter.

"We'd like to sit in there," said the girl with the brightest lip color, tipping her chin in the direction of the dining room.

Their skirts were as short as their bobbed hair, eyebrows especially black, cheeks clearly powdered. Mr. Gilstead hesitated.

"It's better to be together," said the girl and gazed at him steadily, in a way that indicated there was more to it than the pleasure of the other girls' company.

"Yes, of course." His smile had a bit of an oily slick to it that Charlotte hadn't noticed when he addressed, say, an elderly woman, or one with a child on her hip. He indicated to Pablocito the busboy (which seemed a misnomer—though shorter even than Charlotte, the man had to be almost forty) to shift two tables together in the dining room. Gilstead caught Charlotte's eye and gave a curt nod.

Her first table in the dining room, and he was giving her showgirls. Naturally.

They dithered over what menu items would add "padding in the wrong places," emphasis on *wrong*, since there were clearly right places. They wanted to share food but get separate checks. At least two of them were utterly flabbergasted when it was their turn to order, as if Charlotte had descended from the chandelier and asked them to recite the multiplication table beginning with the nines, for goodness' sake.

But she was patient and polite, fully aware of Mr. Gilstead's attention to her courtesy.

Also, there had been a dancer named Marcinda who lived in the room next door to Charlotte and Simeon at the boardinghouse, and Charlotte, desperate for any half-pleasant conversation, had befriended her. Marcinda had been smarter than she looked, and in fact had a penchant for the poems of Sara Teasdale, especially "There Will Come Soft Rains."

"'Not one would mind, neither bird nor tree,'" Marcinda liked to recite after a particularly loathsome night at the dance hall, "'if mankind perished utterly.'"

Desperation walked in all kinds of shoes, Charlotte had learned.

The kitten heel. The sole-worn boot. The expensive black pump with the torn-off bow.

Tildie, a nosy little thing with a penchant for gossip, was the drink girl for the dining room. Charlotte watched as she haughtily poured their coffee, failing to respond to the weary "Thanks, hon" or enthusiastic "You're a doll!" As if waitressing were so many rungs up the ladder from burlesque dancing.

Two, thought Charlotte. *About two rungs.*

She was just returning from the kitchen with a tray of brimming soup bowls balanced on her shoulder when one of the girls walked toward her in the lunchroom, likely on her way to the powder room. Charlotte saw a young man in a new black suit that was a little too large across the shoulders slide his hand behind his swiveling seat, twist at just the right moment, and grab a handful of the woman's bottom.

"Oh!" she yelped and swatted him away, face crimson with fury and embarrassment.

Charlotte was right there, not three feet away. With all that soup.

She felt the ever-present embers of her righteous fury ignite just as they did when Simeon manhandled her. Her fingers on the underside of the tray seemed to press upward of their own accord. She was new at the tray-handling business, after all. The back of the tray tipped upward; she could feel the bowls slide forward until one of them slipped over the tray's edge and onto the young man with the ill-fitting suit.

Regret for such impetuousness crashed over her like a tidal wave before the soup had even landed. She would pay. She knew this for a leaden fact.

"You'll pay for that haughty remark," Simeon would say as he raised a fist balled so tightly it might as well have been a hammer. She had paid for words, or the lack thereof; for her attempts to help him when he was so drunk he couldn't make his way to the john down the hall, or for her lack of assistance; for a look, or for a face so blank it might as well have been an owl's.

The bowl hit the man's lap, thank goodness, not his head. There was a good deal of squawking by him, while his friend next to him went from gargoyle-faced guffawing to silent shock as he stared at his own splattered trousers.

"Look what you've done!" sputtered the young man, bits of barley and carrot sliding down his pant legs in a sluice of beef stock. "How'm I supposed to go back to work?"

Mr. Gilstead was there in a moment, apologizing and calling for a damp cloth. "Terribly sorry, sir," he must have said about six times. "She's new. Terribly, terribly sorry."

"Sweetie, trust me," the showgirl exclaimed loudly to Mr. Gilstead. "She couldn't help it one bit. With me yelling like that, who wouldn't be startled?"

"And why on earth were you yelling?"

"A certain fella who now smells like stew *took a liberty* as I walked by." She said it as if he'd stolen the flag off a soldier's coffin.

Mr. Gilstead turned back to the young man. "Sir, is this true?"

Now it was his turn to flush. "I didn't mean anything by it."

"Sir, this is no saloon. There are standards of gentlemanly behavior by which we expect our patrons to abide."

"How is it *my* fault?" The young man stood and puffed his unimpressive chest toward Gilstead. "I'm not the one sashaying around like a trollop, and I'm not the one who dumped soup, bowl and all, on a paying customer!"

"Sir, I will have to ask you to leave and not to return until you can conduct yourself with propriety."

"I certainly will *not* return!" He looked at his friend. "Geez, get up, will you?"

The other man took one last crocodile-sized bite of his sardine sandwich and the two of them made their way out the door, titters of stifled laughter following in their wake.

"Charlotte . . . ," growled Mr. Gilstead.

"*She couldn't help it*," the showgirl insisted again. "Besides, what are you making your girls carry such heavy loads for? Big guy like you—you shoulda carried that one yourself, then none of this woulda happened."

———————————

Mr. Gilstead had shooed Charlotte back to the kitchen with the tray of now-cooling soup, but he hadn't said another word about the incident. She laid the tray down on the counter and asked Leif to refill the bowls with hot soup from the pot. Then she turned and put her hands flat against the cold glass of the kitchen window, heart still pounding, awaiting the blow. *You're fine*, she scolded her heart. *You're safe now.* But it galloped like a spooked colt nonetheless.

When she returned to the dining room with the hot soup, one of the girls started to clap, but the others quickly shushed her. Then one by one, as she lowered each bowl, they whispered something in her ear: "Nice one, hon" or "You're a peach." One said, "Lucky they're not all like that," and the girl next to her snorted in disagreement.

After they'd paid their bills and click-clacked back out to the waiting train, Charlotte found that every single girl had left a couple of quarters by her plate—nearly the cost of an entire meal—except for the girl who'd been grabbed. She'd left two dollars.

Six

Billie had a hunch that Charlotte had dropped the soup into that man's lap on purpose, and the thought of it thrilled her. She'd learned that you had to deliver a bit of comeuppance every once in a while to teach someone a lesson or simply to keep your own spirits up.

Her mother took in laundry from one of the wealthier families in town, and once when the maid came to pick up the carefully washed and folded clothing and deliver the next load, the man of the house had come along to complain that in the previous batch, there had been a wrinkle ironed into the back of his waistcoat. He announced that he felt it necessary to dock Lorna a nickel for her "lack of diligence."

"An unseen wrinkle, for the sweet love of Jesus!" Lorna had railed as soon as he'd left—more about the insult to her skill than the nickel. She took it upon herself to put an extra stitch into the buttonholes of the man's union suit that had been left for washing.

"Why're you doing that?"

"Take him a good few minutes to get it off when he has to go, won't it?" Lorna smirked.

Some weeks later, Billie was sorting through the family's mending, and there was the union suit, ripped from neck to crotch. They laughed so hard that Billie had to retrieve a set of dry drawers for her mother.

"Well, he got me back and good," Lorna said, wiping a last tear of laughter from her chin. "Made me pee myself, too!"

Billie understood that these acts should be small, untraceable, and private, as was necessary to avoid revenge. The soup event had been none of these.

Charlotte had publicly ruined a man's suit, and not even on her own behalf. She'd done it to avenge a showgirl with whom she'd likely never cross paths again. It reminded her of Paul Revere risking life and limb on that cold April morning to alert townspeople he'd never met. He didn't have to do it. It was the injustice that spurred him to act. The spurs of injustice were particularly sharp, in Billie's experience.

She had wanted to say something to Charlotte that night: that she admired her bravery, or the like. But by the time Charlotte had returned from brushing her teeth, homesickness had hit Billie like the Navajo Number Nine, and she was already starting to sniffle. Charlotte huffed an annoyed little sigh and got into bed, and Billie was right back to hating the woman again.

Their mutual loathing only worsened with comments from the other girls about how noisy their room was at night. Charlotte seemed to think it was all about Billie's crying and had started shushing her, even though Billie took pains to sniffle into her pillow to the point where she'd nearly suffocated herself on occasion. She retorted that it was all that yelling Charlotte did in her sleep. ("No, not that!" and "Stop, *stop*, STOP!"—bossing some poor imaginary servant around, no doubt.) Billie had even thrown a hairbrush at her once in the middle of an unconscious tirade, but it only served to make Charlotte shriek at the top of her lungs as if she'd been stabbed. That made it Billie's fault, of course. Charlotte insisted she slept quietly, though Billie saw doubt behind those fierce brown eyes.

The following Monday, Billie was approached by Phyllis, who, though she had been at the Topeka Harvey House the longest, had never been promoted to head waitress. She was a bit of a sourpuss when she wasn't dealing with customers, and Billie was scared of her.

"Your turn to wash the oyster shells." Phyllis handed Billie a bucket brimming with the ghastly smelling remnants. The oysters were served in shells so everyone would know they came from the sea, but Billie wasn't sure how they actually grew. She wondered why the other fish didn't just eat them up the way they ate worms on a hook.

She had just finished dumping and refilling the enormous coffee urns, wiping down every square inch of her section, and resetting the silverware and bread plates at each place. She'd been on her feet for thirteen hours and wanted nothing more than to take a hot bath and curl up in her nightgown and her mother's green cardigan.

She sighed. "Where do I do it?"

"In back. I already set a rinsing bowl and towel out there for you, and a bucket to put the clean ones into."

"Outside? It's so cold!"

"Because of the smell. You're lucky. It's much harder in the winter when the water keeps freezing on you." Phyllis turned quickly and took the stairs up to the girls' dorm.

Billie got her coat, filled the heavy bucket with hot water and dish soap, and headed out behind the restaurant, where Phyllis had, as promised, laid out all the supplies. She dragged over an old crate to sit on and began the bitter task of washing, rinsing, and drying each sharp shell and depositing it into a clean bowl. Inside of fifteen minutes her hands were red and chapped from the dishwater, with several small nicks from the jagged oyster serving dishes. Why did they have to be served in something with such sharp edges, anyway? Why couldn't they use those dainty little butter-pat bowls? They were the perfect size and so much prettier.

Suddenly the back door of the kitchen flew open. "Did you take my stockings?" Charlotte demanded.

"No, of course not. Why would I take—"

"And what are you doing out here anyway?"

"As you can easily see if you'd bother to look, I'm washing the oyster shells."

"What on earth for?"

"Because they have to be washed! We can't serve oysters in dirty shells, now can we?"

Charlotte suddenly burst out laughing. It was an odd thing to see that somber face go wide with hilarity. For a moment Billie wondered if the woman had gone mad.

"You don't *reuse* oyster shells!" Charlotte chortled. "The oysters grow *inside* them. It would be like . . . like reusing potato skins!" And she fell into another fit of laughter.

Billie's hands had begun to throb and stiffen in the cold, but they were still limber enough to squeeze Charlotte's neck, which was exactly what she wanted to do. "WELL, WHY DID PHYLLIS—"

Then it dawned on her, and she looked up just in time to see four or five girls retreat from the windows of the dorm above. But not Phyllis. She just stood there and waved.

"You can't let her get to you." It was a man's voice. Billie turned to see Leif in the doorway. "They do this with all the new girls."

"Then why didn't they do it to *her*?" Billie pointed at the still-chuckling Charlotte.

"Because she already knew about oysters. It wouldn't have worked." He picked up the heavy bucket. "You go on inside and get warm. I'll clean this up. But, Billie, don't show that you're upset. That just makes it more fun for them."

"He's right," said Charlotte, attempting—unsuccessfully—to stifle a grin.

"Don't you dare speak to me!"

Billie picked up the bucket of clean shells and trudged upstairs. Phyllis's room was the first one on the left and it was empty. Billie pulled back the bedsheets and spread the shells evenly from the pillow to the foot of the bed, flipped the sheets back over them, and smoothed the quilt. "Sleep tight," she murmured and headed for the bath.

An hour later when she heard the groan of annoyance from down the hall and the sound of a hundred shells being swept onto the floor, Billie smiled. It was the first time in a week she drifted to sleep without tears dampening her pillow.

———————————

The next morning when she came down to breakfast, Leif grinned at her, hazel eyes crinkling impishly. She couldn't help but smile back, though she had no idea what she was smiling about. "What?" she asked.

"You know what," he chuckled.

"Darned if I do."

He leaned closer and murmured, "A bed full of oyster shells."

Billie bit down on her lips to stifle her pride. "How'd you hear about it?" she whispered.

"Everyone knows. Phyllis is good and steamed."

"Oh." She hadn't meant to humiliate Phyllis, only to teach her a lesson. Had she set herself up for revenge?

"Don't worry. She knows she deserved it."

This was somewhat comforting, but it was no assurance that Phyllis wouldn't try to one-up her. "Will you keep an eye out for me?"

"I already do." He leaned against the wooden counter and crossed his arms. "Why do you think it took her a whole week to collect that many shells? I kept throwing them out."

"But why didn't you warn me?"

"Because I thought I had her. Besides, it was fun."

"What was fun?"

"Finding the shells and tossing them! Watching her start all over again, thinking no one knew what she was up to."

"You're a wily one!"

His face lit up with a grin, cheeks pink behind pale stubble. He really was quite handsome, Billie realized. Until now she'd been too overwhelmed with work and homesickness to pay much attention, but as Leif beamed at her, pleased with himself, she felt her breath go shallow.

"Billie!"

She spun around at the sound of her name to face Frances, the head waitress. "We're getting some new girls in today. No more coffee for you. You'll wait on customers at the lunch counter." She wagged a finger menacingly. "And I expect no mistakes."

Frances strode away, and Billie turned back to Leif. She didn't have anything particular to say, only wanted to catch his eye again. His face was somehow . . . reassuring. Yes, that was it. Not so much handsome as encouraging, and that was far more important. She had to keep her mind on her work. No time for mooning about bonnie young men.

"You'll do fine," he said.

Very, very reassuring.

She made plenty of mistakes, but the errors were generally fixable. Eggs over easy, not poached. Liver with bacon, not onions. Each time she scurried back to the kitchen, one of the cooks would fry her up a new round, and it would then be expertly plated by Leif with a side order of encouragement.

"Don't worry," he'd murmur. "Happens all the time."

It never happened to Charlotte, but how could Billie compete with all that . . . knowledge?

The spills caused the greatest concern. So public. So humiliating. She noticed that Pablocito, the middle-aged busboy, had taken to hovering near her with a damp rag in hand and a fresh mop just inside the kitchen door, ever at the ready.

Nevertheless, if her tips were any indication, she'd so far never had an angry customer. It was just too easy to make people happy. A sincere apology, a kind word about a tie or a hairstyle, and a free piece of pie generally did the trick. Not that she didn't mean those compliments—if you looked for something positive to say, a little joke to make, or an extra way to be helpful, you could always find it.

"Oh dear," she said as she accidentally sent a fork clattering to the floor. "Clumsy as a newborn giraffe."

"And just as adorable," said the fork's owner, a matronly woman traveling with her old dad, who gummed at his food like a baby and required an endless supply of napkins.

That night, when Billie and Charlotte got back to their room, Billie sifted through her small pile of tips—the first money she had ever earned all on her own. She pulled out three pennies and handed them to Charlotte.

"What on earth is this for?"

"It's for Kansas City, when you tipped the waitress for both of us," Billie said with a hint of told-you-so in her tone. "I said I'd pay you back."

Charlotte scoffed. "You needn't—"

"I pay my debts."

Charlotte looked at the three pennies. "Well, you've overpaid them by twenty percent."

Billie smiled. "Keep the change."

———

As the days passed, the other girls sometimes snickered at Billie's mistakes, but they also seemed to notice that patrons liked her.

"You're a miracle worker with the tough customers," Elsie said one night as they trudged upstairs after the dinner shift. "To be honest, we didn't know how long you'd last."

"To be honest, I wasn't sure, either."

"And then the shells in Phyllis's bed—"

"She was asking for it!"

Elsie laughed and swatted Billie's shoulder playfully. "I didn't know you had it in you to dish it out like that. I thought you were too sweet—you were so kind when I was sick." She stopped at the head of the stairs. "Say, why don't you and Charlotte come and sit in the sewing room with us tonight? You two always head to bed straightaway."

Billie's heart swelled. Maybe she'd make a friend here after all.

Charlotte wasn't interested. "I'm tired" was all she said as she slowly lowered herself onto her bed with a little groan. She never complained about the aches that clearly plagued her, but it was obvious to Billie that this was far more manual labor than the college girl had ever seen in her life.

"Suit yourself." Billie shrugged and happily went off without her.

Elsie, Tildie, and a couple of the other girls were already gathered in the small room that held several couches, a treadle sewing machine, and a nicked wooden table. Billie sat down next to Elsie, who was knitting what looked to be the world's longest woolen scarf.

"It's for my brother," Elsie explained. "He works in a fish cannery up in Alaska."

Another girl, Alice, was stitching red yarn for hair onto a Raggedy Ann doll.

Billie smiled to herself. These were her people, the girls who made things with their hands and had brothers in factories.

"So," said Tildie, who stopped her solitaire game at the table to study Billie. "Do you have a beau?"

Billie reached up to her head self-consciously. "No, I never wear them. My hair's so straight, they just slip right out."

All the girls laughed as Billie blinked in confusion.

"Oh, gosh, you meant it!" said Elsie. "We thought you were being funny."

"Funny about what?"

"Not *bow*," said Tilde, "*beau*! Do you have a fella?"

"Oh!" Billie tried to laugh it off. "I was looking at the doll and thinking how mine has a bow."

"You have a Raggedy Ann doll?" said Alice with a hint of surprise. "This is for my six-year-old niece."

"No, no," Billie lied. "I meant I used to. I gave it to my little sister a long time ago." In fact it was the only plaything she'd refused to hand down to her younger siblings.

"But what about the beau?" Tildie insisted.

Billie shook her head.

"Never?" said Tildie, clearly disappointed.

Billie gave an apologetic shrug, intent on keeping her mouth shut until she could gracefully leave the room. Maybe these weren't her people after all.

On Friday, after four days of waitressing mishaps somehow rewarded with a grand total of six dollars and thirty-five cents in tips, Mr. Gilstead told Billie she could take her dinner break and handed her a piece of mail, her first letter since leaving home. Her first letter ever, actually, which made it a thrill simply to hold.

To ensure that the dining room was never without service, should customers walk in off the street, the girls took staggered breaks, a practice that often found Billie a bit woeful. Left to her own thoughts and without the distraction of work or the other girls' chatter, her mind veered toward loneliness and an endless array of questions. What were her family members having for dinner? It likely wasn't as good as what she was having, and this made her feel guilty and a little sick. What if she finally made a mistake awful enough to get her sent home? What if she stopped making mistakes and *never* got sent home—only farther down the line, to a far and foreign place like New Mexico or even California?

She went out the back door of the kitchen to read the letter. It was still chilly—early April was hanging on hard to winter—but with no wind, if she stayed snug against the building, she almost didn't need a coat.

The letter from her mother included a few details about her siblings (*Peigi's entered an art contest for a baby food company and tied poor wee Dougal into a chair for a model*); her work (*How on earth do the Kriegers rend their clothes to shreds like that? Are they gladiators?*); her hopes that Billie was working hard and making friends; and an admonition to go to church every Sunday.

Oh. Church.

She hadn't forgotten about it, exactly, but last Sunday she was so tired and sad that the thought of venturing out into a strange city to find a Catholic church was completely overwhelming. Instead she'd said two Rosaries and read her favorite passage from the Bible she'd found in the dorm parlor.

It was the one where twelve-year-old Jesus leaves his parents without telling them and returns to the temple. When long-suffering Mary and Joseph backtrack, frantically trying to locate their only child, and finally find him, he answers, "Didn't you know that I would be in my Father's house?"

Once when the passage was read in church, Billie's father had leaned over to his nine offspring spread down the pew and muttered, "If the lad were mine, I'd a skelped his arse for 'im."

The idea of Da spanking the Lord and Savior of the Universe (not to mention saying *arse* in church) made nine-year-old Ian burst out laughing, and in short order every single one of the MacTavish children was in stitches, including baby Dougal, who was only laughing because everyone else was.

"Malcolm!" hissed Lorna.

"Wha'? Cheeky bugger deserved a thrashin', *I* say."

This only served to set off another round of snorting laughter, such that old Father Frazer paused his homily to aim a cold, hard stare in their direction, and Lorna marched them out and made them stand in the damp churchyard until they got hold of themselves. Actually, Ian never did, and was left to sit on the stone steps tittering with his hand clamped across his mouth till Mass was over.

The memory made Billie miss them desperately, especially the part when Lorna brought them back in and Malcolm winked at her. Lorna had tried her best to glare at him but had had to bite down hard on her lips not to smile. Billie had seen it all. Lorna had leaned into her then and whispered "Yer father" with a scoff, but adoration shone through with the warmth of a bonfire. Her parents loved each other, and their children. And no matter what else befell them, it was a good life.

Now, in the tingling chill behind the kitchen with the letter in her hand, she thought it might be better after all to go to a strange church in a strange town—maybe she wouldn't miss her family and their Mass-going shenanigans quite so much.

There was movement in the darkness to her right, and she turned quickly to see something long unfold and straighten up against the bricks.

"For the love of Jesus!" she sighed. "You scared me. What were you doing with your head down by your knees?"

"Stretching my back," said Leif, rolling his neck from side to side. "It aches sometimes." He nodded at the paper in her hands. "Letter from home?"

"Yes. Maw says I must go to church. But I don't know where it is."

"Which are you looking for?"

"Catholic."

"Ask Pablocito. He goes every Sunday."

She studied him a moment, his large hands kneading at his lower back. "Which do you go to?"

"Well, I suppose if I went, it'd be Lutheran."

He didn't go at all!

Billie wanted to ask all sorts of questions about this: *Why ever not? Aren't you worried what God will say when you meet him on the other side? Was it because of the incense?* Because sometimes if they sat too close to the front where the altar boy swung the thurible with all that smoke wafting out, it made her eyes burn.

"Can I ask you a question?"

He turned toward her. "Of course."

"Where do you live?"

"There's a boardinghouse down by the train yard that a lot of railroad men stay in."

"Did you grow up in Topeka?"

He hesitated a moment, and in the fading light she could see his face harden slightly. "I was born in Minnesota."

"My gosh, that's a long way from here. Even farther than Nebraska!"

"Sure is." He gave his long frame one last stretch. "I'd better get back in there. I'll tell Pablocito you're looking for a church."

———————

Most of the girls attended services of one denomination or another, and there was a schedule set up as to who would go when, so that each shift had coverage. The Presbyterians went at nine, the Methodists went at ten thirty, and the like. Billie was the only Catholic, and since there were Masses held on Saturday afternoons, she was expected to go then.

60 — *Juliette Fay*

"Which one?" Frances asked without looking up from the schedule she was sketching out.

"Pablocito says there's a Mass at his church at four."

Frances's gaze came up. "You're going with him? To that one?"

"So I won't have to go by myself."

Frances shrugged and went back to scribbling on her tattered schedule.

———

On Saturday, Charlotte didn't get out of bed.

"Going to be late," Billie said to no one in particular as she tied her apron.

"Day off," muttered the mound of blankets on the other bed.

"Monday is our day off this week."

"Mind your own business."

Billie sailed down the dorm staircase to breakfast with a little tingle of excitement. Charlotte would surely be fired. Then there was the tremor of guilt. What kind of person was she to delight in another's downfall? A bad person.

At least I'll have something interesting to say at confession for once. It beats "I coveted a green velvet hat with a satin bow I saw in the newspaper."

She worked all morning and most of the afternoon, as usual, and was dismissed at three so she'd have time to change into church clothes (also known as just clothes, since she'd never owned anything fancy). Pablocito met her out on Holliday Street behind the Harvey House, and they walked the mile or so to Our Lady of Guadalupe.

"How long have you been going to this church?"

"I've been coming since I moved here when I am sixteen," said the diminutive man. "It is a good place. You will like it. Everybody is very friendly, very nice. Don't worry."

This was more than she'd heard him speak in the two weeks

she'd worked side by side with him for twelve hours a day. She'd thought him shy, or possibly embarrassed that his language skills weren't that good. As it turned out, his accent was strong but so was his English.

"You will meet my wife, Graciela. She is very nice. Very beautiful. But her English is not so good, so don't worry if she don't speak to you. My children, Guillermo and Estephania, will be there, too. Their English is *very* good. Better than me!" At the Harvey House he was always hunched over, pushing a mop, loading a tray with dirty dishes, or hauling water to the coffee urns. Now he strode with his shoulders back, chest high with pride as he described his happy family. "So you will have *three* translators!"

"Translators?"

"Oh, pardon me. I thought you do not speak Spanish, but perhaps you do?"

"No, I . . . Is the Mass in Spanish?"

His face fell. "You do not know this? Guadalupe is our saint. The church is named for her."

Billie smiled her best Harvey Girl smile. "Of course! Isn't that lovely. I'm sure I'll enjoy it." *Even if I don't understand a word.*

Most of the Mass was in Latin anyway, so it wouldn't be too much of a loss. She figured she would have to mouth the prayers in English while everyone else said them in Spanish. As long as she followed the tide up to communion and got the consecrated wafer, she was certain it would count. Or mostly certain. She would say a Rosary when she got back just to be absolutely sure she was in the clear.

Pablocito's wife, Graciela, was just as tiny as he, and truly quite beautiful with her silky black hair twisted into an elaborate knot at the back of her head.

"Billie es una Harvey Girl, Graciela. Es Católica."

Billie offered her hand to shake. "Very nice to meet you, Graciela."

The woman smiled shyly. "Mucho gusto." Her small hand fit like a child's into Billie's large pink palm.

The children, Guillermo and Estephania, appeared to be twins of about eight years old. They stared up at Billie when their father introduced her, little heads craned so far back on their necks they seemed at risk of toppling backward, and the girl whispered to the boy, "*Gigante!*"

Pablocito let out a ringing laugh. "She's not a giant, *bobos!* She's just very, very tall."

Billie smiled to show she wasn't a giant.

"A friendly giant!" yelled the boy, and they took her hands and hurried her into the church and pointed out the pews and the statues—as if these were foreign ideas to her—and the painting of Jesus behind the altar.

"He's like your Jesus, only brown. But he's still Jesus," explained the girl. "You know him."

"Yes," said Billie, understanding that this statement required confirmation. "Definitely the same fellow."

Mass was spent with Estephania and Guillermo translating every single Spanish word, including the songs. "El Señor es mi roca y mi salvación! ¿De quién debería tener miedo?" they sang in high sweet voices, then raced to be the first to whisper, "The Lord is my rock and my salvation! Of whom should I be afraid?"

After Mass, the children, desperate for a few more moments with their friendly giant, clamored to be allowed to walk Billie back to the Harvey House.

"Aye, no cariños. It's getting late. You go home with Mami, now." To Billie it seemed barely evening, but Pablocito was determined not to have his family accompany them. Clearly they lived in the opposite direction.

"I can go back on my own," she offered.

"Oh, no, I cannot let you do that. A woman must not be left to walk alone in the city. Especially not on a Saturday night when people can be . . . " He searched for the right word. "Free," he said finally, "with their behavior."

There were promises to go to church together again next Saturday, and to visit their home, and to go to the park. Finally Graciela took the children gently by their small hands and led them away.

It was after five, and the streetlights flickered on as Billie and Pablocito walked down Branner Street. A few blocks from the train station, a small crowd had converged and was listening to a man with a megaphone standing on the hood of a car.

"Many politicians are squarely in our camp and will ensure the rise of the good men of the Invisible Empire. The Empire, in turn, will ensure the safety and decency of every God-fearing man, woman, and child!"

There was a wide white banner strung along the side of the car the man was standing on: *Ku Klux Klan of Kansas* it read in black lettering. Below it in red was *Join Now!* Several men inside the car hung their arms out the windows and cheered every few sentences the man on the hood spoke. Near Billie and Pablocito, a man with a camera and tall flash-bulb casing stood taking pictures. The flashes went off with pops that sounded like the BB gun her brother Angus used to shoot squirrels.

"The white man is under attack in Topeka today, and all across this fair country. The colored man takes our jobs, our land, and even *tries to take our women!*"

What on earth? wondered Billie. The one colored man she knew in Table Rock never seemed to have any designs on other people's jobs, land, or women. Sked Calhoun, the town barber, had eyes only for his wife, Melasia.

Pablocito came to a dead stop.

"The colored man insinuates himself into our society, pretending at friendship, shuffling along as if no threat exists, all the while aiming his stealthy black eyes at all that is rightfully ours!"

Staring straight ahead, Pablocito murmured, "I will go another way," and sidestepped away from her.

"There! Right there!" The voice seemed to reverberate off the buildings around them, the man's forearm slashing in their direction. "Before your very eyes, a colored man lays claim to a white woman!"

In an instant, the men were out of the car, hurtling toward Billie and Pablocito, the crowd surging apart to let the men through, then back together, like a school of pasty-white fish wearing cloche hats and bowlers.

Pablocito turned to run, but his short legs didn't get him very far before the men were upon him. Billie screamed his name. "He's not colored!" was all she could think to holler as fists rained down on her friend. "He's Mexican!" As if this distinction might matter to these people. As if it might somehow save him.

"Catholic!" she heard someone yell. "And she must be, too!" People surged toward her; a woman with a pink hat and stained teeth came in close and screamed, "Papist pig! You're a traitor to your own race!"

"No, I—"

Suddenly there was a yank on her arm, pulling her back and away from the crowd.

Charlotte.

Hands grabbed at her, and Charlotte screamed, "Stop! Please stop!"

A flashbulb went off, blinding them for a moment as they stumbled backward. Then Charlotte had her by the elbow, dragging her toward the train yard. Sirens howled by them toward the fray.

"Run, for godsake!" Charlotte hissed at her.

"Pablocito!" Billie wailed. "We have to get Pablocito!"

"Don't be stupid. You nearly got your head cracked, and then where would you be? Out of a job, for sure, and possibly dead. How would your dear mother feel about *that*?"

Seven

It was only after they'd safely made it back to the Harvey House dorm and told Mr. Gilstead the horrible news that Billie asked Charlotte, "How did you know where I was?"

"I didn't."

"But you found me. You . . . you saved me!"

"I was taking a walk. I thought a stroll might improve my"—*temper*, she almost said—"outlook. Then I stumbled upon the fracas."

When Mr. Gilstead returned from Christ's Hospital, he told them that Pablocito had suffered three cracked ribs, a broken shoulder, numerous cuts and bruises, and blows to the head which had left him "a bit foggy."

"He's alive?" asked Billie.

"Alive and well."

Not well, you bumbling fool, Charlotte thought. *Not remotely well.*

"Did you tell him I was okay? That Charlotte got me out of there?"

Mr. Gilstead's pasted-on smile became ever more strained. "Well, he . . . he wasn't terribly . . . conversational."

"But he'll be okay?"

"Yes, I feel certain that he'll be right as rain, bussing tables again in no time."

"And the men are in jail?"

"The men . . . ?"

"The ones who did this to him. The police caught them?"

"Well, now, I . . . I'm not entirely sure. The police don't always involve themselves . . . in, uh . . . that sort of . . . Men do fight, you know. This is the West. We don't slap the cuffs on every gent who gets into a scuffle."

"Scuffle?" Charlotte muttered through clenched molars. "He was beaten within an inch of his life by three bullies who were at least twice his size."

She turned on her heel, headed up the stairs, and put herself to bed early, before the tremors she'd struggled to contain broke loose and tossed her to the floor.

The next morning a scream woke her. Her eyes flew open, and she sat straight up in bed with a sense of dread so deep it was as if she already had one foot in the grave.

Billie was also sitting up, long white legs hanging off the side of her bed. She stared at Charlotte.

Charlotte exhaled. "For goodness' sake, what are you looking at? And who screamed?"

"You did," murmured Billie. "It was you."

"I never," scoffed Charlotte.

"You said just what you said to that mob, 'Please stop!' and then you screamed like someone was stabbing you."

Charlotte tucked the covers up a little closer around her chest. "I must have had a nightmare about it."

"Yes, but you have nightmares all the time, and you're always begging someone to stop."

What was there to say in her own defense? *No I don't?* That clearly wasn't working anymore. *I'm secretly married, and my husband, the man who swore to love and honor me all the days of my life, beats me regularly?*

"It's none of your business," said Charlotte.

"No, I suppose it isn't." Billie didn't move, only continued to sit there. "You must be very brave."

"Why ever would you say that?"

"Because you have all these nightmares about someone hurting you, and you went into that crowd to save me anyway."

———————————

That day the dining room seemed particularly full of passengers who dropped their silverware and tipped over their milk while complaining that the soup wasn't hot enough and the oysters smelled off. (They weren't. Charlotte had grown up in the port city of Boston, in a shipping family, and had eaten enough oysters to know fresh from spoiled.) It was Sunday, of course, so they were short-staffed all morning as one group of Harvey Girl faithfuls, and then another and another, attended the services of their choosing. Charlotte, who'd been raised Episcopal but had stopped attending church after her decidedly secular nuptials to Simeon, chose none. Thus she and Billie had to work as hard as those ship-paddling Vikings of yore, and without so much as a moment to lean in a doorway and take a sip of Fred Harvey's world-famous coffee.

"You're in the paper!"

The last batch of churchgoers had returned with the *Topeka Daily Capital*, and the picture glared out from the front page: Charlotte and Billie, faces contorted with fear, clinging to each other as hands reached out from the edges of the photo like demons' claws. The headline read: TOPEKA KKK RALLY TURNS TROUBLESOME.

"Troublesome?" Billie turned to Charlotte. "*Troublesome?*"

But Charlotte was too busy checking the photo credit below the picture.

Associated Press.

As the rest of the girls' heads clustered over the paper to read the article, Charlotte's mind frantically calculated the cascading probability of being discovered.

Would the *St. Louis Post-Dispatch* pick up the piece from the AP? Likely. The Klan was a high-interest story, with many readers passionately for or against it.

If so, would it be printed with the picture or without? Definitely with. That picture was worth more than the entire column.

If so, would Simeon see it? He read the paper cover to cover every single day, so yes.

If so, would he be able to locate her at the Harvey House? Questionable. In the picture she wore street clothes, and they had been several blocks from the train depot. There was nothing to tie her to the restaurant.

"How did the reporter know we were Harvey Girls?" Billie said suddenly, her head bobbing up from the paper.

"Must have followed you back to the station," said Tildie.

"*Oh, dear God,*" Charlotte whispered.

———————

That night, Billie didn't hide her face in her pillow and pretend not to cry as she usually did. She lay on her side facing Charlotte, head propped in her hand.

"Who hurt you?"

"I told you it's none of your business. Besides, you wouldn't understand, so just go back to crying yourself to sleep." It was mean, and Charlotte felt an immediate urge to apologize, which was strange. She didn't like this girl—wasn't she the reason Simeon might now know where Charlotte was? The last thing she should care about was Billie's feelings—or anyone else's. She just wanted to find somewhere she could finally be safe, and it didn't matter if she never made another friend for the rest of her life.

Even more strange, Billie didn't seem to be put off by the comment. "Why were you so upset when you saw our picture in the paper?"

"I was not upset in the least, only surprised. Don't go making a fuss of things where there isn't any fuss to be had. If you're bored and looking for high drama, go to the movies."

"I can keep a secret, you know. I have secrets of my own."

"Yes, well, the way your heart flutters when you see that kitchen boy is no secret."

Billie's pale cheeks went pink. A direct hit. The girl muttered something unintelligible.

"I can't understand your mumbling."

"I said, that's not the secret I was talking about."

"Well, what then?"

"I'm fifteen."

Fifteen? thought Charlotte. *Good Lord, she's a child. No wonder she cries so much.* A memory traced across her brain: herself at that age, terrified on her first day at the Winsor School, which was only across town, not in a different state entirely.

"Years old," Billie clarified. "Not eighteen, like I'm supposed to be."

Charlotte continued to stare. *She hates it here. She desperately wants to go home, but she stays because her family needs the money. Such a hard worker, and never a complaint.*

Billie puffed out a little sigh and rolled onto her back. "Now you think I'm even more of a baby than you already did." She popped up again to face Charlotte. "You won't tell, will you? Oh, sweet Jesus on the cross, please don't tell!"

"No, of course not. Besides, even if I did, I doubt they'd fire you. You're clumsy but you're already a better waitress than half the girls here."

Billie's eyebrows went up. Her surprise at such a small compliment stung Charlotte like a wasp. *My God, what have I become?*

"I'm married," she said suddenly.

Billie didn't move a muscle, but Charlotte could see her putting the pieces together. "My friend Clara . . . her father has a temper" was all she said.

They sat there in the quiet of the dorm, the silence broken only by the sound of the clock ticking from the bathroom. Frances had hung it to remind them not to dillydally, and it echoed off the tile and down the hallway in a comforting sort of way. It had lulled Charlotte back to sleep from bad dreams on several occasions. Now it sounded ominous.

"He didn't know where you were, did he?" said Billie.

"No. He didn't."

Eight

Four days passed. Maybe he hadn't figured it out after all.

Charlotte had tried to leave Simeon several times, and he'd always done a rather miraculous job of convincing her to stay. He was like one of those magicians in the vaudeville shows, waving his charm and compliments around like a magic wand, and *poof*, her resolve would disappear into thin air.

But as his despair over his work prospects, involvement with radicals, and drinking worsened, the apologies and promises to love her as she deserved to be loved had disappeared. In their place rose threats of more violence—the ultimate violence, in fact, if she left.

It had been the black eye that had finally convinced her. He'd never hit her in the face before. Breasts, stomach, back, head, yes, but not the face. She couldn't go to work looking like that. And if she couldn't make money, and he drank up all the money he made, they'd be out in the street. What would keep him from killing her then? She'd be dead one way or another, and it was certainly better to die free than in the cage he had so carefully built for her.

Maybe he'd found someone else to torment. She dearly hoped so, while also feeling terrible for any poor girl who might have fallen under the spell of his poetic sorcery. She'd only been gone for three weeks. Could his charm work that fast?

Maybe he was dead. Fallen down a set of stairs in a drunken stupor, stepped out in front of a trolley car, contracted measles or smallpox or that terrible flu that had killed so many people back in 1918. Of course, it would have been better if the flu had carried him off then, before she'd ever met him. But she would settle for it taking him now.

As disturbing as it was to know he was out there, having practically been given a map as to where she was, there was also something surprisingly calming about having told someone. The terrible truth of her marriage had been hers alone to carry for almost two years now. Then suddenly she'd allowed a fifteen-year-old girl—of all people!—into the darkest corner of her life, and felt some strange relief.

Billie never said another word about it, asked no questions, offered no opinions. Nor had she seemed to pass any kind of judgment. Charlotte had assumed that anyone who learned such a damning secret would shun her. To the contrary, Billie stayed close. If Charlotte served a man eating alone, it was all she could do not to trip over the girl.

"I'm all right, you know," she told Billie. "You don't have to keep an eye on me."

The girl had said simply, "You don't have sisters, do you?"

On Friday, just as the dinner crowd commenced its mass exodus toward the train, a man walked in and spoke to Mr. Gilstead, who showed him to one of Charlotte's tables in the dining room.

At first she didn't recognize him—or rather, she didn't look particularly closely, intent as she generally was at getting on with the business of order taking.

"Good evening," she said. "How may I help you?"

"Hello, Charlotte."

Her eyes flicked to meet the gentleman's gaze.

No. Please, no.

Without thinking, she raised her hands to her chest, in position to protect her face if he attacked her. "Not my face!" she'd begged when he'd raised his fist to give her that shiner. "Please, I can't—" *work if you hit my face,* she'd meant to say, but he'd already cracked her across the cheekbone.

"You're looking well," he said now, without a hint of sarcasm. Surprising, given that she was wearing this ridiculous outfit and he was, well, Simeon. His freshly shaved cheeks looked thinner than she remembered, and his hair was cut short and combed.

Her pulse pounded in her throat. "What do you want?" she managed to murmur.

"I don't want anything from you," he said softly. "I've taken enough already."

"Then why are you here?"

"Just to apologize. And to thank you for teaching me a lesson. One I certainly needed to learn."

The kind words, the gentle delivery. It was the old Simeon, the man she'd loved with such desperation that she'd given up everything—inheritance, social status, home, and family.

"You've cut your hair," she said stupidly, because nothing else came to mind amid the crashing waves of fear and longing.

He smiled. "The anarchist look wasn't for me. Nor the drinking."

"You've stopped drinking?"

"From the moment I came home and found you gone. Turns out it was a sound financial decision as well." He chuckled self-deprecatingly. "I was able to buy this suit so I could present a fresh version of myself."

Something about that phrase, *a fresh version of myself,* struck a minor chord to her highly attuned ear. Why would he need to present anything at all if he wanted only to apologize? But she knew better than to question his motives; that would only set him off, and she couldn't afford a scene. She would accept his apology and serve him some lunch. With any luck, that would satisfy him, and he'd be on his way.

"Please order something," she said, keeping her tone even.

"I didn't come here to eat, I just wanted to see you."

"Yes, but if you don't eat, it will appear as if you only mean to talk to me, and that's not allowed."

"By whom?"

"By my boss. I can't lose my job, Simeon." Why was he purposely being obtuse? "I know you probably don't approve of my being a waitress, but I didn't have many choices left."

His eyes gleamed in a way that could be either amorous or furious, and she instinctively took a step back from the table.

"Not only do I approve, but I admire you. You truly understand the plight of the working class now. The grueling hours, unsafe conditions, low pay, disregard of those above you . . . "

Charlotte felt an unexpected defensiveness rise up. "This is no sweatshop. Look around. It's clean and orderly. I'm paid well and treated well as long as I do as I was contracted to do, which is to serve customers with courtesy and efficiency. So will you please order something?"

He wanted only soup, which she brought him, and he ate slowly so as to have more time to reminisce—about his first sight of her at Wellesley, how adorably serious she was, how smart and purposeful, unlike most of her dithering, husband-hunting schoolmates. How brave she was to agree to meet him at the Boston Public Library, far from the college. His gratitude that such a lovely, deeply curious woman would risk her reputation to sneak off and spend time with him.

He was like a songbird, carefully crafting and performing the precise tune that would woo his chosen mate.

And little by little . . . wooed she was. She had fallen deeply in love in those heady times, laced as they were with the added excitement of a clandestine affair. Could it be like that again?

"Is that him?" Billie hissed, once she'd seen them talking for longer than Charlotte had talked to any customer, ever.

Charlotte felt an urge to lie. It almost wasn't a lie. This wasn't the husband she'd run from, the one who'd turned her life into hell's picture book. This was the one she'd married.

"Yes, but he's . . . he's not . . . he seems fine now. And anyway, he just wants to talk."

"Is that what you want?"

"Yes, I suppose it is."

As she served other patrons, always returning to him and his slowly ebbing soup, she realized that the history of their relationship was like an impossibly complicated math problem. How had Simeon, her Simeon, become a raging animal? And how had she, Charlotte, a young woman with a good head on her shoulders, who'd been raised to think herself better than most, become his prey? How had A become B, and C become D? Every logical calculation she'd ever applied to the problem had failed to solve it. But now she saw that perhaps it needn't be solved at all. Perhaps it could simply be reversed.

Nine

"*I need to ask you something,*" Billie said to Leif as he loaded her tray with seven fruit compotes. "If something happens . . ."

"Just hold the tray steady and don't lean forward when you reach up for each bowl. You'll be fine."

"I haven't spilled anything in days!"

He grinned. "Which means you're due."

She narrowed her eyes at him. "Well, that's just sidesplitting and all, but I'm serious. If something happens, and I ask for your help, will you give it?"

His smile dimmed. "What's this about, Billie?"

"I don't know yet."

"I'm leaving tomorrow morning," Simeon said when the bowl was empty but for the last lick of tomato stock now congealing into brown sludge. "Have to get back to work. I've been promoted, by the way. Covering features."

Not the news desk he'd wanted so badly that he'd stay up for days tracking down a story, fueled by drink and his own fury. Features was less likely to rile him up. Better for him, and safer for her.

"Congratulations."

"Yes, well. It's a move in the right direction, anyway. A stepping-stone to better things." His gaze was humble, loving. "Might I see you one last time before I leave? Perhaps when you get off work, we could take a walk as we used to in the Boston Public Garden? It would mean the world to me."

His words conjured warm memories of strolling along the meandering walkways, watching the swan boats glide across the pond. But something stopped her from agreeing, a little warning buzz at the back of her brain that said, *Don't wander off. Not with him. Not yet.*

"Curfew's at ten, and I won't be done here much before that. But I'll have a short dinner break around eight. You could meet me on Holliday Street behind the depot and say your goodbyes then."

His face lit with gratitude. "I'll be waiting."

———————

That man—Billie didn't like to think of him as someone Charlotte had once loved—finally left. Maybe everything was fine, but Billie still felt skittish. As they cleaned their stations at the end of the shift, her gaze continued to trace across the room, nerves bracing for his return.

When he didn't, she felt foolish. Just another overly emotional teenage girl. Maybe she was bored, as Charlotte had said, imagining turmoil where there was none. Except she'd been right about Charlotte. There was turmoil aplenty.

"Anything happen?" Leif asked when she came into the kitchen to rinse her cleaning rag.

"No, but . . . "

He studied her. "You don't seem the type to make something out of nothing."

"I'm not!"

"You can trust me, you know."

"I do, but I can't . . . say . . . "

He seemed almost a little hurt as he went back to slicing lemons for tomorrow's tea drinkers. "Well, I'm here if you need me."

———————

That night as they changed into their nightgowns, Charlotte said, "Thank you for not asking any questions."

It was bitterly disappointing. Billie had a thousand questions, and Charlotte had just effectively closed the door on all of them.

"I don't want to pry," she said. "As long as everything's all right."

"Yes, I think it is."

And that was it. Charlotte pulled the chain on the wall lamp, and they lay on opposite sides of the tiny room, breathing into the darkness.

"I feel I should tell you . . . "

Billie's eyes flew open. "Yes?"

"I met with him again during my dinner break, and I've decided to return to St. Louis with him in the morning."

It was all Billie could do not to leap out of bed and shake the woman. "He's making you?"

"Not at all. In fact, he didn't even ask me. If he had, I would have reflexively said no. But by not asking and demonstrating the humility to know that he has no right to ask after how he'd behaved . . . he showed me that he's changed."

"He hurt you, Charlotte."

"He's my husband, Billie."

I suppose he must be, thought Billie, *or have cast some sort of fiendish spell, else why would someone so smart have anything to do with a man who'd beat her?*

Charlotte yelled in her sleep just as much as she ever did, and Billie hoped that would give her some pause. But when Charlotte woke in the morning, she packed her things into that battered suitcase with the gold letters. CMC. No *T* for Turner. So maybe that wasn't even her right name. Maybe Billie didn't really know her at all.

"Will you come with me to speak to Mr. Gilstead?" Charlotte said as she slid the faded green day dress over her head. "You can confirm that I told you I was married before Simeon arrived. I don't want him to think I'm running off with some customer."

"Of course." Although why Charlotte cared what Mr. Gilstead thought was a puzzle to Billie. If all went well, Charlotte would presumably never need a job from the Fred Harvey Company again.

"Why are you in street clothes?" barked Frances. "Go back up and change before the train pulls in."

"I need to speak to Mr. Gilstead. I'm resigning my position."

Frances's eyes went wide with fury. "And just before the seven fourteen arrives with a load of passengers! I didn't take you for a quitter." She turned her head and called, "Mr. Gilstead!"

Frances insisted on being part of the conversation, of course, so the four of them stepped out behind the kitchen to the Holliday Street side of the station. Charlotte explained quite matter-of-factly that she'd lied on her application. Her marriage had had some "difficulties," and at the time she'd felt it best to strike out on her own. But now that things were on the mend, she planned to go back and try again.

"What kind of difficulties?" Frances demanded to know.

"Bad ones," Billie muttered. "Very bad."

Frances's face fell.

"Billie, please do not answer on my behalf," said Charlotte. "It's none of your—"

"Are you sure?" murmured Frances.

"Pardon me?"

"Are you certain you want to go back? My sister . . . " She left the sentence unfinished.

"My friend Clara had bruises all the time," Billie whispered. "A bad temper doesn't just go away on its own in a couple of weeks."

"Darling!" The exclamation came from quite a way down the sidewalk, as if the exclaimer was unable to contain himself long enough to achieve a polite distance.

"That's him," said Billie. "He's the one."

"Billie, don't," hissed Charlotte.

The four of them watched him approach as his gaze flicked from one to the next. Then he saw the suitcase.

"Ah, wonderful. You're packed and ready to go. Let me get your bag."

Charlotte watched him snatch up the suitcase, and Billie saw her expression change, as if she were remembering something.

Simeon nodded at the women and stretched out his hand to Mr. Gilstead. "I assume you're the manager?"

"Yes, sir, I am."

"Well, if you'll just arrange for her ticket on the eight-oh-two east to St. Louis, we'll be on our way."

"Arrange for her ticket?"

"Yes, my understanding is that the Fred Harvey Company gives a girl a train ticket home if it doesn't work out." He chuckled merrily. "Well, I guess we can all agree it didn't work out."

Mr. Gilstead straightened up, suit buttons straining against the intrusion. "Sir, a return ticket is provided only for girls who leave in good standing. Your . . . Charlotte has admitted to lying on her application. The contract clearly states that if a girl is married before completing one year of service, the company is under no obligation to provide transportation home. You'll have to pay for the ticket yourself."

Simeon's merry smile seemed to calcify. "Now, see here. She's worked almost the full month and for free. You can't possibly deny her a ticket—one that Fred Harvey receives gratis in a tidy little quid pro quo with the Santa Fe Railway."

He's done some digging, thought Billie. The man knew more about it than she did.

"I most certainly can deny her—and I will. She worked for free because it was her training period. Now all that training is for nothing."

Simeon reached out and placed his hand lightly on Mr. Gilstead's shoulder, a friendly gesture that nonetheless made Charlotte flinch. "Listen, my friend. The company pays its laborers a pittance—*toast crumbs*—compared to what Fred Harvey's greedy offspring suck out of it. And you're trying to tell me—"

"Simeon, don't."

He turned to her. "Don't what, Charlotte? Don't what? Fight against a morally bankrupt system for what's rightfully mine?"

Frances slid her hand into the crook of Charlotte's arm.

Billie took a few strides back to the kitchen windows and gave two little raps. Leif looked up from chopping onions. She crooked a finger, beckoning him toward her. He gauged the look on her face, and in a moment he was in the kitchen doorway.

"It's happening," she murmured.

Simeon's face had slowly advanced toward Mr. Gilstead's until they were practically nose to nose, as Simeon barked into his face about the stink of capitalism and the rise of the proletariat. All the while, Frances slowly tugged Charlotte back toward the Harvey House.

Suddenly Simeon slammed the suitcase so hard onto the ground that it bounced a few feet away. Billie grabbed it and followed quickly behind Frances and Charlotte.

"Charlotte!" Simeon screamed after them. "Charlotte, don't go!"

Charlotte stopped at the kitchen door and turned toward him.

"Now, you listen to me," Frances murmured in her ear. "You can choose to die, or you can choose to leave right now and live."

Simeon's gaze bore into her, and Charlotte stared back. "You come back here right now, or I'll—" He took a step toward her, and Leif lunged into his path. Simeon cocked back his fist, and in a split second everything went from slow motion to fast.

Frances hustled Charlotte through the kitchen with Billie at their heels. "You're going to get on the seven fourteen heading west; it'll pull in any minute. Don't get off till Williams, Arizona. It's about a twenty-hour ride. Don't get off for *any reason.*"

Elsie went by with a tray full of cookies to restock the glass display case, and Frances took the tray right out of her hands. She snatched up a paper sack, dumped all the cookies in, and handed them to Charlotte. "There's your breakfast, lunch, and dinner."

The train whistled as it approached the station, and the three women scurried out toward the platform.

"I don't have a ticket," panted Charlotte.

"I'll take care of that. Williams, you understand? Not before." Frances raised her voice to be heard over the hissing of the steam brakes. "They need girls in California, but they hadn't decided where to place you yet. By the time you get to Williams, Gilstead will have it sorted out with Miss Steele."

"Won't he tell her that I'm married?"

Frances squinted in thought for the briefest moment. "He'll tell her you were receiving unwanted advances from an overly amorous customer, and you need to be transferred for your own safety. It's the truth."

"He won't mention that the customer happened to be my husband?"

"No."

"How can you be sure?"

Frances leveled her gaze at Charlotte. "Because I'll tell him not to."

The locomotive came to a stop beside them. Frances hurried over to a conductor leaning out from one of the compartment doors and gestured back toward Charlotte. The conductor studied Charlotte for a moment, then nodded. Frances waved frantically for her to get on board.

Charlotte looked up at Billie. "Thank you," she said.

"Oh, Charlotte, I hope we meet again! I'm sorry I didn't always—"

Charlotte put her hand on Billie's arm. "You're a smart girl. Smarter than I am, apparently. Don't ever forget that."

Ten

Billie held herself together all day, focusing on the endless delivery and retrieval of what seemed like a thousand pieces of china. Whenever she had a moment to think, the look on that man's face—like he might take Mr. Gilstead's head clean off without a second thought—invaded unbidden. It was utterly terrifying to know how close Charlotte had come to going off with him.

And now what? What if he tracked her down again? How much more furious was he now that she'd slipped from his grasp a second time?

The other girls whispered behind their hands, and that nosy Tildie came over to Billie's station, leaned against the counter in a way that did not seem nearly as relaxed as it was meant to be, and said, "Your friend left in quite a hurry. You must know all about it."

"It's not my story to tell."

With no gossip to glean, Tildie moseyed right back to her own station.

Bunch o' spraffin' eejits, Billie could hear her father say as if he were standing next to her.

After that night with the doll's bow, the other girls had never really included her. They went out on their days off or chattered in the sewing room or did one another's hair, but she'd somehow gotten stuck with Charlotte, who had no interest in any of those things. Billie had blamed Charlotte for this, of course. But deep down she wondered if they sensed how young she was and didn't want her tagging along.

The person she was most worried about at the moment was Leif. The last she'd seen of him, he was heading straight into the fisticuffs with Charlotte's husband. Afterward Mr. Gilstead told her only that he was fine and was just getting "seen to."

"Seen to for what?" she asked.

"A few scratches. Nothing to worry about."

Gilstead had been similarly glib about Pablocito, who still hadn't returned to work a week later.

She hoped Frances might be a little kinder to her after they'd joined forces to help Charlotte escape. That night, as Billie comforted herself with a quick, well-deserved weep, Frances rapped on the door and stuck her head in.

"Charlotte got away," she snapped. "My sister never did, God rest her soul, and your little friend from home probably won't, either. Cry for them if you want to, but don't cry for Charlotte. And you'd *better* not be crying for yourself."

Clearly, Frances's sympathy only extended so far.

The next morning, Billie went down to breakfast early in desperate hope that Leif had returned. She found him with a bruise the size of a ripe plum spreading across his cheekbone and a bandage wrapped around the knuckles of his right hand. With his left he awkwardly rolled a ball of bread dough and placed it on a greased metal tray.

"What happened?"

He shrugged.

Why was it that men became blubbering babies over splinters, yet shrugged off the worst possible things? Her brothers could practically get run over by farm machinery and still claim they were fine, but let them get a head cold . . .

"Leif!" It was all she could do not to stomp her foot.

He stopped pulverizing the little wad of dough and gazed at her with those hazel eyes that looked like the crackled glaze on an old teacup.

"Gilstead left me with that madman so he could go call the

police, and we went at it." A flicker of humor came up in those eyes. "He got his licks in, but I did, too. Broken nose and a bit lighter in the teeth department, I think."

"I didn't know you were a fighter."

He went back to mauling the dough. "Not by choice, but it comes in handy."

"You didn't come back to work."

He tipped his bruised cheek at her. "This fellow gave me some trouble. Couldn't see straight for a few hours."

She held up three fingers. "How many?"

"Twelve?" He laughed, then winced. "Head still throbs a bit."

"You got your bell rung. Here, give that to me." She held out her hand for the dough, and he dropped it into her palm. She quickly went to work on the rest of it, rolling and placing little sticky globes onto the greased metal sheet. "The police came?"

"They were getting ready to cart us both off when Gilstead stepped in and vouched for me. Then he sent me off to Christ's Hospital, which was about right, since I was practically seeing Jesus with every step."

She finished the last bread roll and looked up at him. That beautiful face stamped with another man's rage. "He got you good," she murmured.

"But I got him better."

"I've no doubt."

He smiled. "Your confidence is much appreciated."

Lord, but her heart began to pound, and she knew she'd better fly before her face flushed like stewed tomatoes. She headed for the lunchroom door. "I'll just check on my . . . " Something. She'd check on . . . what exactly?

She stood on the other side of the door, catching her breath for a moment. Oh, yes. That was it. Customers.

———————————

"I meant to tell you I saw Pablocito at the hospital yesterday," Leif said that night, when Billie carried a dessert plate and two forks into the kitchen from her last table, a couple who'd smiled secrets at each other as they shared a lemon meringue pie. At one point, the man had held out a forkful of lemony sweetness to his lady friend, and her mouth opened, rosy and inviting, to accept it. Billie thought she might melt into the floor from envy.

"He's still in the hospital?"

"No, they were letting him out. His shoulder's in a sling and he had a limp, but he was walking, and that's the important thing."

"His face?"

She saw Leif's hesitation, and her heart sank. "The bruises are healing up pretty good," he said a half second late. "Couple of weeks you won't know they were ever there."

"Would it . . . do you think I could ever go see him? I feel so badly."

"It wasn't your fault, Billie."

"I left him there!"

"And what would you have done if you'd stayed? Taken on a bunch of KKK men? If you tried to help a fellow with dark skin, they wouldn't care if you were white and female. Cripes, they wouldn't care if you were Greta Garbo."

"My father says you never leave a friend alone in a brawl."

"Well, he's right about that, but I'm sure he didn't mean *you* you."

"He said it to all of us."

"How many of you are there?"

"Nine."

His eyebrows went up. "And where are you in that mob?"

She smiled. "At the top."

"Might have guessed."

"Why's that?"

"Because you're bossy and—"

"Am not!"

"And . . . you look out for people."

This was true, but she was the oldest; it was her job. He made it sound so . . . nice.

"I wish I could've looked out for Pablocito."

He turned back to the potatoes he'd been scrubbing rather unsuccessfully using one hand and just the fingertips of the other. "We can't always save people."

Where are your *people?* she wondered.

"When's your day off?" he asked.

"Tomorrow."

"Mine, too. I'll take you to see Pablocito."

———————

She was unaccountably nervous, changing from one dress to the next, to the next, then back again. Thank goodness she only had three. Green cardigan on. Green cardigan off. Which way made her look older? It was her mother's sweater, so by rights it should have helped . . . but did it send her past the far side of "older" into matronly?

Och, dinna fash, ye wee eejit!

The fact was, everything she owned looked like it had been passed down for generations. In contrast to the crisp, starched uniforms, which were regularly shipped out to the Fred Harvey laundry shop in Newton, Kansas, and tossed away altogether the minute they looked the slightest bit worn, her own clothes made her seem like a penniless waif.

This would've been a generally accurate description, except that with three square meals a day, she'd gained a few pounds. It was something she'd always hoped for, but now the clothes felt snug, and she worried a button might pop off and fly right into his eye!

She slumped down on the bed.

He doesn't have a whit of interest in you or what you wear. He's just being nice, so stop this nonsense right now.

———————————

"It's not far," said Leif when he met her on Holliday Street. "He lives in the Bottoms just north of here, up by the river."

"So it's at the top of the Bottoms?" she said with a little smile.

"Ha! Sharp as a shearing blade, aren't you?"

She'd only ever seen him in his all-white kitchen clothes, so the man who stood before her now in brown pants, gray vest, and slightly frayed tweed coat looked almost like a stranger. His sandy hair seemed lighter under the brown newsboy cap than it did when he wore the white brimless cook's hat, his eyes less gemlike with the shadow cast by the cap's bill. But there was his smile, slightly wry, always kind.

He had a paper sack tucked under his arm—a gift from the kitchen staff, he said. "Some of the smaller cuts of meat that we can't serve, potatoes, carrots, a couple of tins of sardines, day-old rolls, and all the broken cookies I could find. I may have accidentally broken a few myself." He smiled and held up his bandaged hand. "Clumsy."

As they walked up Adams Street, the homes and businesses got more dilapidated and the children more plentiful. A band of boys rode by on scooters made of scrap lumber and rickety wheels, each one garishly painted and decorated. Two girls trotted past them rolling hoops, occasionally colliding with each other and laughing. All of the children they saw gave extra-long looks to the two tall, white-skinned, pale-haired teenagers making their way deeper into a neighborhood that rarely hosted such specimens.

"I loved my hoop," Billie said wistfully. Actually she'd loved her Raggedy Ann doll even more, but she'd eat soap before she mentioned that again.

"Left it at home, then?" Leif teased as he steered them onto Second Avenue. "Didn't fit in your traveling bag?"

"Oh, I gave it to my younger sisters years ago. I didn't have much time for hoop rolling, once I started helping my maw with her washing and mending business. And when I did have a minute, all I wanted was to sit down!" The day was warming up, spring finally asserting itself over April's vacillations, and she undid the top button of her coat. "What was your favorite toy?"

"Couldn't get enough of checkers."

"Who'd you play with?"

He plucked off his cap, ran a hand back through his wayward sandy curls, then redeposited it. "Whoever was around."

"Did your dad teach you? My dad taught all of us."

"Loves the game, does he?"

"Oh yes. He says it keeps the mind active and the body still. He hauls bricks all day long, so he prefers his arse in a chair."

Billie put a hand to her lips. Sweet Jesus, she'd sworn in public— in front of a young man who was not one of her mouthy brothers, nor any relation to her at all!

Leif let out a ringing laugh. "Don't worry, I won't tell Fred Harvey you cuss."

"I don't!"

"You just did."

"I was only saying what my da would say." She affected a Scottish burr: "*Ge' the board, an' sit yer wee arse doon for a game, lass. Och, there ye go, red or black? I'll take the black now, I'm yer da after all.*"

"*You want to play de sheckers?*" he answered her in a strange accent. "*Yah, sure you do! Black or red, you shoose.*"

Billie laughed and clapped her hands together. "Is that your da? Where's he from—Holland?"

"Sweden."

"And what does he think about you coming all the way to Kansas to work for Fred Harvey? I'll bet he misses you."

"He doesn't think anything." Leif tucked his hands in his pockets and squinted up the street as if something had caught his eye. "He passed."

"I . . . I'm so sorry," Billie stammered. "I shouldn't have . . . "

He smiled in her direction, but only with his mouth. "Don't fret. It was a long time ago."

What about your mother? she wanted to ask but caught herself in time. It wasn't right to pry, despite the fact that she wanted to know every last thing about him.

"My da lost his da at a young age," she said quickly to fill the chasm of silence that had suddenly opened between them. "He had to work and never got past the third grade in school."

Leif only nodded.

"I think that's why he had so many children. He wanted us to have each other if anything happened. Also, he loves my mother."

Lord in heaven, what was she thinking, mentioning such a thing! Leif continued to gaze up the street, but she could tell he was biting the inside of his cheek.

Well, that's that, she thought. *Between cursing and mentioning my parents' private business, he thinks I'm either a trollop or a radical.*

At least they'd gotten off the subject of his dead father, even if it had cost her his good opinion. She wondered if she should turn around on the spot and go back to the Harvey House.

"It's that one," Leif said, pointing to a tiny little one-story house hemmed in on either side by a fruit stand and a livery. Her own home was tight for eleven people, but this looked like a cart shed by comparison. The outer walls were unpainted and water stained, but the front step had been recently swept and the one window was clean.

Leif knocked on the door. No one answered at first, but then they heard slow thumping across the boards toward them. The knob turned and finally a face appeared.

"Pablocito!" Billie smiled brightly, bracing herself against the sight of him, cheeks and nose punctuated randomly with fading bruises.

"Billie," he murmured, and attempted a lopsided smile with the less battered side of his face. "You came to see me?"

"Yes! Leif brought me. He said he saw you at the hospital, and you were on your way home."

Pablocito opened the door a little wider and gazed up at Leif. "Aye! You look worse!"

Leif chuckled. "The bruise spread, but it feels a little better, honest."

Pablocito ushered them into the tiny house, which Billie soon realized was only two rooms: a kitchen area with table and chairs, and a door that led to a bedroom in back. He hobbled over to the cast-iron stove and bent to grab a log for the fire, stifling a groan. Leif put the bag he'd brought on the board by the cupboard and hurried to take the log, as Billie helped Pablocito to a chair. A pot on the stove already had water, and he directed her to a little canister of tea and three mugs in the cupboard. There wasn't much else in there except a half loaf of bread and some rotting fruit, likely cast-offs from the stand next door. He offered them slices of bread.

"Oh, we've just eaten," Billie said, though breakfast had been some hours before, and she could've done with a nibble of something.

They drank their tea and enjoyed some mild conversation about the weather turning warm and Pablocito's imminent return to the Harvey House, which, by the looks of him, Billie very much doubted. The men joked about Leif's future as the next Jack Dempsey.

"Where are Estephania and Guillermo?" Billie asked.

"They play with the kids outside. My wife works at the slaughter-house, and she doesn't want them to bother me. But they are not here, and that is what bothers me!"

"We can go and find them for you."

"No, no. Who knows where they can be. Probably at the river throwing rocks. You will walk in the other direction."

"We could stroll up that way," offered Leif. "We'll make a loop on our way back."

Pablocito made several weak attempts to convince them that they shouldn't go to the trouble, but Billie knew how he loved his children and must have missed them terribly while he was stuck in the hospital all week. As they bid their goodbyes, Billie couldn't help but add, "I'm so sorry, Pablocito. I didn't know people could be . . . like that."

He and Leif exchanged a look so brief she barely caught it, but it was there. *Young,* that look said. *And naive.* She'd grown up poor, the oldest of nine, her mother's confidante, and thus privy to much of the adult world around her. And yet she realized in that moment that none of it had prepared her for the acts of pure malice she'd witnessed in only the last week.

As they headed the few blocks north to the river to search for the children, Billie said, "Strange how he didn't even ask about the bag."

"I brought one earlier this week, and his wife said he'd be mad. But he's not making any money, and a hospital isn't cheap. You have to fight your pride when you've got a family to feed, so I didn't expect any thanks. I'm only glad he didn't make me carry it back."

The street ended at City Park, a lovely small parcel with a little grandstand that overlooked the Kaw River. There were kids playing ball and hide-and-seek. A few dipped their feet in the water, squealing and laughing as they shivered, ran out, and ran back in again. Pablocito's children didn't seem to be among them.

"Mind if we sit for a minute?" said Leif. His pallor, except for the blooming bruise, had gone decidedly gray.

"Are you all right?"

"My head's throbbing a bit. Just a quick rest."

They sat down on the steps of the gazebo, and Leif closed his eyes and leaned his head against the banister. Billie tipped her face up to the sun and enjoyed its warmth in silence.

"You can talk," Leif murmured.

"It's all right. I don't want to disturb you."

"No, actually it would be a nice distraction."

"What should I talk about?"

"Anything. Your family. Tell me all your brothers' and sisters' names."

"Well, there's my brother Angus. He's a fright."

Leif smiled and whispered, "Is he now."

"He'll climb anything. It's true. From the time he could walk, he was up every tree within a mile of us. He practically lived on the roof. My father yelled 'Get down from there, ye wee bastard!' so many times, we felt sure he'd think his name was 'Wee Bastard.'"

Leif's eyes remained closed, and he didn't say a word, but his shoulders shook with laughter, and Billie took this as encouragement to go on. She ran down the list of siblings, giving a little description or story about each. It made her miss them, of course, but it didn't cause the clenching in her chest that she'd come to expect in the last three weeks.

Maybe you're finally getting used to being away from them, she thought. *Or maybe you're just happy to be here. With him.*

———————

Pablocito's children never did show up, and Billie's stomach began to rumble. Leif's color improved a little, and they decided to head back toward the Harvey House so she could eat and he could rest in his room at the boardinghouse nearby. He did seem buoyed by her stories, though.

"That's quite some family you have," he said as they walked, jackets off now in the noon sun.

"Do you have any brothers or sisters?" It was a fair question, but the minute she asked it, she felt his mood turn.

He didn't say anything for a moment, and then it all came tumbling out of him in a rush, as if he knew he owed her an answer and just wanted to get it over with.

"I had a sister, but she died of the whooping cough when she was two. My mother was so overcome she didn't notice a few days later that her skirt had caught fire when she was stirring a pot. She went up so fast. I did everything I could, but I was only five. I couldn't carry the big bucket of water and could only splash her with cupfuls." His voice had gone tight, and Billie was practically in tears. She couldn't imagine how he'd survived watching his mother die in flames.

But then he continued. "It was just my papa and me for a couple of years until he went out to the barn during a blizzard to feed the sheep and lost his bearings coming back. He froze to death not twenty feet from the house. I found him myself the next day, but the snow was so deep I couldn't get down the road to tell anyone, so he lay there half-buried for a week. We had no relatives in the States, so I went into an orphanage."

His gaze flicked momentarily to hers, an apology on his face. "I like your stories better." Then he looked away again.

Struggling to keep from crying, Billie didn't trust herself to speak. Instinctively, she slipped her hand into his, the only comfort she could think to offer, and he grasped it firmly, as if needing something to hold on to in the wake of his tragic revelation. They walked down Adams Street without another word.

A block from the depot, he stopped, but he didn't let go of her hand. He turned to face her, and she saw some small civil war going on behind those eyes, as if he wanted something he didn't want to want.

"Billie," he murmured, and his face came closer until she thought he might kiss her. Her heart pounded in her throat as her lips parted.

But then he tipped his head up and kissed her forehead. "Go on now," he said gently, "I'll see you tomorrow," and turned down a side street toward his boardinghouse room.

Eleven

As the train huffed its way through the grasslands past Dodge City, Kansas, Charlotte found it difficult to keep her brain from constantly replaying the terror of those final moments in Topeka. But by the time it had crossed the state line into Colorado and ran alongside the Arkansas River, her thoughts shifted to Billie.

A bad temper doesn't just go away on its own in a couple of weeks, the girl had said. And she'd known enough to go get that kitchen boy when her prediction came true.

Charlotte had woefully underestimated her intelligence, that much was clear. But she'd also overlooked her loyalty; Billie had barely left her side once she knew about Simeon. Maybe if Charlotte had had a friend like that in college, she might have been persuaded not to leave Boston. Not to make such a ruinous mess of her life.

Charlotte didn't know if she'd ever find another friend like Billie MacTavish, but if she did, this time she was determined to keep her.

She never ate any of the cookies Frances had pressed upon her. The bag sat next to her on the brown leather bench seat until that afternoon when a mother with four children got on at Syracuse, the last stop in Kansas, and crowded onto the bench beside and across from her. The baby was plump and ruddy cheeked. The next child, about three years old, Charlotte guessed, was slightly thinner and paler. This progression held true all the way up to the mother herself.

The woman barely casts a shadow, Charlotte thought.

None of them spoke. The mother and oldest child, a boy of about seven, stared vacantly out the train window, while the next youngest, a girl, held the baby. The three-year-old ran a little wooden train with missing wheels back and forth across the landscape of his knees.

He was the one who smelled the cookies. He suddenly stopped playing with the train, sat up a bit straighter, and made a surreptitious sniffing sound with his tiny nose. Though his head remained still, his gaze darted this way and that until it landed on the paper sack beside Charlotte. He stared up at her for a moment, face solemn, then gave up and went back to his train.

"I wonder if I might give your children some cookies," Charlotte said to the mother.

Each child seemed to freeze on the spot, neither breathing nor blinking, until their mother answered. "We couldn't," she said, in a deep drawl that revealed missing teeth.

"A friend gave me this whole great bag of them just this morning, and they're quite fresh. Only I really don't like cookies, and they'll simply go to waste."

The woman considered this a moment, and then shook her head. "Thankee, no."

The middle boy and girl looked to their older brother, whose frozen face had thawed into a look of determination. He held out his small hand to Charlotte with such finality that she felt compelled to pass the bag to him, even against the express wishes of his mother.

The woman suddenly swung her broomstick arm back and clapped him across the ear. He flinched, then quietly commenced handing the saucer-sized cookies out to each of his siblings before taking one for himself. As if exhausted by the effort of what she'd done, the mother slumped down in her seat and resumed staring out the window. As he bit into his cookie, the boy caught Charlotte's eye and nodded his thanks.

By the time the train pulled into Williams, Charlotte was faint from hunger and sleeplessness. Not that she regretted giving up the cookies. Her stomach had been in knots since Topeka, and she couldn't have eaten a bite. Besides, the look on that little boy's face had been satisfaction enough. He'd obviously mastered a difficult lesson early on: there were things worth taking your lumps for.

Charlotte had felt the same when Simeon started berating her after their first few months of marriage. His loving moments were worth the tirades. But when it turned physical—when harsh words became actual lumps—the seesaw of cost to benefit began to tip.

The dawn was only still thinking about rising behind her as she stood on the Williams platform wondering what on earth to do next. It was so early, the dining room wouldn't be serving yet, and she doubted even the lunch counter was open. The other passengers who'd disembarked hadn't gone into the depot. They'd headed for the waiting arms of friends or family. When the train huffed its way west, Charlotte stood alone.

Frances had said something about California. In the terror of those moments, wondering if Simeon might fly at her from around the corner of the Topeka depot at any second, her brain hadn't registered anything more. She picked up her bag and trudged into the station, knowing only that Williams was where she would receive further instructions.

And who would have those instructions? Not the slack-eyed ticket agent, likely at the end of his shift. She wandered down the hallway into a room filled with artwork the likes of which she'd never seen before. Thick woolen blankets with unfamiliar designs, zigs and zags like thunderbolts on some of them, others woven with stair-like patterns wandering to the four corners. Pottery, some of it decorated with geometric designs, other pieces with intricate figures dancing or playing instruments. And so much jewelry, all of it silver, but differentiated by a variety of stones and patterns. A fire blazed in the great brick hearth on the back wall.

She continued on till she reached a hotel lobby. The desk clerk stood with his arms crossed, his chin down on his chest, but he roused himself as soon as he heard the click of her shoes on the polished floor.

"May I help you, miss?"

"I'm a Harvey Girl. I've just completed my training in Topeka, and they told me to come to Williams and wait for instructions as to where I'll be assigned."

He puzzled at this. "I don't believe I've ever heard of a girl arriving unassigned before. Are you certain?"

"Quite."

"Ah." He nodded, though he surely had no better idea of what to do with her than he had a minute ago. "Well, the manager isn't here yet, and the girls won't be down for another two hours. Would you care to wait?"

"Certainly. Thank you." Charlotte stepped a few feet to the lobby area and dropped down into an overstuffed wing chair that faced the door through which she'd come. Just in case.

She hadn't had more than twenty minutes of sleep in a row since leaving Topeka, convinced that Simeon had somehow made it onto the train and was only waiting for the right moment to pop out and drag her off at some lonesome location where he might easily dispose of her. That hadn't happened, of course, but her sleep-deprived brain couldn't quite latch on to the idea that Simeon had not, in fact, followed her. Or that if he had, his search had been unsuccessful.

She was just so tired.

If her brother, Oliver, were here, he would make her laugh, even if he called her Funereal Fannie or Mournful Myrtle. He understood that she was more than the serious girl most people saw. She wondered if she would ever be known like that again.

"I've a thought." The man's voice startled her, and her hands jumped on the chair arms. "We've got an empty room," he went on.

"If you lie down on top of the quilt and don't touch anything, the maids won't have to go in."

She blinked up at him, barely able to judge what he was suggesting. He would let her stay in one of the hotel rooms—for free? Why on earth would he jeopardize his position for a stranger like that?

"You look real tired, Miss."

He plucked a blanket off the back of one of the chairs in the lobby and took her bag; she followed him up the stairs and down the hallway to the last room. He placed the bag inside the door, handed her the blanket, and said, "I'll give a knock when the dining room manager comes in. This door locks from the inside right here."

Charlotte woke blinking into rays of light streaming from the window. The sun was now sitting on the treetops, and she marveled at how very deeply she'd slept. Her body was in exactly the same position in which she'd laid herself down, trapped as it was under the comforting weight of the thick wool blanket, one like those she'd seen when she'd first entered the depot.

I'm going to buy one of these. It'll be the first purchase of my new life. A life in which I sleep like a normal person.

She wondered why the hotel clerk had never come for her. The breakfast rush must be in full swing. She smoothed down the bed, arranged herself as best she could so as not to look as if she'd slept in her clothes (which she had), gathered her things, and descended the stairs, then quickly deposited the folded blanket back onto one of the chairs before anyone could notice.

There was a different man standing behind the hotel reception desk, and this gave her a prickly feeling on the back of her neck. Had the other man simply forgotten her and gone home . . . or had she dreamed the whole thing?

"Good morning," she said to the clerk. "I'm a Harvey Girl, and I'm to report to the dining room manager."

"Good *afternoon*," he replied with a chuckle, and pointed toward the lunchroom. "Right in there."

Afternoon? She glanced at the grandfather clock beside the reception area. Good Lord, it was half past four! Mr. Gilstead was supposed to communicate with Miss Steele at the Fred Harvey headquarters, who in turn would contact the Williams manager, so they all knew what train she was on and when she was due to arrive. How would she ever explain her disappearance for . . . eleven hours! That early-morning hotel clerk had seemed so kind, and yet he'd likely cost her the job.

She took a deep breath and headed for the lunchroom. Time to take her lumps.

The place was almost empty. Too early for dinner, and apparently they hadn't had a recent train come through. Eight or so Harvey Girls were scattered about at their various stations, wiping, polishing, and straightening everything for the next onslaught. There were no gentlemen except the few who were seated, lingering over cups of coffee or attempting to flirt with their strictly flirt-forbidden waitresses. Where was the manager?

A middle-aged woman in a gray serge dress and upswept hair approached. "May I seat you, Miss?"

"No, thank you. I'm to speak with the manager. I'm a Harvey Girl." *At least I hope I still am.*

The woman stretched out her hand to shake. "That would be me. I'm Mrs. Fleming."

No, the manager, Charlotte almost said, and then it occurred to her that this Mrs. Fleming might actually *be* the manager. She knew that Harvey Girls occasionally rose through the ranks from waitress to head girl and even to assistant manager in a couple of locations. But who'd ever heard of a woman actually running an entire restaurant?

Mrs. Fleming smiled. Apparently, the idea had garnered strange looks before. "I've been with the company for twenty-six years so far," she said patiently. "Are you by any chance the girl we're expecting from Topeka?"

"Yes—yes, I am," Charlotte stammered. "I apologize for any . . . "

"I assume you're fully rested now? That's quite a long trip when you're not in a sleeping car."

"Oh, I . . . The hotel clerk suggested . . . "

"Yes, he mentioned it, and I heard from Mr. Gilstead that you've had some difficulties. Since the room wasn't needed, I thought it best to let you rest before we send you on."

Stunned, all Charlotte could think to say was "Thank you."

"Now, why don't you sit and have a good meal. I imagine you're quite hungry."

Charlotte exhaled. "Famished actually."

"Fine. Order what you like but be ready on the platform for the five twenty."

"Where am I going?"

"To the Grand Canyon."

Twelve

"Another letter from home?" Leif asked.

Billie had gone out the back door during her dinner break to read in peace . . . but not too much peace. She'd been hoping Leif would follow her. The revelations of the previous day—and the near kiss—had made them hesitant, and they'd barely exchanged a word, which for Billie was both a slight relief and a terrible agony.

She smiled and held up the letter. "Peigi got an honorable mention in the baby-drawing contest, and Maw told her she should be proud, but Peigi's just mad she didn't win."

"There'll be another contest. The magazines are always looking for the next great illustrator."

"Yes, and besides, I bought her a charcoal pencil with some of my tip money, and she's drawing on every scrap of paper she comes across. Maw says, 'If I find one more doodle on my customer bills, she's off to the convent.'"

"What else?"

"One of Duncan's lambs died."

"You never told me you had sheep."

"We don't. He works on a farm. He hated school, so he went to work at the brick factory with Da, but he kept getting in fights, and Da said he'd lose his own job if Duncan didn't quit. He's the family tough. He'd be leading up a gang if we had any in Table Rock. But when he's with the animals, he's all kindness. Maw said he didn't come home after the lamb died. Slept out in the woods so no one would see him cry."

"What number is he?"

"Four, after me, Angus, and Peigi."

"How old?"

"Twelve."

"And how old are you?"

Billie looked up at him, and he gazed steadily back at her. She couldn't lie to him, but Lord, she didn't want to say.

"How old are *you*?" she asked.

"Nineteen. Your turn."

"Why are you so keen to know?"

"Because Phyllis says you must have lied about your age. None of the girls think you're eighteen yet."

Damn that Phyllis! thought Billie. *I knew she'd get back at me for the oyster shells!*

But she couldn't lie. Not to him. "I'll be sixteen in June."

His chin dropped. "You're *fifteen*?"

She could feel it all slipping away, any chance she had with him, the closeness of their conversations, the warmth of his hand wrapped around hers.

Rocks, she thought. *That's what's going in her bed next. Rusty nails. Broken glass.*

"You won't tell," she said.

"Of course not." He leaned up against the brick wall behind them and let out a heavy breath.

"I can't help how old I am," she murmured.

"It's my fault."

"What?"

"I know better. I've seen people lose their jobs for . . . being too close. I *got* this job because the fellow before me was caught taking out one of the waitresses."

"We're just friends, Leif. We haven't done anything wrong."

"We don't have to do anything wrong. Even if it just looks like we're keeping company, we could get fired. And you're fifteen, so for me it could be jail."

Alone in her room that night, she didn't indulge herself in a chest-heaving cry, as she'd fully intended to do. She punched her pillow good and hard, but silently so no one else would know. And when her arm got sore from pulverizing the poor feathers inside, she held it close and laid her cheek against it as if it were Leif's chest. Then she tossed it across the room and went to sleep without it.

Work, she told herself in the morning.

And that's what she did. She focused all her energy, like the mighty heat of a brick kiln, on being the perfect waitress. And not just for her own customers, but for others' as well. She fetched replacements for dropped napkins and watered everyone's glasses. Awaiting Pablocito's return, the girls had grudgingly divvied up his tasks of bussing tables, mopping floors, and hauling the huge coffee urns to the deep sink in the dishwashing area to rinse them out at night. Today, Billie did it all.

It wasn't tips she was after, only the relief of having not one spare minute to think about anything else. Nevertheless, her tips doubled. Customers couldn't get enough of her efficient service and genuine charm. And it *was* genuine—the men, women, and children at her tables afforded her the only affable chatter in her life now.

She missed Charlotte! Though the woman hadn't exactly been the lighthearted pal Billie might have hoped for, now she understood why. Charlotte's courage through everything—including the terrifying attack of those awful KKK people—revealed a surprising toughness that Billie admired.

You're a smart girl, Charlotte had told her, and she'd meant it, Billie could tell. None of the other girls thought she was smart. They thought she was a baby.

She ate by herself. Tildie joined her for breakfast one morning, and Billie hoped her interest was sincere. But soon enough she wanted to talk about Leif, how Billie had gotten so close to him when no one else had been able to. Billie picked up her half-eaten bowl of oatmeal and dumped it in the trash. She had wanted that oatmeal, but not at the cost of sitting next to nosy Tildie.

The one person whose appreciation for her grew beyond all bounds was Frances. "You've made remarkable progress—a true credit to the Fred Harvey standard!" she raved.

Cold comfort.

Billie sensed that Leif felt some regret over the course of events—maybe simply for befriending her in the first place, she didn't know—but she couldn't think about that. What was the point? She was pleasant when they had to interact, but otherwise she steered clear.

"Billie . . . ," he murmured when she brought the dirty dishes in from another girl's table.

She looked him in the eye for the first time in three days. "Your bruise stopped spreading," she said. "How's your head?"

"Still hurts."

Sympathy swelled in her. She couldn't help it. *Yes*, she thought. *Everything hurts.*

"It can take a while."

He nodded. "I know."

And then the week was over. Saturday was her day off, so she slept in, washed her hair, rinsed her stockings, ate two pieces of apple pie for lunch because it was her favorite, wrote her mother a letter, and exchanged her tips for a ten-dollar bill to include in the envelope. At quarter past three she dropped it into the box at the post office and made her way to Our Lady of Guadalupe Church.

She hadn't been to confession since she'd left Table Rock, and she almost didn't know where to begin. Her monthlong absence from the confessional was an easy start, and the fact that she'd missed church several times. Lying about her age. The oyster shell incident, even though Phyllis deserved it. Her temporary hatred for Charlotte, and then helping her flee her legal husband. Dumping out that half bowl of oatmeal, because that was a waste of perfectly good food.

The priest gave a little cough and told her to say the Act of Contrition and five Hail Marys and promise to mend her ways.

"Oh, and there's something else," she said.

"Perhaps it could wait until next Saturday. There's quite a line forming out there."

"I won't be here next Saturday. Actually, I have no idea where I'll be, and I'd really like to tell you now."

"All right then, go on."

"I love a boy I'm not supposed to love."

"Is he not Catholic?"

"Oh, um . . . no, he's not. But that's not the reason I was thinking of."

"Is that not reason enough?"

"I suppose it would be, but the other reason is what makes it really difficult, because I see him every day. We work together and it's against the rules."

"God's rules are important, too."

"Yes, of course. It's all . . . hard. It's just so hard, Father."

"But you're leaving soon, and you won't see him anymore?"

Her throat tightened until it nearly strangled the word. "Yes."

"It sounds like that might be for the best," he said gently. "No Act of Contrition necessary."

When she came out of the dark confessional into the stained-glass light of the church, a little voice yelled "Billie!" and was immediately shushed. Guillermo, Pablocito's son, came running toward her, took her hand, and led her to their pew, where she had to squish in awkwardly until Estephania crawled up onto her lap.

Pablocito's bruises had faded to tea stains across his face. "You look wonderful!" Billie whispered.

He raised the arm still in its sling a few inches. "I will come back to work soon!"

Her smile dimmed. "I probably won't be there. My month of training is up on Wednesday, and then I'll be on to the next place. Hopefully not too far."

Actually she was desperately hoping they'd send her back to Kansas City. Table Rock was only a few hours from there by train, and she'd be able to go home on her days off if she wanted.

"Wherever you go, they will love you."

The warmth of the little family surrounded her, and she felt God's love so keenly that, for the first time in over a month, since she'd gotten the letter from Miss Steele inviting her for an interview, she thought that everything might just work out okay.

Thirteen

On Monday, Billie was to have her meeting with Mr. Gilstead to learn where she'd been assigned. The minutes ticked by slow as old honey, and it was a strangely light day for customers, so she could barely find enough to do.

"You'll find out soon," said Leif when she went into the cleaning-supplies closet for more silver polish and he was getting vinegar to wipe down the cutting boards.

"Yes. I'm nervous as a cat."

"Any idea where they'll send you?"

"I'm hoping closer to home. Kansas City, maybe."

"That's only about two hours away." His look was meaningful, but she didn't know why.

"That's right," she said.

"I could possibly . . . visit you."

"We could be friends, you mean."

"We could *stay* friends. I never stopped, you know. Even though you didn't want to talk to me."

"I'll still be fifteen," she said dryly.

He smiled. "Sixteen in June."

The meeting was postponed for a day.

Frances rolled her eyes. "They're all in a dither at headquarters. 'Reassessing staffing needs,' they say. For all I know, *I'm* going to get reassigned, and I've worked here for twelve years."

"But why are they reassessing all of a sudden?" Billie was beside herself with the suspense of not knowing where she'd be living in just forty-eight hours.

"Some places get busier, some get quieter. And, you know, there's the Grand Tour now." Frances shook her head in disgust.

"What's the Grand Tour?"

"Rich people."

"Doing what?"

"*Touring*, for godsake! Don't you pay attention? They all go traipsing around Europe, but now the Fred Harvey Company is pushing this Grand Tour of the Southwest. They're calling it the American Orient, except with Indians and such. All the new Harvey hotels have Indian rooms selling scratchy blankets and strange gewgaws, and some even have real Indians walking around, regular as you please. Why anyone would want to see a bunch of savages is beyond me."

Billie grabbed her arm. "I don't want to go to the Southwest! I want to go east to Kansas City. It's a big station. Enormous! They must need girls there."

Frances shook her off. "Look, all the girls want to go to these big fancy touring hotels. You'd think Albuquerque had champagne flowing from every spigot. If you don't want to go, I'm sure they'll be relieved."

"You'll tell Mr. Gilstead? Tell him Kansas City?"

"Absolutely."

———————————

"The Grand Canyon!" Billie thought her head might explode when Mr. Gilstead told her the next day.

"I knew you'd be thrilled. You've become one of our top girls, so I'm sure they'll be quite happy with you. A place like that requires a real way with people."

Billie began to pace around Mr. Gilstead's office. "But it's all the way in Colorado!"

"Arizona, actually."

"*Arizona*? I can't go to Arizona. I don't even want to go to Colorado!"

"Miss MacTavish, I'll remind you that you work at the pleasure of the Fred Harvey Company, and they are free to send you wherever they see fit."

"And I am free to quit as I see fit!"

Mr. Gilstead stared at her for a full ten seconds. "I didn't take you for the type to vent your spleen so freely," he said menacingly. "Perhaps you'd do better at one of the more out-of-the-way Harvey Houses, like Brownwood, Texas."

Billie let out a desperate sigh and tried to regain her composure. "Didn't Frances tell you I'd hoped for Kansas City?"

"No, she never mentioned it. But if she had—"

The scream Billie almost let loose came out as a strangled squeak.

"*But if she had,*" Mr. Gilstead went on, "I would have replied that Kansas City is overrun with Harvey Girls at the moment, and they would never have assigned you there."

Billie's chin began to tremble.

No crying, she told herself. *No! None!*

Mr. Gilstead's tone changed. "I understand that you're quite close with your family, and that you've overcome a near-historic case of homesickness," he soothed. "Might we send you back to them for a few days to consider?"

———————————

The next evening, Billie finished her last shift at the Topeka Harvey House by hauling the coffee urns back to the big sink. Most of the other girls had tidied their stations and gone up already, and the chefs had finished their preparations for the next day. Only Leif was left to wash the knives and gather up the carrot tops, fish skins, and other refuse for the pig farmer who would come at dawn to collect it.

The dish room was just off the kitchen, and she could hear him scraping food scraps into the big metal pail, just as she knew he could hear her rinsing out the urns. She was leaving early the next day, before breakfast even, and had already pocketed a few biscuits and an apple for her trip to Kansas City. There she had time for a quick meal at the Harvey lunch counter before catching the train north to Table Rock.

This would likely be their last few moments together, and she wondered how to say goodbye. He had been unfailingly kind to her during the hardest month of her young life, and she knew she would never forget him, even if she wanted to. Which she told herself she did, but knew it was a lie as soon as she thought it.

The scraping sound stopped just as she finished her last urn, and a moment later he was there in the doorway. "I'll help you carry those out," he said.

No need, she almost said, because she was perfectly capable of doing it herself. But it was his way of beginning the ending they were about to have, and so she thanked him, and they carried the urns back out to the coffee station together.

"It's warm out," he said.

"Oh, I know. I've been trying not to sweat through this heavy dress all day."

Smiling, he raised an eyebrow.

She pressed her fingers to her lips, mortified, but then she just laughed. "Why do I always say the most unladylike things to you? You must be a devil of some kind!"

"Only a minor one," he said. "No one you've heard of."

"Well, one I won't forget, anyway."

He gazed at her a moment as if memorizing her features. "Would you . . . might you take a walk? Just a short one. I don't think we'll need our coats."

"That would be nice."

He held the door for her, and they headed west on Fourth Street toward Shunganunga Creek. The moon was just starting to wane, a fat crescent in a clear sky, and it shone just enough to light their way, but not so much as to be garish.

"Grand Canyon," he said, breaking the silence.

"Can you believe it?" she muttered.

"I hear it's very . . . dramatic."

"I suppose. Except what will that matter to me, trapped inside during every daylight hour, a million miles from everything I know and love?"

From you, she wanted to say.

"After six months, you can request a transfer."

"I'm fifteen, if you'll remember."

He chuckled. "Yes, I remember."

"Six months is a good portion of a life for someone my age. And besides, they'll only transfer me where they need me. No guarantee it'll be any closer."

They walked in silence for a few moments, until she mustered enough courage to ask, "Do you think you'll stay in Topeka forever?"

"I've no great reason to stay. It's familiar, I suppose, but I have no real ties."

They came to a bridge over the creek and stood side by side watching the water sluice underneath them and away across the city.

"Even if I could transfer, Billie, and be lucky enough to end up . . . where I'd like to, even then we wouldn't be allowed . . . The rules are strict. We could only be friends."

"I'm only fifteen anyway."

"Sixteen in June."

"And if you did come to that stupid canyon place and we were friends, but I hated it and quit and moved back home, then you'd be stuck there."

"Without you."

"You'd make other friends," she said.

"I'm not that friendly."

"To me you are."

He turned to look at her. "You make it easy."

She gazed up at him, the light hitting him in just such a way as to make those lovely teacup crackles in his eyes shine.

And then his beautiful, bruised face was coming closer, his hands lightly resting on her arms, then slipping behind her back. It was slow and sweet, and not scary at all, even though it was the first time a man, a full-grown man, had ever touched her in such a way—in any way at all other than the occasional hug from her da.

She felt herself drifting toward Leif like a little boat in the creek beneath them, being carried along without an ounce of effort. Floating.

His lips were light on hers, not the sort of mashing pressure she'd seen in the movies, but with the tenderness her father showed her mother when they thought no one saw. But Billie saw. And she knew the way a man was supposed to touch a woman. With hope. With reverence.

"Is this all right?" he whispered against her cheek.

"Yes."

He kissed her again, and her arms slid around his waist of their own accord, as if finally finding a longed-for resting place, a slow, lingering dance, each partner doing their part to accomplish, bit by bit, the pressing of their bodies gently but firmly together.

After a few more kisses, he stopped and tipped his head back to look at her.

"Oh my," she sighed.

"Couldn't agree more."

Sadness suddenly swept over her. The futility of it. It seemed to hit him, too, at just the same moment. He pulled her in and held her against his chest the way she'd always hoped he would.

"June'll come," he whispered. "And the one after that. I'll send you birthday letters."

"I can't wait to open them and see what you have to say."

Fourteen

Charlotte tried to convince herself that this was good, this strange, remote place. It wasn't "high iron," as the railroad men called it: the main line, where it would be terribly easy for a passenger looking for someone to get off, conduct their search, then board again and repeat the process at the next stop.

Low iron, she thought, staring out the train window at the endless desiccated bramble of scruffy-looking pines, branches reaching at odd angles as if uncertain about the exact location of the sky. *About as low as one can go.*

She knew about the Grand Canyon, of course. Copies of a painting by famed western artist Thomas Moran often hung in post offices. She'd heard of people going on a Southwest tour when the standard Grand Tour of Europe became old hat. It had never held any particular interest for her. From the pictures, the canyon seemed to have only its vastness to recommend it, as if size alone was an acceptable selling point. She imagined gazing into it, thinking *My, it certainly is big,* and then facing many grueling days of travel to return home. Alternatively, she could simply leave her house on Beacon Hill, take a twenty-minute stroll down to Boston Harbor, and look out at the ocean. It was big, too, and she'd be back by lunch.

Why did I ever agree to leave home? A question she'd asked herself more times than she cared to remember in the last two years.

The train slowed and began to curve into a settlement unlike anything she'd ever seen. To her right, the train rolled past several rustic buildings made of logs or stone, surprisingly large, like those new Lincoln Log toys, but made for giants. On the left, other structures sat at the top of a slight incline, most obscured by trees until the train had come almost to a complete stop. There above her, an enormous brown building dominated the skyline.

El Tovar Hotel, she thought. *My newest prison. At least this one has a view.*

She stepped down onto the platform and stared up at the depot. More logs. For goodness' sake, what was this obsession with dead tree trunks? Had the architect been a lumberjack on the side?

Porters and baggage handlers scurried for trunks and suitcases as passengers patted the wrinkles and dust from their clothes, exclaimed over the rustic grandeur (an oxymoron if she'd ever heard one), and were generally all aquiver to see it.

"It" being the canyon, of course. A gouge in the earth with a river at the bottom. Charlotte was not aquiver in the least. To the contrary, she suddenly felt as if her veins had been filled with sand.

This was where she would spend her days until . . . when? Until she'd saved up enough money to travel on to some even more remote place? Until either she or Simeon died? Because she knew with a leaden certainty that he would feed his obsession until he'd found and captured her. She might be able to beat him at this deadly little game of hide-and-seek . . . or she might not. And either way, what was the point?

What is the actual point to any of this?

The thought stopped her cold.

Someone jostled by her, and her gaze instinctively flicked upward. It was then that she noticed the only other motionless being in all the commotion around her. A man. Standing just beyond the passengers near the depot building. Eyes trained right on her. Waiting.

Fifteen

Fred Harvey had given Billie three days at home. Not Fred Harvey the man, of course. He'd gone on to his reward a quarter of a century ago now and was likely sitting on a cloud up in the heavens, itching to get his hands on the manager who'd let the coffee sit for an extra fifteen minutes, and the chef who'd sent an overcooked steak out to the dining room. Or so Billie imagined. Not God, of course. More like God's caterer, with the extra powers of earthly interference that such an important post conveyed.

She stepped onto the platform in Table Rock and was surprised at how quiet it was. Only a handful of people waited to board—old Mr. Tarkness likely headed down to bustling Pawnee City to conduct some business, and his wife and her sister tagging along to peruse the nicer milliner shops. Highfalutin, the lot of them. Pawnee City might be twice as big as Table Rock, but it was still well shy of two thousand people. Hardly Paris. Or even Topeka.

How different this was from Topeka with its fifty thousand souls noisily to-ing and fro-ing, working, shopping, driving any manner of vehicle, some standing on their soapboxes to decry the state of civilization, some drinking to excess despite all legal interference to the contrary.

Here in Table Rock, once the train had rumbled off into the distance, she could pick out individual sounds: the tree frogs down by Taylor Creek, Floyd Vrtiska's Packard with the stuttering exhaust pipe coughing its way down Grand Street, even the far-off trill of Lulu Mae Beebe practicing the organ at St. John's Church. Devoted to her music, Lulu Mae was, even if it only amounted to accompanying the choir on Sundays.

Was anyone coming to meet her? Billie had been dreaming about stepping off the train into the waiting arms of her loving parents, but now she was alone. She grasped the cracked leather handle of the tapestry bag and started to walk the mile or so home when Da's old Model T truck came careening down Vine Street and pulled up by the depot, Angus spilling out of the bed before it came to a complete stop. "Billie!" he yelled.

Soon they were all crowded round, laughing, hugging, little Isla wrapping her chubby arms around Billie's thigh, talking over one another to ask about the train ride, and did she eat a steak, and did she see anyone famous? Only Maw stood back, holding Dougal, who was lunging toward his oldest sister. Billie pushed forward to take the baby before he fell and used the chance to wrap her mother in a hug as well. She inhaled the familiar scents of Lux laundry soap and Colgate's Violet Talc Powder, Lorna's only indulgence, which she'd run out of months before Billie had left. She must have felt confident enough in their new financial situation with Billie's tips coming in to buy herself another tin of it.

"You look different," Maw whispered in her ear.

"I'm just the same, Maw."

"Ah, well," she sighed contentedly. "Either way."

Duncan took her bag. Angus, as oldest boy, saw this as his right, and tried to wrench it from Duncan's hand. Duncan punched him in the chest, and a fight broke out briefly until Da promised to skelp the both of them.

"But, Da—" Duncan started in. He could never just let it lie.

"Shut your geggie!" Da said and took the bag himself.

Da, Maw, little Isla, and baby Dougal sat in front, while the rest of them clambered into the truck's bed, and soon they were rolling down Grand Street, the wooden boards holding them in clacking and groaning. Six-year-old Elspeth climbed in to sit between Billie's knees and twisted around to say, "I been sleeping in your spot, but you can have it back, I don' mind."

"That's very kind of you," said Billie, smiling.

Elspeth stared up at her a moment, then turned to the others and patted her chest. "That's very kind of me," she announced.

"Oh yes," said Peigi, affecting a high tone. "How *kind* of you, milady." The boys snickered.

"Ah, shut your geggies!" said Billie, and the world order of the truck bed was restored.

The house was the same. Clapboard two-story, white paint peeling off in strips, the yard littered with items of varying usefulness: Maw's big washing tub; a push mower with grass growing up around its tires; Ian's bike (handed down the line from Angus, red fenders bitten with rust); seven-year-old Catriona's hoop and stick (handed down the line from Billie, a split forming along the slat); a small motor of some sort; and several other less identifiable objects. She had never before noticed how cluttered and unkempt it looked and had to bite her tongue from directing Ian and Cat at least to put their things away.

"How're your drawings coming along?" she asked Peigi instead as Maw went in to start dinner, herding the younger ones along with her, and Da tinkered under the hood of the newly repaired truck with Angus.

"Terrible." The girl looked away.

"I sent you that fancy charcoal pencil. Can't be all that terrible."

"I didn't win the contest."

"Oh, now, don't fret. Lots of people must have entered. Some real artists, too."

"Never had a chance," Peigi muttered, and slumped down onto

the front steps. It was a favorite spot, those four wide stairs leading up to the front door—the perfect place to sit and rest between jumping rope and games of kick the can. "Did you know they have whole schools where people go to learn how to draw and paint? That's all they learn! They just do pictures all day long!"

"Art school. I read about that in the paper once. You'd have to be pretty hoity-toity to manage that." Billie chuckled. "Can you imagine?"

"Yes," Peigi retorted. "I can."

"Dinner!" yelled Maw, and they came scurrying like pups to the chow dish, boots clomping down the twisting stairwell, screen door slamming with a clatter.

"Wash," said Maw, and they lined up at the sink to run their hands briefly through the stream from the spigot and wipe them on a graying dish towel that was a good deal darker once the last person had used it. The boys' fingernails seemed to be permanently blackened around the cuticles.

The table had been built by Da himself with boards hewn from a large elm felled by lightning one stormy afternoon. Its trunk had split with a mighty crack, plummeting to the ground with a boom that had made the house jump. After the table was finished, there was just enough timber left over to make two long benches. They weren't terribly wide, however, and if you didn't sit your backside just so, you were likely to tumble backward, an event that happened at virtually every meal, mostly to Ian. Maw always said that if he were ever made king of some foreign land, they'd have to strap him into his throne to keep him from tumbling out in front of visiting royalty and starting a war somewhere.

As with everything Da did, he'd put his back into making the table, sanding and oiling till the wood grain shone like the soft fur of a fox. Maw never put a tablecloth on it; she said it was too pretty to cover. Also, she didn't own a tablecloth.

Catriona and Elspeth had set the table as they always did, with the chipped plates and mismatched silverware. There were only seven napkins, so the younger children shared. A lump of butter, spiky with toast crumbs, sat in the old brown earthenware crock. When Billie turned to the table from washing her hands, the completely familiar sight caught her unawares, and she could hear Frances's bark about Mr. Harvey rolling in his grave. This of course would have been brought on by a salad fork that hadn't been polished to a gleam, or a teacup with the handle facing inward instead of outward toward the customer's easy reach.

He'd rise up out of his coffin and die all over again at the sight of this, thought Billie.

———

That night she slid into her old spot in bed with Peigi, Cat, and Elspeth. Hers was the left side, where she served as a sort of bed rail to keep the younger girls from falling out. Peigi slept on the right for just the same purpose.

Elspeth handed Billie the Raggedy Ann doll. "I was keeping her from being too sad while you were gone."

"She was sad?" asked Billie, suspecting it had been Elspeth doing the missing.

"Course she was—she doesn't have a stone for a heart!"

Her point made, Elspeth curled her back against Billie's stomach and pulled Billie's arm over her shoulder, as she always had. But this night she turned and whispered, "I'm glad you're back. It was cold without you."

"Did you fall out?"

"Just the once."

"Twice," corrected Cat.

"*Ye wee clipe*," hissed Elspeth in her father's strong brogue, and the others burst out laughing at the little one calling her older sister a tattletale.

They soon settled in, and one by one, her sisters' breaths slowed into slumber. It had been a long day; Billie had risen so early and traveled so far. Topeka seemed like it must be continents away from Table Rock. And yet she could see it with such clarity. The Harvey Girls would be finishing up their wiping and polishing, napkin folding, and place setting. And Leif would be cleaning down the cutting boards with vinegar and hauling the scraps out to the pig farmer's bin.

Leif.

She'd staved off the ache of missing him most of the day, anxious to get home and be enveloped by the loud, loving scrum of MacTavishes. But now the loss of his arms around her, his warm breath in her hair, and the bittersweet endearments of their parting, most of all, seemed to coil in her chest like a physical pain.

When would she see him again? Maybe never. Probably never.

Sleep was the only solution, and yet she couldn't seem to drift off. She tried to turn over, but Elspeth had wedged herself in so close, Billie couldn't move.

Pinned by a six-year-old. That lonely single bed in Topeka hadn't been so bad after all.

Leif had been only a little older than Elspeth when he'd been shipped off to an orphanage, mourning his family and likely scared out of his wits. And what was it like for him now, with no people of his own, and only himself to rely on?

Billie smoothed Elspeth's silky hair away from her cheek and breathed a small sigh of gratitude for all the love that surrounded her. Can of sardines as it was.

———————

Slipping back into her old life was easy. She woke early and came down to find her mother perking coffee and slicing an older loaf from the bread box for toasting.

She took the knife from Lorna. "Da and the boys'll be late," she murmured as she began to saw into the crust.

"Already gone."

Billie stopped sawing. "Gone?"

"I've been offering delivery service, now the truck's running. Da drops off the clean and mended and collects the next batch. I charge an extra fee, o' course." She gave a wily smile.

Billie laughed. "How'd you talk him into it? He hates getting up early!"

"The man's happy as a wee lark, isn't he? He's got his truck all fixed now. That bloody bucket of bolts is his secret sweetheart, back from the dead." Lorna gave her daughter's cheek a little pinch. "All thanks to you, lass."

They got the younger ones off to school and put Isla and baby Dougal in the pen Malcolm had built after poor little Sorcha had drowned in the washtub. Isla had her rag doll, and Dougal had Isla, and they both had Lorna and Billie cooing and chattering at them until they each tipped over for their morning naps.

"Tell me everything," Lorna said as they sat at the table with the mending while the little ones slept. "Every detail."

"I told you everything in my letters!" Billie laughed.

"No, you didn't. Come now, there's more to it than customers and coffee urns and that mean old Frances." Lorna's face was lit up, hungry for stories from beyond her own little corner of the world, which consisted of 752 souls, give or take a birth or death on any given day. Billie suddenly had the disorienting feeling of having somehow become worldlier than her mother in the brief time she'd been gone.

Scotland, Billie reminded herself. But Lorna had grown up in a town even smaller than Table Rock. Her travel from there to here had occurred many years before, and all those stories had been told. Billie was the only one in possession of new ones.

"My roommate, Charlotte," Billie began.

"Och, aye," Lorna urged. "The college girl!"

"Turns out there was a bit more to it than that . . ."

The day passed quickly, the two women falling back into their easy friendship, albeit with the new twist of Billie's doing much of the talking. Lorna had her contributions to make, though, providing a running commentary and even helping to explain some of the things that had seemed baffling, like why Charlotte, who was clearly so smart, had done something so stupid.

"Something missing in her own life," Lorna said with a sympathetic sigh. "Something she needed, and he looked like the lad to give it to her."

What's missing for me? Billie wondered.

"And maybe he did give it to her," Lorna went on. "Adventure. Someone smart to talk to. But it came with an extra helping of cruelty."

"How can you know if you'll get an extra helping of something you don't want?"

"Och, that's an easy one. Kindness—to *everyone*, not just to you, and not just so he can crow about it. And hardworking, of course, you must have that. But kindness first. No woman should ever take a man who isn't kind."

———

That night, Billie helped Catriona and Elspeth set the table, folding the few napkins just so and gracing the lip of each plate with its own crumb-free pat of butter.

"What's all this?" asked Malcolm as he thumped down into his seat at the end of his handsome table.

"Oh, it's just something we do at the Harvey House," explained Billie. "Thought I'd show you a little of what I'm learning." In truth, every customer got his own small butter dish with three pats in it, each with a fork-tine print to indicate that the butter hadn't been placed there with fingers. Billie knew personal butter dishes would never find a place in the MacTavish home and had improvised accordingly.

"Waste of butter, looks to me," her father grumbled. His gaze flicked to Lorna's. She fired a warning raise of the eyebrow. He reached across Duncan for a slice from the bread plate and quickly slathered it with the little pat. He took an oversized bite and raised his own eyebrows right back at her as he chewed.

———————————

The next day was Billie's last in Table Rock, and she was terribly sad at the thought of it. Her father's endearing gruffness, her siblings' antics and barely concealed adoration, her mother's friendship and wisdom—she would miss it all mightily. And yet . . . the utter panic she'd felt a month ago watching her mother's back recede into the crowds at Union Station (which had admittedly continued unabated for weeks) was absent. There was trepidation at the thought of such a long journey to such a foreign place, and at having to meet so many new people and prove herself all over again, of course. The work would be hard, the hours long, some of the girls nice, some not so nice.

But there was, strangely enough, no doubt in her mind that she could do it.

"Boys?" her mother said through the steam that rose as she sprinkled water under the iron, a pile of shirts on the board as high as her elbow.

Billie wanted so much to tell Lorna all about Leif, to spout about the many instances of his quiet kindness to her, to Pablocito, to everyone. How hard he worked, even with a banged-up hand and throbbing head. More than anything she just wanted to say his name!

Leif Gunnarsson! He's kind and hardworking, and his kisses nearly make me swoon!

She would not say anything of the kind.

There was no need to worry her mother over the attentions of someone who was almost four years older—a full-grown man with a full-grown man's . . . urges. Not Catholic, and more to the point, whom she'd likely never see again. Lorna herself had married Malcolm and left her maw to follow him away across the ocean, never to set eyes on the woman again. She'd known the risk of letting her own daughter travel far from home. Best not to raise any concerns that Lorna would lose her. And anyway, as far as Billie was concerned, this Harvey Girl business was temporary. A life lived without her mother's regular presence was unthinkable.

"There were some nice men in the kitchen," she said offhandedly. "But I was mostly with Charlotte, and there wasn't much time for anything other than work." All strictly true. And yet the iron stopped moving under Lorna's hand as she peered at her daughter for a long second. Then she turned back to the task, lest she burn a hole in a freshly washed shirt.

The train for St. Joseph, Missouri, her first transfer point, left at 5:12 in the morning, so Billie said her goodbyes to her siblings that night. Elspeth snuggled even deeper into Billie's edge of the bed, nearly pushing her out, and Cat shed a tear or two before slipping off into an open-mouthed slumber.

"You won't come back," murmured Peigi from the far side of the bed.

"Why wouldn't I?"

"Butter pats."

"Who cares about that," Billie scoffed.

"You do." Peigi gave now-snoring Cat a shove and rolled over. "Maybe I will, too, someday."

Billie rose in the dark and moved quietly down the stairs with her packed tapestry bag, careful to place Mr. Gilstead's letter on top where it was easily accessible. Frances had handed it to her as she'd left the Harvey House to board the train home.

"Thank you," Billie had said.

"Don't thank me." Frances had frowned. "It's from Mr. Gilstead."

Billie leveled her gaze at the woman. "Thank you for what you did for Charlotte."

"You keep an eye on her. She'll need it."

That was when Billie began to suspect that Frances had not forgotten to relay Billie's request for Kansas City to Mr. Gilstead at all. Maybe the omission was purposeful. Maybe Frances herself had sealed Billie's fate.

Lorna was waiting for her with a sack of sandwiches, and Billie didn't have the heart to tell her that she could eat whatever she wanted at any Harvey House along the route. Lorna hugged her several times, and the two of them got teary together when she said, "Six months'll go by quick as a jackrabbit, and then you'll come back and we'll see what comes next, won't we? It's not a life sentence, it's a chance to spread your wings a little. Just remember that."

Malcolm drove her through the quiet streets to the depot and waited with her on the platform. She was the only passenger. Table Rock mostly stayed in Table Rock at such an early hour.

He turned to her suddenly, his voice rough with emotion. "Ye dinnae have to go."

"Da, it's all right—"

"The truck's fixed, and your maw's bringing in more than ever, and soon Peigi'll be helping."

"Da."

He looked away. "I dinnae even ken where it is you're going."

"The Grand Canyon."

He let out a snort that turned into a cough. "And what's that when it's at home?" he sputtered.

She tucked her arm through his. "Some great gob of a place."

"Ye dinnae have to, is all."

"I want to."

His eyes searched hers for the lie.

"I don't want to leave you. But, Da, I can send money home so all our lives are better. Now that I'm not in training, I'll get a good wage on top of all those tips. The truck can get fixed if it breaks down again. Peigi can stay in school, and Maw can slow down if she wants to."

"Ye hate it."

"I don't. I did at first, but I don't anymore."

"What's different?"

So many things, she barely knew where to start. "I'm good at it," she said finally, "and it makes me proud to help the family."

The rumble of the train's engine grew steadily toward them, punctuated by two short blows from the steam whistle. Malcolm clutched his oldest child, his first baby, to him, and she could feel his breath rasp through his chest.

"Haste ye back, lass," he whispered. "Haste ye back."

––––––––––

At the St. Joseph, Missouri, station, she would switch to the 7:45 to Topeka. It would arrive at 10:45, and only a few minutes after she stepped to the platform and the train chugged away, the 10:50 California Limited would be fast on its heels. That would take her deep into the Southwest, all the way to Williams, Arizona. The ride would be about thirty-six hours, give or take delays for livestock on the track or passengers whose extensive baggage required more time to load than allotted. But she wasn't thinking of that seemingly endless journey, carrying her farther and farther away from all she held dear.

Five minutes in Topeka. It was the only thing on her mind.

Sixteen

The man now staring at Charlotte hadn't moved. Heart racing, her first reaction was to run.

A moment later, rage hit the surface as if it had been detonated from the ocean floor, a tidal wave of fear and fury that made her want to beat this gawker bloody, to swing her suitcase at his head until he dropped to the ground. How *dare* he?

Compose yourself—it's not Simeon. It's no one.

She took a breath, then another. Set her suitcase down, uncurled her clenched fingers, and straightened. Took another breath to steady her ragged emotions.

When she glanced up again, she realized the man hadn't been staring so much as gazing, and now his features were tinged with concern.

He headed toward her, and what could she do, scurry away into the growing darkness like some desert rodent? She didn't want his concern. Wanted only to be left alone, but there was naught to do but watch him approach. Older than she, but not as old as her father, his body thickened but muscular. Suit jacket strained slightly across broad shoulders. How hard was it to find a suit jacket that fit properly, for goodness' sake?

"I see you're on your own. May I help with your baggage?" His cap was stitched with the words *El Tovar Hotel*.

"I am *not* on my own," she said with perhaps more emphasis than was entirely necessary. "Or I won't be for long. I'm a Harvey Girl."

His brows tensed briefly over dark eyes as he considered this information. "You don't say."

"And this is my only bag, so I won't be in need of your assistance."

He smiled. For what reason, she wanted to know. How was any of this—*any last detail of it*—amusing?

"The girls' dormitory is just up the hill there behind the hotel. It's a short walk, but steep. You're sure you wouldn't like a ride?" He hitched a thumb over his shoulder to the oversized touring car on the road beyond the depot building. Yellow as a buttercup, with a yellow-and-red stripe around its wheels and the words *Harvey Car* printed across the door.

"I prefer to walk."

"Suit yourself."

He turned to an elderly couple who were dithering with their hats and gloves. "May I help—" she heard him say as she hefted the bag and marched toward the incandescent glow of the enormous building.

The road was indeed steep, and the suitcase seemed to grow heavier with every step. With the sun below the horizon and the sky darkening, she tripped over an unseen stone, barely catching herself in time. A bright light came up from behind her, throwing her long shadow against the bushes. As the Harvey Car passed, she looked up, but the driver did not glance toward her, only kept his eyes trained on the road ahead. She looked down again to watch her step. The vehicle's rear lights made the gilded monogram on her suitcase glow.

Charlotte found her way in the darkness to the girls' dormitory, located the dorm mother, was assigned a room, and collapsed into bed.

I have no business being tired, for godsake! she scolded herself. She had slept until afternoon, sat on a train for a couple of hours, hiked up a short hill, and felt as if she'd climbed Mount Everest. The bed was hard, the hall noisy with girls chattering to one another like monkeys in a zoo, the air wafting with earthy fumes from the mule barn down the hill. Nevertheless, a heavy torpor descended on her, and it was all she could do to change into her nightdress before crawling under the covers and dropping into the opening salvo of a dream.

I'm a Harvey Girl.

You don't say.

She woke to the sound of a sigh. Or rather a huff. The other bed, which had been empty when she'd fallen asleep, was now occupied. The girl frowned against the rays of light knifing their way around the muslin curtains. "So *sunny*." She glanced toward Charlotte and forced a polite if unconvincing smile.

"I'm Charlotte."

The effort to smile seemed to have bested her, and the girl's face returned to a look of general grievance. "Alva."

Charlotte was beginning to see why she'd previously had no roommate. "Pleased to meet you, Alva. Have you been here long?"

"Where?"

The State of Stupidity, Charlotte thought. "Here. The Grand Canyon."

"Long enough," the girl snorted. "You always grind your teeth like that in your sleep? Felt like I was bunking in a flour mill."

Teeth grinding—that was new. But at least she hadn't cried out as if she were being bludgeoned. "So sorry about that. I'll try not to to-night."

"Try not to? You'll be *sleeping*."

Charlotte drilled her with a falsely bright smile. "I suppose you're right! Well, sorry in advance, then."

Mae Parnell, the dorm mother, was a comfortable-looking woman, buxom with extra padding, pink cheeks, and a crown of unruly gray curls that cascaded to her jaw, as if the barber had attempted to bob it in keeping with current fashion and Mae was content simply to let the locks flop about of their own accord. Charlotte found her in the dorm kitchen area buttering a small tower of toast.

"How'd you sleep?" Mae asked cheerily, tucking an errant curl behind her ear only for it to pop out again a moment later.

"Quite well, thank you," said Charlotte, anxious for the distraction of work to keep her from ruminating too long on the strange and unholy series of events that now found her stranded in the absolute middle of nowhere. "I know you weren't given much notice of my arrival—"

"Never you worry, my dear. We work for Fred Harvey. We're ready for anything."

"Yes, well, I'm wondering if I'm to work today. Up at the—" She gestured roughly north.

"You're here, so you'll work. But there was a question about placement. You're new, I understand? Just trained at Topeka?" Pale eyebrows rose over bright blue eyes as she chuckled. "Won't *that* be a topic of discussion."

"For whom?"

Mae waved a buttery hand, effectively dismissing the subject. "Do you speak any languages other than English, is the question."

Charlotte had taken French at the Winsor School for Girls, of course, and during her two years at Wellesley, but she hadn't uttered so much as a *bonjour* since leaving the East Coast with Simeon two years before. A second language might place her as translator for the kitchen help, but how many French-speaking busboys were there likely to be?

"I speak French."

"Exactly how well? A bit of parlez-vous, or are you fluent?"

"I'm sufficiently fluent to converse, but I wouldn't trust my skills to translate poetry."

"I'll alert the French poets that your services may not be up to par!" Mae laughed warmly. "The new girls generally start at Bright Angel Hotel—it's much smaller, less formal, and serves fewer foreign visitors. A mistake here or there won't cause an international incident." She blew a lock off her cheek. "You're sure you're 'sufficiently fluent,' as you say? Because they're short of bilingual girls up at El Tovar. It's considered one of the finest and most elegant hotels in all of Harvey-dom, so mistakes of any variety won't be taken lightly, new girl or not."

———————

Mrs. Parnell issued her a calf-length white dress; the dresses had been black in Topeka, which helped to hide stains, but apparently here at the world-renowned El Tovar, they had a bigger laundry budget.

Charlotte dressed, tied her apron, affixed the little black bow tie at the neckline, and headed across the dusty service road toward the employees' entrance at the back of the hotel.

Before she reached it, she saw the wooden walkway beyond the building and some early-bird tourists strolling serenely along in front of a low stone wall. They gazed out over the distance, murmuring in hushed tones.

Might as well see what all the fuss is about.

The sun was ascending its usual path, the sky still purple high in its dome. A nice enough morning. But with every step Charlotte took, another striation of the far canyon wall came into view, and each one—rusty red, sandy orange, chocolate brown, mustard yellow—seemed to glow from within, set off by the cool blues of the sky and the lower still-unlit recesses. The closer she got to the abyss, the deeper it proved to be. Finally she was at the stone wall, which was clearly built to keep visitors, stunned senseless by vast unrelenting beauty, from walking straight into the thing.

"My God!" she gasped and stepped back, fearful that if she wavered at all, she'd be over the edge. And it would be a much farther fall than a fifth-floor walk-up.

"Quite a sight, isn't it?" said an elderly gentleman with a raspy chuckle as he strolled by, knobbed walking stick tapping along the path.

"Sweet Jesus," she breathed. "It's terrifying."

Seventeen

Charlotte stumbled into the large kitchen and kept herself from falling by catching onto a wooden countertop in front of her. Still rattled by the yawning abyss lying in wait like a serpent's maw only a stone's throw away, she hadn't noticed the doorsill.

"What's all this?"

Charlotte looked up into a pink freckled face framed by a lion's mane of orange hair. "I'm . . . I'm the new Harvey Girl."

"Late of the Bolshoi Ballet, I see," the woman said dryly, a faint lilt to her voice that Charlotte couldn't place.

"I'm to report to Nora," said Charlotte, straightening herself to her full, if somewhat unimpressive, height. "I speak French."

"How nice," the woman said without enthusiasm. "I'm Nora. I'm the head waitress here, and I'll want to know a bit about you before we send you out onto the floor. Where've you come from and how long were you there?"

This caught Charlotte by surprise. Nora was far younger than Frances had been, maybe only in her late twenties. Charlotte wondered what special talent had landed the woman such high standing at a relatively early age.

"I was born and raised in—"

"Not where you lived, where you worked. Which Harvey Houses? How long?"

"Topeka, and almost a month."

"Not even a month? Was there trouble?"

Just a bit . . . , thought Charlotte darkly. She forced herself to smile, which she hoped would convey confidence without conceit. "Well, my training was almost over and—"

"Training! You mean to say you've worked for Fred Harvey for *less than a month*? In *total*?"

Yes was clearly the wrong answer for this redheaded Nora, and there was no point in lying. Charlotte wasn't sure she cared enough to lie, or to beg forgiveness for committing such a crime as being *new* at *waitressing*. She met the woman's gaze and said nothing.

Seeing that she would get no satisfying blubbering from Charlotte, Nora let out a snort of frustration. "Are you any good at all?" she demanded finally. It appeared that the woman's commitment to the Harvey standard was even more aggressive than Frances's.

"Good enough to have been sent here, apparently."

Nora narrowed her eyes. "Don't get cheeky with me, sister. I'll keep you on coffee service all summer, and you'll get no tips. Comprenez?"

"Parfaitement."

———

Nora did, in fact, keep her on coffee service all week, but Charlotte didn't mind—except when she remembered how much more money she could be making. The tips for waitresses were plentiful, especially when the customers were wealthy easterners, anxious to show their superiority in such unfamiliar surroundings as "the Wild West" as they still called it, though shoot-outs between sheriffs and bandits were generally a thing of the previous century.

More money. Not to spend or to send home, like most of these girls. Just to have in case she needed to leave quickly.

But Charlotte was fine with coffee service for now. Nerves sometimes came on her at the oddest times, as when she'd seen that Harvey Car driver looking at her the evening she'd arrived. Sometimes a circumstance set her off: once a Spaniard had grabbed her wrist as she'd passed by. He'd only wanted more coffee, but the feeling of a man's fingers closing around her startled her, and she tugged her arm away forcefully.

"Perdóname! Perdóname!" he'd begged as she'd shakily poured the coffee so that it sloshed over the lip of the saucer and onto the table. The brown spots spread into the shape of bullet holes in the fine white tablecloth.

And sometimes her nerves shook for no reason at all.

Coffee was hard enough to control. Trays of heaping plates? She'd surely lose her job.

Sensing Nora's disdain, the other girls steered clear. There were a few, however, who took it upon themselves to give an encouraging smile or a word of thanks for keeping their customers sufficiently caffeinated.

Hendrika, a strawberry blond with skin as smooth as a baby's belly, would give her a little wink and drop a couple of quarters into her pocket at the end of every shift. "You keep my customers happy so they tip better," she said. She spoke with the flat *a* and hard *r* of her native upstate New York—just the opposite of the Boston Brahmin inflections Charlotte was used to. But Hendrika, or Henny as the girls called her, also spoke fluent Dutch.

"Whew," she said, a sheen of perspiration on her smooth forehead toward the end of a particularly busy lunch shift. "Not sure if I can make it through the last half hour!" Her *half* was as long and flat as an acre of farmland.

"Better half than whole," said Charlotte.

"Ha, I knew it!" Henny grinned. "Boston, right? It's the only place in America that *half* rhymes with *cough*."

Charlotte didn't feel this to be precisely accurate, but she stifled an urge to split hairs. "Yes, Boston. And you?"

"Utica, New York! We're a long way from home, aren't we?"

"Quite some distance, yes."

Henny's friendly smile seemed to get a little stale, as if she were waiting for Charlotte to refresh it. Charlotte searched for something interesting to say, but her mind went blank. There was nothing to say about pouring coffee or living in simple quarters on the edge of a chasm. She certainly couldn't share that her nightmares now included falling into that chasm. Or being pushed.

"Have you been to the Hopi House?" Henny said suddenly, saving the conversation from the brink of extinction. "My, they've got a collection over there. All kinds of Indian things. Some real live Indians, too. Are you scared of them? Indians? Because these ones seem real nice!"

Charlotte had heard there was a shop over on the east side of the hotel that sold local knickknacks and curios, but it was a little too close to the canyon for her liking. When she walked, which she liked to do in the early evening, it was always south, away from the canyon. Certainly not toward. The Hopi House was even closer to the edge than the El Tovar dining room, for heaven's sake.

"Oh, that seems quite interesting," she said now, searching for her lost manners. "I'll have to go someday."

"Someday?" Henny was laughing now, a pretty little trill. "Why, it's next door! I'll tell you what. We'll go after our shift. We'll get freshened up and take a stroll before dinner. You and me! What do you say?"

What could she say?

As planned, they went back to the dorm and changed, and then set off for the Hopi House. But instead of walking behind the hotel, as Charlotte preferred, Henny set her long legs on the short path toward the canyon. Charlotte's heart began to tap like a woodpecker desperate for a meal. She lagged slightly behind in hopes of shielding her vision from the enormity of all that . . . enormity.

Henny glanced over her shoulder. "Look at me, dashing ahead when I should let you get the view first!" She waited, then hooked her arm through Charlotte's, the difference in their heights making the configuration a bit ungainly. Not to mention that Charlotte was hardly the arm-hooking type. She hadn't done such a thing since childhood, and only with Oliver, who'd been born silly and overly affectionate.

Ah, Oliver. Sometimes she missed her brother so very . . . hard. *Hard* was the word. It was a very dense and difficult sort of missing.

As much as she couldn't wait for the first opportunity to unhook from Henny, there was something reassuring about being grasped by another person when one was at the brink of a terrible abyss. Charlotte allowed the connection until they were down the path and the Hopi House came into view.

She had never seen anything like it and stopped to take in such an unconventional structure. It was quite large, with multiple floors and flat roofs that seemed to cascade down from the top like giant steps. The walls were built of reddish-brown stone; rustic wooden ladders ran from one level up to the next.

"The lady built it to look like a real Indian house," said Henny.

"Lady?"

"The lady architect. A real stickler, they say. Had to have everything authentic."

A lady architect! Charlotte had never heard of such a thing, and nearly scoffed her doubt aloud. But then she remembered the female manager in Williams and Miss Steele, the head of personnel. The Fred Harvey Company certainly played by a different set of rules from her father's, or really any business that she was familiar with.

Tourists milled about in front of the building, gazing up at it, chatting amiably. An intermittent but steady stream of them unloaded from Harvey touring cars in the roundabout that separated El Tovar from Hopi House and made their way over. The drivers emerged to stretch their legs and have a smoke, one or two wandering toward the gathering crowd.

"Will!" Henny exclaimed suddenly. "Hey there!"

Charlotte turned to look up into the face of the driver whose services she'd resolutely rejected upon her arrival the week before. His brows rose in memory of the small woman tugging her suitcase up the hill, and then his dark eyes—*abysmal eyes, really,* thought Charlotte, *so dark you can't see the bottom*—crinkled in humor.

"Hello, Hendrika," he said, though he was looking at Charlotte.

"I keep telling him he can call me Henny, but will he listen?" the girl teased. "No, he won't."

"It's a beautiful name," he said simply.

"Will, this is my friend Charlotte Turner, and she doesn't have any nickname that I've discovered, so you'll be happy about that."

"Pleased to meet you." He held out his hand to her, not quickly, but not slowly, either. A perfectly moderate offering of courtesy. And yet instinctively she flinched and took a step back.

His eyes, bottomless as they were, remained upon her, the soft crinkle replaced by concern. Or was that anger?

"Very pleased to make your acquaintance," she said quickly, suddenly feeling the need to assuage him in some way, expertly smoothing down any feathers she had unwittingly ruffled.

He nodded, tucked his unshook hand back into his pocket, and stepped back himself.

"Here they come!" said Henny.

A drumbeat started up, a low and steady thumping that Charlotte felt in her breastbone. Then several brown-skinned men emerged from the Hopi House dressed in fringed leather leggings and muslin shirts, crowned with feathered headdresses. They began to dance slowly, purposefully, in front of the drummer, a sound emerging that seemed a cross between humming and chanting, melodic but also communicative. Intimate and yet public.

Charlotte was transfixed.

After a few minutes, the song ended, and the crowd erupted in applause. A woman leaned down to a little girl standing beside Charlotte. "Those are real savages, honey. And you got to see 'em up close!"

There didn't seem to be anything remotely savage about the singing or dancing to Charlotte. In fact she'd been impressed by their reserve, surrounded by a gawping crowd like exotic birds in an aviary. She wondered what it felt like to reveal something so clearly personal—and obviously misunderstood—in front of people who considered one barely human.

"Why do they do it?" she murmured to herself.

"Because they're Indians," said Henny. "That's how they dance."

"Because they're paid to," said Will.

Ah, thought Charlotte. *Paid to serve at the pleasure of others. Just like me.*

Eighteen

As the train slowed, Billie's pulse sped up in response, pounding in her neck like the thumping of a drum. What if Leif wasn't banging the gong out on the platform? Would she have time to run into the station, through the restaurant, and back to the kitchen; hand him the letter; and speed back in time for the California Limited? What if he wasn't even working today?

The idea for the letter had come to her on the train from Table Rock to St. Joseph, Missouri, as her anxiety about whether she might see him generated a strangely unmanageable pain in her chest. Because Leif was in Topeka! And she would be in Topeka! And they would be there at the same time! But somehow the chance that they would miss each other seemed more likely in her mind with every mile of track that sped under her feet. And the very thought of it . . . well, something had to be done.

The letter was a hedge against all that could—and probably would—go wrong. The very fact that they'd connected at all had been so unlikely: the almost kiss, her confession of her age, then the real kisses (oh, those kisses!), and finally her assignment to a place so far away that they would soon be separated by almost half a continent! No wonder her head was "mince," as Da would say.

She had hauled her tapestry bag into Union Station in St. Joseph, found a spot on a bench, and tugged out her letter-writing supplies: a small pad of paper, an envelope, and the fountain pen she'd purchased in Topeka with her first tip money. That pen was dear. Seventy-five cents, for goodness' sake! And the refill ink was a quarter more. But she would have gone without food and water rather than not be able to write home, and you could only borrow pens for so long before you started getting the side-eye.

She'd had to finish the letter quickly, while she was still on solid ground, not on a heaving, shuddering train barreling across the countryside. It wouldn't do to have her one and only contact with him be illegible. She scribbled as fast as her fingers could go to keep up with the flurry of thoughts she wanted to convey.

And now it was all sealed up, tucked into her coat pocket, ready for the handoff . . . except now she was having second thoughts. What exactly had she said? Did it make sense? Was it enough? Or was it too much?

Would he think her head was mince?

As the train slowed through the outskirts of Topeka and huffed through the city, she remembered the last time she had arrived here, only a little over a month ago. It was all different: sunny now, not a flake of snow to be seen. But more to the point, *she* felt different. She'd been so anxious all those weeks ago, so terrified about this new life and whether she could brave her fears and succeed, as her family depended upon her to do. She was anxious now, but for a very different reason. She knew she could succeed. She just didn't know if she could find Leif.

But there he was, easily visible, all dressed in white, his head several inches above everyone else's on the platform. Sweet love of Jesus, she was afraid she might hurl herself at him in gratitude just for the fact of his standing there with that stupid gong!

She had her coat on and her tapestry bag already on her lap when she spied him, and leapt up from her seat before the train had come to a complete stop so as to be the first person down the steps and onto the platform.

"Hot meals served in the Harvey House!" he called out. "Right this way to the dining—"

His eyes met hers and held them, as if needing an extra moment to confirm the reality of her striding toward him. Then he broke into the widest grin his beautiful face could possibly hold. His lips formed a word she couldn't hear. But she could see it.

Billie.

The gong dropped with a clatter, and she let the tapestry bag go. His arms were around her, her face in his neck, his lips against her hair.

"Billie," he murmured. "Billie."

Nineteen

Charlotte dubbed her roommate Angry Alva. The woman gained consciousness with an irritated huff, as if daylight were on par with gum disease. She had not one good thing to say about anything.

Charlotte avoided the room, a territory Alva marked by strewing her clothing about and exuding bad humor like an odious stink. If she wasn't working, inevitably she was entombed there writing letters home—no doubt complaining about Charlotte as well as everything else, from the uniform stockings ("Too thin! They run like a snotty nose!") to the arid climate ("So dry! Makes my skin flake!").

The days when they were on opposite schedules, one serving breakfast and lunch, the other coming in for the late-lunch and dinner shift, were ideal. They missed each other entirely, though Alva often left notes about teeth grinding or what she referred to as "ghostly moans." Charlotte had half a mind to hide some chains under her bed and rattle them in the wee hours.

The days when they waitressed together—and were thus off shift simultaneously as well—were less than ideal. Charlotte steered clear by walking the wooded trails away from the canyon. She particularly enjoyed strolling east to the cemetery, after telling Alva she was off to visit friends. Alva didn't care enough to inquire as to who these friends might be, so Charlotte was never put in a position to comment on their pulse activity. Which was uniformly zero.

She'd become a fan of self-proclaimed "Captain" John Hance when Henny had told her that, for years, the man had given canyon tours so chock-full of myth and hyperbole that they were more fiction than fact. His tales were so tall that he'd been laid to rest under a headstone that was set ten feet from its footstone. Her own stories were similarly sprinkled with untruths, and she had to admire a man who not only had made a decent living at it but had been forever memorialized as an accomplished liar.

In early May, the temperature at Grand Canyon Village could reach as high as eighty degrees during the day, descending precipitously into the thirties in the evening. In either case, when it was too hot or cold for a comfortable walk, Charlotte often found herself at the Hopi House, studying the craftsmanship. It was no Shreve, Crump & Low, the esteemed Boston jeweler who'd made her mother's wedding ring, and yet the items here were somehow charmingly primal, making Shreve's sparkling offerings seem garish in her memory.

There was a young woman named Ruth who was often behind the counter, as petite as Charlotte, with similarly dark hair, though hers was cut in a shoulder-length bob and bangs that ran straight across her forehead, and her skin was several shades darker. Ruth's voice was gentle and precise, and Charlotte supposed that English was her second language, though she didn't have much of an accent.

She rang up purchases and attended to customers' questions, such as "What's this figure with the clarinet and the crazy hair?" (Ruth always answered in the same way: "That is Kokopelli. He plays his flute to welcome the spring.") Or "Why are the blankets so small—they'd never cover a regular bed!" ("They are decorative. But they can also be used as lap blankets. They are very warm.") Charlotte heard such queries and Ruth's unhurried answers over and over as if on rotation. *The patience of a saint* was the phrase that came to mind.

Charlotte herself often answered the same set of questions, generally about the canyon or the menu. "How deep is it?" (Charlotte hadn't a clue, didn't care to know, and often said something along the lines of "Very!") "What's your favorite dish?" (She always said the oysters, mainly because they were very expensive, but also because they reminded her of home.)

"How do you like working here?" Charlotte decided to ask on her third trip to the Hopi House, and it seemed to catch Ruth off guard. She smiled and nodded, but Charlotte suspected she was just stalling for time, trying to come up with an answer that was polite and mostly true.

"I work here, too," Charlotte said quickly before the woman could toss off something pat and uninteresting. "I'm a Harvey Girl in the dining room at El Tovar, and I'm impressed at your ability to answer the same questions over and over as if it were the first time you've heard them. I wish I had your talent for it!"

Ruth's customer-bright smile downgraded a watt or two, and she glanced around to see if anyone else was in earshot. "I tell myself that customers are trying to understand the Hopi way, even if their questions seem silly or even rude at times."

Charlotte saw the wisdom in this: acknowledging that people could be ignorant while simultaneously assuming they had good intentions. She wished she could do more of the latter and a bit less of the former. "But aren't you ever tempted to say 'Mind your own business!'?"

Ruth let out a surprised laugh. "No, but I sometimes worry I'll tell the truth about Kokopelli, that he is a god of fertility and also mischief—sometimes a dangerous combination—and the ladies will run away in shock!"

It was the happiest moment Charlotte had had since arriving at this godforsaken place. "I'm Charlotte," she said warmly, "and I want to know all the shocking things, as long as they're true."

Twenty

On the long journey from Topeka to the Grand Canyon, Billie did a lot of wistful smiling, remembering Leif's passionate embrace and furtive kiss. She replayed that look of shocked bliss on his face when he first saw her coming toward him. So satisfying.

But how would she ever see him again? Her mind spun from one impractical plan to another. By the time the train for the Grand Canyon left Williams, she had resigned herself to seeing Leif in six months, when she got time off to see her family. If she could arrange to take a train that would arrive in Topeka in the morning and catch a connecting train that evening, maybe they could have a whole day together. At least she'd be sixteen by then.

When the train pulled into the station at Grand Canyon Village, she wearily descended to the platform and followed the surge of passengers to the bright yellow cars, rode the few moments up the hill, and got out in front of a building so large, she had to crane her neck to take it all in. Four floors high, built of stone and logs, it had a sort of woodsy majesty that was almost confusing. Was it fancy? Or just big?

She made her way forward with the rest of the group up onto a wide porch dotted with lovely wooden rockers and wicker furniture. Inside they were herded through a large room with log walls and leather sofas, on which guests sat in their stylish clothing, a strange counterpoint to the heads of buffalo and elk mounted on the walls above them. They came to a central area with a dark wooden counter, behind which there were rows and rows of small cubbies for keys.

Two clerks attended to the people in front of her, and when it was her turn, one of them asked, "Name, please?"

"Billie MacTavish."

The young man flipped through a large registry book. "Hmm. Miss MacTavish, could your room have been booked under a different name? We don't seem to have you here."

An older man, clearly in a supervisory position, asked, "Is there a problem here?"

"I'm sorry, Mr. Patrillo, but we don't seem to have this guest listed."

"I'll take care of it." He glanced at Billie, taking her in from top to toe, and his polite smile suddenly seemed to harden slightly. "Please step this way, Miss." Away from the paying guests, he murmured, "When did you make your reservation, please?"

"Oh, I didn't make a reservation. Should I have? Mr. Gilstead said nothing about—"

"Mr. Gilstead?"

"The manager at Topeka. He told me that I'm to—"

Mr. Patrillo's eyes went half-lidded with annoyance. "You're a Harvey Girl."

"Yes, sir. And I can start anytime you need me. I'll just tuck my bag away, and if you could point me to the uniforms, I'll be ready in two shakes of a—"

"Your name, please?"

"Billie—that is to say, Wilamena. MacTavish. But I'm called Billie."

He took her rather firmly by the arm and led her down a back hallway to a door and ushered her through. Once outside, he said quietly but with menace, "Please listen closely, Wilamena. You are never to use the guest entrance again. Once is a mistake, twice is cause for dismissal. Am I being perfectly clear?"

Eyes round with shame, Billie could only nod.

"Excellent. Now go across to the dorm and speak to Mrs. Parnell." He stepped back inside and closed the door, and Billie was left to stand in a little service area by herself, waiting amid the trash bins for the molten flames of embarrassment to cool.

"Why does *she* get her own room?"

Billie had just been shown to her new quarters by Mrs. Parnell. ("Call me Mae," the woman had said, but as she was at least a decade older than Billie's mother, Billie didn't know if she could make herself do it.)

"Alva, for goodness' sake," Mrs. Parnell scoffed at a girl who'd come down the hallway. "You're like an angry duck, quacking at every little thing."

This Alva did look a bit like a mallard, with her lips pooched out in fury, fists flapping onto her hips. "I have *sen-i-ority!* Why do *I* always get the new girls?"

Everyone else knows better than to room with you, is my guess, thought Billie.

"That Charlotte is a one-man band with all her noise!"

"Charlotte?" said Billie. "Charlotte Turner?"

"The very one," grumbled Alva.

"She was my roommate in Topeka," Billie said to Mrs. Parnell. "I'll room with her. Alva can have this to herself."

Mae Parnell smiled and patted Billie's cheek. "You're going to do just fine here."

Billie quickly deposited her bag in Charlotte's room and was soon suited up in her white dress and apron with the little black bow tie at the neck. Mae Parnell was just shooing her off to the Bright Angel Hotel to help with afternoon tea when Billie said, "Oh, am I supposed to give this to someone?" She handed over the letter Frances had given her from Mr. Gilstead.

Mae opened it and gave it a quick read. Her eyebrows rose. "Well, my goodness, dearie, you certainly made an impression!"

"Pardon me?"

"It says here that you are one of the best trainees they've had in years."

"It says that? I thought it was just that I completed my training."

Mae quoted from the letter. "'Always volunteers for the hardest chores . . . excellent with difficult customers . . . and particularly good at thinking on her feet and helping other girls under trying circumstances.'"

Frances, thought Billie. Mr. Gilstead would never have thought to write such things. But Frances knew the value of an ally in a fight. She'd probably been thinking of her poor dead sister, written this herself, and signed Mr. Gilstead's name. Now Billie was certain that Frances had somehow intervened to have her sent to the Grand Canyon. *Keep an eye on her*, she'd said, knowing that Charlotte might need her help again.

Mae Parnell was still holding the letter, but her quizzical gaze rested on Billie. "What trying circumstances is he referring to?"

"Oh, I suppose just general . . . difficulties."

"Hmm," said Mae, "just general ones."

"Yes."

"Because the world can be hard on a girl."

"It certainly can."

"So," Mae said with a sly smile, "what did you do, punch some fella in the snoot?"

"No, ma'am." Billie grinned. "I got a nice young man to do it for me."

Billie didn't end up at the Bright Angel Hotel after all. Mae Parnell suggested she take a walk while Mae went off to "sort some things out."

"Do you speak any other languages?" Mae asked before she left.

"Och no, but ah kin blether in Scots, an ah kin e'en scrieve it doon fer ye."

Mae laughed. "I missed most of that, but I think I got your meaning, even so."

While she waited for Mae to return, Billie took her stroll. She buttoned her coat over the uniform, headed up a little path between the buildings, and soon found herself at a low stone wall. The afternoon sun lit up the canyon walls like a warm-hued quilt as far as she could see.

She let out a little gasp. *Sweet Jesus! It's the most wondrous thing!* In her head she began to compose the letter home to her family. It was just so . . . vast. And gorgeous. And vast!

A couple nearby smiled. "First time?" said the gentleman.

"Yes," said Billie, feeling a bit like a hayseed.

"You'll never get enough of it," he said, and his wife nodded. "We return every year."

As Billie headed back toward the dorm, she wondered at a life that included a grand vacation on a regular basis. She'd surely never know such riches, but at least she didn't have to travel to and fro every year. She lived here now!

When Billie went up to her room to drop off her coat, Charlotte was changing out of her uniform. She startled at first, having just pulled her dress over her head, but Billie understood why now, and simply waited a moment in the doorway.

"Billie! What are you–?" Suddenly Charlotte stepped forward and hugged her tightly. Just as quickly, she stepped away and crossed her arms, collecting herself. "Well, my goodness."

Billie smiled. "I'm happy to see you, too. Can you believe they sent me here?"

"It's quite a coincidence!"

"I'm not so sure about that. I reckon Frances had something to do with it."

"Oh dear." Charlotte's smile vanished. "And you'd wanted to be closer to your family."

Billie shrugged, affecting indifference. "At least it's a beautiful view."

Charlotte's face went flat. "The pit, you mean. Such a fuss over a big hole in the ground. I'll never understand it."

"Oh, but it's amazing! It's . . . it's . . . "

"Big? So is Pennsylvania," said Charlotte. "Ah, well, à chacun son gout."

"Pardon?"

"To each his own taste. Maybe I should teach you a bit of French so you can understand some of the foreign customers. We're not in Kansas anymore."

Mae Parnell appeared in the doorway. "It's all settled then. You'll both be at El Tovar."

Charlotte seemed hesitant. "Has Nora been informed?"

"I'm sure Mr. Patrillo will let her know."

Charlotte frowned.

"What is it?" said Billie.

"She was distinctly displeased about the fact that I'd only just come from training. At least I speak a second language." She turned to Mae. "How will she take it when Billie doesn't even have that to offer?"

Mae's good humor cooled. "I expect she'll take it as she's told to take it. She isn't in charge of placement. Now that it's May, visitors will begin to come in droves, and they'll need the dining room fully staffed." She eyed them before she turned to go. "You two, however, will have to prove yourselves, just like everyone else."

Twenty-One

"Je suis désolée."

"Je suis désolée," Billie parroted.

"C'est ma faute."

"C'est ma . . . " Billie paused. "Why do I have to learn 'I'm sorry, it's my fault' over and over? Aren't there more important things to learn?"

"For you?" said Charlotte. "No."

"I don't spill things anymore! At least . . . well, almost never."

"This isn't Topeka, Billie. Many of the customers are very wealthy people who could go to Europe, but instead they're choosing Fred Harvey's Southwest tour. Actually probably not instead," she muttered to herself. "Probably in addition."

"How do the men take that much time off work?" asked Billie.

"They don't work in a brick factory, that's how."

Billie gasped. "You take that back," she growled.

"Oh dear. I'm sorry." Charlotte shook her head in self-disgust. If she was to keep this friend, as she'd vowed to do on the train, she needed to learn some self-restraint. "I only meant—"

"You can't talk to me like I'm some . . . some . . . little sister!"

"No, of course not. You're a grown woman."

They both paused at the inaccuracy of that statement.

"Well, in any case," said Charlotte, "you're a good friend, and I'll endeavor always to treat you as such."

"I may have to learn to speak another language," said Billie, her anger still pulsing, "but *you* have to learn to keep your trap shut altogether."

Charlotte couldn't help but smile at the girl's truculence. "Now who's the big sister?"

"You *need* one."

———————

The next morning, the two women made their way to the breakfast shift at El Tovar and were greeted by Nora. Charlotte had warned Billie about the steely head waitress, and her first words did nothing to dispel the description.

"And what have we here? Mutt and Jeff?" Nora sneered, playing off the difference in their heights.

Charlotte was about to snap back that if any of them were a comic strip character, it would be Nora, but remembering the previous evening's interchange, she bit her sharp tongue.

"Och, no!" said Billie, leaning into a hint of her mother's brogue. "We've no get-rich-quick schemes in mind, only hard work!"

Nora's pale brows went up in interest. "A Scot, now, are ye?"

Billie wielded her most charming smile and held out her hand to shake. "Billie MacTavish, ever at your service."

"Nora O'Sullivan." She gave Billie's hand an aggressive pump.

"Well, Nora, a pleasure to be in your company. My dear friend Charlotte here speaks highly of you."

Nora flicked a momentary glance at Charlotte, clearly skeptical of such a claim. She turned back to Billie. "You're Catholic?"

"Yes."

"Well, I've some bad news for you. The closest church is in Williams. There's a few of us, and we keep an eye on the hotel register in case there's a priest taking in the sights and he'll do a Mass for us. But that only happens a couple of times a year."

Billie was shocked. A place with no Catholic Church? "What do you . . . how do I . . . ?"

Nora clearly had no patience for such useless questions. "We're

Harvey Girls. We make do. Get to Williams when you can or get on your knees with the beads and make sure the good Lord knows you mean it."

"My maw'll be shocked."

"Then I suggest you don't tell her."

———

Billie was assigned to coffee duty, and she only spilled once at the very end of her shift. However, the incident involved a fair portion of the pot going down her apron, and she was only saved from a good scalding by the thick cotton dress that diverted most of it from her skin. She kept herself from crying out by squeaking at the intended recipient, a matronly woman with a fat pearl choker, "Je suis désolée! C'est ma faute!"

"Oh, sweetie," replied the woman, "I don't parley-voo, but don't you worry about me. You better get yourself out of that outfit right quick!" As Billie scurried away, she heard the woman say to her husband, "Poor little French girl. Leave a good tip, will you, Curtis?"

———

Charlotte had finally graduated to waitressing and found she was better at it here than she had been in Topeka. Most of the customers at El Tovar were of the social class in which she was raised, and as such, she understood them and could anticipate their expectations. Billie had a down-home friendliness that worked with some, but Charlotte's innate aloofness was a better fit overall. Rich customers were less likely to appreciate charm from their servers, and more likely to appreciate the semblance of their not being present at all.

As she silently delivered plates piled high with tender cuts of steak and Delmonico potatoes, she couldn't help but overhear conversations about a nephew's disappointing rejection from Harvard, relegating him to Princeton, "in *New Jersey* of all the unfortunate cesspools!" Or a sister's promising alliance with a Vanderbilt cousin, "though he is a bit of a tippler . . . " Comments such as these had been commonplace at the Crowninshield table at which she'd sat for the vast majority of her life, and she'd never had any reason to question them.

Yet now, from this side of the apron, Charlotte found herself evaluating such conversations with a different lens: that of a working girl who counted every nickel and spent her time in the company of those for whom a Harvey apron was a step up.

"You might try the Blue Point oysters," she suggested gently to a young man with a silk bow tie who was dithering over what to order. "They are excellent."

"And how would you know?" he snapped back. "You've probably never had decent seafood in your life."

"No need to chastise the girl," said an older woman at the table, likely his mother, Charlotte guessed. "The manager probably instructs them to recommend the most expensive items. It's not her fault she wouldn't know an oyster from a sardine."

"He can order for himself," insisted an older gentleman at the table. "He doesn't need some scullery maid telling him what to do."

Charlotte did what she knew was expected: stood at attention with her gaze cast into middle space as if she couldn't hear the insults being lobbed in her direction. They spoke as if she didn't exist. It was her job to pretend that this was a correct assumption.

But later she couldn't help thinking back to all the times her parents—and even she herself, occasionally—had behaved the same way toward the household staff or others in service to their every want and need. Of course, Simeon had ranted endlessly about the disregard of the poor by the rich, but his arguments were always about "systematic oppression," not the practice in everyday life. The wrinkled nose. The disapproving glance. The expectation of always having one's messes cleaned up by some other lesser being.

Besides, as the son of a man who owned a local printing shop, he'd never really experienced it, either.

If I exist, thought Charlotte, *so did all those nameless others*. And if life were a footrace, she'd been born at the final lap. Of course, she'd lost her advantage and fallen behind the pack, but for that she only had herself to blame.

———

"Tomorrow's our day off, and we're going for a ride," Henny told them as the three women walked back to the dorm after a dinner shift.

"Yes!" said Billie.

"Possibly," said Charlotte. "What's our destination?"

"The trading post in Cameron! Will says he doesn't have many guests signed up, so we can come if we want to."

"Who's Will?" asked Billie.

"One of the Harvey Car drivers. He's a dear."

"A dear?" said Charlotte. "He's very quiet. How do you know he's not secretly planning a takeover of the mule barn or something?"

"Well, *you're* quiet," said Henny. "Should we be worried about the mules?"

"She's had her eye on them," said Billie.

"Oh, for goodness' sake, I only meant—"

"We know what you meant." Henny gave Charlotte a friendly little pat on the arm. "But Will's harmless. And we need a change of scenery!"

———

At nine in the morning, they headed for the roundabout in front of El Tovar where Will and the long yellow Harvey Car, a Packard Eight, were waiting. The vehicle, with its convertible top and extra tire mounted on the side, could hold seven passengers plus the driver. There were only four other people there: a young couple on their honeymoon and two elderly sisters with their soft white hair done up in identical Gibson Girl buns.

And there was Will, broad and black-eyed. He wasn't as tall as Simeon, but he was powerfully built, and Charlotte found herself wondering how much damage he could do to an eye or a breast.

Stop this, she commanded herself. *You're safe. Just stay with the others and there's nothing to worry about.*

"Will!" Henny sang out. "How's your magic carpet flying these days!"

"I wish it were a magic carpet. I should warn all of you that the road is a bit bumpy."

"Oh dear," said one of the elderly sisters. "Bumpy, you say?"

"Bumpy!" the other chimed in. "We've had enough of that for one lifetime, haven't we?"

"We grew up on a farm in Maine," the first explained to whoever was listening. "*Rocky* doesn't *begin* to describe it."

"The roads were *full* of *rocks!*"

"It's a wonder our spines aren't in pieces." They started to titter at this.

"We're lucky to be standing at all!" Their giggling surged into laughter.

"Bumpy?" cackled one. "No thank you, sir! *No thank you!*"

"I didn't want to go in the first place," said the other, wiping a tear from her eye.

"You didn't?"

"No. I didn't."

"Neither did I!" At this they burst into giggles all over again. Unable to choke out a proper adieu, they simply waved, linked arms, and made their way back up the porch steps.

Charlotte glanced over at Will, who was watching the ladies, a warm little smile of amusement playing around his eyes. *Kindness*, she thought. It was a wonder she could recognize it at all anymore. Simeon could make a show of kindness, and occasionally even *be* kind at times. But this was different, somehow. It wasn't for show.

The newlyweds said not one word. They simply glanced at each other. The wife smiled shyly. The husband's brows shifted upward. She tipped her head. He slipped his hand into hers.

"Well, um . . . ," the husband said to Will. "Maybe another time."

"Of course," Will replied with a nod. As the couple turned to go, he watched them for an extra moment, and Charlotte sensed a touch of sadness come over him. She had grown so acutely aware of Simeon's moods, gauging every twitch of even the tiniest facial muscle, and she found herself reading Will's face in the same way. Sadness. Yes, that was it exactly.

"Well, now what are we supposed to do?" said Henny. "You can't take us, can you? With no guests going? Just us Harvey Girls?"

Will thought for a moment, glanced away and then back at the women. "I'll take you."

"Would you get in trouble?" asked Billie. "We don't want to cause any problems."

"Well, strictly speaking, the trips are for guests," he admitted. "But since they canceled last-minute, I'm not assigned anywhere else. As long as I fill the tank after, it should be fine."

Kindness.

"I'll pay for the gas," said Charlotte.

His gaze flicked to her. That smile again. "That's all right—"

"I want to."

"We'll all chip in!" said Henny.

"No, you girls have families to send your money home to," said Charlotte. "I can afford it." A few less dollars in her getaway fund wouldn't hurt. Maybe she'd never even need it . . .

Will took note of this. "We'll split it," he said.

The road was like nothing Billie had ever experienced, and she'd been on plenty of bumpy roads in Nebraska.

"Get comfortable," Will told them at the beginning of the trip. "It's about fifty-five miles to Cameron, and the road is rustic, as I said, so it'll be at least two and a half hours."

Henny sat up front with him, peppering him with questions. They headed east toward the rising sun, skirting the southern border of the park, and Will pointed out vegetation. ("Pinyon pine, mostly, and sagebrush over there, and that's some Indian ricegrass.") He talked about the history—until they came to some terrifyingly steep descents and he had to concentrate to keep the vehicle from skidding off the sandy, unpaved, one-lane road.

"This was a trail made by the Indians," he told them. "They traveled along here, back when the Grand Canyon was theirs."

"Theirs?" said Henny skeptically. "How'd they get it?"

"Well, they didn't actually own it. They don't really think about land like that. They were here, and so was the land. Then back in the 1800s the military scouted it out, and they didn't want it. Eventually miners and frontiersmen came along and set up camps. Then the Santa Fe Railway fixed the tracks up from Williams. Fred Harvey built the El Tovar in 1905, and suddenly everyone wants to stay in a nice room, eat decent food, and look at the canyon. When they made it a national park in 1919, the Harvey Company made a deal to provide all the food and lodging at the rim. They turned this trail into a road—such as it is. Hold on now, ladies."

They were suddenly at a hairpin turn, and Will had to focus on keeping the wheels connected to the earth. Billie sat directly behind him and saw what he saw: on their left was an unimaginably steep drop down to a river far below—and it was only a few feet away! They might have gone right off the cliff if Will hadn't had his wits about him. Billie gasped in fright.

Charlotte, sitting next to her on the passenger side, startled. "What? What is it?"

"We almost—"

"But we didn't, did we?" Will interrupted. "The road gets a little close to the edge on our side, but it's fine. We're safe and sound."

Despite the hair-raising twists and turns, the long car ride was a nice chance to get to know one another better. Will, in his quiet, matter-of-fact way, asked them general questions—nothing terribly probing or personal—but this seemed to have the effect of allowing them to be more forthcoming than they might otherwise have been in casual conversation.

Henny, it turned out, was one of five daughters on a dairy farm in upstate New York, and when she saw the Harvey Girl job description, she'd jumped at the chance "not to smell cow manure every waking minute of the day. And a lot of sleeping minutes, too. I'd be having some sweet dream about one thing or another, and that stink would sneak right in!"

As the middle daughter, she was neither a marrying-off priority nor a parenting priority. "If I hadn't packed my suitcase and hugged them all goodbye, they wouldn't have noticed I'd left for weeks." But once she started sending money home, they all became quite aware that daughter number three was no longer milking Holsteins out in the barn. "My next-younger sister, Astrid, can't wait till she turns eighteen so she can join me."

Billie and Charlotte exchanged glances. "Won't that be nice," said Charlotte.

"How about you, Billie?" said Will. "Any brothers or sisters?"

Billie happily described her colorful family and found herself talking about her brief trip home. "I never noticed . . . well, I mean, of course I knew we weren't well off. But after working for Fred Harvey for a month, making sure every last napkin was perfectly folded and every oyster fork gleamed . . . I'd never even seen an oyster fork before. I'd never seen an oyster, either. But now I have. And once you know how napkins are supposed to be folded, well . . . "

"It was the same for me," said Henny. "I went home after six months in Rincon, New Mexico, and suddenly I was horrified at the grease stains on my mother's apron. I took it and scrubbed it real hard. She asked me why, and I said, 'Well, it's got spots.' And she said, 'It's an apron—that's what it's for!'"

"Fred Harvey's turned us into a bunch of fussbudgets!" laughed Billie.

————————

When it was Charlotte's turn, she said she was from Boston and had one older brother, Oliver, who worked on ships like their father. In truth, Oliver rarely set foot on the deck of anything other than the Crowninshield yacht moored in Newport, Rhode Island, but "working on ships" was close enough.

"Do you miss them?" asked Will. This was the most personal question he'd asked since the trip began.

Charlotte had to think for a moment. It had been some time since she'd had the luxury of considering how she truly felt about anything other than evading Simeon's fists. She certainly missed Oliver. But her parents? They'd been so utterly disgusted with her for wanting to spend even a moment with a lowly college professor. After she eloped with Simeon, she had sent them a letter explaining the choice she'd made, begging for their forgiveness if not their blessing. For weeks she'd gone to the post office hoping for a response, and eventually she realized she'd gotten one: silence.

Charlotte was certain of one thing—if Simeon had been the man she'd thought he was, she would have been happy. She would have made peace with her disinheritance and lived a middle-class life, relieved to avoid all those dreadfully boring social engagements and fussing about who had outdone whom this season. Of course she would have liked to be comfortable, with a housekeeper and maybe a maid or two. But even without that, if she'd had a husband who loved and honored her . . .

Her parents were right in a sense. She'd made a terrible mistake; they were wrong only about the particulars. Did she miss them?

"Yes," she said. "I do."

"You'll go back to Boston someday, then?" he asked.

"I don't know," she said truthfully.

"Life has its twists and turns, doesn't it?"

She gazed out over the vast arid wilderness. "Indeed it does."

When Henny asked Will about himself, he was as brief and circumspect as Charlotte. He was an only child who grew up on a ranch near Ash Fork, Arizona. His parents had passed.

"What happened to the ranch?" asked Henny.

"I still own the land, but I sold off the livestock and rented the house to a nice family."

"Not the life for you?" she asked.

"No," he said. "Not anymore."

Why not? was the question that hung in the air, but none of the women ventured to ask it. In his quiet way, Will had made clear that no answer would be forthcoming.

Twenty-Two

They'd been driving for almost two hours when Will stopped the Packard in the middle of the road—there was no shoulder except sand, and he explained that with so few cars, there was little chance of causing a traffic jam. He led them to a promontory of rock that afforded a wondrous view both up and down the river, which sparkled pale blue far below.

"The Little Colorado River," he said. "Sometimes it's completely dry, sometimes it's roiling with sediment so dense it's a river of mud, and they say it's too thick to drink and too thin to plow. It has flash floods that come out of nowhere, and quicksand in places that can swallow you up."

Charlotte's stomach lurched at the thought, and though she stood well behind the others, she backed away another few feet. Will turned toward her in that moment, studying her. "But for all its unpredictability," he went on, his voice slightly softer, as if trying to soothe her discomfort, "the place can be a salvation, too."

He told them that in 1864, the US government forced all the Navajos off their land and made them walk hundreds of miles through the desert to Fort Sumner, New Mexico. "The Long Walk, they still call it," he said, "and it was so grueling that many didn't make it. The story goes that a young woman was pregnant, and feeling sure she would die, her relatives hid her in a cave down in the gorge. When a treaty was finally enacted, and the Navajos were allowed to return, her family threw down a braided yucca rope to help her climb out, and the place was called Pull Up the Baby Canyon after that."

"Imagine giving birth all alone in a cave," said Billie. "She must have been terrified."

"It was the worst of times for the Indians," said Will. "Even those who hadn't been born yet don't forget it."

"I wouldn't forget it, either," said Henny.

Will's gaze flicked to Charlotte, then away. "Getting beaten down over and over has a way of sticking with you."

They reached the Cameron Trading Post in late morning, a large wooden structure with a tin roof. It sat on Route 89 just before a one-lane suspension bridge that crossed the Little Colorado River. Above the door was a cameo picture of an Indian man.

"That's Roy Huskin. He's the manager when the owner isn't here." The owner was Hubert Richardson, or Naa' Dootlizhii, as he was called by the locals. "The name means 'blue eyes,'" said Will.

The Richardson brothers had built the trading post ten years before, in 1916, as a place for the local Navajos and Hopis to barter wares—blankets, baskets, jewelry, sheep—and dry goods. There were Indian houses called hogans set up out front for traders to stay in. Inside the main building was a large room of tables and shelves piled with all sorts of handmade goods.

"It's like our Hopi House," said Billie.

"Only giant sized," said Henny.

"Grand Canyon sized," murmured Charlotte, transfixed. Like the canyon, she felt as if she could fall into this cornucopia; unlike the canyon, she would enjoy it.

The women wandered through the piles of blankets and displays of jewelry, and Charlotte soon found herself on the other side of the room, not far from the payment counter.

"Sisters?" said a man's low voice.

"Do they look like sisters?" said another man with a chuckle. It was Will.

Sisters? thought Charlotte. *We couldn't be any more different!* She peered over a shelf of pottery.

Standing behind the counter, a large man with brown skin and dark hair that fell around his shoulders shrugged. "They look like white women."

Will laughed. "Well, they certainly are that."

"Rich?"

Will shook his head. "Harvey Girls."

"They'll buy a little bowl or two, then."

"They're saving their pay to send home to their families." Will gave the other man a pointed look. "Just like you are, John."

The man gave a snort, as if to say that their circumstances were not the same. And Charlotte supposed he had a point. Besides, she had only herself to think of. Her family certainly didn't need her paltry tip money.

Her eye caught on a nearby pile of folded blankets that appeared to be made like the one under which she'd slept so soundly in that hotel room back in Williams. Remembering her vow to procure a blanket like that when she had enough money, she picked up the top blanket and walked toward the counter. It would also prove her to be no buyer of trinkets.

"I'd like to purchase this, please," she said to the man behind the counter. Now that she had a better look at him, she guessed that he was about her age.

He put on a customer-service smile. "Yes, of course, Miss."

Charlotte glanced at Will just long enough to see the concern on his face. "Is there a problem?" she asked.

"No problem at all. It's just that . . . "

"What?"

"It might be more than you intended to spend."

Charlotte looked at the man behind the counter.

"It's eight dollars, Miss. But it's very fine quality."

Charlotte opened the folded blanket. The pattern was completely different from the one in Williams, with three large red diamonds in a row on a light brown field. The design was enhanced by borders of concentric black and beige triangles around the con-joined diamonds and along the edges of the blanket.

"My goodness," she murmured, running her fingers gently across the weave. "It's beautiful." She looked up at the man. "I'm sorry. I don't have eight dollars. That is, I do, but not with me." She turned to Will. "Do you think, if I gave you the money, when you're here next, you could . . . "

Will nodded. "Can you hold it for her, John? I'll be back next week."

"I'd have to ask Roy."

Will gave him a smirk. "John . . . "

John's expression softened. "I suppose I could."

"Thank you. I'm Charlotte, by the way. Charlotte"—she paused to get it right—"Turner."

"Pleased to meet you. I'm John Honanie."

"I appreciate your help, Mr. Honanie."

"I appreciate your eye, Miss Turner. This was made by my aunt. She's a very good weaver."

"Please tell her I'm honored to consider myself a patron—one of many, I'm sure."

John's gaze cut momentarily to Will, then back to Charlotte. "I'll do that."

Charlotte felt a sudden wave of anxiety. Had she said the wrong thing? "Well, I'm going to keep looking around," she said, and slipped away from the men.

"'Honored to consider myself a patron'?" she heard John murmur skeptically before she was out of earshot. "There's more to *that* story."

"None of us was born in the shoes we're standing in," replied Will.

Truer words were never spoken, thought Charlotte. It made her wonder about Will's shoes. . . . What kind was he born in? And where had they taken him?

Twenty-Three

After they'd completed their purchases (a silver charm with a tiny pebble of turquoise for Henny's charm bracelet and a lovely little earthenware bowl that Billie planned to bring home to her mother), they ate their packed lunch at the rustic tables behind the trading post and watched the wind rustle the scrub brush across the desert and the occasional car or truck trundle over the one-lane suspension bridge.

When they returned to the Harvey Car, Henny climbed in back with Billie—"I might rest my eyes for a minute," she said—and Charlotte was left to sit in front with Will. Now it was late afternoon, and they were heading west along the Little Colorado toward Grand Canyon Village, the sun sliding down behind a patchwork of wispy clouds.

Unlike the ride to Cameron, no one spoke, but to Billie it seemed a satisfied kind of silence. It reminded her of the picnics she took with her family beside the Big Nemaha River, where they would wade and splash and run after one another for the better part of a Sunday afternoon. On the ride home the kids would hunker down like a litter of piglets, tangled up and drowsy in the truck bed or against Maw's shoulder in the cab. (All except Duncan, of course, who spent his time trying to ping road signs with rocks fired from his slingshot. "Got one!" he'd yell occasionally, and someone would rouse long enough to give him a half-hearted punch.)

This Harvey Car was certainly more comfortable than her father's cantankerous truck, but Billie wouldn't have minded if the now-snoozing Henny had tipped over like one of her siblings and laid her head in Billie's lap. She had never had so little bodily contact in her life, and she missed the comfort of it.

Billie was nodding off, too, when Will said quietly, "I hear Boston's quite a city."

"Yes," Charlotte said after a pause. "It is."

"Nothing around here quite like it."

"No."

Well, this is some fascinating conversation, thought Billie wryly.

Her eyelids were almost closed when Charlotte said, "I like the newness here."

"The newness?" Will's tone was so casual he almost sounded bored. This in itself made Billie blink herself fully awake. Will wasn't bored, she sensed. He was being careful not to scare Charlotte off.

"Yes. It barely has a history."

"Well, it does," Will said mildly.

"Oh, yes, of course," Charlotte corrected herself. "The Indians."

"Only it's not recorded."

"Ruth at the Hopi House says the stories are handed down orally."

"So then it is recorded," said Will. "Just not in a way we recognize."

Neither of them spoke for a moment, but Billie could feel their alertness to each other.

"I suppose what I meant," said Charlotte quietly, "is that I don't have a history here."

Will only nodded.

"It's a fresh start," said Charlotte.

"I know what you mean."

Sitting behind Will, Billie could see Charlotte glance briefly at Will for the first time. "Do you?"

"Yes," he said. "I do."

Again they paused, each absorbing this new information about the other.

"Recently, I've been wondering," said Charlotte.

"Wondering?"

"Maybe the word is *ruminating*."

"Pondering," said Will.

"Yes. Pondering."

The car slowed almost imperceptibly, the motor growling at a slightly lower volume. *He doesn't want to miss a word,* Billie realized.

"I've been pondering fresh starts," said Charlotte, "and whether they exist at all. Whether one can simply disconnect oneself from the past as a train uncouples from cars it no longer requires."

"That's a very good question."

"Do you think so?" Now Charlotte was the casual one. Having revealed what was perhaps her most central worry, she retreated to a lightness she certainly didn't feel.

"I do."

Billie wanted to give him a little slap on the back of his head as she would any of her brothers. *I do?* What sort of answer was that?

But then he went on. "I think there are cars that we're welded to, that we'll always pull along behind us. And others we might be able to let go of."

"Which ones do you think we can let go of?"

"Not many," he said. "The past is the past, and there's no changing it. But . . . " He tipped his head slightly in thought.

Charlotte turned to gaze at him.

"I'd like to let go of the pain," he said. "I can accept the past. But there's a carload of pain I'd pull the pin on."

Charlotte smiled. "Pulling a pin. Wouldn't that be nice."

Will glanced over at her, and Billie could see his cheek go round as he smiled back.

And then they were quiet again.

Billie watched them, eagerly hoping that more would be revealed, but the two sat in what seemed to be a contented silence as the car rumbled along.

A memory came to her of a time she was watching the little ones while her mother delivered dinner to a sick neighbor. Duncan was riding Ian around on the back of his bike and Ian's big toe got caught in the bike chain somehow—Billie still didn't know how he'd done it, but leave it to Ian—and Duncan carried the wailing boy into the kitchen yelling for Billie to save the damn toe and yelling at Ian to stop his damn howling. Duncan felt guilty, Billie knew, and his response to an unpleasant feeling was always to yell at someone else.

There was blood everywhere, and Angus came in and gasped, "Holy feckin' Christ!" which only made Billie's skyrocketing worry rise even higher, and Catriona threatened to tell Maw about his awful dirty mouth, and all the while Ian was howling and wouldn't stay still to let her look at the wound.

When Da came in from work saying "What in the bloody hell . . . ?" and took over, Billie had been so relieved.

That's how she felt now about Will talking in such a way with Charlotte.

Finally there was an adult in the house.

Twenty-Four

Billie had only been at El Tovar a week and a half, and Charlotte just shy of a month, when they saw their first celebrity. And it was not just any famous person.

"Oh, Lord!" Alva's sour face suddenly lit up like a fireworks display. "It's him!"

"Whom?" asked Charlotte. They were standing by the coffee urns as two men approached the reservation desk across the dining room.

Alva's expression returned to its usual state of distaste for everyone and everything. "Where've you been living—under a rock on Jupiter?"

Billie came up beside them with a coffeepot in hand. "Is that . . . ?"

"The Latin Lover!" breathed Alva. "I'm certain of it!"

Charlotte was more concerned about serving her guests than who the random—though rather good-looking—man might be. She turned quickly to see if a table of ladies quibbling over what to order had laid down their menus yet and nearly crashed into Nora.

"Jaysus, watch yourself!" hissed the head waitress. "Maybe if you'd had more than fifteen minutes of training, you'd have learned not to plow into people by now."

"I apologize," Charlotte said coolly.

Nora narrowed her eyes. "Meaning you think you're in the right."

Charlotte certainly did think she was in the right. Nora had collided with her just as much as she'd collided with Nora, and training had nothing to do with it. But the woman had an ear for derision, and Charlotte's tone was doing her no favors.

"What? No!" Alva suddenly whined. "Why does *she* get all the good ones? I'll bet he tips bags of money!"

Charlotte looked back across the room as the men were being seated at one of her own tables.

Still glaring at Charlotte, Nora said, "You'll take the table, Alva. Important patrons go to the *seasoned* girls."

"That's not fair," said Billie. "Charlotte's just as good as—"

Nora's face went wide with mock disbelief. "Did you miss the bit about my being the head girl with prerogative over who gets which tables?" Her eyes continued to bore into Billie. "And about who stays on coffee service until her hair goes gray?"

Billie tucked her chin and cast her gaze at the floor.

Nora turned to Alva and snapped, "You got what you wanted, now don't dawdle."

Alva practically skipped to the table.

When Nora went off to harass some other poor soul, Billie whispered, "So unfair. Alva's the worst girl on the floor."

"It's fine, Billie," said Charlotte. "I don't even recognize the man."

"You're joking, right?"

"I most certainly am not."

"Charlotte, that's Rudolph Valentino."

———

By the time Charlotte had taken the ladies' orders (finally), and Billie had caffeinated half the room, Alva was scurrying back, her face ashen.

"I can't do it. I can't even *look* at him, he's so beautiful."

"Well, don't look at him, then," said Charlotte. "Look at his friend or cast your eyes into middle space and just listen to what he wants to eat."

"I can't!" squeaked Alva. "I think I may have had a teeny, tiny accident . . . "

Billie pressed her lips together to keep from laughing, but it came out as a weird snort. Nearby patrons looked up to see if someone was choking.

"Oh, for goodness' sake," muttered Charlotte, squinting in disgust. "He's just a man."

Alva shook her head. "He's a god! No woman could look in those eyes and not—"

"Pee herself?" Billie snickered. She clamped her hand over her mouth and whirled to face the urns so no one would hear her snort again.

"I can't go back there," Alva whined. "Charlotte, you *have* to take the table."

"After you begged for it? Absolutely not. Besides, Nora would have me shot at dawn."

"Please, *please*! I have to go change my drawers." Alva scurried away before Charlotte could protest again.

Charlotte shook her head and turned to Billie. "What should I do?"

"Try to keep your drawers dry?" Billie erupted into another burst of giggles.

As Charlotte approached the table, she had a vague memory of a movie poster she'd seen. Mr. Valentino was the titular character in *The Sheik*, a film that had generated a worldwide, collective female swoon. Charlotte hadn't seen it, of course, but girls at Wellesley had gabbled about it endlessly.

But as she came in close proximity to that face—the smooth, tan skin; the sultry brown eyes; the charming smile—she had a notion of what all the fuss was about. The man *was* a god. Or looked like one, anyway.

"Is everything all right?" Voice faintly scented with Italian, the Latin Lover's words seemed edible. "The other girl, she is . . . "

"Everything is fine," said Charlotte crisply, as her knees started to quake just a little. "Please allow me to take your order."

When she returned from the table, Nora was waiting for her. "The bloody gall!" she hissed. "After I specifically—"

"Alva begged her to!" Billie was suddenly at Charlotte's side. "She . . . she . . . " Billie started to chuckle. "She wet her—"

"Apron," Charlotte interjected. "She got a spot on her apron and asked me to step in while she procured a new one."

Nora narrowed her eyes. "If I find *one word* of this to be false, you're both on the morning train." She turned on her heel and left them.

Charlotte closed her eyes. "I should never have—"

"Go serve the sheik," said Billie. "I'll make sure Alva knows you *didn't* tell Nora that she wet herself in the middle of the hotel dining room."

That night they lay in their beds deeply relieved. Alva had been all too happy to corroborate the apron story.

"What did he look like up close?" Billie whispered into the darkness.

"To be perfectly honest . . . "

"Yes?"

"He was absolutely beautiful."

Twenty-Five

"*There's a party at the* community hall tonight," Henny told them the following Saturday. The last guest had left the dining room, and all the girls were scrubbing their tables and resetting for breakfast.

"What kind of party?" Billie had been to birthday parties and church suppers in Table Rock, but the way Henny's eyes twinkled with enthusiasm made her wonder if this particular gathering might be less about cake and raffle tickets and more about . . . well, she didn't even know what.

"You know," said Henny conspiratorially, "a *party*."

Charlotte's expression went flat. "Drinking," she explained to Billie.

"There might be a little bit of that," said Henny, feigning innocence.

"We're not going." Charlotte was still addressing Billie. "You're too young for that kind of foolishness."

"What are you, her maiden aunt?" said Henny. "She's an adult, isn't she?"

She's no maiden, and I'm no adult, thought Billie. She blinked at Charlotte, wondering how to turn this worrisome conversation around.

"Well, of *course* she is," said Charlotte a little too emphatically. "But she's from a very sheltered background, and . . . and her father wrote to me asking that I protect her from . . . from certain elements."

"He did?" said Billie, astounded by this revelation.

"I'm sorry, but he asked me not to tell you. So I think it best if we simply—"

"My *father* wrote to you?" In Billie's memory, Malcolm MacTavish had never written a letter to anyone, ever.

Charlotte drilled her with a look. "Yes, he did. He was very concerned that you not be exposed to inappropriate language."

Billie almost laughed. Her father would no more have said that than worn a gold crown to work. He actually prided himself on *using* inappropriate language.

"Well, I don't think there'll be much of that," said Henny, who now seemed a bit stumped by the whole exchange. "It's just a community dance, not a Wild West saloon. In fact, the boys will all be on their best behavior. We're the only females for miles and miles, and you don't impress nice girls like us with rough talk."

"I thought the Fred Harvey Company had strict rules about men and women in their employ mingling," said Charlotte.

"Oh, they do!" said Henny. "When I was at the Harvey House in Rincon we were forbidden to even *look* at the fellas in the kitchen, much less get friendly with them. We had to get the manager's approval just to keep company with men who didn't work there."

"Well, then—"

"But it's different here. There aren't any outsiders to choose from, so it's sort of a wink and smile about dating coworkers. There was a waitress a couple of years back who started going with one of the pastry men, and didn't they get hitched right in the chapel!"

"So it's just a party, but with dancing?" said Billie.

"And alcohol," said Charlotte.

"Well, so what?" said Billie, getting tired of Charlotte bigsistering her again. "I drink a little alcohol from time to time." A weekly sip from the communion chalice, anyway, though she hadn't even had that since Topeka. She'd been good about her prayers and Rosary, though.

"Do you," said Charlotte skeptically.

"Yes, I do, and if it's all right with you, *Auntie*, I think I'll go."

"Look at the state of these dresses," Charlotte scoffed as they changed into civilian clothes in their dorm room that evening. "They're hardly fit for public view."

Billie eyed herself in the mirror. "They are a bit tired."

"Why don't we stay in tonight?" said Charlotte. "I saw Mable with a Sears, Roebuck catalog. We could look through it and pick out some inexpensive things to order. They wouldn't be fashionable, but at least they'd be new."

Billie smiled over at her, and for a moment Charlotte thought the girl might agree. But then she said in an overly mild tone clearly meant to coddle, "Why don't you want to go?"

"It's not that I don't want to go—"

"It's clear as crystal you don't."

"These things can be rough affairs, Billie."

The girl's eyes went flat. "Not fancy enough for you?"

"That's not it at all—"

"Isn't it?"

"I never liked galas and soirees—I hated them, in fact. All that folderol, and for what? So the ladies can gossip behind their silk-gloved fingers about who wore the wrong shade of blue or patronized a less fashionable seamstress? So a match can be made with some boorish son of a boorish family, and all the silver can be passed around the same old circles?"

Billie's eyes went wide. "You *are* rich."

Charlotte indicated her faded garment. "As you can see, that particular problem no longer plagues me."

"Are you ashamed?"

"It's not the dress!"

"What is it then?"

"Don't you listen? It's exactly what I said it was."

"The alcohol?"

"Yes, of course! It makes people do terrible things. Things they might not do otherwise. They might be intelligent, loving—" Charlotte stopped abruptly and pressed her lips together.

"Your husband's an alcoholic."

Charlotte took a breath to calm her roiling emotions.

Billie dropped down onto her bed. "We won't go then."

Charlotte sat on her own bed. Her heart was still thumping a little too hard. "I'll ask Mabel for the catalog."

"That's okay," said Billie. "We don't need new clothes if we're not going to parties. I should really send that money home anyway."

Charlotte looked at the girl. Not a hint of disappointment showed on her smooth, pale face, though Charlotte knew how much she'd wanted to go.

Billie smiled at her encouragingly. "Maybe we can practice that card game Henny was trying to teach us. What's it called?"

"Euchre."

"Right! I still don't get how the dower works."

"Bower," Charlotte corrected.

"I thought it was 'dower.'"

"'Dower' means to give money or property to a man in exchange for his marrying your daughter."

"You have to pay a fella to marry your daughter?" said Billie. "Doesn't he just want to?"

Charlotte chuckled. "He should, shouldn't he?"

Billie shook her head. "Rich people are funny."

"Oh yes. They're absolutely sidesplitting!" Charlotte laughed, and Billie giggled, too. She really was such a sweet girl.

When their laughter subsided, Charlotte said, "You were really hoping to go, weren't you?"

"Well, yes, but maybe it's better if I don't." She smiled slyly. "Especially if my father is so concerned about bad language."

"Sorry about that."

"No, it's just that my da swears a blue streak!"

"Does he?"

"Yes, but not in an angry way. He knows it annoys my maw, so he teases her with it. I don't think she actually minds it that much. It's just the way they joke."

"It sounds like they understand each other."

Billie smiled and gave a little nod that said there was more than just understanding between her parents. There was love. And contentment. Charlotte had loved Simeon—quite passionately, in fact. And she knew that in his own way, he had loved her, too.

But there had never, ever been contentment.

Twenty-Six

The community hall was past the train depot and the Harvey Car garage, and up the hill toward some of the smaller residences of park and railroad workers. It was built of logs on the outside—as so many buildings in Grand Canyon Village were—and was just one big room on the inside with a stage at the far end. Chairs had been set up around the edges of the space, and there was a long table on one side with light refreshments. Someone had popped a huge bowl of popcorn, and there was a jar of jelly beans in every color. There were also bottles of Coca-Cola and Dr. Pepper. In the middle was a large punch bowl surrounded by glass cups.

At the moment it was empty, but it wouldn't be for long.

"Make way! Make way!" called a distinctive brogue that could only belong to Nora. She was cradling about eight bottles of Royal Crown Ginger Ale in her arms and barely made it to the punch bowl before several slipped and fell the last few inches to the table. Billie and Charlotte quickly reached out to corral them before they rolled to the floor.

"Well, look at you two early birds! Party girls like you don't want to miss a minute, now do you?" she said sarcastically. "All right, since you're here, make yourselves useful and start uncapping those bottles." She pulled a short metal bottle opener out of her pocket and tossed it onto the table before leaving again. Billie picked up the well-used item and read the writing on the handle.

"'Drink Ballantine Ale & Beer,'" she read.

"I'm *sure* it's only been used for soda pop since Prohibition," said Charlotte wryly.

Billie chuckled. Her father's friend, Klaus Becker, brewed beer in a shed in the woods behind his house. As long as everyone minded their manners, the police looked the other way. "Cap'n Fogerty likes a swig himself now and again," Da said.

Nora soon came bustling back with two large cans of pineapple juice and a bottle of some sort of red syrup. "Don't tarry," she scolded them. "Start tipping those bottles!" All went into the big bowl, as well as a bucket of chipped ice from the hotel kitchen that one of the other Harvey Girls hauled in. When it was done, the punch was a hazy orange-pink color that looked more like liquid taffeta than something you might actually consume.

A steady stream of people came spilling in, and the piano playing started up, a bouncy tune called "When the Red, Red Robin Comes Bob, Bob, Bobbin' Along." The hall quickly filled with music, the chatter of friends, bursts of laughter, and the tapping of feet on the dance floor. Billie was thrilled!

Charlotte gave her arm a tug and Billie hunched down so the shorter woman could whisper in her ear. "Have a cup of that punch now, if you like, but then don't touch it. It's only a matter of time before something illegal goes in, and then suddenly your head's spinning."

"Hey there!" called Henny when she spied them across the room. She was wearing a light blue dress that matched her eyes. It had a square neck, dropped waist, and delicate white embroidery across the inset belt and cuffs. The dress had seen some wear, but it was fairly fashionable by working-girl standards. "Let's claim a few chairs while we can!" she said.

The three of them slid folding chairs into a little arc at the far side of the floor so they could talk and watch the dancing. Henny did less watching than Charlotte and Billie, however; she was a spirited dancer, so her hand was requested over and over. Billie got up to do the Charleston when a crowd gathered on the floor—she felt less conspicuous that way. She'd only done it a few times before, mugging around with friends back in Table Rock, never in public. But she found she wanted to be part of things, to join the group laughing and pumping their arms. She didn't want to spend her life sitting next to Charlotte, who declined every request to dance.

"Well, you're an old sack of flour," Henny told Charlotte as she collapsed back into her chair, dabbing at the shine on her forehead with the back of her hand. "You're sitting there as cute as a button, making all the boys weep!"

This was not true. *Cute* was not really a term that applied to Charlotte, though she was attractive in a dark-eyed, pensive sort of way. Nor had she declined many offers to dance. Once she turned down a few, the fellows seemed to sense that it wasn't worth the effort of asking.

"Don't you know how?" asked Henny after a few thirsty gulps of Dr. Pepper.

"I do know," said Charlotte. "I just don't really care for it. I'm happy to sit here and watch."

"Just one dance!" said Henny. "The way the fellas outnumber us, every girl has to do her part."

Charlotte glanced at Billie, who said, "If you will, I will. And I know you're a much better dancer than me."

"How do you know that?" said Henny. "We haven't seen her so much as tap her feet!"

But now that Billie knew just how wealthy Charlotte had once been, she could guess that she'd had dance lessons—and likely a lot of other sorts of lessons, too.

"Well," Billie stammered. "She just seems graceful, doesn't she?"

Henny narrowed her eyes at Charlotte, then nodded shrewdly. "She does at that."

The door to the community hall opened, and in walked Will. His thick black hair was neatly combed and recently cut. He was clean-shaven and wore a light blue shirt with navy serge trousers and suit jacket, both of which were better cut than his Harvey driver's uniform. His broad shoulders had room to move, and his sleeves came down over his wrists properly. It gave him a far more dignified air than the ill-fitting uniform.

Charlotte saw him first and took a moment to absorb this adjusted version. *My goodness*, she thought, and smiled. He caught her eye and smiled back. He headed across the room toward her just as another song started up.

Henny had waved over a couple of young men, and suddenly one was standing right in front of Charlotte, obstructing her view of Will.

"This is Ernie. He's a brakeman for the railroad," said Henny. He was a bit doughy in his tweed jacket and slightly grease-stained shirt, and he grinned at her like she was his next meal.

"Oh . . . dear," said Charlotte, shaking her head at his extended hand.

"Now, come on, you promised!" said Henny.

"Just one dance," murmured Billie. "It's not a jail sentence."

Charlotte glanced up at the man with his toothy smile. *That's just what it is*, she thought, but her hesitation was becoming uncouth. She took his hand—did it have to be quite so clammy?—and allowed him to lead her onto the floor.

The song was "April Showers," and whoever had taken over at the piano was belting out a slightly up-tempo version. "Life is not a highway strewn with flowers. Still, it holds a goodly share of bliss," he crooned.

Well, this highway certainly isn't strewn with flowers, thought Charlotte as she pasted on a good-sport smile and let Ernie muscle her around the dance floor. It was a simple foxtrot, for goodness' sake, not a tango. Why was he gripping her so tightly?

————————————

A man named Robert—a park ranger, he inserted quickly, as if it were a part of his name—came to claim Billie's hand for a dance.

He was tall and so cleanly shaven as to look almost baby-faced. His smile was warm when she accepted.

"I'm really not very good," Billie warned as Robert led her to the dance floor. She looked over at Charlotte, who was already dancing quite elegantly with Ernie.

"Oh, I'm sure you're just fine," Robert said good-naturedly.

She didn't know how to tell him that she wasn't being modest. He figured it out soon enough when her knee slammed into his shin. He let out a stifled yelp of pain.

"I'm so sorry," whispered Billie. "We can stop."

"Not at all! Say, would you . . . "

Like to do anything but dance? she thought. *Yes, I'd rather dig ditches, as a matter of fact.*

"Would you like me to give you some pointers?" Robert wasn't dancing so much as shuffling back and forth at this point, avoiding any sudden moves that might result in more bruises.

"You don't have to," said Billie.

"I really would like to! That is, if you don't mind."

"I could use the help," she admitted.

"It's easy. Just look down at your feet and follow what my feet do, only backward. So when I move my left foot forward, you move your right foot back."

Billie practiced for a few steps. It really wasn't so hard.

"Hey, you're good at this!" Robert was a bundle of enthusiasm, despite the fact that a four-year-old could have followed such simple directions. "Now you're going to do two slow steps back, one quick step to the side, then feet together, like this." He held her firmly at the waist so she could feel which way to go, murmuring "Back, back, side, together. Slow, slow, quick-quick" as he guided her around the dance floor.

After a few minutes she didn't have to look at her feet anymore, but only had to pay attention to the gentle pressure from his hands to know where to go. She grinned at him. "I'm doing it!"

He beamed. "You're the next Zelda Fitzgerald!"

———————

Charlotte glanced over at Billie, who was dancing with a boy with slicked-back brown hair. He'd certainly overdone it with the pomade, but Billie didn't seem to mind as she smiled and tried to keep up with him. Charlotte could see he was murmuring to Billie, who kept looking down at her feet as if trying to follow instructions. They got in step and Billie grinned gratefully.

Charlotte was glad for the girl. She'd had so few opportunities to experience the world. Of course, at such a tender age, she needed someone to keep an eye and make sure she wasn't taken advantage of or hurt in any way. Charlotte could be that person. She could steer Billie away from the kinds of rash and unfortunate decisions Charlotte herself had made.

Ernie must have noticed Charlotte's momentary reverie and assumed it was aimed at him. "There, now!" he said loudly, as he leaned in too close to her ear. "I knew you'd enjoy it!"

You haven't any idea who I am or what I enjoy, she wanted to say, but the song was ending, and she'd make her escape from this oaf soon enough. As he danced her around, she saw Will sitting with Henny, and any second now she could join them . . .

———————

When the song ended, Robert clapped for Billie. She made a little curtsy, and they both laughed.

"Say, I'm thirsty," he said. "Stay right here!"

In a moment he was back with two cups of punch.

"Oh . . . thank you." Billie took the cup from his outstretched hand. She didn't want to be rude, and she actually was quite thirsty. She'd just take a sip and then set it down somewhere.

It was sweet and bubbly, and she didn't taste anything amiss. In fact it was delicious! Maybe Charlotte had been wrong about someone adding alcohol. She looked around; there were plenty of punch cups in plenty of hands. No one was acting the least bit drunk. She took another sip but felt nothing.

That Charlotte. Always so gloomy. And bossy! She didn't know everything.

"'It Had to Be You'!" said Robert. "This is a nice slow one. Now you've got the basics down, I can give you a few of the finer points." He tossed back the rest of his punch, and Billie did, too.

———

Charlotte's plans to return to her friends were thwarted when the piano player segued into another song—was that the opening bars of "It Had to Be You"?—and Ernie didn't let her go. In fact, with the tempo decelerating, he pulled her in even closer.

"No, I—" she said, attempting to release herself.

"Oh, now, you can't give a fella just one dance," he said.

"Yes, I certainly—"

"Come on, sweetheart, I just want—"

"I am not your sweetheart—"

He was about to say some other inane thing when he suddenly looked over his shoulder. "Taken," he growled. He turned back to Charlotte, but then his head spun around again. "I said taken!"

Charlotte peered around him, and there was Will. With a very unbecoming yank, she wrenched her hands from Ernie's and reached for Will, who quickly inserted himself between them and danced her backward, away from the unpleasant scene.

Will did not grip her hand, only held his out so that she could lay her fingers across his palm. His other hand was like a butterfly alighting at her waist, exerting its presence just enough to lead. He held his body so far from hers that it reminded her of dancing with her brother, Oliver, who would no more have clung to her than kissed her on the mouth.

"Thank you," said Charlotte.

"Happy to help." His dark eyes crinkled warmly at her.

The singer crooned, "It must have been that something lovers call fate, kept me saying, 'I have to wait.'"

"We don't have to keep dancing," said Will.

"Oh . . . ," said Charlotte, surprised to find herself disappointed. "We might as well stay until—"

Suddenly a hand was thumping Will's shoulder. "Cut in?" Ernie snarled.

"No," Will said simply; he gripped her a little more forcefully and moved her away.

But in another moment, there was Ernie, thumping him again. Will stopped dancing, dropped his hand from Charlotte's, and turned to face the other man straight on. His expression was relaxed; there was nothing specifically menacing about it. He only looked Ernie in the eye and said, "Stop."

Ernie glared at him. Charlotte tensed, prepared to protect herself if the other man tried to retake possession of her. Will's other hand was still resting lightly at her waist, and his fingers gave a reassuring little tap. *I'm still here*, those fingers seemed to say. *I'm with you.*

Thus emboldened, Charlotte said quietly but firmly, "I don't want to dance with you anymore."

Ernie's face fell. It was no longer a manly competition to get the girl back. It was a rejection. "Well, why didn't you just say so?" he muttered and slunk away.

The singer was delivering the song's final lines: "It had to be you, wonderful you. It had to be you."

Will released her. They both stood there a moment. Charlotte might have liked to dance to the next song; there was a strange easiness with Will . . . an odd sense of . . .

"Something to drink?" he asked.

"Yes, thank you. A Coca-Cola?"

He nodded. "I'll meet you at the seats."

Out on the dance floor, Robert continued to whisper instructions to Billie, and she concentrated on following both his words and his actions: the way he gently steered her this way and that, the way his torso tipped slightly to one side or the other. She liked his attentive, confident leadership. She really felt quite wonderful!

At the end of the song, Robert seemed keen to stay together. "I'll get us some soda pop," he said. But when Billie's gaze followed him to the refreshment table, she saw that the bottles were gone. He returned with two more cups of punch, apologizing that this was all that was left. "You don't have to drink it," he said.

"Oh, no," she told him. "I like it!"

Another song started up, and they finished their punch and headed for the dance floor. Relaxed and happy, Billie felt she was dancing better than ever. By the end of the song, however, she felt a little funny. The room had gotten warmer.

"My, isn't it hot in here," she said to Robert.

"It's all the people," he said. And he was right. Suddenly she felt strangely hemmed in by the bodies swirling all around her. And so hot!

"I'll just get a little ice from the punch bowl," she told him, and headed across the dance floor toward the refreshment table.

The punch bowl itself having been "refreshed" with a variety of beverages several times over the course of the evening, there were only a few scattered ice chips left. Billie corralled as many of them as she could into the ladle, tipped it into a cup, and downed the whole thing.

Robert was beside her. "Say, that stuff's pretty strong. I don't know what kind of hooch they put in there—probably just some swill somebody cooked up in a bathtub."

"A bathtub!" Billie's tongue felt thick, but this only made her giggle.

Charlotte rejoined Henny in their folding chairs at the edge of the dance floor. "Sorry about that," said Henny ruefully. "Ernie seemed sweet. Who knew he'd be so grabby?"

Charlotte looked at her blankly for a moment. "Oh, yes . . . " She'd nearly forgotten already, her memory blurred by the agreeability of dancing with Will.

Henny patted her arm. "I sent Will over to save you as soon as I saw it."

Charlotte felt as if she'd been slapped. Will hadn't actually *wanted* to dance with her. He'd be sent on an errand, which he'd completed quickly and efficiently.

"Oh," she said, trying not to look as crestfallen as she felt. "Yes, thank you."

"Well, don't thank me. Thank him. He did all the heavy lifting."

Heavy lifting, thought Charlotte. *Meaning me.*

Will was suddenly in front of them, handing out soda pop. "I got you one, too, Hendrika. We were lucky—these were the last three bottles."

"Thank you," Charlotte said coolly. "And thank you for rescuing me. You've certainly done your good deed for the day."

Will went motionless for the briefest second studying her. "It was nothing," he said.

Nothing. Charlotte's spirits sank even further.

Then she saw Billie.

Twenty-Seven

Billie felt a little unsteady, went to put her cup down on the table, and met only air. She tried again, but she couldn't get the cup to land on anything solid.

Suddenly it was being lifted from her hand, and she heard a familiar voice hiss, "What kind of man gets a young girl drunk? You should be ashamed of yourself!"

Billie would know that high-and-mighty tone anywhere. She turned toward the voice and Charlotte's face looked slightly wavery. Billie closed her eyes.

"I didn't!" she heard Robert say. "I had no idea that she'd have so little tolerance for the stuff. She's like a drunken Indian."

"It tastes like candy!" said Billie.

"Oh, for the love of . . . " Charlotte again. So bossy.

"I've got her." This voice was low and soft and very kind. Like a nice warm blanket.

Billie opened her eyes. "Will! How *are* you?"

"I'm just fine, thanks," he said, taking her arm. "Now, let's get a little fresh air before anyone catches on."

"We could go for a ride in your car!" said Billie.

"Something like that," he said.

"Whatever you do, don't let Nora see her!" The Queen of Sheba was giving orders again.

"Henny," said Will, "why don't you strike up a conversation with Nora." He tucked Billie's arm tightly into his and said, "Hang on tight, okay?"

"Okay!" said Billie. He smelled good. But not as good as that candy drink. "Wait a minute, where are my manners. Robert?"

"Yes?"

"Thank you for teashing me t'dance. I hope we can do it again sometime!"

"All right, Emily Post," murmured Will. "Let's get while the gettin's good."

————————

"You'd better go," Charlotte said after she and Will had taken off Billie's shoes and tucked her under the covers. "If Mrs. Parnell sees you, I'll lose my job."

Will chuckled.

"Is that funny?" After the disappointment of learning that their dance had been at Henny's behest and the guilt of having let herself be distracted from Billie's descent into sot-hood, Charlotte was on her last nerve.

"It is a bit," said Will.

"I'm glad you can find humor in a night that mainly consisted of errands of mercy," she grumbled, "even if it is at the expense of my livelihood."

"Mae Parnell isn't going to get you fired. She's too busy managing her own herd of suitors to pay much attention to the comings and goings around here."

Charlotte frowned. "But it's precisely her *job* to pay attention to—" She blinked several times. "What herd of suitors?"

Billie made a mewling sound like a kitten and rolled over. Will walked quietly from the room and waited in the hallway. Charlotte thought he was leaving until he tipped his head, beckoning her to follow. She sighed and followed him down the hall. After all, he had saved her not once but twice this evening. It was the least she could do.

Will descended the stairs to the parlor and sat in one of the overstuffed armchairs. Charlotte wasn't sure what was happening. Were they to have a visit now? She thumped down onto the couch.

"What errands of mercy are we talking about?" Will asked. He certainly was a plainspoken sort.

"Rescuing me from that oaf and Billie from the punch bowl. I'm sure you would rather have had a relaxing evening."

"Did it seem like I found dancing with you to be a chore?"

"Henny said she asked you to do it."

"Only because she saw him manhandling you before I did. I would've gone on my own."

"You're a gentleman," Charlotte said sullenly. "Gentlemen do that sort of thing."

"It was no chore."

She met his gaze. He really was very . . . honest.

"Was it a chore for you?" he asked.

She thought of how gently he'd held her, and of those finger taps letting her know that it was safe to stand up to a bully, and she felt herself soften. "No," she said. "It was nice."

"I thought so, too." His gaze was warm.

Simeon could gaze warmly, too, though, couldn't he? He'd so often made her feel appreciated and interesting and loved. Safe in the embrace of that warmth. It wasn't all a lie. Only the most important part.

Charlotte decided that the best approach to a plain-spoken sort was to speak plainly. "You seem like a good man, and I believe you are. However, I think I should make it clear that the only thing we will ever be is friends. I don't intend to be here long, and I certainly don't intend to participate in any . . . entanglements."

She watched him absorb this information for a moment before he nodded and said, "I would be very happy to be your friend."

"And I would be happy to be yours. As long as you don't try to prevail upon me for more."

His eyebrows went up. "I'm not in the habit of *prevailing* upon women for anything, much less . . . entanglements." He stood to go, and Charlotte rose, too.

"Thank you for all of your help tonight," she said. "I don't know what we would have done without you."

"You would've managed. I imagine you've seen your fair share of predicaments and lived to tell the tale."

Lived to tell the tale, Charlotte mused as she lay in bed a short time later with Billie snoring noisily in the other bed. With any luck, it would be chiseled on her headstone.

Twenty-Eight

The next morning Billie knelt on the floor as she did on Sundays, rosary beads in hand. *Hail Mary, full of grace . . .*

Billie herself felt distinctly lacking in grace. Her head throbbed, and her teeth felt sticky. Blinking hurt. It was all she could do not to lean against her bed. She finished the Rosary and prayed for each member of her family, thinking in particular how disappointed her maw would be in her. She was finishing up with prayers for Leif, Henny, Will, and Charlotte, when the latter's eyes fluttered open. Billie braced herself for a tongue lashing.

But Charlotte said only, "How do you feel?"

"Peely-wally."

"I don't know what that means, but it sounds apropos."

"You don't have to lay into me." Billie hung her head. "I know everything you're going to say already."

"I'm sure you do, seeing as I said it last night *before* you went and got yourself soused."

"It tasted fine!"

"Like candy, I believe you said several times."

Billie's worried gaze came up to meet Charlotte's. "What else did I say?"

"You didn't reveal any secrets, I'll give you that. But you were rather effusive about that young man's 'teashing' abilities."

"Oh, Lord. He must think I'm daft."

Charlotte pushed back her quilt and sat up. "It's his fault for foisting alcohol on you in the first place."

"He wasn't foisting. It was only that we were thirsty, and there was no more soda."

Charlotte thought for a moment. "Oh dear. I believe Will brought Henny and me the last ones."

Billie smiled wanly. "So it's *your* fault."

Charlotte rolled her eyes. "Yes, it's all my fault. And I suppose if I took the last biscuit and you decided to eat rat poison instead, that would be my fault, too."

"It was so sweet, how was I supposed to know there was anything bad in it?"

"Because I specifically warned you about that very thing, didn't I?"

"Yes," sighed Billie.

"And that's exactly why they spike punch—to hide the taste. If straight alcohol tasted that good, we'd all be drinking it straight from the jug like hoboes."

Billie winced. "I'm not sure if I can work like this."

"Oh, you'll work," said Charlotte. "If you stay in bed, Nora will surely know why, and then Lord help us both."

———————————

Down in the little dorm kitchen, Mrs. Parnell poured them cups of coffee. "Toast?" she said, offering her usual leaning tower of buttery bread.

"Thank you." Charlotte took two slices and offered one to Billie.

"I don't think—"

Charlotte put it in Billie's hand. "You don't want to work on an empty stomach, do you?"

"I suppose not."

Charlotte eyed Mrs. Parnell. "I don't think I saw you at the dance last night."

The older woman smiled. "No, I had other plans."

"Visiting with friends?"

Mae pushed a lock of gray curls off her rosy cheek. "You might say."

"I expect you've made many friends over the years," Charlotte said innocently between sips of coffee. "I don't think I ever asked how long you've been with the Fred Harvey Company."

"It's been some time now. Since my husband died."

"I'm so sorry. That must be very sad for you," Charlotte prompted.

"Yes, indeed," said Mae. But she didn't look particularly sorrowful about it. In fact, she might have been reacting to unpleasant weather, rather than the death of the man to whom she'd pledged her love and obedience.

"And were you ever a Harvey Girl?"

"Oh, no. I'm too old for that. Besides, I like being a dorm mother. It gives me a bit of freedom when you girls are off working." Mae nodded in the direction of El Tovar.

"Freedom to . . . " Charlotte knew she was being impudent. Her mother would have been appalled at such prying. But Charlotte couldn't stop thinking of Mae's "herd of suitors."

Mae offered a guileless little smile that clearly hid a multitude of secrets. "Well, freedom in general, I suppose. If you ever marry, you'll know what I mean."

When they headed out the door, someone was waiting for them.

"Robert!" said Billie. She almost didn't recognize him in his Park Service uniform—a dark green belted suit with four large patch pockets and pants that looked like horse-riding jodhpurs. His black boots came up almost to his knees, and his Stetson hat sat high on his head.

He cut a quick, worried glance at Charlotte, then said, "Billie, I feel terrible."

She nodded grimly. "Did you drink too much of that punch, too?"

"No, I feel terrible about . . . Well, I should have stopped you."

"Yes," said Charlotte, "you should have."

"I didn't realize you didn't know it was spiked. I just thought—"

"That I was a bit of a lush?" said Billie.

"Well, I suppose I thought you knew what you were drinking. And you're of age. It's not my place to tell a grown woman . . . "

Billie and Charlotte exchanged a fleeting glance.

"Anyway, I'm glad you're okay," he said. "I hope you won't be mad at me for too long."

"I'm not mad at you," said Billie. "I am a grown woman, as you say, and I should have known better."

Robert smiled. "We've all made *that* mistake. I remember once—"

"Yes, well, Billie and I don't want to be late for work," said Charlotte. "Apology accepted."

She took Billie's elbow and started in the direction of El Tovar, when Robert said, "I was hoping maybe we could take a walk someday. I could show you some of the trails."

Billie stood her ground and Charlotte had to let go. "I'd like that. I always hear customers talking about how beautiful it is in the canyon."

"It's a wonder. I'll be in touch!"

In a few long strides, Billie caught up with Charlotte. "He'll be in touch," she whispered.

"Oh, I'm sure he will," said Charlotte dryly.

Billie hooked her arm in Charlotte's. "Would you like to come with us?" she teased. "Way down deep into the canyon?"

"Enfant terrible," Charlotte scoffed in French.

"Hey, I know what that means now," Billie said with a laugh. "You're the one who taught me!"

In the El Tovar kitchen, they were tying their apron strings when Nora emerged from the pantry. "And how is everyone this morning?" The comment was clearly directed at Billie.

Billie grinned gamely and laid on the Scottish burr. "Ah feel pure tidy!"

Nora gave her a knowing look. "Well, I'm just pleased as *punch* to hear it."

A week later, while Nora was berating her for a linen that wasn't quite as crisply folded as the others, Charlotte had a revelation.

"You've been here a month already," chided Nora. "You should've graduated from napkin school by now!"

Graduated.

It was May 23, 1926. If her life had taken a different course—if Charlotte had *chosen* a different course—she'd be graduating from Wellesley College today, not "napkin school."

Good Lord, it was beyond depressing.

When was the last time she'd even read a book? She'd always been a voracious reader—in fact it was her love of the written word that had first attracted her to Simeon, her English instructor. But after they were married, he berated her for her choices. If she declined to choke down some manifesto about workers' rights, it had to be "real" literature, like *War and Peace*, or *Les Misérables*. He'd torn *The Age of Innocence* by Edith Wharton from her hands and lit it on fire on their bed.

"It's a Pulitzer Prize winner!" As the words tumbled from Charlotte's mouth, she knew she was in for a screed about how Joseph Pulitzer was a sellout and Edith Wharton an heiress whose novels served only to whine about how hard life was for rich ladies. As far as Charlotte knew, the scorched hole in their only blanket was there still.

She'd stopped reading altogether when she'd gotten the hat shop job. Working six days a week, ten hours a day, didn't leave much time for anything other than cooking, housework, and sleep—which she got little enough of, being on constant alert for Simeon's ire.

As usual, thoughts of Simeon made her anxiety rise. Her name hadn't been printed in the newspaper back in Topeka, so she was fairly certain he didn't know her alias. But he knew she'd been a Harvey Girl a month ago, and with the help she'd gotten from Frances, Leif, and even Mr. Gilstead to escape, he might rightly assume she still worked for the company. There were about eighty Harvey Houses and hotels, so it could take quite some time for him to find her . . .

She needed a distraction before her pot of worry boiled over. Books had always been a great respite for her, and here in the women's dorm there was an entire bookshelf, mostly dog-eared and spine-cracked by rereadings. Charlotte perused these titles and found many to be a bit on the silly side for her mood. There was *Gentlemen Prefer Blondes* by Anita Loos and *The Inimitable Jeeves* by P. G. Wodehouse. There was even a copy of a new children's book called *Winnie-the-Pooh* about a stuffed bear with a pig for a friend. *Who on earth would read that?* she wondered.

She plucked a book at random from the bunch, tucked it under her arm, and retreated to her room to change out of her uniform. It was only when she tossed the book onto the bed that she saw its title: *The Grand Canyon of Arizona: How to See It* by George Wharton James.

Serves me right for not looking first, she thought gloomily as she tugged on her most worn day dress.

One of the other Harvey Girls poked her head in the door. "We need a fourth for euchre!"

Charlotte was in no mood to be social. "I was just sitting down to read," she said, thumping onto her bed.

"You can read anytime!"

"Yes, but I've been looking forward to diving in all day." Charlotte made a show of opening to the first page. "I'm sure you'll find someone."

The young woman left grumbling about strange girls who *dive* into books.

The tome now in hand, Charlotte decided she might as well start reading, but the author's florid style soon got on her nerves.

"Those who have long and carefully studied the Grand Canyon of the Colorado do not hesitate for a moment to pronounce it by far the most sublime of all earthly spectacles."

The Colosseum in Rome! she wanted to yell at old George Wharton James. *The pyramids of Egypt!* How he could so smugly deem that big crack in the earth more sublime than these was beyond her.

Then she came to a sentence that stopped her cold. Commenting that if one were to throw a rock over the edge, the sheer depth of the canyon meant that no sound reverberated back, James proclaimed it "the grave of the world."

She tossed the book on the floor and left the room.

———————

"What do your parents think about you working here?" Charlotte asked Ruth in the Hopi House a few minutes later. She often found herself there when life became dull or upsetting. The beautiful objects soothed her, and Ruth was always good company.

There was a lull in customers and Ruth was refolding blankets that had been unfurled, admired, and discarded by the last gaggle of tourists.

The young woman sighed. "My mother is happy. She is a potter." Ruth picked up a low, wide bowl of blond-colored clay with a band of black geometric designs around the rim. "This is one of hers. Sometimes she comes here and makes pots while the people watch her. She's proud of her work. Also, she likes the money she makes, and the money I make working here. Life can be hard in the villages if the harvest isn't good."

"And your father?"

"He does not like the way the white people have taken over this land that is sacred to us, how they have thrust their way in and changed our ways with their cars and food and . . . well, everything. It is not good for our spirit as a people."

"And what do you think?"

Ruth ran her fingers over her mother's bowl. "I work here. I sell my mother's work. And then I go home and try to be my father's daughter."

A few days later, when they both had a day off, Robert met Billie in front of her dorm to go on the hike he'd promised her.

"We'll follow the South Rim Trail out to Mather Point," he said. "It's only a couple of miles and it's quite flat."

Billie was disappointed. She'd hoped they'd take one of the steep trails down into the canyon. She'd been here almost a month and looked at it an awful lot, but she hadn't really experienced it. She wanted to touch those wide stripes of stone all the way down, back to the dinosaur age.

Robert clearly had no such adventure in mind. He was in regular clothes—dark trousers and a blue cotton button-down shirt—and he was carrying a picnic basket. Maybe it was too heavy for him to lug down and back up again.

They chatted amiably as they walked. Robert was a friendly, upbeat fellow. He was as enthusiastic about the Grand Canyon National Park as he'd been about dancing, and he was very proud to be a member of the Park Service. He told her all about his plans to advance to a park supervisor one day.

"Maybe not here," he said. "Grand Canyon, well, she's a doozy. You might have to be a rich man's son or have gone to Harvard or both to rise that high. But maybe one of the less busy ones, like Zion."

Billie was fascinated. Her maw had wanted her to see the world, and here Robert had all kinds of plans to do so. She marveled at his

202 — Juliette Fay

bravery to sally forth wherever he chose. They were having a marvelous time. And to think, Charlotte had tried to keep her from going.

"Why on earth shouldn't I go?" Billie had said. "He seems like a nice enough fellow, and we're only taking a walk." She felt the need to toss in, "Besides, you're not my mother."

"You have no idea what young men are capable of."

"Of course I do! Do you think my *real* maw didn't tell me about girls going off in cars with boys at night, and then a couple months later, there's Maw taking out the seams on their dresses? But Robert and I aren't going out at night, and he's not driving me to some lonesome place where no one can hear me if I scream. We're walking in broad daylight on the most traveled path in the whole darn park!"

Billie could tell she was making her point, but Charlotte wasn't ready to let it go. "He could pull you off into the bushes."

"You're right, he could. And a masked man could come into the restaurant in the middle of the lunch rush and drag me away at gunpoint."

Charlotte huffed a sigh. "Does he know how old you are?"

"No, of course not."

"Okay, then please promise me you'll act like a woman of the world who knows better than to be taken advantage of."

"Fine, I'll act like—" Billie was about to say *you*. But then she remembered that Charlotte, for all her worldly college-girl wisdom, had been taken advantage of quite ruthlessly. "—Mae West!" She put her hands on her hips, arched an eyebrow, and grinned sultrily.

This had made the taciturn Charlotte burst out laughing. "Oh dear," she said, "now I know we're in trouble."

Mather Point was an open promontory of rock that thrust out into the canyon, and Billie felt both awestruck by the beauty of it and also a little woozy at how a few steps in the wrong direction would mean the end of her.

"It's ten miles across to the North Rim over there," said Robert.

"And a mile down to the Colorado River." Billie could see it far below, like a garter snake winding its way through the rocks. She stared in silence, barely able to take it all in.

"I hope I'm not talking too much," Robert said suddenly. "It's my job to know all these things and to tell people about them, but I don't mean to sound like some wrinkled old professor."

"Not at all. It's like having a private tour guide."

Robert gave a little sigh of relief. "Sometimes I get excited about things, and I don't stop to take a breath."

"My brother Ian is like that. Maw says he's in love with the whole world."

"You have a brother?"

"I have four, and four sisters, too."

"Gosh, that's even more than me!"

Robert, as it turned out, was the youngest of seven. He was from Barstow, California ("We have a Harvey House there, too—it's huge!"), and his family owned a small orange grove. He joked that they were the stickiest family in town. He told her stories about being an altar boy with his older brothers. One time he tripped over his robe during the holy consecration and went sprawling. His oldest brother started to chuckle, and that set off his middle brother, and the more they tried to stop, the harder they laughed.

"Father Marchand got so mad, he practically threw the chalice at us!"

Robert was fun and funny, and their afternoon together flew by.

He was also twenty-four years old, a full nine years her senior.

Charlotte isn't going to like this one bit was Billie's first thought. But this wasn't a date; they were only having a picnic and being friendly. Besides, who cared what Charlotte thought?

As they walked back toward Grand Canyon Village, the wind picked up and eddied around them with the scent of juniper trees and sage brush and an earthy smell that wasn't quite like Nebraska but felt familiar all the same. It was May 26; Billie had been here almost a month. She didn't know how long it took to get accustomed to a new place. It would never be home, but it was where she lived for now, and she was strangely happy about that.

Robert walked her to the dorm entrance, and for the first time in three hours neither of them seemed to know what to say.

"Thanks for a nice lunch," Billie offered.

"I hope I didn't talk your head off."

She tapped her temple. "Still firmly attached."

"Would you . . . do you think you might . . . want to get together again sometime?"

"Yes, that would be nice."

"Okay!"

"You know where to find me. I'll be right here at the—"

"Dorm! Yes, good."

"Thanks again."

"Thank you!" He nodded and grinned his big grin, then he hurried off.

When Billie went in, Charlotte was sitting in the parlor with that book she'd left lying around their room. But she wasn't reading; she was pressing her lips together to keep from smiling.

"What are you smirking at?" demanded Billie.

Charlotte glanced pointedly toward the front windows, one of which was open.

"We actually had a very nice time! It only got awkward at the end."

"And did he ask your age?"

"Thankfully not."

"Good." Charlotte lowered her book to her lap. "Was he well-behaved?"

"Yes, he's very nice, and he certainly knows a lot about the canyon."

Charlotte rolled her eyes.

"Fine. I know you hate it, but I'm interested."

Charlotte gazed at her a moment. "I thought you still had feelings for Leif."

Leave it to Charlotte to find trouble where there was none. "This has nothing to do with him. Robert and I are just friends, so mind your own beeswax."

Twenty-Nine

When Billie got up to their room, there was an envelope on her bed.

Leif!

She'd secretly started to hope he might send her a letter sooner than her birthday, which was a month away. She'd written him one and delivered it personally. Was it too much to ask that he respond?

But the return address on this envelope was her own in Table Rock. The handwriting wasn't her mother's, though. It was from Peigi, dated a week before.

Dear Billie,

Da is sick. Right after you left, he started coming home tuckered. He said it was just a little cough, but after a while it got worse, and he ran so hot he couldn't work. Maw had him over a pot of steam with some mint in it for days, and that helped some. They didn't want to call the doctor because we were losing money as it was, with him not working.

Finally a couple of days ago, the doctor came. He said Da's lungs crackled like a bonfire. He's got the newmonia.

Maw says not to tell you, because she doesn't want you to worry, and by the time you'd get a letter, he'll be right as rain. And God willing, he will be. Also, she thinks you'll want to come home, and we can't afford it. We need your tips.

But I'm thirteen now, and I have my own mind. You've a right to know about your own da, and he needs all the prayers he can get. Just don't come home, because she's right about the money.

All the rest of us are fine, so don't worry about that. If I have to quit school and help Maw with the laundry business, it won't be a calamity.

Yours very sincerely,
Peigi

"What's wrong?" Charlotte asked when she came up to the room an hour later. "Are you sick?" The girl was positively ashen.

"I got a letter from my sister. Da's got the pneumonia. Peigi sent it a week ago, so he might be better by now. Or he might be . . . " Billie chewed her lip to keep from crying.

Charlotte scoured her brain for words of encouragement, but she had never been good at false cheer. She had never really been good at genuine cheer, either. She wasn't a cheery person.

"I'm so sorry" was all she could think to say. "You must be very scared."

Billie nodded, chin trembling.

"Do you want to go home? I'm sure they'll let you—"

"We can't afford it. What with him laid up and having to pay the doctor, they need me to stay here and work."

Charlotte frowned in thought. These were the types of problems she'd never had to worry about in her old life. Her mother called the doctor every time she felt the least bit lightheaded, and it was always just that her corset was too tight.

"I've been praying," said Billie. "I don't know what else to do."

The poor girl looked so alone in her worry. "Could I . . . ? I'm not Catholic, but I do know how to pray." She hadn't in quite some time, but she assumed the general idea hadn't changed.

"Oh, Charlotte, would you? That'd mean the world to me."

Charlotte pulled her dress up a little so as not to get dust on the hem and knelt by the bed. Her knees immediately began to ache against the wooden floorboards, and she wished there were a nice thick carpet like there was in her room in Boston. But this was no time to be a fussbudget.

Billie dropped down beside her and clasped her hands together in prayer. "Whenever you're ready."

Charlotte had thought they would pray in silence, but clearly Billie expected something different. She cleared her throat to give herself a moment to think.

"Dear Lord, we pray that . . . um . . . Billie's father—"

"Malcolm MacTavish," whispered Billie.

"—that Malcom MacTavish returns speedily to good health. He is a hardworking man and a loving father, and we ask your intercession on his behalf. We also ask that you hold the entire MacTavish family in your heart and comfort them as they await his recovery. Amen."

Billie crossed herself and whispered, "In the name of the Father, the Son, and the Holy Ghost, amen." She opened her eyes with a grateful smile for Charlotte. "That was nice."

Charlotte was relieved that her rusty prayer skills had served their purpose. She reached under the bed for her little string purse, extracted a ten-dollar bill, and held it out to Billie.

"Oh, no, I can't take that."

Charlotte put it in Billie's hand anyway. "Doctors are expensive."

"But you need that in case . . . And anyway my maw would never accept it."

"Put it in the envelope along with your own money the next time you write to your mother, and don't mention me. Just think of it as sending my prayers to your family, but going by way of the US Postal Service."

Thirty

When Charlotte wasn't working at El Tovar, she was working her way through the limited library in the dorm parlor. She even read *Winnie-the-Pooh* and found it surprisingly philosophical for a children's book. She admired the characters' devotion to each other despite their differences in temperament, species, and food preferences.

But as hard as she tried to keep busy, she often found herself alone with her thoughts. One morning on her day off, Charlotte woke in a funk, and she didn't know why. She was concerned for Billie and her father's health, of course, but this felt more personal. Perhaps she was nearing her time of the month, which sometimes served to make her think dark thoughts about humanity in general and herself in particular. But she'd just dealt with all that two weeks ago. She felt at a loss. As if something important had gone missing.

Maybe I'll buy myself a little trinket at the Hopi House and have a chat with Ruth, she thought, trying to muster some reason to rise from bed. It was then that she remembered the blanket she'd picked out at the Cameron Trading Post. She'd never given Will the money for it.

She felt a sting of shame—how thoughtless of her to say she would pay for it, ask that it be laid aside for her, and then not keep her word. But she also felt the blood thrumming a little harder in her chest at the thought of having a perfectly good reason to search out Will.

She hadn't seen him since that night a couple of weeks ago when she'd insisted that they would only be friends. It hadn't occurred to her that he would cut off all contact between them. Perhaps she'd been too plainspoken. Perhaps he'd misinterpreted it as a complete lack of interest on her part. Which, if she were honest, was not the case. Not even a little.

Face washed and wearing her new dress, a dusty rose poplin with buttons at the waist and a tiered skirt, Charlotte and her eight dollars went in search of Will. She'd ordered the dress from Sears a couple of weeks ago when the weather turned warm. She had only three dresses: two were a weighty serge material and one was wool. She'd left St. Louis so quickly, stuffing whatever clothing she could fit into the monogrammed suitcase, with little thought to the future and rising temperatures. In truth, she hadn't been sure if she'd be alive in April, much less June.

Will was standing with one foot on the running board of a Harvey Car, reading a newspaper. The line of vehicles stretched along the road by the train station, and other drivers were smoking or talking in small groups as they waited to be called up to the hotel to collect riders. As she approached, she saw him glance up from his reading and go still at the sight of her. Then he tucked the newspaper under his arm and nodded as she walked toward him.

"Hello, Charlotte."

"Hello, Will. How are you?"

"I'm just fine. How are you?"

How was she? She was terrible. Lonely and cranky and sick of reading. She'd missed him, she realized. She'd missed the sight of him with his kind face and direct gaze. That gaze was trained on her now, but not in a way that made her skin prickle with fear as it had when they'd first met. Anonymity had been her greatest desire when she'd set off on this desperate journey as a Harvey Girl. Will made her feel noticed in a way that ought to be terrifying but wasn't.

"To be honest," she said, "I feel a bit guilty."

The brows rose above his dark eyes, and she could see she'd piqued his interest. "Oh?"

"I said I would give you the money for that blanket, and I forgot all about it."

"Oh, yes. John asked me about that. I told him to hold on to it a while longer, and if you didn't . . . well, if I didn't see you, I'd buy it myself."

She liked the thought of it, Will having her blanket. Perhaps sleeping under it. Perhaps thinking of her.

"That was considerate of you, but I should have kept my word." She thrust the dollar bills out toward him. "I'd like to rectify that now, if you're still willing to make the purchase for me."

He looked at the money, then at her, then at the car, then back up at her. "Are you working today?"

"No, it's my day off."

"Would you like to come along and buy it yourself? I only have two passengers."

Charlotte stood mute before him, the seconds ticking by as he waited for her response. It had never occurred to her that she might go, too, spending the better part of a day with him. Her highest hope when she had tugged on that new dress this morning was that she'd be able to find him and have a small conversation about a blanket she barely remembered.

He stood as still as granite as he waited for her to decide how she wanted to spend her day. How strange to be in the company of a man who allowed her the complete freedom to choose her own path.

"Yes, I think I'd like that very much."

The couple they picked up in front of El Tovar were college professors—both of them!

Charlotte judged them to be in their midforties; they introduced themselves as Dr. and Mrs. Randolf.

"You're a doctor, too, dear," murmured the man, who had a bushy gray mustache. "You mustn't shy from that."

"I'm quite proud of it, actually," she replied, hazel eyes twinkling. "However, on vacation, I prefer not to think of all the lecturing and paper grading I'll have to do in the fall."

He chuckled and patted her hand. "Ah, sounds quite freeing. Maybe I'll join you, and we'll go incognito this summer."

Will introduced himself, and then he said, "This is Charlotte Turner. She's a Harvey Girl here, and she's quite knowledgeable about the Grand Canyon, so I asked her to join us and contribute to our tour."

"Wonderful!" said Mrs. Randolf. "How nice to have not one but two guides."

As the couple climbed into the car and situated themselves in the middle bench seat, Charlotte glared at Will. "What have you done?" she whispered. "I don't know anything!"

"I needed a reason for you to be here. Just tell them what I told you when we went a couple of weeks ago."

"I don't remember—"

"Sure you do."

Charlotte got in beside him and racked her brain. There was that story about the pregnant woman hiding in the canyon . . . She shook her head. This was not nearly enough material for an eight-hour excursion!

But there was all that time she'd spent with George Wharton James and his florid prose. As it happened there were three of his books in the dorm library: *The Grand Canyon of Arizona: How to See It*, of course, but there had also been *The Indians of the Painted Desert Region: Hopis, Navahoes, Wallapais, Havasupais* and *What the White Race May Learn from the Indian*.

Charlotte doubted that the two professors would be terribly interested in the latter two. Tourists generally seemed to find it inconvenient and distasteful that anyone else might have a claim to the canyon. But she had to make do with the information she had.

"As you may know," she began, "the Atchison, Topeka and Santa Fe Railway completed the track to the rim of the Grand Canyon in 1901. El Tovar was built by the Fred Harvey Company in 1905 for a quarter of a million dollars. But there were people here before the tourists came. There were miners and adventurers. And there were Indians."

George Wharton James had quite a bit to say about the tribes with which he'd become familiar. He'd apparently spent a good deal of time with them, was able to converse in their languages, went to their ceremonies, and traveled with them. Vehement about how profoundly they had been abused by missionaries, the US government, and whites in general, his words were striking:

"In our treatment of the Indian we have been liars, thieves, corrupters of the morals of their women, debauchers of their maidens, degraders of their young manhood, perjurers, and murderers."

While he made clear in the first sentences of his book that there were things about Indians he did not admire—mainly that they smoked, wore dirty clothes, and enjoyed coarse humor—he'd written twenty-four chapters about the aspects of tribal life that "Americans" would do well to emulate. He was particularly taken with the Indians' ethos of hard work without complaint, frankness and truthfulness, and the manner in which they educated their children. In this last category, James included the teaching of sex education for adolescents.

Charlotte had been taken aback by this at first. She herself had received no such information from her mother and barely knew what to expect on her wedding night. Upon further consideration, however (and she'd found herself thinking about it quite a bit), it would have been helpful—*very* helpful—to have had some prior knowledge of the details. Simeon certainly could have used some instruction as well. As it was, there was a bit of fumbling and confusion. After that, the goal was quickly accomplished, thank goodness.

"There are a number of tribes who've made their homes in and around the Grand Canyon from time immemorial," Charlotte now told the couple. "The Havasupai, the Hualapai, the Hopi, and the Navajo, to name a few."

She told them about the excellent gardening and basket-making skills of the Havasupai; the remarkable horsemanship of the Navajos; and how Hopi women built their multi-floor homes with minimal help from the men.

"The three-story Hopi House across from the hotel is actually a replica of a building in the Hopi village of Oraibi," she said. "Built by women."

"You have quite extensive knowledge on this subject," said Dr. Randolf. "I'd be interested to know how you came by it."

"I've read books," said Charlotte. "And I've become acquainted with one of the Indians at the Hopi House. Her name is Ruth. I like to go in and chat with her from time to time."

The professor addressed Will. "I can certainly see why you brought Miss Turner along. This trip is delightfully informative!"

When they arrived at Cameron, they all got out of the car and took a moment to stretch after the bumpy ride. As the men began to walk across the dirt parking lot toward the trading post, Mrs. Randolf put a hand on Charlotte's arm. "Please forgive me in advance for any offense I might inadvertently give, my dear, but I find you quite well-spoken for a waitress. Where were you educated? You're from Boston, I take it," said the older woman. "I hear those soft *r*'s in your speech. My mother was from Boston before heading west with my father."

"Yes, Boston," Charlotte said.

"And I suspect you are not a product of the public schools." The woman held up her palm. "Not that I have anything against public education. I teach at a public university, after all. However, your vocabulary, diction, and use of syntax are quite impressive. I'm a professor of English, so I notice these things."

Simeon would be so proud, Charlotte thought ruefully. "I did attend college for two years," she admitted, "but I wasn't able to complete my course of studies."

"Ah, what a shame. This is so often the case for young women. Families tend to prioritize the education of their sons over their daughters."

"Yes, they do." This hadn't been true for Charlotte, of course, but if the Crowninshields hadn't had the money to send both of their children (as well as half the high school graduates of Boston) to college, they certainly would have prioritized her older brother, Oliver, over her.

As they reached the door of the trading post, which Will held open for them, Mrs. Randolf said, "I hope you'll find a way to finish up those last two years and graduate. You have a sharp mind and a wonderful curiosity about the world. You could accomplish great things."

The Randolfs were understandably agog at all that the trading post had on offer. "Please let us know if we can help you with a purchase," said Will (as if Charlotte would have two words to contribute on that subject). But the couple was content to wander admiringly amid the piles of rugs and blankets, the racks of jewelry and pottery, and the walls hung with baskets.

"College?" asked Will as they headed across the large room.

He'd evidently overheard the tail end of the conversation with Mrs. Randolf, so there was no use denying it. "Yes."

"But you didn't finish."

"No."

"Because?"

She stopped and turned toward him, intending to tell him to mind his own business. But instead she said, "Because I was foolish and trusted the wrong person."

"Bad advice?"

Oh, if it had only been advice. "Bad everything."

Will's expression didn't appear to change at all, but suddenly she felt a silent fury come over him, and instinctively she put a hand up to her chest. He glanced down at that hand and then back up to meet her wary gaze. "He's the one who hurt you."

Charlotte tried to present a confidence she did not feel. "I lived to tell the tale."

"My mother almost didn't."

She understood now how he'd known not to intrude or frighten her, how protective he'd been about that bully on the dance floor. "I'm so sorry," she murmured. "Your father?"

Will nodded. "He was a charming brute. I spent my earliest years trying to protect her. He was thrown from a horse and broke his neck before he could do her in, thank God."

"How old were you?"

"Twelve." He took a breath and let it out slowly, as if needing to remind himself that it was in the past. "Where is he now?" he asked. They both knew who he meant.

"St. Louis, I think."

"I want you to know that I'm a friend. You can call on me."

She smiled. He really was so kind. "I'm sure I won't need to."

"It's there for you all the same."

Thirty-One

Billie was getting very little sleep. Each night, she prayed as long as she could before her mind spun off in a tangle of worry. What if Da never recovered and became an invalid? How would Maw pay the bills, even with Billie's contributions? Peigi would certainly have to quit school (though she found it boring and spent most of her time doodling on her homework anyway). Ian was only nine, too young for most jobs and too silly to work very hard even if he got one.

What if her da . . . passed? Maw would be heartbroken—they all would be—and they'd need Billie to be there for them. Besides, she didn't know if she could withstand the immensity of such sorrow without her family around her. But leaving El Tovar would be absolutely the worst thing for their finances. She had to stay and earn as much as she could.

This was, however, no easy task. She no longer spilled things (almost never), but there was a certain . . . je ne sais quoi with the "upper crusties," as she thought of them, that she just couldn't seem to master, no matter how much French Charlotte taught her. The pace was different here from Topeka, where trains came and went every few hours and patrons generally sat for a mere thirty minutes. At Grand Canyon Village the trains arrived only twice a day and people often lingered at their tables for hours. It gave them so much more time to scrutinize and fuss about every little thing!

She had complained to Charlotte about it—for instance, the other day when a man with an overplucked mustache that looked like two bobby pins stuck on his upper lip had commented to his companion in a spotless ivory linen suit that Billie looked so "milk-fed," she might as well be a newborn calf.

"Right in front of me!" Billie had howled as they took off their uniforms that night. Nerves frayed by sleeplessness and constant worry, she had far less patience than usual for difficult customers.

"I agree it's quite rude," Charlotte said calmly, "but they just don't see you."

"Charlotte, I am almost six feet tall! Are they blind?"

"The rich don't see the poor. They're taught from infancy the fine art of disregard."

"*Why?*"

Charlotte had sighed wearily. "I suppose it's convenient. If you don't see someone, you don't have to consider their feelings or circumstances. You can say and do as you like."

"I *hate* them!" Billie had flopped down onto her bed. She no longer seemed to care if Charlotte saw her undergarments.

Charlotte had lowered herself slowly. She was a small person who conducted herself admirably in the dining room, lifting huge trays of soup, lugging away dinner plates still loaded with the half-eaten remains of prime rib and Cornish game hens. But she had not been raised with any kind of manual labor or exercise; to the contrary, she'd been consistently warned against exerting herself for fear of building muscle "like a housemaid." As a Harvey Girl, Charlotte went to bed with an ever-changing constellation of aches.

"Hate them all you like, but you must never, ever show it. The rich are also trained to spot a social snub at fifty paces. Disdain from a waitress will not be borne." She rubbed at the small of her back. "And neither of us can afford to lose our jobs, no matter how rude they are."

———————————

Not all of the upper crusties were condescending; most, in fact, were reasonably polite and generous tippers, though they rarely exchanged comments with their servers that didn't have to do with their meal. But every once in a while, Billie got a group that was crustier than usual, and try as she might, she felt like she was holding a rattlesnake by the rattle.

Today, a customer threw a cocktail shrimp at her, claiming it was not sufficiently chilled, though it was sitting in a dish of ice. It was all Billie could do not to pick it up and throw it back. She'd held her tongue, only to turn and see Nora watching. Back in Topeka, bad behavior was not tolerated by the management. Of course, back in Topeka, the customers tended to be regular folks, not the senators, titans of industry, and movie stars the El Tovar catered to and indulged.

Today was Charlotte's day off (where had she disappeared to, anyway?), and Billie was left to steam furiously to no one after work. Then Henny peeked her head in the door.

"Sunset?"

They headed west from the Grand Canyon Village out along the rim path to Hopi Point. Billie had only been there once before, and the sky had been overcast, so it hadn't been quite the spectacle she'd been made to expect. But tonight the conditions were perfect: the sky was a limpid blue, save for a few frothy clouds that drifted along the horizon, bit players ready to do their part in reflecting the sun's last rays across the vast stage of the canyon.

Billie spent most of the hour-long walk brooding about nasty customers and worrying about her da. There had been no word from Peigi, and Maw's most recent letter had been brief. Caring for her ill husband and picking up extra laundry work had probably left little time for the kinds of informative, chatty notes Maw usually wrote. Billie hoped desperately that no news was good news . . .

The two women arrived at Hopi Point about fifteen minutes before sunset. Gazing out across the timeless tapestry of cliffs and crags and hoodoos, Billie fell silent.

The world was big. She was small. (The shrimp-throwing customer didn't even exist.)

The sun shimmered, the clouds radiated pink and orange, the sky went purple, and the walls of the canyon pulsed with red and ocher and cinnamon.

She sent a silent prayer for her father into the colorful heavens.

Henny hung her arm around Billie's shoulder. "It's something, isn't it?"

Billie slipped her arm around Henny's waist and smiled.

Will went off to answer a question for the Randolfs, and Charlotte headed to the back counter where her blanket had been stowed for her. John was there as he had been the last time.

He leveled a momentary stare at her. "You're back," he said.

"Yes. I'm sorry it took me so long."

"You had to earn your eight dollars from the tourists."

"Oh, no, I had it. I just forgot to give it to Will. It had slipped my mind, you see."

He shrugged. "I suppose I do."

He wasn't terribly friendly, was he? Nothing like Ruth in the Hopi House. He lifted the blanket from behind the counter, and as he handed it to her, his hand slipped across it one last time.

"It's very beautiful, isn't it?" she said, taking possession and cradling it against her.

"It's a lot of work. Many, many hours."

"Yes, I know. I see the weavers at the Hopi House by El Tovar. They're artists."

He let out a wry grunt of a laugh. "So you won't be using it as a dog blanket?"

She glared at him. "Why would I *ever* . . . "

"They do, you know. I've heard them. Or they say they'll leave it in the trunk of the car for cold days."

"I have neither a dog nor a car. I can't afford them, and I may never in my life be able to. So I suppose I'm left to treat it with the respect it deserves." She dropped the money onto the counter. "I hope that doesn't disappoint you."

He laughed. "Not at all, Miss."

Charlotte walked toward the front of the store to wait for Will and the Randolfs. The couple was at the register. The clerk was wrapping up a lovely large pitcher they'd bought.

Will came to stand beside her. "They picked a good one."

"What makes it so good?" Charlotte asked.

"It's a normal size, for one thing. Most tourists need things small so they can pack them in suitcases for the train. The Indians started making smaller items to accommodate the market, but they'd never use such tiny pots themselves. The Randolfs drove up from Tucson, so they can just put their nice big water jug in their car."

"Glad they didn't buy a blanket then," Charlotte muttered. "Your friend John would accuse them of throwing it in the trunk."

"Sounds like you and he had some words."

Charlotte relayed the conversation. Will smiled. "He must like you."

"Certainly not," huffed Charlotte. "He was bordering on rude."

"What were you saying in the car about all the things that author thinks white people should emulate? Something about frankness, if I remember. John is straightforward with people, as many Indians are, when he feels he can be. He'd be much more deferential with tourists, but that's an act he puts on. Sounds like he was himself with you."

Charlotte ruminated on this. It was a little like serving customers who treated her as a person rather than just a vehicle for them to get their food. They smiled and said thank you and maybe even asked her where she was from. She didn't have to work so hard to be invisible; her existence was acceptable.

The ride back to Grand Canyon Village was quieter. The four of them were full of the lunch they'd had at the trading post—piki bread and mutton and roasted corn—and the bouncing carriage of the Harvey Car lulled them. Charlotte didn't dare doze, of course. It wouldn't do for her to nod off on the job. But when she sensed that the Randolfs were not responding with ever more questions and comments, as they had on the ride to Cameron, she left them to the sounds of the wind in the pines, the rush of the Little Colorado, and the hum of the motor.

Undistracted by her own gabbling about whatever she could remember from those books, she became acutely aware of Will sitting next to her, his strong hands on the wheel, his broad shoulder occasionally grazing hers as they went around a bend in the winding road. There was a certain bearlike maleness to him. She imagined for a moment that she was sharing the bench seat with a grizzly bear—physically powerful, able to do damage with the mere swat of one large paw. And yet he lacked the tightened-coil energy of a predator. Of Simeon.

Will would not strike without provocation; she was somehow certain of this. She felt strangely, unaccountably, undeniably . . . safe.

———

When they arrived back at El Tovar, the Randolfs extricated themselves slowly from the Harvey Car. "My goodness," said Mrs. Randolf. "I feel as if I've had my spine tied in a knot!"

"I hope I wasn't driving too quickly for you." Will took her hand to guide her out. "I try to get my passengers home in a speedy fashion, but not so much that their heads hit the roof on the bumps."

She patted his arm when she was safely on the sidewalk. "I can't imagine anyone doing any better on such a rustic old trail."

Dr. Randolf tapped his now-dusty pockets to locate his billfold, then pulled two ten-dollar bills off the stack. He handed one to Will and one to Charlotte.

"This is far too much!" Charlotte gasped.

"Not a word of it." Dr. Randolf tucked his billfold back into his pocket. "The two of you gave us a full day of edifying information and expert guidance. You've earned that and more."

Mrs. Randolf squeezed Charlotte's shoulder and whispered, "College. You've got to finish that degree, my dear."

As the two professors made their way up the wide stairway to the El Tovar porch and into the Rendezvous Room that served as the lobby of the hotel, Charlotte was struck silent by their kindness. Finally she turned to Will.

"Well, I don't know what to think," she murmured.

He grinned. "You should be thinking of asking me for my tenner, since you did practically all the work."

She let out a laugh. "I don't think I've ever talked so much in all my life."

"It was a piece of cake for me. All I had to do was drive. And besides"—his dark eyes were on her, the faintest hint of a smile crinkling around them—"I like the sound of your voice."

Thirty-Two

"There's a movie at the community hall on Friday." Robert was waiting for Billie when she came out of the service entrance at the rear of the El Tovar dining room.

"Hello, Robert." Work weary, she swiped a stray lock of fine blond hair off her cheek. "How long have you been out here?"

"Not long," he said. "A few minutes." He blushed. "Maybe twenty or thirty."

"You could have left a note at the dorm."

"Yes, but then I wouldn't have been able to . . . I just wanted to . . . " He looked down at his shiny black boots. "See you."

It had been a week since their trip to Mather Point. Billie had started to wonder if the awkwardness of their last exchange had dampened his interest in spending time with her, which was a bit of a disappointment. She liked having someone to do things with other than Charlotte, and Robert's bubbly personality distracted her from worrying about her da.

If she were honest with herself, it kept her from worrying about something else, too. Leif still hadn't responded to her letter. True, he had only said that he'd write for her birthday, but the more she thought about it, the more uncomfortable she felt. She had poured out her heart in that letter. Maybe he'd been put off by it. Maybe he didn't want a girl who was so free with her feelings.

Robert seemed to like her just as she was. He was a lot older than her, but he didn't act like it. In fact she felt she was almost as mature as he was. Sometimes even more so.

"I'm glad you tracked me down," said Billie.

Robert looked up. "You are?"

"Yes. I love movies."

"Okay! That's dandy. I'll, um . . . " He wagged a finger as if trying to jog his memory.

"What time?" she prompted.

"Right! Seven o'clock. That's when it starts, so I'll swing by and get you at six thirty."

"Perfect!" She smiled at him. He really was very sweet.

———————————

Charlotte wasn't terribly worried about the movie idea, despite her concern that this Robert might have hopes that Billie was trying to ignore. Billie claimed she and Robert were "just friends," and at this point, it was technically true. Charlotte felt certain the girl was smart enough to know that eventually he might want more, and she would have to deal with that when the time came.

At the moment, however, what Billie needed most was a respite from her worries, and Charlotte gauged that nothing untoward would likely happen in a room full of people. It wouldn't hurt to keep an eye on things, however, so she decided to go, too.

"It's a just silly movie," said Billie. "You won't like it."

"Don't worry, I'm not going to sit with you."

"Yes, but you'll be lurking around, watching us."

"I do not *lurk*. And why would I watch you when there will be actual entertainment on-screen?"

"You'll think it's foolish and boring, and you'll be waiting to gallop in like the cavalry if he so much as puts an arm around me—which he won't because, as I keep telling you, it's *not a date*."

"You vastly overestimate how intriguing you and your little friend are to me."

"*We are not little!*" Billie stamped her foot. "*You* are!"

Charlotte started to laugh, and Billie, knowing her performance was indeed laughable, could do nothing but stomp out.

Charlotte was not laughing, however, when Vincent Patrillo, the El Tovar general manager, called her into his office on Friday afternoon after the lunch shift. She was terrified.

"Miss Turner," he said as she stood at attention before a mahogany desk the size of a billiard table, "I'm told you took a trip to the trading post in Cameron earlier this week." He was seated behind the desk, yet he commanded the entire room with his booming baritone and faint Italian accent. His thick black hair was slicked back from his forehead, and his large brown eyes pierced hers with their directness.

Charlotte felt herself go cold. She was about to be fired.

"Yes, I did, sir," she stammered. "I . . . I insisted on going."

"You insisted?"

"Yes, sir. It was my responsibility entirely. I had wanted to purchase a . . . a blanket."

Good Lord, she sounded ridiculous, but she had to protect Will. She would not have him lose his job over this, even if she lost hers.

Mr. Patrillo's face went quizzical. "A blanket?"

"It's . . . " She could feel her lip beginning to tremble. "It's very beautiful."

Patrillo crossed his thick arms and squinted in annoyance.

"I'm so sorry, sir." Her voice went breathy with dread. "It will never happen again."

"But that is the point," he said. "I want it to happen again."

"Pardon me?"

"A couple—the Rudolfs, I believe—"

"Randolf," she murmured.

"Hah?"

"The name is Randolf."

"Yes, well, this couple of the undetermined surname, they spoke very highly of you. They said you are very smart and told them many things about nature and the Indians and all of this kind of business."

"Yes, I did, sir. I've been reading books about the area, and—"

"Yes, yes." He waved his hand. "This couple, they come back every year. They often stay in one of the suites. This year they stayed in the El Tovar Suite, the most expensive room in the hotel."

"But . . . they're college professors, sir."

He shrugged. "Apparently there's money."

Of course there is, thought Charlotte. *How else would a woman have the financial means and social clout to be allowed to earn a doctoral degree?*

"It is good to keep them happy," Patrillo went on. "And you did."

"Thank you, sir."

"Now." He put his hands flat on the enormous desk as if he were about to conduct some important business. "Will Rosser."

Charlotte realized he had never heard Will's last name before. *Rosser. Possibly Welsh*, she thought. Like her grandfather. "Yes, sir?"

"Are you and he . . . ?" Patrillo tipped his head vaguely, though the implication was clear.

"Absolutely not."

He eyed her skeptically, and it unnerved her to the point where she almost explained that she was married and therefore unavailable for such a connection. Almost, but not quite.

She held his gaze with the certainty of the righteous.

He nodded and moved on. "Fred Harvey is starting a new business, the Indian Detours."

"Detouring around the Indians?" The Indians had been here since time immemorial, and despite the fact that the mighty US government had done everything in its power to contain and diminish them, they were still here. How did Fred Harvey propose to avoid them?

"Not *around* them," said Patrillo, clearly questioning the Randolfs' assessment of her intelligence. "*To* them. The tourists take a detour from Harvey Houses to the Indian villages and see how they live."

He went on to explain that the Detours had already begun, with passengers disembarking in New Mexico for a three-day excursion into Indian country. "De-tourists" would visit pueblos and cliff dwellings, see the Indians in their own environment, witness their rituals and their rustic industry. The cost of the three-day tour, including meals, lodging, and the services of a male driver and a female guide, was $135.

"I suspect we will be starting Detours from here in the next year or so, and I would like you to be part of it. There will be training, of course. You need to know what you're talking about, and not just from books. The pay is very good. Better than serving food."

Charlotte's eyes went wide. She was already interested in learning more about the Indians; the increased salary made it all the more appealing. "I'd be delighted."

"For now, you will continue to do the tours to the trading post and around the South Rim with Will Rosser. It seems that you are a good team, as long as there is no . . . reason for concern. Of course, it is high season in the restaurant, so I will need you there, as well. Are you prepared to work hard?"

As if she'd been sitting on a satin cushion eating chocolate eclairs these last two months.

"Yes, sir. I am prepared."

———————

Charlotte did not go back to the dorm to change out of the white uniform with the little black bow tie. She went directly in search of Will.

In the afternoon heat, she walked down the line of Harvey Cars by the train depot, and the drivers tipped their hats or nodded as she passed. (A couple of them ogled her, but she was too distracted to muster her usual outrage.) When she came to the end without locating him, she said to the last driver, "Pardon me. I'm looking for Will Rosser. Do you happen to know where he might be found?"

The man chuckled at this—why did people find her so peculiar?—and said, "He just got off. Reckon you'll find him back at his place."

It was a strange way to refer to the men's dormitory, but she thanked the man and strode off in that direction. She knew it was southwest of the village, a bit farther out than most of the buildings. The women's dorm was right behind El Tovar; Harvey Girls had almost no distance to walk at night to return to their rooms. Grand Canyon Village seemed like a safe place—far safer than the crime-ridden St. Louis neighborhood where she'd lived with Simeon—but Charlotte would have been ill at ease making a trek like this in the dark.

She rapped on the dormitory door, and it was soon answered by an older man with a cook's apron around his waist. He looked her up and down and sighed. "No women allowed in the dorm. You'd best get back to your own."

"I don't want to come *in*," said Charlotte curtly, offended at the implication. "I need to speak to Will Rosser, so I'd like him to come out. Would you be so kind as to retrieve him?"

"Oh, you want Will."

"I don't *want*—"

"They gave him his own place. Seniority and all. Plus everyone likes Will." The man gave directions to the National Park Service housing.

The little neighborhood of small rustic cabins wasn't far, and as she walked, her thoughts lingered on the man's comment about everyone liking Will. She'd never heard anyone referred to in such a way in her old life. People might say a man was respected or admired. But to be liked was another thing entirely, wasn't it?

The last cabin in the row was a bit more dilapidated than the rest, with a shingle missing here and there and a bit of paint peeling on the columns that held up the little front porch. Charlotte barely noticed, however, because Will himself was sitting in a chair on the porch next to an upturned wooden crate. On it sat a bottle of Bevo, a brand of the nonalcoholic near beer that was the only legal option these days. Will was reading a newspaper in his lap.

"You certainly do keep abreast of current events," said Charlotte from the short walkway.

Will's head snapped up from the paper. When he caught sight of her, warmth spread across his face as if he'd suddenly been hit by a ray of sun on an overcast day. Charlotte could only smile back, the stiffness she seemed to carry constantly now melting into softness.

"I like to know the news of the world, even if I'm only in a quiet little corner of it."

"I have some news," said Charlotte as she trod the couple of steps onto the porch, "though it might not be as fascinating as what's going on out there."

"I always like to hear what you've got to say, new or not." He stood in greeting, as a gentleman should, and she thought for a moment that he might embrace her—as a gentleman should not. She could imagine such a greeting with great clarity, however, almost as if it were happening in some alternate universe, and she had only to shift somehow into that other reality to feel his arms around her.

"Let me get you a chair." The screen door squeaked, and he disappeared inside. She watched him go and saw a tidy room with a short brown upholstered sofa and a kitchenette to the left with a little round table—oak, she guessed, like the much larger one in the breakfast room back in Boston. There was a doorway on the right through which she could see a made bed. Will's bed.

"Here we are." He came back through with the chair and set it on the opposite side of the crate. "It's cool out here."

"It's lovely," she said, and she meant it, though a couple of battered kitchen chairs and a crate were hardly beautiful. The breeze lifted the last bit of dampness from the back of her neck.

"Can I offer you a drink? Water? Bevo, if you like?"

"No, thank you, I'm fine." She was a bit thirsty, but she was anxious to tell him her news. "Mr. Patrillo called me into his office just now."

His face fell. "What did he want? Are you okay?"

"I'm fine, Will. Apparently the Randolfs were quite pleased with the trip and told him so. He'd like me to accompany you on future excursions."

His face broke wide with delight and he tapped the flat of his hand on the table. "No kidding!"

She grinned back. "No kidding."

They sat on the little porch talking and eventually she accepted a Bevo, which she did not like at all, and he laughed at the face she made. As the sun set and the temperature dropped, the breeze grew chilly, and he invited her inside. It would have been a reputation-incinerating event for a young woman to enter a man's home alone back in Boston. But this was not Boston.

Will sliced up an apple, a wedge of hard cheese, and some bread. "I'm sorry I don't have much to offer. I generally eat meals at the men's commissary."

"How did you end up in this place?" she asked.

"I've worked for Fred Harvey for seven years. That's a long time at the Grand Canyon, where there isn't much of a town, and most everyone is single. It's not the ideal place to raise a family. Folks meet their mate—or don't—and they move on."

"But you've stayed."

He shrugged. "I like the work, I'm paid well, and I have a bit of freedom with the driving."

"You haven't met your mate here."

His expression dimmed slightly. "No."

Charlotte hoped he would expand on this one-syllable answer, but he did not.

"So you've been here long enough to earn your own little home."

"House, I guess," said Will. "Not sure if it qualifies as a home. The Park Service doesn't need it at the moment—you may have guessed that from the maintenance they've neglected. But if their ranks expand, I expect it'll get a paint job, and I'll be back in the dormitory."

The apple, cheese, and most of the bread were gone, and they were sipping tea when Charlotte noticed the surprisingly ornate clock ticking away on a side table. It read eight o'clock.

"Is it really that late?" she asked, startled.

"I've never known it to be a minute off," Will said. "I wind it regularly."

"I was planning to go to the movie at the community hall."

"What's it called?"

"I don't know. Some silly thing. I was only going to keep an eye on Billie and that Robert. There's something about him I don't like."

"And what's that?"

"Well, he made a crass comment about drunken Indians that I didn't particularly care for when Billie was . . . under the weather. But it's his age, mainly. I'm fairly certain he's much older than she is."

"He didn't look that old. Early twenties? No older than twenty-five, I'd wager."

Charlotte glanced again at the clock. It appeared to be an antique in good condition. The base was dark wood, beautifully carved with branches and little birds. The glass domed out from the face, encircled by a thin brass band.

"How old is she?" Will asked in the silence.

"Young."

"How young?"

She turned her gaze to him, and he tipped his head. "You know you can trust me."

Charlotte let out a resigned sigh. "She'll be sixteen in three weeks."

"*Fifteen?*"

"You're sorry you asked."

"Well, it certainly solves the mystery of why you're so protective of her." He wrapped up the last bit of bread in paper and took the plates over to the small sink. He looked back at her still sitting at the table. "We'd better get going."

Thirty-Three

Robert was apologetic about the movie. "It's four years old. We don't get first-run movies here in the wilderness. You've probably seen it already."

"That's all right. I love movies, however old they are, and even if I've seen them before." When Billie was twelve, Maw had started letting her take the older children to the Ideal Theater in Table Rock whenever she had some extra change, which wasn't often. This movie had come out when she was eleven, so there was little chance she'd seen it.

The community hall was laid out with benches and a screen set up on the stage. A cantankerous two-wheel projector was hauled in. Robert suggested they sit near the front so the machine's loud whirring wouldn't distract them. It was a silent film, which would have come with sheet music for an orchestra to play throughout the show, but there wasn't even a pianist tonight.

The movie was called *Fox Trot on the Congo*, and the story followed a wealthy couple who goes on safari, gets separated from their tour, and stumbles upon a society in the middle of the jungle that is just as ostentatious and party loving as their own—only more "African," of course. The couple becomes so enamored of the tribe that they create a big ruse to protect them from the outside world when colonialists threaten to invade.

Billie was thrilled. "I saw the sequel, *Charleston in China*, but I never got to see this one. I love Gertrude Turner!" The leading lady was known for her comedic chops and physical humor. She could slip on a banana peel and do a pratfall better than any other actress in Hollywood. "She was an acrobat in vaudeville," Billie told Robert. "I read it in *Photoplay* magazine."

"She's my favorite, too!" said Robert. "And boy, what a knockout with that blond hair and big blue eyes."

Billie had a strange moment of jealousy. It wasn't that she wanted Robert to think she was pretty—she'd told herself over and over that they were strictly friends. So why did she care if Robert thought some other girl was "a knockout"?

Robert seemed to intuit that he'd said the wrong thing. "You're pretty, too," he said quickly. "Actually, you're beautiful, Billie."

"You don't have to say that. And Gertrude Turner is truly gorgeous."

"You're not mad?"

"No, why would I be?"

He stared at her a moment, frozen in uncertainty. Then the lights went down, and the screen flickered to life.

When the lights came up, people stood and stretched the blood flow back into their extremities after two hours on the hard benches. They greeted one another as those at the back slowly filed out. Billie was surprised that Charlotte had never shown up to scrutinize them in the dark, but she was nowhere to be found.

Billie and Robert walked down the road together chatting about the movie, the best parts ("All of it!" said Billie), and how the costars, Gertrude Turner and Henry Weston, had met on set and were a real married couple now.

"It's very romantic," she sighed, and he agreed.

They walked up the short steep hill to the women's dormitory, and Robert suggested they keep walking. "It'll be easier to see the stars if we get away from the lights of the buildings."

It was past nine, and most of the tourists had gone to their rooms or to have a nightcap at the El Tovar lounge. Billie and Robert strolled along the Rim Trail past the homely and aging Bright Angel Hotel with its gaggle of tent-cabins, the Lookout Studio and its competitor, the Kolb Studio. They passed the Bright Angel Trailhead, and then there was no one around at all.

Billie stopped. "I think we've gone far enough. It's so dark here we could step right off into the canyon without seeing it."

"Just a little farther," said Robert.

But Billie suddenly thought of Charlotte warning that he could drag her off into the bushes. "I'm going back," she said.

"I'll walk you back, but before we go . . . and before I lose my nerve . . . could I please hold your hand?"

Billie hesitated. "You want to hold my hand?"

Robert stiffened. "Is there something more you had in mind? Because if that's the case, you're not the kind of girl I thought you were."

Billie was confused now. "What kind of girl did you think I was?"

"A good one! Chaste and respectable and—"

"I *am* a good girl," said Billie. "*You're* the one who wanted to come all the way out here in the dark!"

"Because it's beautiful! The stars and the canyon and the scent of *Artemisia tridentata!*"

"The what?"

"Sagebrush." His shoulders slumped. "Oh, never mind."

"Robert, you worried me. I don't know you that well."

"I'm sorry if I scared you. I guess I'm not very good at this."

She sighed. "I'm not very good at it, either. I don't go around with boys at night."

"No, of course you don't. I didn't mean to accuse you of being . . . "

"A trollop."

"I apologize. Sincerely I do."

They stood there for a long moment, each gazing off toward the darkened canyon. "If it would be all right with you," he murmured, "I would still like to hold your hand."

Billie thought for a moment. Was there any harm in it? Holding hands seemed pretty tame. It wasn't nearly as romantic as kissing. And even though Robert was a good deal older than her, there was a boyish innocence about him that reminded her of her brothers.

"It would be all right with me."

He reached out and gently took her hand in his. It felt warm and good. She'd had so little bodily contact since she'd left home, where there was always someone on her lap or an arm around her waist. She missed that comfort especially now, with Da so sick. Outside of her family, the only person who'd touched her was Leif. And who knew if she'd ever even see him again?

"Thank you very much," whispered Robert, and they made their way back to civilization hand in hand.

Crouched behind a large *Artemisia tridentata*, Will and Charlotte watched them go.

"Seems like he might be harmless," murmured Will.

"So far," said Charlotte. "He's still a grown man, and she's still fifteen."

The next evening when Billie and Charlotte came in late from the dinner shift, there was a letter on Billie's bed. She snatched it up and studied it, her heart pounding in her throat, frozen in fear. "It's from Peigi," she murmured.

"Do you want me to read it first?"

Billie thrust the letter at Charlotte, whose fingers shook slightly as she tore open the envelope.

As soon as she looked at it, Charlotte smiled. "He's all right."

"Really?"

"See for yourself." She handed back the letter.

It was exactly as Charlotte had said.

> *Dear Billie,*
>
> *Da is all right. It took a while for him to get his strength back, and there was one or two days when he seemed to get worse, but he's better now. He says he's going back to work tomorrow, but Maw will have the last say on that.*
>
> *You must be working hard. That was a lot of money you sent. I'm staying in school for now.*
>
> *Yours very truly,*
> *Peigi*
>
> *PS. Don't tell Maw I told you. She'd have my hide.*

Tears rolled down Billie's cheeks as she hugged Charlotte so hard she nearly smothered her. But Charlotte didn't mind; it helped to hide the tears in her own eyes.

Thirty-Four

Charlotte greatly enjoyed her conversations with Ruth at the Hopi House. Not only was the young woman knowledgeable and patient with Charlotte's questions, but there was a certain elegance to her demeanor. She had a sense of humor but didn't engage in the kind of crass jokiness and silly giggling that many of the Harvey Girls were prone to.

Charlotte often thought that Fred Harvey should hire Ruth or one of the other Indians to be tour guides—they would have far better answers to the some of the questions that came up. But there were clear lines about who was allowed to do which jobs.

Every Harvey Girl she'd ever seen was white. A few Mexican girls worked as maids or kitchen help, but they were not allowed in the dining room. There were Indians who worked for the railroad or on construction projects around the village, but these were never public-facing jobs. Apparently, the Fred Harvey Company wanted Indians to be seen only as artistic primitives, not people who might serve you a meal, take you on a tour, or be your neighbor.

Will said as much. "Most white folks only know about Indians from the movies—savages who'll scalp you and take your women. I suppose it's better that the Harvey Company presents them as exotics who make pretty things, but it's a long way from saying that they're people like us, just trying to feed their families and live their lives in peace."

In the beginning, Charlotte's conversations with Ruth focused mainly on the types of items for sale at the Hopi House that were also carried at the Cameron Trading Post. Charlotte wanted to know how the baskets and jewelry and the like were made, of course, but more than that, she wanted to understand the symbols and artwork and what it all meant. She wanted to know the history.

Ruth was happy to talk when there was no one else in the shop, but their discussions were often cut short by the needs of actual customers. And if Fred Spencer, the Hopi House manager, was in the vicinity, Ruth went silent, busying herself with whatever small task she could find.

"I cannot lose my job," she murmured to Charlotte one day. "It is a very dry year. My father's melons and peaches are not coming in well."

This gave Charlotte an idea. "I shouldn't bother you while you're working."

"It's no bother. It's just that . . . "

"You're very kind, but I don't want to jeopardize your career. And it's unfair to ask you to provide me with an education out of the goodness of your heart. What I really need is a tutor, and tutors get paid."

"A tutor? I don't know if there is anyone like that around here."

"You! You're a wonderful teacher. And if we meet when you're not working, you won't have to worry about Mr. Spencer firing you for talking to some gabby Harvey Girl."

They agreed that they would meet in the early morning before the Hopi House opened on the days when Charlotte had the dinner shift. Ruth balked at being paid, but Charlotte said, "Information has value. You are in possession of a valuable commodity that I would like to have. It's only right for me to compensate you."

———

During their first tutoring session a couple of days later, Charlotte said, "One of the things tourists often ask is where Indian children go to school." She assumed they learned by following their parents around, an apprenticeship of sorts, but she wanted to be sure.

It seemed like a simple enough question, but Ruth gazed into middle space a moment before answering. "Many children go to boarding school."

"My goodness, that must be expensive."

"It's free."

"Free boarding school! Well, don't let white families hear about it," Charlotte joked. "They'll all want to go."

Some strong emotion flashed briefly across Ruth's smooth features. Anger? Disgust? Sorrow? Charlotte wasn't sure.

"No white family would ever send their children to these schools. Most Indian families don't want their children to go, either."

Charlotte blinked in confusion. "But then why do they . . . can't they just keep them home?"

"No. We are given no choice. They send the military, and we are forced to go. These are not white schools. These are Indian schools, and their purpose is to teach us to be white."

"Why on earth do they want you to be white?" It seemed like a lot of effort and expense spent on people who were happy as they were and doing no harm.

Ruth leveled her gaze at Charlotte. "It's what all conquerors do. They take the land and make you speak their language, and use their customs, and worship their god. Then you don't exist anymore, so you are no longer a problem."

———————————

Charlotte thought about that a long time after the tutoring session was over. At the next one several days later, she asked, "How can they make you worship their god? Can't you worship whoever you want in the privacy of your own heart?"

Ruth let out the tiniest breath of a sigh. "Religion is not private in our culture." She tapped her head. "It's not just in here. It is at

242 — Juliette Fay

the center of our community, a part of everything we do. Our cere-
monies have been outlawed by the Indian Religious Crimes Code.
We still do them, because they are necessary, they are who we are.
But it is a risk every time."

"Your ceremonies are *illegal?*" said Charlotte.

"Yes."

Charlotte was appalled. "Do they think that if they take away
your religion, you'll happily pick up Christianity as if it were a new
pair of socks?"

"The government might think that, but the missionaries know
it's not that simple. So they offer things to make us go down the
Jesus Road."

"What do they give you?"

"It could be anything. Food or gifts—yes, including socks! Or it
could be sewing lessons. They give you just enough cloth for part of
a quilt, and they read the Bible as you sew. You have to come back
again and again to finish the quilt, and they keep reading."

"Does it work?"

"A few of the Hopi in my village have gone down off the mesa to
live in the tiny Pahana houses by the church." Ruth smiled. "But not
many."

"Pahana?"

"White people."

Charlotte studied Ruth, trying to imagine how frightening it
must be to have everything important to you—your very life—in jeop-
ardy. It was like being trapped in a bad marriage, only on a much
grander scale. She thought of the alias she'd taken to avoid her own
tormentor.

"Your name isn't really Ruth, is it?"

"My name is Ruth here in the white world. With my family, it is
Yoki, which means 'rain.'"

"Which should I call you?"

The young woman considered this a moment. "I think it's best if you call me Ruth. It's less confusing for me if I keep my worlds separate."

On the tours, Charlotte now found herself expounding on the virtues of tribal cultures and how important it was to protect them from eradication. Some tourists were interested; most, however, were more focused on getting the best prices on Indian crafts.

"I agree with your argument, and I admire your persistence," Will murmured to her one day as they watched tourists wander through the trading post like ants at a picnic, "but it does no good to bash them over the head with it."

"I am not *bashing*," she hissed back.

"You are, a little."

He was right. And if tourists felt they were being lectured, they would complain, she would lose her job, and what good would that do?

She railed to Billie about it one night. "No one seems to care that the US government is trying to erase Indian culture and make them all Jesus worshippers!"

She was caught off guard by the girl's response, though if she'd thought about it for even a moment, she wouldn't have been.

"What's wrong with that? *I'm* a Jesus worshipper."

"Yes, but that's by choice, Billie. No one tried to take away everything that makes your family Scottish and ram a new religion down your throat."

A ping of memory flashed in Charlotte's mind: her British history class back at Wellesley College. "Actually, that's exactly what happened," she said. "Since the First War of Scottish Independence around 1300, the English had been trying to take Scotland, and in the 1700s they finished the job with the Battle of Culloden. The

Highlanders' way of life was decimated, their lands taken, their clans abolished, and their Catholic faith persecuted. It's likely the reason your ancestors immigrated to the United States."

Billie's gaze clouded for a moment as she measured what she knew about her family history against this new information about the Indians.

"Oh," she said.

"Right."

"But Jesus isn't a bad thing."

"No, he's not, if you choose him of your own free will. Your people left the only home they'd known for a thousand years and came all the way to America—which purports to have freedom of religion—so they could practice their faith and live their lives in peace. But where can the Indians go?"

———

Charlotte toned down her message about what the US government and the missionaries were doing to the tribes—but she didn't like it. She hoped that if Mr. Patrillo was given the green light to start the Detours, people might be able to see Indian cultures for themselves, and their appreciation would grow. She was proud to be first in line as a guide who would see that to fruition.

In the meantime, she had to be content with sneaking her message in subtly as she described the artistry of Indian crafts or tribal reverence for the Southwest's harsh beauty. It was frustrating to have to spoon-feed the truth in tiny sips, but her growing friendship with Will—someone who knew this truth and admired her for trying to impart it—was a comfort at least.

If she were completely honest, it was also a bit of a thrill.

You're lonely, she tried to tell herself. *It's just an infatuation.*

But she knew it was more than that, and she suspected he knew it, too.

Billie had settled into a sort of tentative contentment, now that panic over her da no longer simmered constantly in her veins (though she was now painfully aware that, at any given point, one of her family members could be injured or ill, and she'd never know unless Peigi decided to tell her).

Spending time with Robert was fun. He took her for walks and told her interesting things about the canyon or funny stories from home. On Sundays they said the Rosary together. They held hands sometimes, and that was nice, especially because he never pressed for anything more. It felt uncomplicated and safe.

Occasionally he made some mention of the difference in their ages, and this worried Billie. If he knew the truth, would he be angry? Would he tell Mr. Patrillo? But it was not just anxiety she felt; it was guilt. Robert had never come right out and asked her age, as Leif had. He just knew she was younger than him and assumed she was eighteen or nineteen—he'd referred to her as a teenager on occasion.

It was true, she *was* a teenager! And she'd never outright lied. She'd never had to. Nevertheless, it made her feel a little sick inside. She told herself it would be easier once she turned sixteen and wasn't quite as far off from his guess.

But as her birthday approached, she knew that her anticipation was not only for the relief of being closer to the age she purported to be, nor for whatever little celebration her friends might cook up. It was the hope of a letter from Leif.

"Have you heard from him?" Charlotte asked out of the blue one day when Billie was reading a letter from home. Charlotte herself never received any mail.

"Heard from who?" asked Billie.

"You know who."

"No. I guess he's not much of a letter writer. A lot of boys aren't." She'd never known her brothers to so much as leave a message on the kitchen table as to where they were going. "He said he'd send one for my birthday, though."

"I'm sure he will then."

"What makes you so sure?"

"He seemed like a man of his word. Not the type to make promises he wouldn't keep."

Billie had told Charlotte what had happened that day in Topeka when Simeon tried to take her back to St. Louis: how Billie had put Leif on notice that there might be trouble, and he'd stepped in just as he said he would. He'd been the one to hold off Simeon so Charlotte could escape, and he'd gotten cracked in the face for his trouble. Billie knew that Charlotte would never forget such a selfless deed on her behalf.

She certainly didn't seem to have the same regard for Robert. But Charlotte had proved she wasn't always such a good judge of character when it came to men, Billie reminded herself. Robert was kind and hardworking, just as her mother had said a man should be. And secretly she had to admit he was quite handsome in his Park Service uniform. They still hadn't gone into the actual canyon, but Billie had dropped a hint or two and was hoping he'd take her soon. Possibly on her birthday, which was coming up in just a couple of weeks.

She tried to keep her thoughts from straying to what might happen that day. "The world is full of the unexpected," her mother would say. "It's a fool's errand trying to imagine every possibility."

But with this, there were only two possibilities: Either Leif's letter would come. Or it wouldn't.

Thirty-Five

"Can I take the table in the corner?" Billie whispered excitedly at Charlotte.

Charlotte was loading a tray with perfectly scooped ice cream in cut-glass parfait bowls, and she had to serve it before it melted. Late June had warmed up aggressively in the last week, and so had the dining room. Also, with the growing influx of visitors, the shifts were busier longer. It was almost three in the afternoon, and the tables were still full of lunching tourists. She was hot, irritable, and even more on head waitress Nora's bad side since she'd started taking occasional days off to go on tours with Will.

"Absolutely not," she said, surreptitiously dabbing at her face with a napkin. "I can't have Nora after me for one more thing. If you take my table, she'll think I'm shirking."

"Please," whined Billie. *"Pleeeease!"*

"For goodness' sake, why is this one table so important?"

"It's my favorite actress, the one from *Fox Trot on the Congo!*"

Charlotte heaved the tray of ice cream expertly onto her small shoulder. "Nora will use it against me. The best I can offer is to let you bring her coffee."

"Thank you!" Billie let out a strangled squeal of glee and hurried off to the coffee urns.

Charlotte didn't know why this one actress was so thrilling. By now Billie should have been used to the comings and goings of famous people. Why, movie stars Mary Pickford and Douglas Fairbanks had dined there only last week. You'd have thought they were

Mary and Jesus, the way the entire staff of El Tovar practically genu-flected in their direction.

Charlotte had been far more intrigued by Western author Zane Grey. She'd just finished reading *The Vanishing American*, about a Navajo boy who is adopted by whites but returns to his village in adulthood to try and protect it from corrupt missionaries and gov-ernment agents. As Mr. Grey sat there contentedly eating his liver and onions, it was all she could do not to express her deep regard for the book and ask a question or two.

If it made Billie happy to serve a cup of coffee to the actress in the corner, Charlotte didn't mind indulging her.

———————

Billie knew Nora would lambaste her if she was caught bothering a customer, even with praise. She didn't want an autograph or anything. She only wanted to tell the woman how much her talent was appreciated. What was so wrong with that?

"I'm a huge fan, Miss Turner," Billie murmured as she poured coffee into the upturned cup. "You're just wonderful!"

"Gee, thanks, that's sweet of you!" The woman's bright blue eyes twinkled happily. Blond hair fell just below her ears in soft finger waves. Her dress wasn't particularly fancy for a movie star, but who wore ermine and pearls at lunch? The light green cotton sleeveless showed her toned upper arms. "Do you get to see many movies here in the wilds?" she asked.

"Not very many," said Billie, her eyes darting away to see if Nora was watching. "We only saw *Fox Trot on the Congo* a couple of weeks ago. It was a hoot!"

"What was your favorite part?"

"Oh, goodness, all of it! But I really loved when the African women were teaching you that dance, and you added in all those flips—I know you were an acrobat in vaudeville."

Gertrude Turner's gaze cut to her dining partner, a petite brunette wearing a high-neck blouse with long sleeves. She must have been roasting!

"This is my sister, Winnie. She was in the act with me. She could fly through the air like a cannonball." The two women shared a meaningful, bittersweet glance. "But that's all behind us now—we're here celebrating Winnie's acceptance into medical school at the University of Southern California. I'm especially happy because it's not far from where I live in Hollywood."

"Medical school!" Billie said to Winnie. "My, you must be very brave."

Gertrude Turner nodded. "The bravest."

Charlotte was waiting for Billie to leave the table so she could approach and take their order, but the girl was nattering on with the blond as if they were old friends at a cocktail party. The other woman at the table seemed to be all but forgotten, and Charlotte wondered if she might be annoyed, but as her back was turned, Charlotte couldn't tell.

Nora had just come into the dining room (likely from berating some poor busboy for a crumb below a table), and it was only a matter of time before she noticed Billie's criminal fraternizing. Charlotte strode toward the table to physically block Nora's sight line until she could shoo Billie off.

"Good afternoon," she said crisply as she approached, lobbing a quick glare of warning at Billie. "How can I be of—" When she glanced at the smaller woman, she froze.

Familiar green eyes blinked up at her in surprise. "Charlotte?"

Winnie Turner. That poor, damaged girl from Wellesley College. They'd been friendly freshman year—the other girls shied away from all those scars. When Charlotte began spending time with Simeon, she'd avoided her friends, especially those like Winnie who might be smart enough to figure it out.

Lifetimes had passed since then. Charlotte barely recognized herself from that naive girl she'd been only two years ago. How did Winnie?

"Pardon me?" she said coolly.

"Charlotte Crowninshield!" The woman's face lit up with warmth. "It's me, Winnie Turner—from Wellesley!"

Charlotte kept her expression perfectly neutral. "I'm sorry, you must have mistaken me for someone else."

Winnie's gaze remained trained on her. "But—"

"This is Catriona!" Billie said quickly. "Catriona MacTavish!" She turned to Charlotte. "Thanks for your help, Catriona, but I can take this table."

Charlotte nodded curtly and walked back to the coffee station to hide behind the urns until she stopped shaking. Billie found her there after taking the Turner sisters' order.

"Crowninshield?" she whispered. "That's your last name?"

"It was."

"Sounds fancy."

Charlotte almost laughed. Fancy didn't begin to describe it. "And who in the world is Catriona MacTavish?"

Billie handed Charlotte the coffeepot. "My sister."

———————

Charlotte was relieved that Gertrude Turner had given her sister the seat with the view. Facing the windows overlooking the canyon, Winnie couldn't study Charlotte to find the lie. But just knowing the other woman was in the room, Charlotte felt shaken as she went about serving her tables like an automaton. It wasn't fear of being found by Simeon—Winnie Turner wouldn't know how to contact him and wouldn't try if she did.

It was shame.

Shame for her foolish choices, her lost potential. Shame for being caught in this damned apron.

But there was also shame about being ashamed. Every Harvey Girl in the dining room was working at full capacity with a smile on her face; they were proud of that apron.

As she served chocolate pudding to a family in homespun clothing who'd likely broken the bank to eat at world-famous El Tovar, Charlotte realized that of all the fates that could've befallen her once she'd married Simeon, this was one of the best. The work was hard, of course, but she had a nice little nest egg growing, and when she wanted to move on—whether to a different Harvey establishment or to somewhere else entirely—the choice would be hers.

It wasn't just control of her own life that Charlotte cherished. She had friends here, too. Billie MacTavish had gone from an uneducated, blubbering klutz to . . . well, possibly the most quick-witted and loyal friend Charlotte had ever had. There was Henny, funny and kind.

And Will. In his quiet way, he had become a friend to her, too. He still didn't know she was married, but other than that, she'd had deeper, more revealing conversations with him than she'd had even with Billie.

When the shift was over, Billie and some of the other girls decided to "take a stroll in the late afternoon light." It wasn't the light they craved, Charlotte knew. They wanted to hear all about Billie's brush with stardom. They reminded her of that silly Tildie back in Topeka, always nosing around for intrigue.

Charlotte returned to her room. As she sat there considering her past in a new light, she felt a strange sense of calm come over her. Yes, she'd made mistakes (or one big one, at least). Yet through all the terrible things that had happened, she had persevered, devising an arguably ingenious plan to save herself. Not only had she achieved it, but she'd landed in a place many young women would envy. Maybe she could stop castigating herself quite so much.

Maybe instead of shame, she could indulge in a bit of pride. She was alive, after all, engaged in honest work, surrounded by friends.

Maybe she could even be grateful.

———————————

"Dish," commanded Billie as she thumped herself down onto the bed later that night. Since getting chummy with the other young women, her vocabulary had taken a turn for the vernacular, a change that Charlotte found grating.

"Pardon me?"

"You know what I mean. Who's Winnie Turner? And why does she dress like somebody's granny?"

"She went to college with me."

"You were friends?"

"Yes, I suppose we were. Until I began secretly seeing Simeon, and then I cut myself off from everyone." Now that she thought of it, Simeon was the one who'd urged her to stop seeing friends—out of caution, he insisted—and spend time with him instead. He'd made her positively paranoid that other students would be jealous and alert the administration.

"Winnie came from a relatively poor family from upstate New York. She and her three sisters turned to performing as an acrobatic act in vaudeville to make ends meet." Winnie had told her this once while they were up late studying for a philosophy exam. It had been a warm night, and Winnie had absentmindedly pushed up her sleeve, revealing terrible burn scars. She caught Charlotte surreptitiously glancing at them and decided to explain.

"The Tumbling Turner Sisters had become quite successful," Charlotte went on, "until they were caught in a hotel fire in Seattle. Winnie narrowly escaped burning to death by jumping from a high window just in time. Gert caught her and broke her fall. She wears long sleeves and high collars so no one pities her for her scars. The Tumbling Turner Sisters never performed again."

Billie gazed at Charlotte a moment. "You borrowed her last name."

Charlotte nodded. "She had a good life until tragedy struck. But she didn't let that be the end of it. She decided on a new path and followed it resolutely, even as damaged as she was. I tried to take inspiration from that, as well as the name."

"She was poor, but she went to college. And Gertrude went to Hollywood and became a movie star!"

"Oh, I don't think it was that easy. Winnie told me that in the beginning Gert had to survive 'any way she could.'"

Billie's eyes went wide. "Jeepers!"

"Yes, well, apparently paying for Winnie's tuition at Wellesley helped to fuel Gertrude's determination to make it in the film industry."

Billie's focus went soft, and she smiled to herself.

"What is it?"

"Nothing, really," said Billie. "It's just . . . sisters. We'd do anything for each other."

As Charlotte lay in bed that night, she wondered if having a sister to guide her—or even to yell at her as Billie often did—would have kept her from marrying Simeon. Her older brother, Oliver, had done his best to advise against it, but she had been stubborn, so certain she was in the right. Besides, she'd had no one to worry about but herself.

But if I'd had a younger sister like Billie, it would have given me pause.

And perhaps a pause would've been all she'd needed to think—*for goodness' sake, think, Charlotte!*—and change course.

———————

The next day, Charlotte and Will did three tours to Hermits Rest, a structure built at the edge of the canyon that was designed to look like an old miner's cabin. It was seven miles west from El Tovar; the trip took over an hour as they trundled over the dirt road built by the Fred Harvey Company, making stops along the way at Hopi Point and Pima Point.

The first tour began at nine in the morning with three couples in their thirties. They had left their respective children at home with "the staff." As they passed flasks between them, it became readily apparent that they had no interest in Charlotte's tour guide services. They wanted only to make bawdy jokes, screech with laughter, and take full advantage of the curves in the road by mashing suggestively into one another as the car leaned to one side or the other.

Will and Charlotte kept their eyes on the road and their faces neutral. Occasionally one of the passengers would tell a joke that was actually funny without being overly lewd, and Charlotte caught Will biting the inside of his cheek to keep from smiling.

When they arrived at Hermits Rest, the six tourists tumbled out and stumbled up the path to the structure. Charlotte muttered to Will, "I am not completely without a sense of humor, you know. You can laugh if you want to."

He stopped and turned to her, about to respond, but instead he let out a belly laugh. "The one about the blind dog and the mink stole!"

Charlotte rolled her eyes. It wasn't the cleverest joke she'd ever heard, but Will's laughter was contagious, and she found herself smiling at the sweetness of his happy face and then giggling right along with him.

Oh dear, she thought as their laughter subsided and they continued to grin at each other for an extra moment. *I really do want to kiss him.*

This thought (and whatever he might have been thinking) was cut short, however, by one of the ladies screeching, "Are you two *ever* coming?"

By the time they returned to El Tovar, the group was so inebriated they forgot to tip. But Charlotte and Will were still smiling anyway.

The second tour included the family Charlotte had served in the dining room the night before. Mother, father, and two children in their clean but well-worn clothes seemed to greatly enjoy all that she had to tell them.

Everyone loved the stories of the pioneers who settled along the rim before it was a national park. "Ada Bass was the first white woman to raise a family at the Grand Canyon," Charlotte told them, "but that's only one of her many accomplishments. As wife of William Bass of the Bass Camps, Ada kept the business humming with food, shelter, laundry, livery services, and procuring provisions from as far away as Prescott, enduring the elements and every possible hardship. She once said she had either slept or prepared a meal under every tree from here to Ash Fork."

"What about the Indians?" asked the younger child, a boy of about ten named Charles, clearly unimpressed with Ada's tenacity and extensive wilderness skills.

"We are right now on the traditional land of the Havasupai Indians," she told him.

Charles stuck his head so far out of the car window Charlotte was afraid he'd fall out. "Well, where are they?"

Charlotte recalled the book by the indomitable George Wharton James called *Indians of the Painted Desert Region*. James was, as usual, furious about the treatment of the Native people, while also crowing from time to time about outsmarting them, despite their "wily" ways.

"This area around the rim of the Grand Canyon was their hunting ground until the US Park Service evicted them about thirty years ago," she told them. "They're now confined to a small reservation deep inside the canyon walls by the river. Not being able to hunt up here is a real hardship to them, and they go hungry far more often than they ever used to."

"Why did the park kick them out? What did they do?" Charles's eyes went wide. "Were they scalping people?"

"No, it was just that the Park Service wanted this land for a national park, and they didn't think white people would come if there were Indians here. Also, apparently they didn't think the Indians appreciated how beautiful it is, though of course that's silly. Indian cultures venerate art and beauty. You only have to look at their blankets and baskets and jewelry. In fact their designs often take inspiration from the landscape."

"They're artists?" said the quiet older sister, a girl of about seventeen named Jane.

"Many are, yes. Go into the Hopi House sometime and watch the Indians there weaving or making baskets. You can also talk to Ruth, behind the counter. She's an expert."

"Artists," said a clearly disappointed Charles. "I thought they were warriors."

"They're both," said Will. "Workers when they need to feed their families, and warriors when their families need protection. Like all parents."

"My dad just works in the railyard," grumbled Charles.

"And I bet he'd beat the snot out of anyone who tried to hurt you," said Will.

"I surely would," said Charles's father. "No doubt about it."

Out of the corner of her eye, Charlotte saw his wife lace her hand through his.

When they got out of the car at Pima Point and the others headed toward the edge to enjoy the view, Charlotte hung back as usual. She'd been here at the Grand Canyon for two months now, and her distaste for the abyss had not wavered.

As she stood in the shade of an Apache plume bush, Jane, the teenage girl, approached. "You served us dinner last night," she said shyly.

"Yes, I did. Some days I'm a Harvey Girl and some days I'm a tour guide."

"I've heard about the Harvey Girls all my life." The girl let out a little sigh of longing. "They can go to new places, live in a dorm with their friends, and meet interesting people. I didn't know they could run tours, too. And you get to learn all about the place and tell people what you know. It must be wonderful."

Charlotte smiled. "It is. If your parents agree to it, you should apply."

With a glint of determination, the girl said, "Oh, they'll agree. I've already got the application filled out and waiting."

———————————

Before the last tour, Charlotte hurried over to the women's dorm to use the lavatory. When she returned, Will was standing by the car with their new passengers. There were only two of them.

"Here's Charlotte now," she heard Will say. When the women turned to look in her direction, she saw their faces.

It was Gertrude and Winnie Turner.

Thirty-Six

For the briefest moment, Charlotte considered turning on her heel, running back to the dorm, and letting Will handle the tour himself. He'd been doing it on his own for years, after all. But that would have meant conceding to shame, and Charlotte hoped to be done with that.

"Hello," she said. "Nice to see you again."

The two women stared at her, and then Gertrude Turner spoke. "Listen, I don't know what you're playing at—"

Winnie put a hand on her sister's arm. "Gert, why don't you and this gentleman give us a moment."

Gertrude frowned at her sister. Winnie raised an eyebrow, and Gertrude gave her blond head a little shake of frustration. She turned to Will and hooked her arm in his. "Mister, you and I are getting the bum's rush. Let's take a walk, and you can tell me what's so great about this hole in the ground."

When they'd gone, Winnie turned her gaze to Charlotte without a word and waited.

"I'm sorry I lied to you yesterday," said Charlotte. "I was embarrassed."

"I'm not one of those society girls, Charlotte. You know I wouldn't think less of you for doing honest work."

"Yes, but I *was* one of those society girls, and I've been thinking less of myself. That is, until I realized that lying to you was far more shameful than working here."

Winnie's expression softened. "I don't want to pry, but if you'd like to tell me what happened, I promise to keep it between us. I did always wonder why you disappeared after sophomore year."

Charlotte had been keeping the secret of her relationship with Simeon for two and a half years now: guarding it, lying about it, acting like a felon running from the law. But she was no criminal, and the only thing she was running for was her life. Winnie Turner was smart and worldly and, most important, compassionate.

"I would like to tell you, if you don't mind hearing some unpleasant details."

Winnie smiled. "I'm going to be a doctor. I imagine I'll be hearing unpleasant details all day long."

———————

The next day, in the wee hours of June 25, a newly minted sixteen-year-old woke with a smile on her face. She suspected that Henny and Charlotte were cooking up a surprise for her birthday, maybe even some sort of party, because there had been some switching of work shifts that she wasn't supposed to know about.

But what she was really hopeful about was hearing from Leif. Finally. He'd said he would send her a letter for her birthday, and while it had been disappointing that he hadn't sent one sooner, she felt certain he would keep his promise. Almost certain, anyway.

This made Billie feel strangely guilty. She'd spent a lot of time with Robert over the last month, and she really liked him. They were friends, she told herself again, though that was becoming harder and harder to believe. They held hands all the time now.

"Are you going steady with that park ranger?" one of the other girls had asked her last week.

Billie didn't know how to answer. Going steady where?

"You know, is he your sheik?"

"Sheik?"

"Ah, for the love o' Mike. Your *beau*."

"Oh!" said Billie, filing this all away for later use. "No, we're just friends."

The other girl looked at her like she was dumber than a bag of rocks.

———————

When Charlotte got back at five o'clock from a tour to the Cameron Trading Post, she found Mae Parnell, the dorm mother, soothing a bawling Billie.

"Whatever is the matter?" she asked.

"The mail came," said Mae.

"What did he say?"

"NOTHING!" Billie wailed. "He said NOTHING!"

Charlotte looked at Mae. *No letter*, the older woman mouthed.

"After I wrote him the sweetest, nicest—" Billie dissolved into tears again.

"Oh dear," said Charlotte. "I was sure he would write." She shook her head. Why were men so utterly contrary? You wanted them to contact you, and they didn't. You wanted them to leave you alone, and they tracked you to the ends of the earth.

"Let's have a bite to eat and maybe a little rest."

"I DON'T WANT TO EAT! I WANT TO . . . I DON'T KNOW WHAT I WANT!"

Mae met Charlotte's eye. "You want to give him a piece of your mind!" Then she gave Charlotte a little nod.

Charlotte got the gist. "You want to say, *How DARE you treat me with such disregard?*"

"You want to kick him in the shins!"

"Report him to the authorities!"

"Stab him in the neck!" said Mae. The other two women stared at her. "All right," she conceded, "maybe not the neck."

This made Billie giggle through her tears.

Mae smiled. "Come on. Let's get you some toast."

———————

After Billie ate toast and a bit of leftover chicken and drank a glass of milk, she went upstairs and took a very long soak in the tub, even though another girl banged on the door and said she was being selfish. *The whole world is selfish*, she thought bitterly as she studied her prune-y finger pads.

When she finally got out and went back to the room to change, Charlotte had laid out a dress that Billie had never seen before. It was light cotton voile fabric in lilac with cap sleeves and a simple V-neck with a lovely long tie that dangled down. It had no waist at all and ended in a stylish hanky hem. It was simple yet striking.

"Henny made it," said Charlotte. "I bought the fabric."

"Charlotte, it's . . . it's wonderful!"

"Put it on."

"Oh, no. I don't want to wrinkle it. I'll wear it when there's another party at the community hall."

"Well, you should try it on, in case Henny needs to make any adjustments."

"Where is Henny, anyway? Shouldn't she be here to see me in it?"

"She has the dinner shift."

Billie was fairly certain that wasn't true, but she tried the dress on anyway. It was so light and airy it felt like a cloud against her skin. Charlotte held their small mirror in front of her so Billie could see the skirt swish back and forth around her calves.

"Let's take a walk so you can really see how it feels."

Now Billie knew something was up. Charlotte never walked at night if she could help it.

"That'd be the bee's knees!" she said, knowing it would go right up Charlotte's spine.

Satisfyingly, Charlotte rolled her eyes and puffed out a little sigh.

They strolled south, away from the canyon, and over toward the community hall.

"Do you mind if we stop in?" Charlotte asked. "I think I left my sweater in there."

"The windows are dark. It's probably locked."

"Let's just check." They walked up the steps, found the door open, and stepped into the shadowy room.

Suddenly all the lights were ablaze, and the room was full of people yelling "Surprise!" and Billie felt a little bit swoony.

Until she saw her idol, Gertrude Turner. Then she felt *very* swoony.

Thirty-Seven

Everyone was there: Robert and Henny and Will and some of the other girls. They all crowded around her, all talking at once: "Did you know?" and "You look beautiful!" and "Your last year of being a teenager!"

Billie had to take a moment to catch her breath, but then she smiled and answered as many questions as she could while trying not to gape at Gertrude Turner.

Gertrude Turner! What was she even *doing* here?

Charlotte was standing with Winnie, and Billie knew they must have had a talk and cleared things up.

She turned to Henny. "I absolutely love my new dress!"

"Oh, honey, I'm so glad," said Henny. "It feels okay?"

"It feels dreamy." She turned to the others. "Henny made this!"

Suddenly the lights went out again, and a faint glow came from a little side room. Mae walked in carrying a cake, and they all began to sing "Happy birthday to you, happy birthday to you . . ."

Billie was so overwhelmed, she almost cried.

"Make a wish!" someone insisted. Billie closed her eyes. Leif sprang to mind, but she wouldn't waste a wish on him. She thought of her family, but they had each other.

Keep Charlotte safe.

She inhaled all the air she could and blew out what she knew were three more candles than she had a right to. Maybe those extra little flames would help carry her wish to the stars.

Charlotte was quite pleased. She'd never thrown a party before. Robert had borrowed a phonograph from one of the other rangers, and everyone was eating cake and dancing. Billie and Gertrude Turner were leading the other women in the Charleston, and Billie looked happier than Charlotte had ever seen her. And to think, less than three months ago, all she could do was cry.

"What a wonderful party," said Winnie. "She's lucky to have a friend like you."

"I'm just as lucky," said Charlotte. "She really is a remarkable girl."

Winnie studied her a moment. "I know this isn't the life you would have chosen, but it seems to suit you."

Charlotte smirked. "You mean I'm not the snobby rich girl I once was?"

"Well, yes, but it's more than that. You never quite fit in with the society crowd. I imagine that marrying Professor Lister seemed like a solution to that problem. But here you are, in a place you never meant be, making the most of it. It's impressive!"

Charlotte felt her cheeks go warm at the compliment. "I borrowed your last name for my alias because I so admired your perseverance in the face of adversity."

"Charlotte, I'm honored. But you should know that I have my self-doubts and setbacks, too. I've made my share of bad decisions."

"Well, you've certainly made far more good ones than bad. Your family must be so proud of you. And Joe must be bursting his buttons." Joe Cole was the young piano player she'd met on the vaudeville circuit, and he was far more devoted than any of the other girls' boyfriends at Wellesley.

Winnie looked away. "Actually, Joe is engaged to someone else."

Charlotte gasped. "No!"

"He'd waited four years to settle down and have children with me. He didn't want to wait anymore."

"You must have been devastated."

"I was. Am, really. But in my heart, I'm a doctor, and I knew if I gave that up, I'd regret it for the rest of my life. And I'd resent him. What kind of marriage would that be?"

Charlotte knew very well what kind of marriage comes from one person giving up too much for the other. She was impressed that Winnie had somehow understood that before making a terrible mistake.

The song ended and Billie and Gertrude collapsed into each other, laughing and gasping for breath, their pale blond hair sticking to their damp cheeks. "Look at those two," said Winnie. "They could be sisters."

Charlotte was not by nature or upbringing an overly affectionate person, but she found herself hooking her arm in Winnie's. "I'm coming to understand the importance of honorary sisters. I truly don't know where I'd be without them."

It was late, the cake was gone, and people were starting to trickle away, bidding Billie final *happy birthdays* and telling Charlotte what a lovely night they'd had. The Turner sisters headed back to their suite at El Tovar; Mae and the other Harvey Girls made their way to the dorm. Will and Charlotte were collecting sticky plates, crumpled napkins, and empty soda bottles.

"Billie," said Robert. "Can I walk you home?"

Billie glanced at Charlotte. Charlotte glanced at Will. "We can finish up here," he said.

As they made their way down the path, past the mule barn and the train depot, Robert reached for her hand and clasped it warmly in his.

"Have you ever had a beau?" he asked.

"No, I never have."

"Would . . . would you like to?"

Billie stopped. "Are you asking me to go steady?"

"Yes, I believe I am."

She looked into his handsome, expectant face and realized she'd never really thought they would be romantic. She'd been secretly holding out hope that she could someday be reunited with Leif.

Clearly her time with Leif was in the past. Her time with Robert was now.

"Then my answer is yes."

He grinned his biggest grin. "May I kiss you?"

"Yes, you may."

He leaned forward and gently pressed his lips against hers, and it was very nice.

Will shut off the lights and locked the door behind them. "That was some soiree you just pulled off."

Charlotte smiled as they walked through the cool night. "I never knew throwing a party could be so satisfying! Back home it always seemed like such a bother. But this was fun, and everyone helped." She rested her hand on his forearm for a brief moment. "Especially you, convincing Mr. Patrillo to let us use the community hall and setting everything up."

"It was my pleasure. Besides, there wasn't much convincing needed. As soon as I told him it was for you, he said yes. Apparently your tours are a real hit with the clientele."

"*Our* tours."

"I just drive. You're the star attraction."

Charlotte laughed. "I wouldn't be doing them at all if you hadn't tricked me into it! And I wouldn't want to do them with anyone else."

In the silence she could hear the breeze tickling the tops of the ponderosa pines, their wide limbs brushing gently against one another, and she wondered if she'd said the wrong thing. Finally he responded.

"Nor would I."

Charlotte was surprised to find Billie still awake when she reached the room. The girl had had quite a day, emotions flying from fury to bliss, dancing for hours with her movie idol, not to mention ten long hours of hauling tray-loads of food to hungry tourists. But the girl was bright-eyed as she sat perched on the side of her bed, knees tucked up under her nightdress.

"This was the best day I ever had!" she said before Charlotte had even completely closed the door.

"I'm so glad you were able to enjoy it, Billie. I was a little worried when you were so upset this afternoon."

Billie's grin faded. "I was very disappointed. People should keep their promises."

"You're absolutely right. They should. And yet, sometimes they don't. I'm just happy you were able to recover so quickly."

"It's pretty hard to be a sourpuss when you get to dance with a movie star! She told me to call her Gert!"

"She seems to like you quite a bit."

Billie grabbed her pillow, held it up to her face, and squealed into it. Charlotte couldn't help but laugh.

When they were finally both in bed and Charlotte reached up to pull the chain on the light, Billie said, "Oh, and Robert asked me to go steady!"

"Go steadily where?"

"You know, be my sheik."

"Your . . . ?"

"My beau!"

Silence grew until Charlotte said finally, "I see."

"You don't like him."

"It's not a matter of my liking him, Billie. It's just that he's much older than you."

"I'm sixteen now! My mother was sixteen when she met my father."

"And how old was your father?"

Billie didn't respond, which meant he was sixteen, too, or nearly so.

"I know you don't want to hear this, but a man his age will want more from you—if not now, then eventually."

"He's Catholic! He knows I won't do any of that business before marriage."

"Yes, but that very thing might make him more eager to wed. He thinks you're nineteen."

"Robert is sweet and patient. He won't press me to do anything I don't want to do."

Charlotte sighed. In some ways the girl was so wise; in others she was as naive as a toddler.

"Billie, if you had an older sister, maybe someone like Gert Turner, who'd known and loved you all your life and wanted only what's best for you, what do you think she'd say?"

"I guess she'd say 'Be careful,'" Billie grudgingly conceded.

"That's all I'm saying. Please be careful."

The next day, after a long, hot lunch shift at El Tovar, Billie came back to the dorm and started to trudge upstairs to her room, untying her apron as she went. Before she could reach the second floor, however, she heard Mae Parnell call out to her.

"Billie? There's someone here to see you."

Maybe Robert had come by to ask her for a date. Or maybe he wanted to give his new steady girlfriend a little kiss! Billie smiled to herself and came back down the stairs, pulling off the apron, dropping it on the banister, and smoothing her white dress as she walked.

Mae was standing in the kitchen doorway. She had a funny look on her face, as if she were trying to decide whether to smile or frown. "He's waiting in the parlor."

Winnie went down the hallway and stepped into the parlor to find a man who was definitely not Robert sitting on the couch. When he saw her, he stood quickly and held out an envelope.

"I wanted to deliver this in person. Sorry I'm a day late."

Thirty-Eight

"Leif!" she yelled and threw her arms around him.

He hugged her tightly, picking her up off the floor for a moment, then he returned her to the ground and pulled back to look at her. His smile was as wide as a prairie.

"Are you surprised?"

"Of *course* I'm surprised! How did you . . . what are you doing here?"

"I got myself transferred. After I read your letter, I knew I had to."

Her letter. The one in which she told him that it seemed as if she'd known him all her life, and he felt like family to her, and she loved him. And now, in slightly less than two months since she'd written those words, she'd gone and gotten herself a sheik.

Leif took her hand and pressed the envelope into it. "I have to go. I was supposed to get here yesterday, but the train crew got the grippe, and we sat on the tracks for half a day waiting for a new crew, and I missed my connection in Williams. They've got me on the dinner shift, and I don't want to get fired before I even start. Can we talk tomorrow?"

She blinked at him, her heart in her throat at the thought of having to tell him what she'd done. "Of course," she said.

"Don't be sad," he murmured, those teacup-crackle eyes looking into hers. "It's only a few hours. Then we'll have all the time in the world."

Billie stood stunned in the parlor for a few minutes after he left, the pain in her chest growing until her whole body hurt. She walked woodenly back down the hallway. As she passed the kitchen, Mae said, "That was him, wasn't it? The one who didn't write."

Billie stopped and nodded. She looked at the envelope still clutched in her hand, and tears started to roll down her face. "I didn't think . . . ," she whispered. "I didn't know . . . "

"Oh, now," soothed Mae, taking Billie by the shoulders and guiding her to one of the wooden chairs at the table. "None of us knows anything until we do."

"Knows what?" Charlotte appeared in the doorway. She'd been on shift with Billie, but then headed off to Will's to discuss their tour schedule, or some such nonsense. Billie knew she just liked his company.

Mae sighed. "He came. Just showed up out of nowhere."

"What?" Charlotte's head swiveled to look over her shoulder. "*Where?*"

"Not him," said Billie quickly, swiping at her cheeks. "Leif. He got himself transferred here."

Charlotte sank against the doorframe, visibly relieved. "Leif," she echoed, as if to reassure herself. Mae eyed her but said nothing.

"What's this? A tea party?" Henny appeared behind Charlotte in the doorway, strawberry blond hair swept up in a ponytail, cheeks flushed. She was wearing an old white shirtwaist blouse tucked into a pair of men's trousers.

"Where have you been?" asked Mae. "Panning for gold?"

"Just a little hike." Her eye caught Billie's tearstained cheeks. "Oh dear, what's the matter?"

Charlotte had regained her composure. "Apparently she suffers from an excess of suitors."

Mae chuckled. "No such thing."

Henny moved into the room and sat next to Billie. "Why don't you tell us all about it, and we'll sort it out together."

Mae brewed tea and broke out some biscuits she'd been saving, and the four of them sat at the long table listening to Billie's tale of friendship with Leif that became a little something more on her last night in Topeka. And she told them about the letter she wrote.

"He's all alone in the world with no family. I just wanted him to know that I cared for him and that I felt . . . a bond."

"Felt or feel?" asked Henny.

"Given the little shriek of joy I heard all the way down the hall," said Mae, "I'd say the answer is 'feel.'"

Billie slumped in her seat. "But I told Robert I'd go steady, and Da always says you can't go back on your word."

"Which do you like better?" asked Mae.

"I like them both."

"Who's a better kisser?"

"Mae!" said Charlotte. "That is no way to make a decision."

Mae crossed her arms under her bosom. "Well, what's your advice, then?"

"She should choose the man who will respect her and treat her with courtesy."

"You're a real barrel of monkeys," muttered Mae.

"They both do that," said Billie. "They're both very nice to me."

"There *is* one big difference . . . ," offered Henny.

"What's that?"

"I don't mean to be snooty, and I respect any man who works hard at any job. Leif's kitchen help, right? He could rise through the ranks—and I bet he will. But Robert's already a park ranger, and he's the ambitious type. If you stick with him, you could really go places."

The room fell silent as they all considered this.

"I think maybe the most important difference," said Billie, "is that Robert is Catholic and Leif isn't. My maw wouldn't like me dating someone who doesn't share our faith."

"Well, there's your answer then," said Henny.

"But Leif is a good man, too."

"Why don't you open that letter and see what he has to say for himself?" suggested Mae. "Maybe that'll help you decide."

"Letter?" asked Charlotte, and Billie raised the now crumpled paper in her hand. "Oh, no, that's private. You can't read it here. Go up to our room to open it."

"She just poured her heart out," said Mae. "We know the whole story. The least she could do is let us hear what he has to say."

"Perhaps another time, after she's had a few moments to digest it herself." Charlotte was tugging at Billie's arm to get her to rise.

"*Digest it?*" laughed Henny. "What's she going to do, swallow it whole?"

"I don't mind—" Billie began.

Charlotte glared at her. "How would Leif feel if he knew you were reading his words aloud for the entire world to hear?"

Billie colored in shame. "It's bad enough I went and got a steady beau."

Charlotte patted her arm as she walked her to the door. "Don't be too hard on yourself. You go read your letter, and I'll take a walk to give you some privacy."

When Billie had left, Mae said, "Wet blanket."

"Busybody," Charlotte retorted and headed for the front door.

Henny was soon at her side as they headed down the path in the direction of the Bright Angel Hotel. "Why'd you get so hot under the collar?"

"Because Billie is a young, impressionable girl, and I don't like that woman telling her to choose a man based on his kissing skills."

"Don't worry. Billie's smarter than that . . . no matter how young she is."

Charlotte sensed the edge of something in the way Henny said those last words. She needed to change the subject and fast. "Who did you go hiking with?"

Henny didn't answer for a moment. "Just a friend."

"You don't have to tell me who, but I'm guessing it was that brakeman who's been following you around like a lost puppy."

"No, not him. Actually it was Nora."

"Nora?" Charlotte could imagine the foul-tempered head wait-ress chastising the rocks for being in her path.

"She can be nice, you know."

"I'll have to take your word for that."

"She's just very serious about the Harvey standard and doing her best. But she can be funny and even silly when she's not on the job."

"You should try your hand as a lion tamer."

Henny smiled. "They're just big kitty cats, after all!"

Dear Billie,

Happy 16th birthday!

So that was why Charlotte insisted that she not read the letter out loud.

> *By the time you are reading this, I will have said it already face to face, but I told you I would write, and it is not right to break a promise.*
>
> *I have read your letter so many times, it is a wonder the words have not worn right off the page. It has warmed my heart, but it has also made me think. Until I met you, I was alone in this world, and I told myself that is just how I like it. When you lose people, you do not like to put yourself in the way of heartbreak again.*
>
> *You gave me hope that I could have friends and love and maybe even be part of a family someday. I told Frances that she had to get me sent to the Grand Canyon so I could protect Charlotte, which I certainly will do. But there was selfishness in it, too. I want to be near the only person I have loved since my father died.*
>
> *Yours always,*
> *Leif*

The only person he loved since he was eight years old. Billie couldn't stop thinking about that. She also couldn't stop thinking about how he said it wasn't right to break a promise. Hadn't she made a promise to Robert to be his girl?

When Charlotte came back to the room, Billie showed her the letter.

"Now I'm doubly glad you didn't read it out loud," Charlotte said, sinking down on the bed next to her.

"Why?"

"Because Henny has become friendly with Nora, and if she learns your age, you'll be sent packing without so much as a farewell."

"With *Nora?*"

"Apparently she can be nice. So says Henny."

"The woman could curdle fresh cream with a look!"

"I hate to say it, but I suspect there could be some ulterior motive. Nora has always disliked us for our inexperience and how fast we rose up the Harvey ladder. I wonder if she's befriended Henny to find reason to fire us."

Billie was crestfallen. "At least Leif is the only one who knows our secrets. And he won't tell."

"Actually . . . "

Billie turned to eye Charlotte. "Actually what?"

"I did tell Will how old you are."

"Charlotte, how could you!"

"I'm sorry. But honestly there's no one more trustworthy than Will."

"So trustworthy that you've told him you're married and using someone else's name?"

Charlotte looked down at her hands.

"Oh, so it's fine to spill my secret, but not your own!"

"Billie, I promise you, he won't breathe a word—"

"You had no right! I've never told anyone about you—"

"Not even Robert on all those long walks you two take?"

"How could you accuse me of such a thing?" Billie sputtered with fury. "Unlike *you*, I can keep my trap shut!" Blind with rage, she stormed out, down the stairs, and out into the night.

She wanted to scream, but what was she, a five-year-old? Instead she continued to stalk down the path away from the village, past the buildings and the nighttime strollers until there was no one around. Winded, she stopped and glared out over the canyon.

She *hated* Charlotte! Billie picked up a rock and threw it over the edge. Then she picked up another. And another.

She smelled it before she heard a sound. Smoke.

She whirled around and there suddenly was Nora.

"Jaysus!" said the woman, clearly startled. Tobacco use was a clear infraction of Harvey Girl rules. She hid the cigarette behind her, but it glowed all the same. "What in the world are you doing out here so late?" she demanded.

"Well, I'm not *smoking*, am I?"

Nora narrowed her eyes and pointed at Billie, the cigarette wedged between her fingers. "If you tell a soul, so help me—"

"I'm not going to *tell* anyone," Billie snarled. "Trust me, I'm the best secret keeper you ever met!" And with that, she stomped right back toward the dorm.

Charlotte had changed into her nightgown, but she was sitting up in bed with the light on, waiting. "I'm sorry," she murmured. "I should never have told him without your permission."

Billie put her hands on her hips. "That's all you have to say?"

"It's all I can say. I can't undo it."

Billie thumped down onto her bed. Suddenly she felt more bone-weary than she ever had in her life. She wasn't really so mad at Charlotte—she knew Will wouldn't reveal her secret any more than Leif would. She was mad at herself for getting into this mess in the first place.

"What am I going to do?" she said, her voice going tremulous.

"Well, I suppose the only thing you can do is to tell Leif the truth. Very gently."

———————————

He was waiting for her when she got off shift the next afternoon.

"I meant to catch you before you started," he said, "but I didn't wake up in time. It's noisy in the dorm. I didn't get to sleep until the wee hours." He smiled bashfully. "I guess I was excited to see you again, too."

They walked east past the Hopi House and along the Rim Trail. Leif hadn't had a chance to explore, and he was awestruck by it all. Billie relayed many of the things Robert had told her, and was pleased with her tour guide skills until he asked, "How'd you learn all this?"

She hesitated. "I've been spending time with one of the park rangers."

Leif's gait slowed. "Spending time."

"Yes."

They walked in silence for a few minutes, Billie's mind spinning like a top to think of any way she could spare him the hurt of what she had done.

"Is he your beau?"

"Yes, but, Leif, I didn't know if I'd ever see you again."

"You wrote me that letter." His voice was low, as if he were sinking into himself.

"I meant every word of it."

"Billie." He stopped. "You said you loved me."

"I do! I do love you! I just . . . I thought . . . And when I didn't get a letter from you on my birthday, I figured you'd forgotten me, so I promised I'd be his girl."

This seemed to land the hardest. "Forgotten you? *Forgotten?*"

When he said it like that, she realized how silly it sounded. "I . . . I lost faith."

"I guess you surely did."

"I'm sorry," she whispered. "I'm so sorry."

He nodded. "Is he good to you?"

"Yes. He's very kind."

"And he knows how old you are?"

Billie didn't answer. Leif shook his head. "So you're lying to him."

"I didn't lie, I just didn't—"

His look stopped her cold, and it scared her.

"Leif, you wouldn't . . . "

In that moment she was fairly certain she saw his heart break completely. "You really have lost all faith in me," he murmured, and turned and left her there.

Thirty-Nine

July had always been Charlotte's least favorite month. July was the price you paid for June. The blooms and scents of springtime and early summer were a thing of the past; in Boston, July brought the briny stench of low tide doing battle with the wet-wool feel of humidity.

Here in northern Arizona, it was just the opposite: smells parched in the sun and the air was so dry it hurt. Charlotte woke every morning with a tongue so desiccated that she took to keeping glasses of water on the floor just under her bed. She was certain that Billie would make fun of her: *See the dainty daisy whose delicate constitution requires constant infusions!*

But Billie had grown quiet since her last conversation with Leif over a week ago. On shift in the dining room, she folded napkins, polished silver, and set and cleared tables like it was her last best hope for salvation. Charlotte had witnessed the occasional crossing of paths between Billie and Leif in the restaurant kitchen, and while it was always cordial, it seemed to pain them both.

One night Charlotte caught her crying into her apron in their room.

"He came all this way," the girl sobbed. "For me!"

"If it makes you this unhappy, why don't you break it off with Robert?"

"Because Leif isn't Catholic—my mother would be beside herself. And I like Robert, I really do. I didn't promise to be his girl for nothing. Shouldn't a promise mean something?"

How to explain that the ways of love don't conform to the gen-

280 — Juliette Fay

eral expectations of a handshake? "It's not a business transaction, Billie. You're not cheating Robert out of his savings if you say you like someone else better. And dating Leif doesn't mean you're going to marry him. Your mother doesn't even have to know."

"But I don't actually know if I like Leif better, do I? We've never even had a date. Maybe he'd be a terrible beau. And then I'd be lying to my mother for nothing."

"You liked him well enough to tell him you loved him."

Billie threw her damp, mucus-y apron on the floor. "You don't have to remind me!"

"I'm not trying to shame you. I'm only saying that you cared very much for him—"

"I still do! But what kind of caring is it? It could be friendship or . . . or it could be like one of my brothers, and you just love them because their yours. Maybe it's a sort of a . . . a . . . "

"A kinship."

"Yes! It's as if we belong to each other, and it's not about dates or kissing or any of that. It's—" Billie shook her head, and the tears began to flow again. "I miss him so much."

Charlotte sat down next to the crying girl and gently laid an arm around her back. She had never been given to shows of affection. Her kind didn't embrace at the slightest provocation like some did. But she wasn't with her kind anymore. Perhaps they had ceased to be so. She laced her other arm around Billie's waist and gave a little squeeze.

Billie inhaled a sniffle. "You're a hugger now?"

Charlotte smiled up at her. "And who's to blame for that?"

———

As the heat rose, so did Patrillo's pressure that Charlotte be prepared for the Detours.

"I had hoped they would offer them here, once they got the

business up and running, but it appears that they will keep them in New Mexico for now." He showed Charlotte the brochure.

The cover was a line drawing done in red, black, and white. In the foreground sat a blanket-shrouded figure next to an impressive piece of pottery. In the middle ground a touring car with white faces in the windows was approached by more blanket-wearing figures. The background was composed of a simplistically drawn Indian village and a train.

There was quite a bit of flowery language: "Words are futile things with which to picture the fascination of this vast enchanted empire, unspoiled and full of startling contrasts, that we call the Southwest." And there would be "none of the usual petty worries of a motor trip." For $135, the Harvey Company would take care of everything on the three-day trip: comfortable accommodations, baggage handling, meals, the driving services of a local man dressed as a cowboy, and tour and hostess duties performed by a female "courier" who was trained to provide information about all that "detourists" would see.

"But how can I be a courier when they're headquartered in New Mexico?"

"At this time, you cannot. However, I've been boasting about you to Major Clarkson, who runs the Detours, so he'll know we are ready to start whenever he gives the word." Patrillo took the brochure back from her and began to thumb through it. "Either that or you will relocate."

"Relocate?" Charlotte felt her blood pause in her veins. "To *New Mexico*?"

"It's beautiful there. You'll like it. And he will owe me a favor for letting him have my best tour guide."

Charlotte couldn't sleep that night. She was furious at the idea of yet another man dictating where she would go and how she would live. She had barely been able to keep herself from telling

Patrillo right then and there that she would damn well do as she pleased.

Her instinct for self-preservation had stopped her. The fact of the matter was that, as her boss, Patrillo did have a right to relocate her if he chose to. She could quit, of course, but then what? She had money, but did she have enough? And what other employment could she pursue? Waitressing at an ordinary diner was not nearly as respectable as being a Harvey Girl, and far less lucrative.

The brochure he'd given her said that the women were trained to "provide interesting and authentic information on the archeological and ethnological history of the Southwest." Their value was in their brains, not their ability to carry tray-loads of pork chops. She liked the idea of learning more about the Indians. It would be like taking a class.

Maybe relocating wasn't the worst idea. She'd grown complacent, she realized, enjoying doing the tours, spending time with Will. But the fact was, it wasn't wise to stay in any one place too long. Doing so only made it easier for Simeon to find her . . .

A few feet away in the other bed, Billie wrestled with her own quandary. Leif had accused her of lying to Robert, and this was not true. She had never said anything at all to him about her age. Was it her fault if he'd guessed wrong?

But the very fact of her being a Harvey Girl was supposed to mean that she was eighteen or older. Hadn't she been lying to every person she'd met for the past three and a half months?

And what business was it of theirs if she embroidered the truth a little? She worked at least as hard as any other girl there. The only person she had outright lied to was Miss Steele, the woman who'd hired her back in Kansas City. And boy, she'd told that lady some whoppers. Billie didn't even know she could lie like that.

Had her mother ever lied to her father? She was Robert's steady girl now. Was this any way to start a courtship? Were they courting? Didn't courting lead to marriage?

She didn't want to get married! But if she did someday get married, shouldn't it be to someone of her own faith?

Around and around both women's thoughts swirled until the canyon wrens began their song and dawn light slowly suffused the room.

———————

Billie was desperate for advice. Charlotte was biased toward Leif, so she was no help. Henny seemed to have a good head on her shoulders, but she was friends with Nora now. Billie thought about writing to her mother . . . who'd be fit to be tied that she was dating a man eight years her senior while simultaneously pining after a non-Catholic. She might insist that Billie quit and come home. She even thought about talking to Will, since he knew most of it already. But that would get back to Charlotte.

There was one person she might like to talk to. But he wasn't speaking to her unless you counted the occasional "Your soups are ready" or "That mutton chop is missing a garnish."

It was painful to be near him almost every day and not be able to talk to him. But she had made a promise to Robert, and she didn't know how to break that promise, or if she even wanted to. Henny had made a point that Billie had never thought of. Should she decide which man she liked better based on what he could provide?

Well, if so, there was one thing Robert could provide that Billie wanted very much and that was to hike down into the canyon. She'd seen other girls do it, and she'd even hinted at wanting to go along with Henny one of these days.

"Robert hasn't taken you yet?" said Henny. "Seems silly to go with me and Nora when you have an actual park ranger to show you the sights." (Billie did find it a little strange that Henny and Nora went hiking so often and never invited anyone to go with them.)

Finally Robert agreed to take her. He'd even found a pair of cast-off boots for her. She'd borrowed Henny's trousers with a mind to get a pair for herself one day.

When they met outside the dorm at five thirty in the morning, Robert was pleased. "Why, look at you! You're a regular prospector! You won't need that heavy coat, though." It was about fifty degrees out, and Billie was certain she'd freeze without it. "It's cool for July, but it will be blistering hot at the bottom," he said, "and you'll warm up as we walk." She went inside and exchanged the coat for her mother's green cardigan, hoping she wouldn't shiver too much.

Though the trail was in the shade as far down as she could see, it soon became clear that Robert was right. Once they began, she could feel her body warm with exhilaration. She was finally going into the canyon! The sun had just risen behind them as they headed west along the trail, casting a rosy glow against the rock walls ahead of them.

As she knew he would, Robert began telling her about the trail and surroundings. "It used to be called Cameron's Trail, after the man who built it. He's one of Arizona's two US senators now."

"Gosh, that must have been hard work, cutting into the canyon walls."

"Oh, there was a path that the Indians used, but he improved it tremendously. He had some mining sites down in the canyon, and he wanted to be able to reach them easily."

A little farther along he pointed up the cliffside to their left. "The Mallery Grotto," he said, and once she located it, she could see red markings under a shallow ledge in the canyon wall. "It was named after Garrick Mallery, an expert in Indian pictographs. See the deer figures marching along? Those are several thousand years old!"

"Imagine people living here thousands of years ago," Billie said with wonder, "heading down this trail where we are now, just like we are."

"They weren't really like us, though. They were primitives, not people the way we think of it. No industry, no advancements, not even written language, just scratchings on rock."

As they proceeded down the interminable switchbacks, they had to flatten themselves against the canyon side of the trail several times to let the mule trains carrying tourists go by. She was glad they were on foot, traveling like people had thousands of years ago. She wondered what those long-ago humans thought about. Did they marvel at the beauty, or were they mostly concerned with getting from one place to another? Did they hope there was a good meal waiting for them? Did they tell jokes, worry about their children, plan their futures?

As Robert expounded on flora, fauna, and geology, Billie found her mind wandering back to her family. Angus had completed his apprenticeship at the brick factory, and Maw suspected he was sweet on Maybelle Watkins, "bewitched by that silly giggle she has." Peigi would be fourteen in a month; however, she was still in school, thanks to the money Billie sent home. Elspeth had lost her first tooth. "She wanted to send it to you, and I said I would, so your next letter home better make mention of it." Billie chuckled to herself at the thought of a baby tooth traveling all this way. She would say that she tossed it into the canyon so Elspeth could claim she was the first person in the family to go all the way to the bottom.

Robert pointed out the slow circling of hawks and the screeching of the blue-winged pinyon jay, the prickly pear cactus, and where the sandy yellow rock dust turned to red as they moved down on to another geologic striation.

As they descended, the temperature climbed, and soon Billie had stripped off the cardigan and tied it around her waist. They stopped occasionally to drink from Robert's canteen. He carried an entire day's worth of food and water for the two of them in his ruck-sack, and Billie felt as if he'd attended to her every need.

He really was quite wonderful.

She, on the other hand, was a liar. The time had come to own up.

———————

Charlotte yawned as she waited for her next tour on the steps of the El Tovar porch. Billie had gotten up so early for her canyon trip, and though she'd been quiet, Charlotte had woken. She hadn't been able to keep herself from whispering into the darkness, "Please don't fall in."

"I plan to get to the bottom quickly, but not *that* quickly," said Billie.

Charlotte hadn't been able to go back to sleep after that.

Will pulled up in the Harvey Car and stepped out to wait with her as she stifled another yawn. "Hello, sleepyhead."

"Billie's in the abyss."

"She'll be fine. She's with a park ranger, after all."

"I just wish . . . " She wasn't sure how to complete the thought; there were so many wishes to choose from. But she didn't have a chance to consider any of them, because they were suddenly bombarded by three young women all talking at once.

"We're here!—Sorry we're late!—Oh dear, where's my hat?—Are you the ones? The Harvey Car people?—Of course they are, you ninny! Look at them!"

They finally stopped prattling long enough for Charlotte and Will to introduce themselves. The women did the same and shared that they had just graduated from college.

"Radcliffe," said the one with an unfortunate underbite. "Have you heard of it?"

"It's near Harvard." This one's nose turned up, reminding Charlotte of the little pig in *Winnie-the-Pooh*. "You've heard of *that*, right?"

"I believe I have." Charlotte surreptitiously pinched her thumb to keep herself in check.

"Well, of course they have, Lillian!" scoffed the third, pulling a monogrammed handkerchief out of her purse to swipe at nonexistent dust on the car seat. "Everyone's heard of Harvard, for goodness' sake."

"This is the West, Mildred. Who even knows if they have regular mail out here?"

The women squeezed themselves into the middle seat and immediately began tittering to each other about one of their classmates "from Colorado, of all places!"

On the long trip to Cameron, Charlotte tried to do her job of providing commentary on the surroundings and the history, but the girls seemed more interested in gossiping about their classmates—who was getting married, and to whom, and where they planned to honeymoon, and whether each had made a good match or was doomed to "marry beneath her."

When they walked into the trading post, suddenly they were stuck to Charlotte like glue.

"Tell us about the jewelry!"

But they didn't want to know about how the lovely items were made or the significance of their forms or detailing; they were mostly interested in how to buy the biggest items for the lowest prices.

"Look at this!" Mildred pointed to one of the larger necklaces. "It's huge!"

The chain of the necklace was laden with silver beads the size of peas, interspersed with beads that flared out at the ends like the petals of a flower. The pendant was a large silver horseshoe imbedded with smooth pieces of turquoise.

"It's a squash blossom necklace," explained Charlotte. "Squash is one of the four sacred plants of the Navajo, along with corn, beans, and tobacco—"

"It looks heavy—those Navajo ladies must have strong necks!"

"Try it on, Mildred!" the other two urged.

Charlotte looked around for a clerk to help them and caught John Honanie's eye. "Would you mind opening the case, John?" she asked him.

"Certainly."

The young women gawked at John as he lifted the necklace from the display. He was a large man with brown skin. His straight dark hair was parted down the middle and fell to his broad shoulders. He wore a plain blue muslin shirt, slightly wrinkled but clean.

"You know him?" one of the women whispered to Charlotte as if he couldn't hear her.

"Yes, I do tours to Cameron often, and John is one of the most knowledgeable clerks here."

"Thank you, Miss Charlotte." He called her this only when customers were near. As she'd grown more comfortable around him, no longer taking his bluntness for disrespect, she had asked that he call her simply by her first name alone.

He held the necklace out to her, knowing the women would be uncomfortable if he came too close. She took it and placed it over the young woman's neck.

"Oh, Mildred, it's smashing!" said Lillian. "You look like a squaw!"

Mildred made a hooting sound as she patted her hand over her mouth, and the other two convulsed with laughter.

John gave Charlotte a hard, blank look. Charlotte raised her eyes to the ceiling as if praying for patience. This made him smile, and she smiled back. Though they had been born worlds apart, they both knew a mean-spirited fool when they saw one.

By the time Will pulled up to the curb back at El Tovar, the car loaded with a variety of items including the three largest squash blossom necklaces to be had, Charlotte felt as if the trip had taken eight days, not eight hours.

"Let's go back and sit on my porch, and I'll make us some sandwiches," Will said after the women had departed with their loot.

That was how it often began: "We'll sit on the porch." But that was not how it often ended. He would go into the kitchen to prepare a snack or a meal, and she would wander in to slice the tomatoes or collect the dishes. And then they would remain inside, sitting at the little oak table. At the end of the day, they sometimes talked until well after the sun had set and the evening had cooled.

As he sliced bread and she tore lettuce, she glanced over at the ornate clock that seemed so out of place. She had often wanted to ask how it had come into his possession, but decorum kept her from prying. Now, though, with the heat and the lingering irritation of the three college girls, Charlotte asked quite bluntly, "Wherever did that clock come from?"

Will didn't answer for a moment, and in the distance, the sound of the mules braying in the barn seemed to fill the room. "From my mother," he said finally.

"It's an heirloom?"

"Yes. Her father brought it from Wales. It had been his father's and he refused to sell it, even when his family was near ruin."

"It's got a bit of a checkered past, then," said Charlotte.

"You could say that."

"I take it that, under similar circumstances, you would have sold it?"

Will began to assemble the sandwiches, swiping the bread with a thin puddle of French's Cream Salad Mustard and arranging the tomato slices. "I did sell it."

Charlotte shifted into his sight line and waited for him to lift his gaze from the lunch he was now preparing as if it might detonate if he didn't pay close enough attention. He glanced up at her. She tipped her head.

"My wife . . . "

Charlotte felt a brief pain below her clavicle, as if someone had thrown a small but very sharp rock at her. "You're married."

"Not anymore."

She let her fingertips graze a knot in the wood tabletop. "I would like to know about that, if you'd like to tell me."

"She was from Phoenix." He said this as if it explained half of what would come next.

They met in Flagstaff. Her family had a summer place there as a respite from the Phoenix heat. His farm was near Ash Fork, but he often went to Flagstaff for supplies or to see a show at the Orpheum. They fell hard and married quickly.

"What's her name?"

"It was Cora."

Was.

"Oh," Charlotte said softly.

"Farm life wasn't for her. She'd been so certain it would be. As much as I tried to be realistic about it, I think she got caught up in my enthusiasm. Maybe I made it sound romantic in some way. I don't know." He sighed. "She loved the lambs, but she hated the sheep."

"She left?"

"Went back to Phoenix."

"Her family took her back?"

"Happily. She'd finally come to her senses."

Charlotte nodded. *Lucky girl.*

"But then she got sick. A lot of people go to Phoenix for the cure, you know. Tuberculosis. The heat and dry air are good for them. She must have picked it up somewhere."

Her sister wrote to Will. He pawned the clock for the money to take care of her and headed straight for Phoenix.

Charlotte looked at the lovely ornate piece, so out of place in the rustic cabin. "But . . . "

"She didn't need it," he said simply.

"Her parents paid for her care?"

"They had been, but by the time I got there . . . "

"Oh, Will. I'm so sorry. Did you arrive in time?"

"She told me she wished she'd stayed on the farm." His hands had stopped moving over the sandwiches. "The money paid for her funeral."

Charlotte felt his sorrow reverberate against her body and had to bite at the inside of her cheek to keep from crying. He glanced over at the clock and then resumed his sandwich making. "Ash Fork is a small town. When the owner of the pawnshop heard, he dropped it off on my porch. Wouldn't take a nickel for it."

Charlotte stepped toward him, slid her arms around his waist, and held him. It felt a little like when they'd danced together that night at the community hall, except she was the one rescuing him this time.

After a moment, he pulled back to look at her. "You're married, aren't you?"

Charlotte nodded.

"To the man who . . . "

"Yes."

"What did you do with your wedding ring?"

"I pawned it, and I never want it back."

Forty

The sun had risen high enough now for its rays to sweep against them on the trail, and Billie unbuttoned the neck of her white cotton blouse to invite the air. She gazed out at the verdant valley far below tucked between the massive walls of canyon. Robert was explaining something about the Bright Angel Fault and how it was the place where the something-something met the something-something.

Billie had fallen into the hypnotic rhythm of motion, listening mostly to the mesmerizing drumbeat of her boot heels hitting the stony path. Her thoughts wandered, but they always returned to one thing: she would tell Robert her age and ask his forgiveness for misleading him when they stopped for lunch. It was only right.

After several hours the trail leveled out and was lined not by rock but by grasses and low bushes. The dry air seemed to moisten, and soon she could hear the tinkling of a stream.

"We're almost there," said Robert. "Indian Garden. I know it's only nine in the morning, but for us it's lunchtime!"

Amid the greenery, the place was scattered with low, mostly decrepit buildings and tent frames. "Ralph Cameron's campground," explained Robert. "He's been fighting the Park Service for decades for control of this place, and the last few years he's barely put a dime into upkeep. Apparently they even found a still for making hooch in one of the abandoned buildings! But we finally got him, and we'll come in and clean up his mess soon enough. I hear Fred Harvey has plans to build a hotel down here. The possibilities are endless."

"Why do they call it Indian Garden if it's Mr. Cameron's?"

"Oh, well, I suppose before him this used to be Indian land.

They had their farms down here with all kinds of vegetables and fruit. With the springs here, it's one of the best places to grow things in the whole canyon. The place was crawling with red men. Cameron let a few of them stay, but we'll clear them out as soon as it's legally ours."

Billie's thoughts swung to the conversation she'd had with Charlotte about missionaries trying to turn the Indians into Christians. *Clear them out*, Robert had said. But to where? And why couldn't they just stay here on their own land?

They found some rocks to sit on by the spring-fed creek and took off their boots and socks to cool their feet in the water. Robert refilled his canteen and began to set out the lunch he'd brought: cream cheese and olive sandwiches, apples, biscuits, and even a couple of Oh Henry! bars. Billie was surprisingly hungry and felt she'd be better prepared to make the admission about her age once she had some food in her stomach.

"I'm glad my girl likes to eat," said Robert admiringly. "Those delicate flowers who just pick at their dinner—I don't understand that at all."

As soon as they'd finished the last of the chocolate bars, he started to pack up and put his boots back on. "The hike back will take five or six hours, and we want to do as much of it as we can before the hottest part of the afternoon. It's a cool day for July, but it's still July."

"Yes, but can't we take an extra minute to—"

"You want to do a little exploring before we head out?"

"Oh. Sure."

As they walked farther down the trail, he took her hand in his and gave her a grin. He looked so happy . . .

"Robert?" she began.

He stopped suddenly, and Billie thought he was turning to answer her, but his gaze went past her. Then she saw the man. He was bent over, working at the ground with a sturdy stick. His black hair was shoulder-length with a thick row of bangs across his forehead. He wore an old button-down shirt and a pair of canvas pants. There was a bandanna knotted around his head, just like Billie's da sometimes wore to keep the sweat out of his eyes. In fact the whole messy getup reminded her of her da's when he was trying to make some semblance of order out of the yard.

Under a nearby tree sat a woman of about her maw's age. Similar to the man, she had thick bangs across her forehead, though the rest of her dark hair trailed down over her upper arms. She had a long dress and a shawl over her shoulders pinned in front, both a bit dusty. She was working on something in her lap. At first Billie thought it might be a sewing project, but then she realized it looked to be the beginnings of a basket.

As Billie studied her, the woman's eyes came up from her work and met Billie's. She gave a little smile and a nod. Billie smiled back, and she was about to go toward the woman and ask if she could look at the basket, when Robert muttered, "Filthy heathens."

"Robert, they're just—"

"You there!" Robert called out, and the man suddenly stood up from his work. The woman was no longer smiling. "You won't be here long, you know!"

The man dropped his stick and moved cautiously toward his wife. Neither looked at Robert and Billie, only gazed mildly at the ground. They did not cower, but they went still as if to prepare themselves for whatever this large white man might do. Billie herself wasn't sure what he might do.

"Robert, let's go."

He glared at them a moment longer, then turned back up the trail.

They walked in silence for a few minutes, Billie's heart pounding with anger. Why had he felt the need to yell at them like that?

They weren't hurting anyone, only going about their chores as her own parents were probably doing this very minute a thousand miles away. And soon people like Robert would come and "clear them out," just as her own ancestors had been forced to leave their native land.

"These cottonwoods were planted by Cameron to increase the shade," said Robert, recommencing what Billie now knew would be five to six hours of lecturing. "The stupid Indians keep cutting the branches of the willows to make their baskets, so he took matters into his own hands and planted trees they couldn't use. You have to admire the man for that, at least."

I don't admire him, thought Billie, *and I don't admire you.*

———

Robert's canteen had run dry a mile below the rim, and Billie felt as limp as a week-old bouquet. She wanted nothing more than to leave this man behind and head straight for her dorm, gulp gallons from the kitchen faucet, and then sink into the claw-foot tub to wash away the dust and the disgust she felt.

He was unkind. And she was foolish.

"Robert," she said as they reached the trailhead, "thank you for taking me."

"It was my pleasure!"

"I don't want to be your girl anymore."

Pride slid down his face and melted into alarm. "What?"

"I don't want to go steady anymore."

"But we just—" He threw his long arm out toward the canyon. "We had such a nice . . . "

As limp as she felt, Billie pulled herself to her full height. "I don't like how you treated those Indians. You scared them, and you scared me."

His mouth went slack with surprise. Then he clamped it shut

again and put his fists on his hips. "The *Indians*? You're breaking up with me over the way I spoke to a couple of dirty—"

Billie didn't want to listen anymore. And in fact, she didn't have to listen to him ever again. She turned on her heel and left him standing there.

———

Charlotte and Will held each other far longer than a friendly, consoling hug between an unrelated man and a woman would ever—should ever—go on.

Billie had accused her of becoming "a hugger." Wouldn't her brother, Oliver, have a good laugh over that. As children they hadn't been cuddled or taken onto laps, and Charlotte wasn't the type to fawn around hanging an arm over the shoulders of her girlfriends.

She and Simeon had embraced quite often—in the beginning, anyway, and secretly, of course. It had made her feel tingly and daring and special. It had been an act of defiance, a symbol that she'd gained her freedom from the straitjacket of polite society. That she'd won.

Perhaps she'd won the battle, but she had most assuredly lost the war.

Now, with Will in her arms and she in his, Charlotte didn't feel tingly or brave. She felt safe and comforted and right. And yes, a bit flushed in the places a woman flushes, craving his hands and his mouth.

Finally they slowly, gently pulled apart, both aware that they'd arrived at a point beyond which neither was quite yet prepared to trespass. No longer touching, eyes averted in sudden shyness, Charlotte felt bereft and unsteady, as if the very thing she'd needed all this time to hold her up had been suddenly removed.

Silence filled the cabin for several long moments until Will asked, "Have you filed for divorce?"

Her gaze came up to find his. His cheeks were pink and his breathing shallow. He, too, looked unsteady.

The question, though reasonable, felt pointed to her, as if there was some judgment in it.

If he was so terrible, Charlotte, why haven't you legally excised him from your life?

It wasn't his question, she realized, but the question she'd been asking herself.

Her answer had an edge of defensiveness to it. "If I do, he'll find me."

"I can protect you."

"You can't be with me every minute of the day and night, Will."

"You could use a lawyer who won't disclose your whereabouts."

"He's a brilliant bloodhound, and sleuthing is his favorite game. It's what makes him such a good newspaperman."

"He's a reporter?"

"Yes, and he'll track me down like the story of the century. Believe me, I know my own husband."

The words *my own husband* seemed to hit him like a slap.

"Charlotte," he breathed, "I want *so much* to . . . but you're a married woman."

It hadn't really occurred to her, she realized, that after all that she'd gone through—the cascading heartbreaks of losing her family, the man she loved turning on her so viciously, being reduced to squirreling away her tips like acorns for the looming winter—that there was anything left of her heart to break.

Will was a good and honorable man. And he was right; whatever they wanted and however much they wanted it, a romantic entanglement was ill-advised for them both.

"Yes, I am," she said simply. "And I won't be here for long."

The next morning, Charlotte asked to speak to Mr. Patrillo.

"What can I do for you?" he said without looking up from the papers on his enormous desk.

"I'm ready to relocate."

Forty-One

The first half of July had been very dry, but the weather gods made up for it in the back half. It poured almost every afternoon, and tourists shied away from tours in the rain. For this, Charlotte was very glad.

It was nice to have some small thing to be glad about, because mostly she felt miserable. The few excursions she did have with Will were polite, and they exchanged small pleasantries while they waited for passengers in between. She never went to his cabin anymore. Instead she distracted herself with books, specifically those oriented toward the history of the Southwest. She wanted to be prepared when Patrillo secured her spot with the Detours in New Mexico.

She and Ruth had continued their occasional tutoring sessions, but she hadn't told Ruth about becoming a guide for the Detours. If she did go, she felt it was important that Billie, who was her dearest friend and what Charlotte had come to think of as an "honorary sister," be the first to know. And though she knew Ruth wouldn't tell a soul, if word ever got to Billie before Charlotte had told her personally, it would hurt her terribly.

Having read most of what there was in the women's dorm, Charlotte occasionally snuck into the Ladies' Lounging Room in El Tovar to pilfer and then quickly return what she found. There wasn't much to choose from. She avoided novels, which often had some romantic thread, no matter how informative they might be.

She decided to take a chance with the immensely popular novel *Ramona* by Helen Hunt Jackson, and every page nearly tore the breath from her chest. Set in California in the mid-1800s, it follows the titular character, a half-Scottish, half-Indian orphan. She falls in love with another Indian, and they are constantly abused by whites as they try to find a place to settle. Their only daughter dies because a white doctor won't treat her. Charlotte found herself crying through most of it.

Billie was relieved (though not exactly happy) now that she'd dispensed with that lout in a Stetson, Robert. They had discussed it with Mae and Henny, and three out of four of them had agreed that it was best to put a little time between beaus.

"You don't want to take right up with some new guy and then give him the boot, too," counseled Henny. "You'll get a reputation as a heartbreaker."

Mae had shrugged. "It's not the worst thing in the world. Getting right back in the saddle and all that."

"I think *Billie* should be the arbiter of what's best for her," Charlotte had said. "And she should take all the time she needs to determine what exactly that is."

Billie had given her a grateful smile. "Thank you," she'd murmured.

Why had it taken so long for Charlotte to remember that young people approaching adulthood were practically allergic to being told what to do? She had been just the same at that age. In all honesty, she still was.

Gossip being what it was in any small town, word of the breakup spread quickly. Charlotte had seen Billie and Leif talking a little when they were on shift together, though that seemed to be all it was. They never saw each other outside of work, and with Charlotte no longer seeing Will socially, the two women spent more time together and with the other Harvey Girls.

———

Angry Alva stuck her head in their door one late July evening. "Are you two coming or not?"

Billie was leafing through an old copy of *Photoplay* magazine. Clara Bow graced the cover with the glaring headline WHAT IS IT? DO YOU HAVE IT? Billie was pretty sure she didn't have it.

She looked at Charlotte. "I'm not much in the mood, are you?"

Charlotte peeked over the top of a book that was making her eyes leak, though she tried to pass it off as an allergy of some kind. "I'm very happy here reading." She did not look the least bit happy.

Alva gave her foot a little stomp. "You know we can't do the tournament without you!"

Billie shrugged. "Oh, all right." She turned to Charlotte. "Come on now, sniffles."

"I am not sniffling! I have allergies—"

"The only thing you're allergic to is that book."

The sewing room was much larger than the one in Topeka, with five square tables set up for a variety of hobbies and activities. The knitters sat at one table, the crocheters at another, though they did make room for one girl doing needlepoint. There were two tables at the back for card playing, and woe to the girl who tried to sit at one of them and darn a sock!

Euchre, the partners card game Henny had taught them, had become a bit of an obsession this season, and some games went well into the wee hours. (Mae Parnell was never strict about eleven o'clock lights out, as she often wasn't in the building to enforce it.) Head waitress Nora was one of the nocturnal players, yet she brooked no subpar performances at breakfast the next morning.

"If you can't get by on only a few hours of sleep, then don't play the damn game all night!" she'd chastise the bleary-eyed. She and Henny had become partners (the other girls secretly grumbled about Nora having the advantage of the best player, and Henny currying favor with the head girl), and they'd been unbeatable . . . until Charlotte and Billie suddenly had plenty of time on their hands to practice.

Tonight they played their first round against Alva and the only person who could stand her: a German girl named Ursula. Billie and Charlotte suspected Ursula suffered from a bit of deafness, which she played off as learning English as a second language.

They made short work of Alva and Ursula, euchering them twice.

"You shouldn't have played that jack so soon!" Alva railed at her partner.

"Thank you!" said Ursula.

Henny and Nora were simultaneously wiping the other table with their opponents. Soon enough, it was time for the showdown everyone had been waiting for.

To no one's surprise, Nora was the most competitive. She never missed an opportunity to call the trump suit even if she didn't have enough of a hand to back it up. Henny, the best player of the four, was more strategic, often holding back cards that others would've wasted early in the game. But she was remarkably patient with Nora, even when the older girl's impetuousness got them euchred.

Charlotte was the card counter of the group. At any given moment, she knew what had been played, what was still in somebody's hands, and the statistical likelihood of getting trumped. Billie was all enthusiasm; she played erratically but with gusto and left the others scratching their heads at how often she won with so little strategy.

Nora and Henny were one point away from winning, and Charlotte and Billie were three points behind, when Billie called a "loner." She would play her hand with Charlotte sitting out, and if she took the round, they would get four points and win the game.

Charlotte looked at her own hand and saw cards that Billie would likely need to win. She raised her eyebrows at the girl.

"That's cheating, right there!" Nora barked.

"I didn't say a thing!"

"Don't give me that, ye little sleeveen. You gave her the eye!"

Henny's sweet face went serious. "Did you?" she asked Charlotte.

"I only . . . " Charlotte trailed off.

"She did," said Billie. "She gave me the eye." She turned to Nora. "What's a sleeveen?"

"A cunning one." Nora smiled imperiously. "And now you don't get your loner."

Henny, ever the strategist, said, "Maybe she should have to take the loner, seeing as she already called it. I like our chances if her partner doesn't think she can win."

"Let's just redeal," insisted Billie. "Charlotte promises not to be a sleeveen."

Henny and Nora looked at each other.

"You're playing that hand," Nora told Billie, "and you're going alone."

When Billie won the hand, and thus the game, the other three sat there with their mouths agape. Even Henny was stumped. "How did you . . . why did you want to . . . ?"

"I wasn't sure if I could make it, but I figured we had to try. When Charlotte gave me that look, I knew she had good cards, meaning you two probably didn't. So I decided to say we should redeal, knowing that Nora would then *make* me play."

A roar of approval went up. Even the knitters dropped their needles and clapped. Nora went red-faced. And Billie and Charlotte went to sleep with smiles on their faces for the first time in weeks.

———

One afternoon near the end of July, Billie and Leif both came out of the service entrance at the back of the hotel at the same time. Leif was just tugging off his white brimless kitchen cap and Billie saw his sandy curls tumble down to his shoulders.

"You need a haircut," she said.

"I keep meaning to go down to Williams and find a barber, but when I get a day off, I just want to sleep in and relax."

"I can cut your hair."

Leif didn't respond for a moment, which was just long enough for Billie's insides to curdle with embarrassment. "I used to cut my brothers' hair," she said quickly, "but you'd probably rather see a real barber."

"Actually, I . . . I'd like that, if you don't mind taking the time."

"I'll see if I can borrow some haircutting scissors."

He chuckled. "Once my papa did it with a pair of sheep shears because that was all he could find."

"That must have been an awful cut!"

He shook his head so the curls bounced around. "Who could tell?"

She smiled at him; he smiled back; they kept walking.

A while later, they found themselves passing Will's cabin and its lone resident sitting on the porch with a bottle of Bevo and the newspaper. As Billie called out a hello, the heavens opened, and arrows of rain began to torpedo them.

"Come up where it's dry!" said Will, and the two white-clad adolescents scurried up the steps to the cover of the porch. "And who've we got here?" he asked.

"This is my friend Leif. We met when I was in training back in Topeka."

Leif stretched out his hand. "Pleased to meet you, sir."

"He's not *sir*, he's just Will."

The older man smiled. "Just Will. That's me."

He brought out two more chairs, a Bevo for Leif, a bottle of Moxie for Billie. Then came a box of saltines and a tin of marmalade. In his mild, respectful way, Will asked Leif about himself and learned that he'd been raised on a sheep farm.

"Me, too," said Will. "In fact, I still have it."

"You have a sheep farm?" asked Billie. "What are you doing driving a car for Fred Harvey?"

"I suppose I wanted to try something different for a while."

"It's hard work," Leif told Billie. "You can't just play with the lambs all day."

Will gazed out into the pines for a moment. Then he nodded and took a swig of his Bevo.

Leif looked at the last saltine. "Why don't I run over to the dorm and get us some dinner?"

Billie started to rise. "I'll come with you."

Leif laughed, and Will shook his head. "No girls in the dorm."

"Stay here and drink your Moxie," said Leif. "I'll be right back."

As they watched his form recede through the trees, Will said, "He seems nice."

"He is."

"How old is he?"

"Nineteen. And before you ask, he knows I'm sixteen. And no, we're not going steady or anything like that. We're just friends."

"For now."

"Well, everything's for now, isn't it? Life is for now."

Will smiled. "No wonder everyone thinks you're older than you are."

Billie picked up the last saltine and turned it in her fingers like a toy. "Are you and Charlotte still friends?"

"I'd like to think we are."

"But you don't spend time together anymore."

"We work—"

"That's not what I'm talking about. She used to be over here all the time, and now she's not."

"We felt it was best under the circumstances."

Billie put the saltine back on the plate and rested her hands in her lap.

"I know about her husband," he said.

Her eyes flicked up to his.

"And I know you've been a good friend to her," he continued. "I'm trying to be a good friend, too."

"Just not anything more."

"No. It wouldn't be right."

"You'd be looking over your shoulder all the time."

"It's not that," he said. "I'd welcome the chance to give that fellow a dose of his own medicine. I just can't be with someone who's half in."

"Because she's married. Other than that," said Billie with a sigh, "I'm pretty sure she's all in."

The man didn't move. Just sat there with one hand wrapped around an empty bottle of near beer. Billie took the other hand and squeezed it.

Will squeezed back. "Keep being a good friend to her."

"The best I can, till the day I die."

———————————

Later, when Leif walked Billie back to her dorm, he said, "That man is very lonely."

"He misses Charlotte."

"Lonelier than that," he said.

"How can you tell?"

"I know what it looks like, because I know what it feels like."

"You're not alone anymore," said Billie. "You have me."

"And you have me," he said. "Tricky thing is figuring out how to keep it that way."

They walked in silence for a while, shoulder to shoulder, their long legs keeping pace with each other.

"Do you like it here?" Leif asked.

"Sure I do."

"No, I'm asking if you mean to stay here, or are you going to take your first chance to move back to Table Rock?"

Billie turned the question over in her mind. "My family needs the money."

"If that's your answer—"

"It's not my *only* answer. I do like it here. I like the work and the people. I have friends now, and it's just so . . . so beautiful here. I suppose I do mean to stay. But I don't think it'll be forever."

As they walked, they startled a young ringtail, who let out a worried bark and scurried up a tree. It reminded Billie of the baby raccoons she'd seen around her house growing up.

"What about you?" she asked. "Do you like it here?"

He chuckled. "Well, Chef Giuseppe is impossible to truly please, but I'm learning how he likes things done, and I'll be prepared when the time comes to be a line chef. No matter where I go, I can say I worked at the great El Tovar, and that'll get me a job."

"I didn't know you wanted to be a line chef."

"Not sure if it's my life's work, but it's the next step."

"What else do you like?"

He thought for a moment. "I guess I like that everyone here is either working for the Santa Fe Railway, the Park Service, or Fred Harvey, and we're all trying to accomplish one goal: a good experience for the people who come. Back in Topeka, there were fifty thousand people going in fifty thousand directions. It was easy to feel lost."

"And lonely."

They slowed as they approached the dorm. It was late, but there was a light on in the parlor. *Probably Charlotte and one of her many books,* thought Billie. They stayed in the shadows for a few moments longer.

"What I like best is that you're here," said Leif.

That was it exactly. Just his nearness. She realized in that moment that, no matter the official status of their relationship, she never wanted to be far away from him again.

She smiled. "I like that you're here, too."

"I don't want to lose you again."

"Me, neither."

They stood silently for a moment. The breeze sent his shaggy curls swaying around his head, and Billie felt she could see what he must have looked like as a little boy. And yet there was a timeworn-ness to his face that also made her imagine him as an old man.

She could sense so much about him, but the truth was she didn't actually *know* that much. And if she wanted this friendship— or whatever it turned out to be—to last until she got to see what he'd really look like in old age, she had to be more mature about it than she had been with Robert.

"Leif?"

"Yes."

"I know you're a good man."

He gave her a wary look. "But . . . "

"But I think maybe I went too fast and let my feelings get ahead of me. We really haven't spent that much time together. I want . . . I'd like to . . . "

"Take it slow."

"Yes."

"Me, too."

He pulled her into a loose embrace, but he did not kiss her. He only said, "Good night, Billie," and turned to walk back to the men's dorm.

At the end of July, Charlotte made a trip to Flagstaff on her day off. She told Billie she missed Boston and wanted to window-shop in a town with more than three stores. In truth, she had no intention of perusing the scant retail offerings of this "city." Her true mission was to find out what, if anything, could be done about being legally bound to a vicious bully.

After inquiring with several attorneys with shingles out on Santa Fe Avenue, it became clear that the options were extremely limited, and there was a year's residency requirement in the state of Arizona before she could even begin. She returned demoralized.

It had been raining for days, and this, too, conspired to dampen her spirits. To calm herself, she headed for her favorite place in Grand Canyon Village.

"Hello, Ruth," she said. "How are you today?"

"I'm fine." Ruth's eyes flicked to the office door behind which sat the Hopi House manager. "But I can't talk very much."

"That's all right. I just came because it's my day off and I needed to get out of my room. I'd take a walk, but with this rain, I thought it would be nicer to stroll around in here, and maybe buy a little something for myself."

"Then you're a customer, and we *can* talk," Ruth said with a smile.

Charlotte was about to respond when she saw Ruth's gaze shift to something behind her.

"May I help you, sir?"

"Yes, thanks, we'd like to purchase this—"

That voice!

Without thinking, Charlotte spun around.

"Charlotte?"

"Oliver!"

Forty-Two

Though they had never in their lives embraced before, Oliver threw his arms around her and clutched him to her. "Charlotte, my God! I thought you might be dead!"

Tears sprang to Charlotte's eyes. "Oliver, I can't believe you're here . . . "

There was a little gasp behind them, and a woman's voice said, "This is your sister?"

Oliver pulled back but didn't fully release Charlotte, as if she might somehow disappear if he didn't keep a hand on her. "Yes, darling, this is long-lost Charlotte."

The woman was about Charlotte's age, and quite beautiful, but the first thing Charlotte noticed was the color of her skin. It was not the pale goose flesh of the Brahmin families of Boston; it was a creamy tan.

"This is my wife, Gianna. We're on our honeymoon."

Gianna reached out her hand. "I'm very pleased to meet you. Oliver has told me so much, and I always hoped that somehow, I would come to know his beloved little sister." Her eyes were shiny with emotion.

"Gianna is a Rossi," Oliver said, and no further explanation was needed. The Rossi family owned a rival shipping company, and though they'd been established for decades, Casper Crowninshield always referred to them at "those upstart Rossis."

Oliver had married an Italian! A rich one, but an Italian nonetheless. Perhaps their parents had decided that losing two children to "unacceptable" mates was one child too many.

310 — Juliette Fay

Other customers came in, and Oliver quickly paid for a lovely turquoise bracelet and hurried them all up to his suite.

Once he'd ushered them into the sitting room, he wanted to know everything. Why had she left St. Louis? Where was Simeon? Why was she here at the Grand Canyon?

Charlotte had written to Oliver only three times in the two years since she'd left Boston. The first letter had been to tell him about her wonderful new life with the man she loved, free of all the tedious requirements of high society. He responded that he missed her terribly, but if this was what it took to make her happy, he would accept it.

A year later, her second letter delicately tested the waters about a possible "visit" home. Oliver had tried to convince his parents that Charlotte deserved such a chance, but they were vehemently opposed to hosting her. She had "made her bed." He sent word that it wasn't a good time.

Oliver had reached out to her once more not long before she'd left St. Louis. He asked how she was and suggested that maybe she should simply turn up on the Crowninshield doorstep. He felt that if their parents saw her in person, they wouldn't be able to deny her. But Charlotte now knew that Simeon would track her there and would likely make a scene in order to induce her to return with him. It would ruin the Crowninshields in the eyes of the other society families, after which she was sure her parents would be forced to permanently disown her. She couldn't take that chance. Instead she headed in the opposite direction: west.

She had written Oliver one last letter to tell him she was departing St. Louis and not to write to her there anymore.

"That letter confirmed all my worst fears," Oliver said now. "You spoke in the singular, which suggested that you were leaving him. I assumed he was not the man you thought he was, and that in fact he might be dangerous. I relayed my concerns to Father, who hired men to locate you. But you had vanished!"

"Father wanted to find me?"

"He did. Mother quibbled a bit about what we would tell people. When you left Boston, she concocted an elaborate tale of how you'd gone on a European tour with a college friend who'd introduced you to Danish royalty, and you were now living in Denmark, the happy wife of a baron or some such nonsense."

Charlotte couldn't help but laugh. "A baron? I wasn't even worthy of a viscount?"

"Well, she had to make it believable, you see, and hard to trace. I imagine Danish barons are a dime a dozen. Now," he said, "tell me what really happened."

Charlotte was glad that she had already faced Winnie Turner on the matter. It had helped her come to a new perspective, one that involved far less self-excoriation. "As you say, he was not the man I thought I married, and he became . . . quite unpleasant."

"He hit you?" asked Gianna.

Her frankness reminded Charlotte a little of John Honanie. Apparently the Italians shared that trait with the Indians. Or maybe everyone in the world was more forthright than the Protestant elite. Charlotte did not respond directly, knowing her silence would speak volumes. "Fred Harvey offered both the perfect escape and a far better wage than I could find elsewhere."

Oliver's eyes went wide. "You're a *waitress?*"

Charlotte smiled. "A Harvey Girl, if you please. And quite a good one."

"Won't Mother absolutely froth at the mouth!"

"You can never tell Mother."

"Of course not, but just imagine how fun it would be!"

"Oliver," chided Gianna, "be serious. Charlotte has gone through a terrible ordeal, and here you are, making light of it."

"It's all right. It has been an ordeal, but it's nice to find a little humor in it, too."

"What's this?" said Oliver. "Has Mournful Myrtle suddenly gone lighthearted on me? Maybe consorting with the great unwashed has done you some good."

Charlotte leveled her gaze at him. "Harvey Girls are known for their spotless dress, impeccable manners, and unmatched hospitality."

Gianna patted Charlotte's hand. "My grandmother ran a boardinghouse, and she was just the same."

"Your grandmother ran a boardinghouse?" Oliver was incredulous.

"She was a strong woman, and she raised a strong son who has more ships than you," Gianna said plainly. "Now, what will we tell your mother when we bring Charlotte home?"

It was late when Charlotte arrived back in the dorm, but Billie was up darning a sock. "For cripes sake, where've you been? I caught up on all my mending waiting for you!"

"I . . . I met with someone."

A look of fear came over Billie's face. "Not him."

"Whom?"

"*Him.*"

Charlotte blinked at the girl a moment before realizing she meant Simeon. "Oh, goodness, no."

Billie continued to study her. "It wasn't Will."

Was this some sort of mind-reading exercise? "How do you know it wasn't?"

"Because you've been off him for a while. And anyway, you'd just say you've been with Will."

"I haven't been *off* him."

Billie grinned slyly. "You're saying you've been on him?"

"What kind of talk is this for a young girl!"

"Charlotte, *who was it?*"

Charlotte put her hands to her cheeks. "It was my brother," she whispered. "He's on his honeymoon."

"Your brother! Oh, Charlotte, was he kind to you? I hope he didn't—"

"No, no, he was wonderful. And his wife is a lovely, smart Italian woman."

"Italian? I thought—"

"Yes, I know. I'm sure my parents went positively Vesuvian over it." Charlotte sank down onto her bed. "Billie, they want to take me back to Boston with them."

"Gee, that'd be . . . " Billie gazed uncertainly at Charlotte. "I mean, would it?"

"Well, yes, of course it would be wonderful to be accepted back into the family."

"You'd be rich again."

"Yes, I guess that's true."

"No more polishing silver. No more running ragged for bossy tourists. You can read all day long, every day of the week, if you feel like it. You won't have to have a job at all."

Charlotte could hardly imagine what it would be like to have control of her days!

Though of course, she'd never have full control. Mother would insist she attend every last tea, garden party, dinner, and soiree. In fact, Charlotte would have to be on her best behavior to make up for how deeply she'd disgraced the family. She'd have to play the very essence of decorum, the perfect picture of someone she wasn't.

"Would we still be friends?" asked Billie.

"Yes, of course!"

But would they? Charlotte would be chained to her social calendar, and Billie could never visit. How would the Crowninshields ever explain playing host to some working-class girl from Nebraska?

Billie seemed to intuit this just as quickly as Charlotte. "We could write, I suppose."

"Yes, and maybe in a year or so I could come and visit." The brightness of her tone didn't fool either of them. Charlotte would be a tourist; Billie might even have to serve her.

But Billie knew Charlotte needed to continue the ruse. "On my day off we could go driving with Will and Henny."

Will.

Charlotte felt tears sting her eyes.

Billie came over to sit next to her on the bed. She put her arm around Charlotte's back. "I won't forget you, and neither will they. We'll all just be happy that you're happy."

"Billie." Charlotte's throat constricted with emotion. "Your kindness and friendship these last four months—"

"Och, dinna fash," the girl soothed. "My maw would sew you an entire Sears, Roebuck catalog if she knew all the mothering you've done in her place."

Charlotte laughed through her tears. "Not that you've enjoyed it!"

"Ha! Fought you tooth and nail, but I'll miss it when it's gone." Billie squeezed her shoulder. "It'll be good to know you're finally safe."

Neither of them fell asleep as quickly as a day of manual labor usually compelled. But it was Charlotte who lay awake in the darkest hours contemplating this shocking reversal of fortune.

But was it? Or was it just a return to an even stricter version of the life that had made her run in the first place? They'd never let her go back to college. Beatrice Crowninshield hadn't even finished high school, and had she needed that degree? No she had not. She had simply married the wealthiest eligible bachelor available to her, and that was exactly what she would expect her daughter to do. Finally.

Father would have his lawyers arrange a divorce, of course, which was more than Charlotte could accomplish on her own. The Crowninshield lawyers could find some way around whatever obstacles there were, but Simeon would still have to be notified. There was no doubt in Charlotte's mind that once he knew she had returned to her family, he would show up in the most public fashion, creating a scene that would have tongues wagging all over the city.

Possibly her father could hire protectors of some sort, though sooner or later even this would be noticed by the sharp eyes of the Beacon Hill matrons and provide endless fodder for gossip. More likely she would be confined to the house except for events that required her presence. And wouldn't Boston society life, with its widely publicized social affairs meant to let the world know who was included (and more specifically who was *not* included), be the obvious place for Simeon to look?

Yes, it most certainly would.

It would be like shooting fish in a barrel.

Forty-Three

Oliver didn't take it well.

He waved away concerns that a man with so few resources and connections as Simeon could really pose such a problem to a family like the Crowninshields. But he did agree that every last decision, from where to go, to what to wear, to which friends Charlotte could have, would be firmly in the hands of their mother. But was that such a sacrifice if it meant returning to a life of ease and leisure?

"At least you wouldn't have to *serve* people, for goodness' sake."

In the end, the only thing that seemed to make sense to him was that Charlotte was having an adventure, and she wasn't ready for it to be over. She told him about the Detours—all the training she would receive, the chance to be an authority on a subject she found so intriguing, journeying into lands few white people had ever visited.

"Old Teddy Roosevelt doesn't have much on you," Oliver had said with wonder. "You've become quite the explorer!"

"Will you tell our parents that you've found me?"

"I'd like to tell them, if you'll give me permission. They've been so worried, it would be cruel not to let them know you're all right."

"But what will you say about where I am?"

The room was quiet as each tried to think of what version of the story they could present.

"May I suggest something, Charlotte?" said Gianna. "Oliver could say that you realized your marriage was a mistake. You moved to the Southwest for a fresh start, and you're so happy here, you plan to stay for a little while longer. You've made wonderful friends, and you're under the care of an upstanding benefactor." She smiled. "He just won't mention that the good man's name is Fred Harvey."

They hadn't been to the trading post in weeks. Heavy rains had washed the road out in places, and it took Fred Harvey's entire road crew to clear it of mud and debris. Consequently, when the first day of August dawned crisp and blue, hotel guests signed up for tours like a run on the bank. The drop-off loop at El Tovar was bumper to bumper with Harvey Cars.

Charlotte and Will's group consisted of a young couple with a new baby to whom they cooed incessantly; an older gentleman whose large extended family had decided to head west to Hermits Rest, so he had chosen the tour going the farthest east; and two law students who'd been disappointed to find that El Tovar wasn't a dude ranch.

"On our left," Charlotte called out to the passengers as they exited the El Tovar loop, "is the Park Service administration building and home to Park Superintendent Mr. J. Ross Eakin!"

The law students grumbled that they didn't come all this way for a lecture; they could get that back at law school. The elderly gentleman began to snore, and the young couple compensated by simply cooing louder at their young progeny.

"Nice try," Will murmured.

As the tourists wandered around the trading post, Charlotte made her way back to find John Honanie. Much of what she'd learned from Ruth was about the Hopi culture, and Charlotte knew that Navajos had their own traditions, customs, and beliefs that were quite distinct. She needed more information, and as her initial testiness with John had grown into something more friendly over her many trips to Cameron, she hoped he would be willing to tutor her as well.

"Can I talk to you?" she said.

John was hauling a heavy box in from the storeroom. "What is it now, small Boston lady?" He had taken to calling her this, and after getting over the impudence of it, Charlotte had to agree that she was, in fact, a petite woman from Boston.

"I have a proposal, large Navajo."

He put the box down. "This will be interesting."

"I'd like to pay you to teach me about your culture, specifically the types of things I can't learn from books. I have an opportunity to become a courier for the Indian Detours and I want to be fully prepared." Surely Billie would never hear of it from a place so remote as Cameron, so it was safe to discuss with John.

"The what?"

She explained about de-tourists visiting Indian ruins and villages, viewing their customs and ceremonies, and purchasing artwork, jewelry, and wares.

At first she couldn't read the look on his face—surprise, certainly. But what kind of surprise? Was he happy that the artisans would have more opportunities to sell their work without having to travel far from home? Did he like the idea of white people learning about Indian culture and traditions by viewing and interacting with them in their villages?

No, he most certainly did not. In fact, he was boiling mad.

"Why doesn't Fred Harvey just round us all up and put us in zoos? Then the whites wouldn't even have to leave their wretched, stinking cities to gawk at us!" he hissed, trying to keep his fury from booming across the showroom. "Isn't it enough that we've had our lands stolen and been corralled onto reservations like prisoners? Isn't it enough that the government takes our children, makes them speak English and forget all their families have taught them? Now you want to treat our homes and sacred ceremonies like some kind of peep show?" He dropped the box with a thump and stormed out the back of the store.

Charlotte stood there stunned.

"What did you do to John?" Will asked mildly, his casual delivery belied by the fact that he was suddenly at her side as if she might be in some sort of danger.

"I . . . I asked him to . . . help me with something."

"Seems like he doesn't want to do it."

"No, he very much doesn't."

The cooing couple's baby started to squawk, and the law students were bored. The older gentleman sighed and said his family was likely wondering where he'd wandered off to.

"You didn't let them know where you were going?" asked Charlotte.

The older man grinned slyly. "It's good to make them worry every once in a while."

Back at El Tovar several hours later, they found that his family had in fact made the Park Service conduct an exhaustive search, fearing he'd fallen into the canyon. His sudden appearance, fully intact (if a little dusty), prompted a great outpouring of teary gratitude and relief, to which he smiled innocently and apologized for any consternation he might have caused.

"'Might have caused,' my eye," Will whispered to Charlotte as the group trundled him off to get him a cup of tea with a splash of something more fortifying in it if he felt the need.

Charlotte thought of her own family and wondered if they would receive their wandering daughter with quite so much affection and forgiveness. Likely not, but their willingness to accept her back into the fold at all would be a remarkable gesture of goodwill.

And she wouldn't be so alone in the world. Nor would she have to devise yet another plan for what do next. Her mother would take care of that with great pleasure.

"You've been quiet," said Will before she could leave for the dorm. "Ever since John stomped off."

She'd been quiet all right, her mind churning on what John had said.

Peep show.

Is that what the Detours were? Or a zoo of sorts? The more she thought about it, the more it did seem like a safari, only with exotic people instead of exotic animals, the trophies to take home a bowl or a blanket instead of a pelt. And would the de-tourists really want to learn about and understand another culture, or would they be like the tourists in the car with her today, who hadn't really wanted to listen to her anyway?

"Seems like you've got something on your mind," Will prompted.

She turned to look at him, his face all kindness and concern. "I don't know what to do."

"Let's take the car back, and you can tell me about it."

"I don't think I can do it." They were now sitting in his cabin, and she had told him everything: about her attempt to procure a divorce, Patrillo's insistence that she join the Detours, Oliver's insistence that she come home, and John's reaction to her request. "I keep hearing John's words in my head, and I think he's right. But if I don't do it, Patrillo might very well fire me. I don't want to go back to Boston, but I may not have much choice."

Will had been silent as he'd listened to all of this, and she'd been grateful for that. Unlike the other men involved, he hadn't immediately felt the need to insert his own wishes and opinions into the situation. But when he did speak, his wishes were clear.

"It seems like you're eager to leave."

"I need to stay one step ahead of Simeon. I can't remain in any one place for long."

"Is that all it is?"

She felt her blood surge in her veins, and she was just so angry. Furious, really, that everything she tried to do, every plan she made, every effort to avert misery, was thwarted. Every single thing she dared to want—even simply to protect herself from harm, much less to experience real love—was yanked from her reach.

"To be quite frank," she said, "I find it excruciating to be near you."

For a moment he said nothing, only gazed steadily at her. "I find it excruciating to be near you, too," he said quietly.

"I wish you would just kiss me."

"You're—"

She slammed her hand on the oak table. "Yes, I know, I'm married! Tied like a prize pig to a man who'd rather see me dead than happy! He could show up tomorrow and claim me or kill me, and then what good would your precious morals be?"

"It's not morals, Charlotte, it's for your own good! If you do someday file for divorce, you'd be an adulteress."

"Which means I'd have no right to his vast fortune. Except that he doesn't have a vast fortune; he doesn't have a plug nickel. My problem isn't that he'd leave me without a cent, it's that he won't leave me at all!"

They glared at each other a moment, his dark eyes flashing with a kind of torment. She was his tormentor, she realized, and the thought of herself as an evil temptress suddenly seemed silly. She sighed, bested. "Of all the things I've done in the past two years that I never thought I'd do, I never, *ever* thought I'd beg a man to take me to bed."

He exhaled heavily. "You didn't—"

"Yes, I did," she said with a sad smile. "And you said no."

"I didn't actually."

"But you did call me a would-be adulteress."

He shook his head. "I didn't mean it like—"

"You did, I think."

He placed his hand on the table very close to hers. "In the eyes of the law you would be, and I just don't want you to have to pay any sort of penalty for . . . You've paid enough, is all I mean. You've been through enough, Charlotte. I would never want to feel that I pressed you in such a tenuous time. I wouldn't want you to regret . . . "

"I have many regrets, Will. Many. Being with you would never be one of them."

He turned his hand up on the table, and she slid hers into it. He looked at her hand as if someone had laid a jewel in his palm. His eyes came up to hers. "You mean the world to me. I want to treat you with care."

"I want to treat you with care, too." A little smile played across her lips. "But not *too* much care. We're not porcelain dolls. At least I'm not."

The color rose in his cheeks as he tugged her toward him onto his lap, their faces close. "Oh dear," she murmured, "have I made you blush?"

"What you've done," he whispered, "is made my heart pound. And not for the first time, by the way."

As they held each other's gaze, Charlotte had a momentary thought of how unlikely this was: she, a well-bred, educated woman of pedigree, sitting on the lap of a chauffeur. But that wasn't what they were at all, really. She was simply human and so was he, and they had found each other in the vast sea of humans—old, young, male, female, cruel, kind. They had found each other in this great and terrifying world. It was something of a miracle.

And so she moved not as a woman of the upper class, nor as an unimpeachable Harvey Girl, but as a human who had finally found her home. She kissed his lips and his warm cheeks and felt the muscles of his back flex under her fingers as he held her closer and closer still.

"Will," she breathed. "Please take me to bed."

He stood, lifting her easily in his arms, and carried her into the other room.

Forty-Four

Early the next morning, as Charlotte glided through the restaurant serving corned beef hash here and stewed prunes there, handing a fallen napkin to its owner with a beneficent smile, she felt like the cat that ate the canary. She wondered giddily if there might be a metaphorical feather or two sticking out of her mouth.

The night with Will had been a revelation.

He had, in fact, treated her with great care. His attention to her—how *she* felt, what *she* wanted—had made her realize that even at his most loving, Simeon's intimate moments with her had been mostly about him. He had playacted a great lover; he had never actually been one.

Will, though . . . he had paid attention not just to her words but also to her subtle reactions to a touch or a kiss. And yet he hadn't treated her like a porcelain doll, either. He had shown her how he felt and what he wanted. She had learned some things!

I do love learning, she thought as she turned away from customers to indulge in a wicked little grin, her insides fluttering at the memory. She hadn't known that she was capable of such reactions— of such pleasure, yes, but more than that, of such joy.

Resetting her lunch tables for dinner, Charlotte felt as relaxed as she could ever remember. It wasn't just the night with Will (though that had left her so limp as to feel positively boneless). It was that her limbs didn't throb as they had at shift's end when she'd first started as a Harvey Girl. In fact, she had noticed in the tub recently as she smoothed soap around her body that there was a sizeable (though not manly!) lump of muscle under the smooth skin of her

upper arms. Her calves didn't ache. Her neck didn't feel as if someone had let the air out of her spine. She was tired, of course, and
ready to change out of her slightly sweaty, heavy white cotton dress
into a light sleeveless one. But such ordinary things aside, Charlotte
felt good.

Almost, dare she say . . . happy. Truly happy.

Yes, her future was still an open question, and Mr. Patrillo could
upset the tentative balance of her life with a word. But he hadn't yet.
Perhaps he'd forgotten her, and she wouldn't have to face his ire when
she told him she would not take part in the Detours. Because she
wouldn't; that was for certain. John Honanie's words rang too true.

After she changed, she and Will would take a walk, and possibly
have dinner together. Actually they would definitely have dinner,
but until now there had been an unspoken agreement that they
would make a pretense of spontaneity. That way it wasn't a date,
only two people who happened to be hungry at the same time. Perhaps now they might begin to be honest about their desire to spend
every waking (and sleeping, she hoped!) minute together.

Two nights ago, she had been sitting on the porch with Will
when Billie and Leif strolled by. Will invited them up, and Charlotte was surprised to learn it wasn't their first visit.

Billie explained, "I didn't tell you because I didn't want you to
feel . . . "

"Forgotten?" said Charlotte.

"You were not forgotten." Will had a way of saying things so quietly and simply that they were unquestionable. The truth needed no
emphasis. Nor did his love for her, which was evident in everything
he did and said.

The comment had been so strangely moving that out of the
corner of her eye, Charlotte had seen Leif's hand alight briefly on
the small of Billie's back. Real love required no grand gestures, she
realized, only gentle constancy.

Had she done enough to show the people she loved that she loved them?

She hoped she was a kind and thoughtful friend, but had she done *enough*? Or would this be a question that dogged her to her deathbed?

Life was fleeting, and death would come whenever it damn well pleased. The last two years had taught her that as the previous twenty never had. *The rich always assume they'll die of old age*, she mused. Well, poverty and violence had set her straight on that score.

As she polished one last water spot off a steak knife, Charlotte resolved to improve and increase her expressions of affection. She would study Billie. Love shone from the girl's pores, for goodness' sake, no doubt taught to her by her parents and that vast gaggle of siblings. Charlotte would study love, and it was a test she intended to pass.

———

That afternoon, Billie finally cut Leif's hair.

"I thought I was going to have to order a pair of scissors from Sears," she told him as she slid her fingers down a curl to straighten it for trimming. They were in the parlor, the only place men were allowed in the women's dorm. Billie had put an old sheet down under Leif's chair to keep little snips of hair from imbedding themselves in the braided wool rug.

"Where did you find these?" He had his eyes closed. Billie could tell he was enjoying having her hands on him, and she had to admit she liked having an excuse to be so close. But it was innocent enough: everyone needed a haircut now and then, and someone had to do it, didn't they? Might as well be her.

"I was talking to Henny about it, and she said, 'Oh, now don't go buying them.'" Billie imitated the upstate New York accent. "'Someone around here must have a pair.' And the next day she handed me these. I think they might be Nora's. They're best pals now."

"That's odd company," said Leif. "They couldn't be more different."

"Well, I'll say one thing. Nora's a lot nicer now that she's got such a good friend. I dropped an egg cup with a half-eaten soft-boiled egg right in the middle of the dining room, and the yolk splattered everywhere. I thought I was in for a tongue-lashing, but she just said, 'These things happen,' and helped me clean it up. I almost fainted dead away!"

"It's easier to be bighearted when you're happy."

Billie ran her fingers through his locks a little more than was absolutely necessary to ensure the cut was even. "Are you happy?" she asked shyly.

Leif laughed. "I'm very happy. You could trim my hair down to the scalp and I'd just sit here and—"

"Jesus!"

Leif opened his eyes and spun around to look at her, but she was staring out the window, a look of horror draining the color from her face.

Forty-Five

Charlotte smiled as she headed out the service entrance toward the dorm, thinking of her self-imposed love exam. She stopped short, however, when her happy gaze took in something so contradictory as to seem almost impossible.

Him.

He was standing in front of the dorm, his head swiveling to scan the area so he could see her approach from any direction. He did not look spruced up as he had back in Topeka. His hair had grown down over his ears, and his beard was patchy and unkempt. His clothing was deeply wrinkled as if by multiple nights of sleeping in them.

No! she thought. *Not now!* Now that she'd finally found true friends and real love.

She froze in her steps for only the briefest moment, but it was long enough for him to catch sight of her across the road. "Charlotte!" he barked.

It was not the pretense of remorse that he'd constructed so carefully back in Topeka. Now his face showed only fury.

She turned and ran.

Back through the service entrance into the dining room. Where to hide?

But then she heard the commotion behind her ("Sir, you can't—") and she dashed past the hotel reception desk.

"Miss Turner!" It was Mr. Patrillo's voice, but she couldn't stop for him. She would stop for no one until she was safe.

She ran through the Rendezvous Room with its ghastly severed animal heads mounted around the upper walls, leaving a wake of grumbled comments from hotel guests—"My word!" and "Goodness me!" and " . . . Harvey Girl!"

From the porch she scanned the Harvey Cars lined up in front, searching for Will, but he wasn't there. *He's sitting on his own porch waiting for me*, she thought. And all she wanted was to get to him. But first she had to lose the predator who now stalked her.

She headed left toward the canyon, thinking she might slip into the constant stream of tourists strolling along the edge of the abyss. But her damned white dress stood out against the tide of colorful garments and the rusty reds of the canyon. She didn't know if he was behind her, but she had to keep running.

Up ahead was the Lookout Studio, and she considered slipping in there, but if he saw her go in, she'd be trapped.

"Charlotte!" His voice came from her left. He must have turned right out of El Tovar and come around the south side of the building, but he had located her now, even if he was still some distance away.

She ran harder down the path, and then she saw her chance.

As sure as she had once been that the infernal hole in the ground would be the death of her, now it would be her refuge.

The canyon would save her.

Down the Bright Angel Trail she went, spinning so fast around the first hairpin turn that she almost ran right into a hiker. "Hey, watch it!" he yelled, but she had no time to apologize. Her heart pounded so hard from fear and exertion that she thought it might leap right out of her chest and drop off the side of the precipitous cliff to her right. She knew she had to stop and catch her breath, but he could be right behind her.

When she felt she might collapse, she saw the tunnel ahead. It wasn't deep, only ten or so feet through an enormous rock outcropping that jutted out over the canyon. Before a hole had been bored through, the old trail had required a death-defying climb around it

on a narrow ledge. On the other side of the tunnel, Charlotte scrab-
bled out onto the ledge on the back side of the rock. If he came
through looking in front of him, he would miss her altogether and
keep running downhill. Then she could climb back onto the trail,
reverse direction up through the tunnel, and head straight to Will.

All she had to do was wait.

As she stood there, muscles quivering, back pressed painfully
against the jagged stone, she saw two women in the distance coming
up the trail from below, one redheaded and one blond. They were
chatting amiably, smiling at one another, and then the blond said
something that made the redhead roar with laughter.

Henny and Nora.

They hadn't spied her yet, too engrossed in their conversation
and each other. Charlotte could only hope either that Simeon
would pass by them before they saw her, or that he hadn't come
down the trail at all.

"Charlotte!" Henny called out, just as Simeon dashed through
the tunnel. He stopped short, his shoes skidding in the dusty gravel,
his head craning around to track her.

And there she was like a bird in a cage. Like a fish in a barrel.

"Charlotte," he growled and moved toward her. "Your hiding
days are over."

"How . . . how did you know . . . "

"One of the Harvey Girls in Topeka. You remember Tildie." He
smiled, proud of having charmed yet another source into revealing
things they knew they shouldn't. "I secretly visited stupid little
Tildie every month until I'd gained her trust. Then I got her to find
out from that oaf of a manager where you'd gone." He took a step
closer. "It was easy."

Throat clenched in a knot of fear, Charlotte couldn't breathe,
much less call for help. She could only stare at the man who would
end her right now on this godforsaken cliff.

The graveyard of the world, George Wharton James had called it. Her graveyard.

Simeon's left foot was so close to the edge that several rocks gave way and tumbled over the side. She never heard them land, just as the author had promised. Simeon paused a moment to adjust his footing. His hair was plastered with sweat, and she could tell that he, too, was terrified. But his terror would not keep him from accomplishing the task at hand, and that was to punish her for leaving him, humiliating him, disobeying him, not once, but twice now.

Well, if she was to die, she had something to say—had always had something to say but had lived in soul-crushing fear of saying it. Now there was no reason not to.

"You are a fool."

His face contorted in confusion, and it occurred to her that it was possibly the most surprising thing he'd ever heard in his life, this man who thought he was smarter than everyone else on the planet.

"You had a wife who adored you, who supported your dreams and left her entire world behind to be with you, something most men would dream of—and you squandered it. Squandered all that love and happiness. And for what? To feel large and powerful when the world showed you that you were small, to beat and bloody your true source of pride. You should have been proud to have me by your side, but you were too stupid—so unbelievably stupid—to see it. And now you have *nothing* when you could have had *everything*."

Billie sped down the trail, hoping desperately that Leif had found Will and they were close behind her. But whether they were or not, she had to get there. She had to help her friend.

She ran through the short tunnel and heard Charlotte's voice. She turned quickly, searching for its location, and saw her friend cornered on the ledge, a man standing motionless with his back to Billie as Charlotte drilled him with the ferocity of her words.

"Charlotte!" Billie called out, uncertain what to do, how to keep the terrifying scene from getting immeasurably worse.

The man startled and spun toward her, kicking up dust and sending small rocks flying out into the canyon. Billie locked eyes on Charlotte, whose face had gone from fury to sorrow and almost . . . was that an apology of sorts?

Suddenly Charlotte scrambled forward between the rock and Simeon.

He grabbed her arm as she tried to pass.

No, thought Billie. *Please, God, no!*

She lunged forward to stop him, but Charlotte wrenched free. The motion destabilized him, and suddenly his arms were windmilling in the air, his face a rictus of terror as he teetered and fell away from them, back, back, back . . .

And down.

Forty-Six

Billie latched on to her friend's arm, the one that Simeon had so recently laid claim to, and for one terrible moment as their eyes met, Charlotte's saucerlike with horror, Billie thought Charlotte might pull away from her, too.

"Charlotte," Billie soothed. "It's me."

Charlotte let herself be guided to the safety of the trail and collapsed into Billie, quaking uncontrollably.

"I've got you," Billie murmured into dust-caked hair. "You're safe now."

The two women sank unsteadily to the ground as Henny and Nora reached them.

"My God." Henny sat down in the dirt and put her arms around both of them.

Nora peered over the edge and muttered, "Holy feckin' Christ, who in the hell was *that?*"

Will and Leif ran down the trail panting, and Will dropped to his knees. Charlotte reached out a hand to clasp his.

"Where is he?" demanded Leif as he prepared to fend off a madman.

"Bloody bugger's gone." Nora tipped her head toward the chasm.

A crowd had gathered, and someone called out to a park ranger.

"Step aside, please. Ma'am, step aside."

Billie turned toward the voice only to find Robert staring down at her. "What on earth?" he demanded.

"Someone fell."

Robert took charge: he commanded bystanders to move away from the scene and ordered a young man to run ahead to the park administration building and inform them of the accident, all while herding Billie, Leif, Will, Nora, Henny, and Charlotte back up the trail.

As the bedraggled group made their way down the service road, rangers ran past them toward the trail.

"Will they find him?" Charlotte asked Robert.

"They'll do their best," he said gently.

———————————

As this involved several of his Harvey Girls, Mr. Patrillo was summoned.

"Your *husband?*" he said to Charlotte once he'd heard all of it.

She nodded. Billie wondered why she didn't lie and say it was an old suitor or some such tale. But it was clear that Charlotte needed to tell the truth. To say it publicly. To confess.

Patrillo glared at her. "You understand this is cause for termination."

Charlotte nodded again.

He shook his head. "I had such hopes for you," he muttered.

Will was standing behind Charlotte's chair. "Is it any wonder she lied? That animal tracked her across half the country. She nearly lost her life today, and all you can think of are your staffing needs?"

"You knew."

"I did."

"Now you're *both* fired," said Patrillo. His gaze scanned the others in the room. "Did any of the rest of you know she was married?"

Billie was about to admit that she did, but hesitated because she knew Leif would follow suit. Then Charlotte drilled her with such a fierce look, Billie stayed quiet.

Patrillo turned back to Will and Charlotte. "You have twenty-four hours."

"We'll need to get the Williams police up here to take statements," said Mr. Eakin, the park superintendent. "They can't leave before that's done."

"Fine. Everybody better show up at work tomorrow," Patrillo warned them. "Except you two. You start packing your bags."

Everyone stood up to go, but Robert pulled Billie aside. "Are you okay?" he murmured.

She was not in any way okay; she had watched as her friend was nearly murdered and a man had fallen to his death, but she knew that if she gave into her feelings now, it would keep her from what she would need to do in the coming days. She nodded. "Robert—"

"Yes?" The hope in his eyes pained her.

"Thank you for taking charge like you did and getting us all out of there safely."

He stiffened. "That's my job."

"Of course. You did it well, and I'm grateful."

He gazed at her a moment. "Is he your new beau?"

"Leif? No, we're just good friends."

He made a skeptical little grunt and turned back to Superintendent Eakin. "I'll go and help with retrieval, sir."

Body retrieval.

Billie hurried after the others.

Henny was pale as a sheet and said her head was throbbing. The hike out of the canyon had been so hot and then . . .

"You need water," said Nora, and walked her back toward the dorm.

Except for answering Eakin's and Patrillo's questions, Charlotte had been mute. Now that Nora and Henny were out of earshot, she turned to Billie and Leif, eyes blazing. "You will not admit that you knew."

"The police—"

"Absolutely not. A man died today." Charlotte bit her lip to keep from crying. "Will has lost his living. I will not be the cause of any more destruction. Promise me. Both of you promise me *this minute*."

"She's right," said Will. "It won't help her case, and it certainly won't help yours."

Billie looked at Leif. He would follow her lead, and he'd have nowhere to go if he were fired. "I promise," she told them.

"Me, too," said Leif.

"Why don't we all go back to my cabin," said Will, "and figure out what to do."

Charlotte hesitated. "Is it safe for Billie and Leif to be seen with us, now that we've been fired?"

"Wherever you go, I'm going with you!" said Billie.

"She's your roommate, Charlotte," said Will, "and we were all there. I believe that horse has left the barn."

Forty-Seven

"*How did you know where* I was?" Charlotte asked Billie as Will put the kettle on. Though it was long past dinnertime, tea was all anyone could imagine wanting.

"I saw him from the parlor window and sent Leif to get Will," explained Billie. "Then you came out from the restaurant, and I ran after the both of you."

Charlotte looked down at her hands. "I'm so sorry to put you all through this."

"None of it was your fault," said Will.

"I'm the reason he's . . . "

Mr. Eakin had questioned her quite plainly: "Did you push him?"

Charlotte wasn't sure. Had pulling away from him involved an inadvertent push of some kind? She had to admit, if only to herself, that she had often wished him dead. But she had never meant to be the means of his death.

"Will's right," said Billie. "You're not at all to blame."

"You're just saying that because you're my friends."

"I'm not your friend." Leif had been silent until now, and they all turned to him in surprise. "I barely know you. But having taken a few punches in the face from that fellow back in Topeka, I'm quite certain that if he wanted to come here and hurt you or worse, that's exactly what he would've done, and without a moment's regret."

Charlotte let her gaze rest on the young man across the table. "Thank you," she whispered.

As Will poured the tea into chipped ceramic mugs, quiet descended on them, and the sounds of Grand Canyon Village—sounds that all of them would soon no longer hear—filtered in the windows: Harvey Cars returning to the garage, tourists calling to one another, a mule braying in the mule barn. The obvious question floated about the room: Where would they go?

"Boston?" Billie asked Charlotte, breaking the silence.

"I think it's best."

"What about you?" Leif asked Will.

"Back to the farm," he said. "It's time I checked on things anyway." He glanced at Charlotte, and she nodded.

"I'm hungry," said Leif. "Shall I get us some food?" No one was hungry. "Billie, will you come with me?"

"I thought it was no girls in the dorm," Billie said peevishly. What was it with teenage boys and their always-rumbling stomachs? They'd ask for a sandwich at their own funerals if they could.

"You can wait outside," he said. "Come on."

She had never known him to be so insistent. Perhaps there was something he had to say that he didn't want the others to hear. As she rose, she gave Charlotte's hand a squeeze.

When they'd walked far enough away, Leif said, "We need to leave them be."

"What? Why?"

"Because this is their last night together."

"But . . . " Billie felt tears well in her eyes. "It's my last night with her, too."

"Billie, they're in love."

She swiped at the drops on her cheeks. "How do you know?"

"All you have to do is look at them."

Billie started to cry in earnest then, the need to keep herself to-gether having melted away now that everything was over: the abject terror of those moments that had seemed like years, the shocking death, her dear friend soon to be gone from her life, possibly forever.

How would she go on here as if none of this had happened?

How would she pour the coffee and serve the tapioca and polish the silver like it was just another day as a Harvey Girl?

Leif put his arms around her and said nothing as she sobbed. He didn't try to soothe away her feelings or promise that everything would be okay. Leif, she knew, had plenty of experience in the area of life not being okay.

Her crying slowed. Leif used the cuff of his shirt to wipe her eyes and her nose. "You're going home, aren't you?" he said.

"I really don't know. But I don't think I can stay here. I'll be reminded of that horrible scene every single day."

He nodded. He'd known the answer before he'd asked the question.

"Leif." She gripped him hard around the waist and gave him a little shake. "Leif!"

He pulled away from her. "I'll be all right," he said.

"I don't want you to be all right!"

He gave her a sad smile. "No?"

"Wherever I go, I want you with me."

Charlotte looked down at her uniform. It was caked with dust and smelled terrible. *She* smelled terrible: sweaty and sticky with the terror that had leaked from her pores.

"I need to bathe."

"I could draw you a bath."

"Yes, but then I'd have to put this back on again."

He nodded and started to collect cups filled with the tea that had gone cold. "You're going back to the dorm then."

"I don't want to do that, either."

He looked over at her.

She reached out and laid her hand on his. "I don't want to miss a moment with you."

He turned his hand palm up and held hers. "You could stay here."

"Not to . . . I couldn't after . . . "

"Of course not. I'll sleep on the couch."

Charlotte looked at the couch. It was a love seat; he'd barely fit. "Or you could lie next to me."

"Is that what you want?"

"Is it what you want?"

"The only thing I've wanted since I saw you on that trail is to hold you."

He drew her a bath in the small claw-foot tub and delivered a clean set of his pajamas when she was neck-deep in water. He took her uniform, scrubbed it in the sink, wrung it out, and spread it over a chair to dry.

When Charlotte emerged from the bathroom with his light blue pajamas puddled around her feet, her dark hair in wet waves, Will had set out a plate of toasted bread.

She picked up a piece. "I've eaten more toast in these last four months than I have in my entire life."

"Not quite as good as French pastries?"

"I think I actually prefer it." She took a bite, and a few crumbs sprinkled onto her chin.

He reached over and gently brushed them away with his thumb. Suddenly tears sprang to her eyes. "What is it?" he whispered.

"One moment I'm here with you, and I'm so grateful that he's gone. Then I feel terrible for being glad that he died in such an awful way." Her throat clenched around her words. "I hated him, but I never meant to . . . "

He laid his hand on her shoulder. "Of course you didn't. You were only defending yourself. What happened was his own fault."

"But I benefit enormously." She dropped the toast onto the plate and gazed at his beautiful clock.

"Being relieved that you're no longer in danger doesn't make you a bad person, Charlotte."

"I caused the death of someone I once loved, Will. And I caused a scene of horror that Billie can never unsee. When I made the decision to bolt for freedom, I didn't think it would work. I thought she would watch me die." The idea of saddling her dear young friend with such a gruesome image made her tears flow. "But I had to try, Will. Even though I thought I was doomed, I couldn't let my last act on this earth be acquiescence."

The panic of that moment came back to her as clearly as if it were still happening. "I thought I would never see you again," she sobbed, "and you'd have to carry around another ghost for the rest of your life!"

Will pulled her toward him and held her against his broad chest. When her sobs finally quieted, he whispered, "You don't have to go to Boston. We could be together. You could come to the farm with me."

She picked her head up to gaze into those dark eyes that had once so frightened her. "I want to be with you, Will—I want that more than anything. But I have to go home. This is my chance to reconcile with them, and if I put it off, it will only make it harder."

"I'll wait for you, then."

She put her hand to his cheek. "Please don't. I don't know how long it will take. I just don't know what will happen. It's possible that I'll choose to stay. Also I . . . I need to think before I leap wholesale into something else, with someone else. I've made so many mistakes, Will. I don't trust myself. I need to try and trust myself again. I hope you can understand."

He nodded. "I love you, Charlotte. That won't change. But I won't wait."

―――――――――

Leif went to the men's dorm and picked up a couple of his sweaters. He and Billie walked west along the rim until they came to

Maricopa Point. From there they could look back across an inlet of the canyon and see the lights of El Tovar twinkling in the distance.

"I'll miss it," she said.

"Me, too."

"Maybe we'll be back someday."

"We have to figure out where we're going before we make plans to return."

They lay on their backs on the sun-heated rock and looked up at a sky that was noisy with stars. They talked, Billie cried, and Leif shed some tears, too, thinking about his own mother's horrific death.

"Leif, I know you're not Catholic, but you were raised to pray, weren't you?"

"I stopped after my father died. Mine didn't seem to work."

"Would you . . . would it be all right if we prayed to ask God what to do next?"

He clasped her hand. "I'll follow your lead."

They prayed in thanksgiving for Charlotte's courage in the face of such evil, and that she had not been called to heaven so soon. Then they prayed for guidance in the days to come.

"One more thing," said Leif. "Thank you for bringing Billie into my life. She is smart and fierce and beautiful inside and out. I'll try always to be worthy of her."

"Fierce?" said Billie.

He kissed her temple. "In the very best way."

They curled together for warmth as the night air cooled the canyon, and eventually drifted to sleep.

By sunrise, they had a plan.

Forty-Eight

Mae Parnell dropped a plateful of toast when Billie came in early that morning. She stepped over the mess and pulled Billie into a tight hug against her soft form. "I've been so worried about you!"

"I'm sorry I didn't come back to the dorm last night."

Mae released her and said, "Oh, I didn't care about that. I knew you were probably with Charlotte. But with all you've been through, goodness, you must be ready to faint!"

Billie collapsed onto a chair. "Actually I wasn't with Charlotte the whole time."

Mae bent down to pick up the broken plate and scattered pieces of toast. "You were with that kitchen boy." She heaved the detritus deftly into the trash bin.

"Leif. He's a good man."

"And you love him?"

Billie almost started to explain that while, yes, she did love him, it was a wider kind of love than all that sheik business, and they hadn't really defined what it was or what it could lead to. But none of that was going to get her Mae's help, which was what she needed at the moment.

"I do," she said. "I love him eternally."

Mae put her hand to her chest and heaved a great sigh.

"But I can't stay here." Billie felt herself tear up. "I can't stop seeing it."

Mae sat down in the chair next to Billie and patted her knee. "Of course you can't."

"Charlotte almost died. She was truly just inches away . . ." Billie put her hands to her face and began to cry, and while the tears were real, she also knew they would aid her cause. Mae stroked her hair, and it felt like her own mother doing it, which made her cry even harder.

"There, now," soothed Mae. "We'll get you out of here."

Billie inhaled a sniffle and wiped her nose on the shoulder of her wrinkled dress. "I need to keep working, though. My family needs the money, and Fred Harvey pays better than anything I could get at home."

"If that's what you want, it's easy enough to get yourself transferred to another Harvey House. Do you have one in mind?"

"I thought maybe the Escalante at Ash Fork." It was near Will's farm; Billie and Leif had decided he would need their company. "But what about Leif? I can't just leave him here."

Mae pursed her lips in thought. "Mr. Patrillo doesn't like complications, so he'll be happy to have this whole episode behind him. He won't mind seeing the backs of you two."

"But how can we get him to send us both to the same place?"

"You leave that to me."

Charlotte barely slept, and when she did, she was right back on that ledge, cornered by Simeon. Or watching him fall.

She woke with a start to find the room lit by pale light, a breeze fluttering the thin white curtains. Will's arm was across her waist, and she was clutching it like a life raft.

"You're safe," he whispered. It was a phrase he'd repeated often during the night.

She turned toward him, into him, and he corralled her against him, their bodies molding to accommodate each other as if they'd been formed that way.

"You're the kindest man I've ever met," she murmured.

"And you're the most surprising woman I've ever met."

"Yes, well, I'm a bit less exciting now that I'm no longer on the lam and using an alias."

"I didn't say *exciting*, although you are that, too. I said *surprising*."

"That such a smart woman could be so stupid?" she said ruefully.

He sighed. "You really do need that time to learn to trust yourself, don't you?"

"Clearly. But I'm interested to know what you think is so surprising about me."

"How much you care about people who are so different from you, even though you weren't raised with any notion of the plight of others. John and Ruth, Billie, even me. That first trip to Cameron, the talk we had on the way home—I could feel you absorbing me."

"I could feel you absorbing me, too. But gently, without intruding. Just listening so carefully."

"You fascinated me."

She pulled away and leaned up to face him, gazing into those dark eyes for a long moment. "Are you going to be all right without me?"

He ran a finger along a lock of her hair and tucked it behind her ear. "Yes," he said. "Are you?"

"I aspire to be. Also to not hate myself or live with bitterness." She smiled sadly. "'Without you' will be the hardest part."

It didn't take Charlotte long to pack the battered suitcase with the gold monogram. The only things she put in it were her Navajo blanket and a couple of changes of clothes for the three-day trip to Boston. Her family would be horrified to see what was now her best dress. A day with her mother's favorite seamstress would surely be scheduled within minutes of her arrival.

"Alva, would you like these?" she said, holding up her few remaining dresses and her winter coat in the girl's doorway. "I think we're about the same size."

Alva didn't say anything for a moment, and Charlotte was certain an unpleasant comment was about to come her way.

But Alva reached for the clothes and said, "Thank you. That's very kind of you."

"Oh. Well, good. I'm glad they'll get some use."

"I'll be proud to wear them, Charlotte. After all you've been through, you're a bit of a hero to me and the girls."

"Oh dear, I'm not . . . Do people know about . . . all that?"

"Of course we do. Word spreads, and a Harvey House is the smallest small town there is. We all know someone—an aunt or a neighbor or a friend." Alva gave her a meaningful look. "He got what he deserved."

———————————

Questioning by the police that afternoon took surprisingly little time. They weren't interested in any of the history—that Simeon had physically assaulted Charlotte for years, or that he'd gotten into a fistfight with Leif over it back in Topeka. They didn't care about the why, only the how.

Charlotte repeated what she'd told the park superintendent, that she had wrenched her arm away when he'd grabbed her. With Billie, Henny, and Nora all separately corroborating that Simeon had cornered her, and she had been trying only to escape, the death was quickly ruled accidental.

At the Hopi House, Charlotte went to the register holding a squash blossom necklace that was smaller than most, almost dainty with its tiny silver beading and lovely turquoise pendant.

"Hello, Ruth," she said.

"Charlotte!" The surprise on the young woman's face made it

clear that she, too, had heard the news. "I'm so glad that you are . . . that you . . . "

"Lived," said Charlotte.

"Yes!"

"Thank you." Charlotte laid a hand on the young woman's arm. "And thank you for your friendship these last few months. Being with you and learning all that you taught me was a bright spot in the midst of my worries." Charlotte showed her the necklace. "I've had my eye on this. It will be the perfect memento of our time together."

Once it was rung up, Ruth came around to help with the clasp. Then she gave Charlotte a brief hug and whispered, "I will remember you."

"And I you, my friend."

Later, Charlotte dropped a postcard into the mailbox addressed to John Honanie at the Cameron Trading Post. It said, "I apologize. You were right." She signed it "Small Boston Lady."

The train sat on the tracks huffing to itself like a hibernating dragon. Passengers arriving thrilled and wide-eyed had finished their descent to the platform; those starting to board were happy, filled with the wonder of the place, and a little tired. Some would be dozing even before the train rounded the great wide bend and headed south to Williams.

Billie and Leif stood with Charlotte and Will as they waited to board. Once they got to Williams, Will would take a train west one stop to Ash Fork. Charlotte would take the first of several trains east toward Boston.

"You'll write to me?" Billie said to Charlotte.

"Of course. And you'll write back. I know you're a good letter writer."

"I'll tell you everything."

Charlotte smiled. "And I'll tell *you* everything, though I'm sure my letters will be much less interesting than yours will be."

Billie's eyes went shiny. "Whatever you have to say, I want to hear it. Even if it's bossy."

Charlotte felt her own eyes fill, too. "Dear girl," she murmured, and gave Billie one last hug.

Then Billie hugged Will. "We'll be out to see you soon," she whispered. "We're working on a plan."

"I have every faith in it."

Leif shook the older man's hand. He went to shake Charlotte's, but she used it to pull him in. "You saved my life," she told him. "A handshake doesn't feel quite right."

Billie laughed through her tears. "Didn't you hear? She's a hugger now."

As Charlotte and Will turned to climb aboard, someone called out, "Wait!"

It was Henny. Followed closely by Nora and a small stream of women in white cotton dresses with little black bow ties, interspersed with men wearing Harvey Car caps.

Charlotte gave Henny a hug, and she and Will ascended the steps. At the top, they turned to wave, and the small crowd waved back and called out good wishes.

Billie and Charlotte exchanged one last glance before Charlotte followed Will into the car. As the train began to chug back down the track, slowly picking up speed, each woman wondered if she'd ever see the other again.

Part 2
1996

Forty-Nine

Billie had insisted on taking the train from Williams.

"Be cheaper if I drove," the girl had said. "Route 64 goes straight to Grand Canyon Village and takes a lot less time. Not like there are any stoplights."

They had chuckled over that. No stoplights. Barely even a road to cross.

"I'll pay for it," said Billie.

"I didn't mean it like that, Grandy," said the girl. A nickname from her first grandchild. All the little ones had called her Grandy ever since.

The girl touched her arm. Sweet as pie, she was. Whoever she was.

She looked to be in her thirties and had long silky brown hair. Like . . . her mother. Yes, that was it. Freddie had married a Hopi girl. This was one of their brood. But what was her name? *Come on, now. Your own grandchild.*

"Carrie," said the girl.

"Pardon?"

"I'm Carrie."

Still didn't sound completely familiar, more like a few notes from a toe-tapping song she'd danced to a long time ago.

"It's a nickname for Charlotte," the girl prompted.

"Oh! Yes, of course!"

The girl laughed. "*That* you remember."

It was a marvel to Billie what she could remember. And what she could forget. The doctor had given her the news about six months ago.

"You mean senile," she'd said.

He'd smiled uncomfortably. "We don't use that term anymore."

Maybe not, she'd thought. *But it doesn't care what you call it, now does it? It doesn't care about you or me or anyone else on God's green earth. All it wants to do is eat my brain.*

They leave Carrie's car in the parking lot in Williams—a lot that certainly wasn't there seventy years ago when Billie first came through. Back then, whoever was rich enough to own a car just parked it along Railroad Avenue, often with the keys left right in the ignition.

The Grand Canyon Express is sleek and clean with windows that frame the arid Arizona landscape, coarse grasses sprouting from rusty-red soil dotted with ponderosa pines. And quiet—there's so much less noise than the steam engines she rode across the Southwest all those years ago.

Billie settles back in her seat. It's sixty-five miles to the end of the line, and even with no stops it will take over two hours to get there. It will give her time to think . . . and to remember. She needs to retrieve those memories before she faces the place again.

One last time.

"Happy birthday, Grandy," Carrie says. "Is this what you wanted?"

"It's exactly what I wanted."

"I know you were a Harvey Girl at the Grand Canyon, but I don't think I ever heard how you got there."

She smiles. "That's a long story."

"We've got some time."

She has to think.

Think, for goodness' sake!

The older the memory, the more likely you are to keep it, she reminds herself. It's the newer things that give her the most trouble. She gazes out the window and watches the scrim of pines against a sky so blue it nearly hums.

"It goes by fast," she says.

"The scenery?" asks Carrie.

"All of it. Everything."

Fifty

She's never talked this much in her life. The train speeds along, and so does her mouth. Every time she thinks she can't remember one more thing, another scene tumbles into her mind's eye like a key into a lock, *click*, and there it is.

The girl asks good questions.

Grandchild . . . Freddie's girl . . . Carrie!

Billie repeats the name in her head three times as she taps the back of her hand. *Carrie, Carrie, Carrie.* For some reason this seems to help.

"We're almost there," Carrie says now, and Billie can feel the train's engine ease, the effort needed to pull itself along releasing, slowing, surrendering to its terminus.

"Does it look the same?" Carrie asks as buildings come into view, many more of them than Billie remembered. But the depot building—that hasn't changed a bit. Still looks just like an oversized Lincoln Log project.

"Some of it does, some of it doesn't. But it's been seventy years. My brain might be playing tricks on me."

"Your brain did just fine telling me the first part of the story!"

Billie smiles. "It's hard to forget, even for me."

"How did you feel when you first got here?"

She'd stepped off the train with Maw's tapestry bag, a dry wind blowing with a strange mix of smells: mules and laundry soap and pine. Tired, scared.

And so very far from home.

———

"Are you sure you're up for this?" Carrie asks as they climb the steep road to El Tovar.

"My legs work just fine," Billie says, lengthening her stride a little to prove it. "It's the noodle that doesn't always keep up."

And there it is, the grand hotel, just as she remembers. Billie can almost see Mr. Patrillo standing on the front porch, making sure she doesn't come in through the guest entrance again.

Let him stand there. Billie's not ready to go in anyway. She wants to see the canyon.

The beauty—oh, the beauty of it! Even now she can feel that hunger to hike down into it, touching all the stripes, the layers of history as she descends. If she had stayed longer than four short months, would she have gotten used to it? Would it have become old hat?

Oh, yes, that thing, I barely even see it anymore.

No, she can't imagine anyone feeling that way.

As they make their way along the rim path, Carrie urging her to continue the story, Billie notices all the improvements they've made in the seventy years since she last laid eyes on the place. There are many more buildings, but most of the old ones are still here, too. They pass the Lookout Studio with its rocky exterior made to look like a part of the cliff wall.

"Do you mind if I take your arm?" Carrie asks. "I really don't like heights."

Billie holds her elbow out, knowing full well it's to keep her from falling down. Maybe she isn't as spry as she once was, but she can still hike like a sixty-year-old.

"I can't believe you had a park ranger boyfriend," says Carrie.

Billie smiles. "He was handsome in that uniform."

"But not as handsome as Farfar."

"And nowhere near as nice."

As they slowly stroll the mile and a half out to Maricopa Point,

Billie continues the tale. When they arrive, they sit down on the rock outcropping overlooking the canyon.

"I can imagine you and Farfar lying right here," says Carrie.

"The nights can be chilly here even in August, but your grandfather had gotten us a couple of sweaters, so we weren't cold."

Carrie smiles. "You snuggled."

Billie laughs. "We were a couple of snugglers, weren't we?" How she misses that man. It's been five years now, but she knows she'll long for his arms around her till the day she catches up to him.

"And you made your plan."

"We did. As soon as we woke, I went straight to the only person I knew would help."

"Don't tell me . . . " Carrie gazes out across the canyon in thought. Then her expression goes wide with delight. "Mae Parnell!"

"You got it, smarty. She was the one who thought of telling Mr. Patrillo we were cousins. 'You look just alike with all that blond hair,' she said, 'and you're practically a couple of giants!' That woman was on the side of love, even if you had to fib a little." Mae had gone to Patrillo herself, telling him quite truthfully she was worried that if Billie continued to live and work so close to the terrifying scene she had witnessed, she might break down in front of the guests.

"Can't have that," says Carrie.

"Certainly not. Crying in front of patrons is strictly against the Harvey standard."

As Billie had requested, Mae had suggested that Patrillo send them to Fred Harvey's Escalante Hotel in Ash Fork.

"Near the farm!" says Carrie. "Is that how you and Farfar started working for Great Uncle Will?"

"Oh, I never worked for Will."

"But I thought . . . "

"Your grandfather went to the farm when I left the Escalante."

"Wait, you *left* him there?"

Billie gingerly pushes herself up and slowly rises to stand. "Come on, doll, we don't want to miss why we came."

Carrie gets up and takes her grandmother's arm again. "But you told him you always wanted the two of you to be together!"

"Listen. I know I said that, and I meant it. But after six months at the Escalante, things between your grandfather and me were getting a bit . . . heated," she says with a sly smile.

The girl's eyebrows go up in mock shock. "Grandy!"

"Farfar wanted to marry me, but I was sixteen years old. I wasn't ready. As a Harvey Girl with a free train ticket wherever I wanted, I had the whole Southwest at my feet. So, every six months or a year, I moved to a different hotel, a different town, sometimes a different state. I worked at the Alvarado in Albuquerque; the Casa del Desierto in Barstow, California; the Cardenas in Trinidad, Colorado; and La Posada in Winslow, Arizona."

"You went from a weepy little homebody to a great traveler!"

"Oh, I was still a homebody. The first thing we did when we left here was head straight for Table Rock."

Carrie's eyes twinkle mischievously. "You took a boy home?"

Billie smiles. "You can imagine the looks on my parents' faces. I explained that we were just friends, but my maw saw through that quick as a fortune teller. She made sure there were always a couple of siblings with us wherever we went. Of course, my brothers were in awe of him, and my sisters were all sweet on him inside of an hour."

"Was he overwhelmed by your enormous family after living alone so long?"

"Oh, Lord, no, he was like a pig in slop! Should have seen him chopping firewood for my da and hauling laundry baskets for my maw. Tripping over himself to make them love him as much as he loved them." Billie's heart fills with the memory of it. "That was the first time he asked me to marry him. But I said no, you just want to marry my family."

"Heartbreaker."

"It was true! I knew he loved me, but we were too young. Besides, Maw didn't like that he wasn't Catholic."

"What about your da?"

Billie laughs. "The man nearly had to be dragged to church every Sunday. He saw how hard Farfar worked and how much respect he had for me and all of the family, and he said, 'He's a braw laddie. Whit's fer ye'll no go by ye.'"

"I'm going to need a translation."

"He's a good man, and if it's meant to be, it'll be."

"What made you finally say yes? What was it—four years after you'd met?"

"Yes, it was 1930. He was managing the farm by then, and he already had my brothers Angus and Duncan working for him. Maw had finally given up caring that he wasn't Catholic. I was serving at the new Harvey House in Winslow—La Posada—and it was a relatively quick train ride to Ash Fork, so I visited on my days off. Peigi was working with me by then—all my sisters became Harvey Girls at some point. Maw and Da eventually came to live on the farm when the brick factory closed. Little by little, the MacTavishes all became southwesterners.

"Anyway, one day Farfar just said, 'I miss you.' Your grandfather was never one to put his own needs ahead of anyone else's, so I recognized it for what it was."

"Pleading?"

"More like 'fish or cut bait.' I gave Fred Harvey my notice the next day."

"*Fred Harvey* Fred Harvey?"

"Goodness, child, the man had been dead almost thirty years by then. But Harvey Girls always said 'I work for Fred Harvey' till the day the company was sold in the 1960s."

They climb the steps onto the El Tovar porch and head through what used to be known as the Rendezvous Room, now just the lobby. It looks almost the same, with its log cabin walls and mounted heads of bison, moose, and deer. They pass by the registration desk where the old built-in key cubbies still line the back wall.

When they get to the restaurant, Billie stands for a moment to gaze at the place she worked for four of the most pivotal months of her life. There are no Harvey Girls in their spotless white uniforms and little black bow ties—in fact, there are even a couple of male waiters. But other than that, it's much the same.

As the hostess leads them to their table, Carrie breaks her grandmother's reverie with a question. "But where did Great Aunt Charlotte go after she left here?"

"Well, doll, why don't you ask her yourself?"

There at the best table in the house, with the closest view of the canyon, sits Charlotte Crowninshield Lister (Turner) Rosser. Naturally, she has chosen a chair with her back to the window.

Fifty-One

Charlotte's squash blossom necklace catches the light as she struggles to rise. At ninety-two, she's never been quite as physically strong again as she was seventy years ago in this very room. There is a man next to her, and he quickly gets up to help her. His presence has no meaning to Billie. Only Charlotte's does.

Wordlessly the two women embrace.

"You're still a hugger," Billie whispers in her ear.

"And you're still my honorary younger sister."

When they settle themselves around the table, Billie asks, "How was your trip? You came from . . . " She trails off as she realizes she's not sure.

"I flew in from Boston."

That's not right. Billie is certain that Charlotte left the East Coast long ago. "But you and Will live in . . . in LA. You're a professor."

"I went back to Boston thirty years ago, after Will passed," Charlotte says gently. "I wanted to spend time with my brother, Oliver, and his family. I taught at Wellesley College until I retired. You came and visited a couple of times."

Billie can't remember those trips. All she can focus on is "after Will passed." She knows Will is gone, or at least she knows it somewhere in the recesses of the haunted house that is her brain now. But it hits her like a gut punch, even so. That wonderful, kind, generous man is no longer with them. She feels her eyes go shiny with tears. Embarrassed, she smiles and says, "And who's this fine young fellow?"

"This is my grandson Ted."

"Olivia's boy?"

"Not exactly a boy anymore, Aunt Billie," says the man with a smile. "But at forty, I'll take the compliment."

"Oh dear," says Billie. "I'm sorry, I—"

"No need to be sorry. I'm just glad to see you, Auntie. I have fond memories of visiting you and all the Gunnarssons at the farm when I was young. I should get over to Prescott more often. It's only an hour and a half away."

Prescott? Oh, yes. The kids moved her down to be closer to them when Leif died. She had a little house there . . . but that's not where she lives now . . .

"I heard you moved to Flagstaff," Carrie says to Ted, tucking a strand of her long silky brown hair behind her ear. "Great town. A little different from LA."

"Little bit." His dark eyes twinkle just like his grandfather's once did. "My grandmother tells me you're teaching high school history. I'm in the history department at NAU. I'd love to hear about your curriculum sometime."

Is this flirting? Billie glances at Charlotte, who meets her eye at just the same moment.

A waitress approaches wearing a white button-down shirt, black pants, and a black apron tied around her waist. There's a little fleck of something on her sleeve that looks like ketchup.

"Welcome to El Tovar," she says. "Can I offer you all something to drink?"

They order their beverages—iced tea and hot tea and two coffees—and the woman goes off to fetch them. Billie and Charlotte both start to giggle.

"I see the cup code has gone the way of the dodo," says Charlotte.

"Did you catch the spot on her sleeve?" says Billie.

"And that outfit. At least the color palette hasn't changed."

"Needs a black bow tie, if you ask me."

"Harvey Girls still," Carrie says to Ted. She turns to Charlotte. "Which brings me to my first question. Grandy has been telling me all about your time in Topeka and here at the Grand Canyon, but where did you go when you left?"

"To Boston. I needed to reconnect with my family. I stayed for a year, but I was always longing to come back to the West."

Billie remembers the letters she received every week from Charlotte about life in the unfathomably big city of Boston. The fraught tea parties and ghastly galas she was forced to attend, keeping up the ruse of her Dutch baron husband tragically drowned in the Baltic Sea. Her ongoing and seemingly fruitless efforts to convince her parents to let her return to college, and then the flurry of applications she sent once she finally succeeded in wearing them down. The way her heart ached every day missing her friends. Missing Will.

Charlotte got into every college she applied to. She chose the University of Southern California in Los Angeles. When Billie wrote and asked her why that one, Charlotte responded simply: *It's the best school on the Santa Fe Railway, and Winnie's there.*

Billie still has those letters. Somewhere. At least she thinks she does.

Will left the farm in Leif's capable hands and moved to nearby Hollywood where he worked as Gertrude Turner's chauffeur. He and Charlotte married quickly and spent summers at the farm. By the time Charlotte graduated, however, it was clear that sheep were not for her . . . though she did think the lambs were cute.

Will did not make the same mistake twice.

"I got my degree at USC," Charlotte tells Carrie, "stayed for a doctorate, and taught sociology there for many years. We raised our daughter, Ted's mother, there. Will was a train ride away from the farm, so he could go and help out when needed. He made your grandfather a co-owner—they had a great partnership."

The drinks come; they order their lunch. They catch up on where all the children and grandchildren are. It's a good refresher for Billie, though she somehow knows she'll lose it all again before she gets home. Or not home, exactly, but that new place.

She finds herself drifting while the others talk, and she gazes around the room. There's Henny over there with her smooth skin and wide smile, carrying a tray full of fruit cups. There's Nora, ordering that waitress with the spot on her sleeve to go get a fresh uniform. There's Will standing by the entrance in his Harvey Car cap. And there's Leif peeking out from the kitchen, looking straight at Billie with those teacup-crackle eyes . . .

This world is just as present to her as the "real" one. Even more so these days.

Soon enough the lunch plates are cleared, and Billie thinks it's time to go. But suddenly that pants-wearing waitress is before her with a beautiful thick slice of chocolate cake lit by a small pink candle. "Happy birthday!" they all say.

Billie is frozen in confusion. Carrie lays a hand on her arm. "It's today, Grandy. This trip is the only present you wanted, remember?"

Billie blinks at her a moment. No, she doesn't remember, but she'll go with it. What choice does she have? She has only one question. "How old am I?"

"Eighty-six."

Billie bursts out laughing. "I'm *what*?"

Carrie grins. "No lie!"

Billie shakes her head, still chuckling. "If you say so . . . "

"The last time I celebrated your birthday with you, you were sixteen," says Charlotte. "I'll bet you remember that."

"Of course I do. I danced with a movie star because of you." She sighs. "Boy, that was some party. Thank you again for that."

Charlotte's gaze is full of warmth. "You're welcome."

They all share the rich cake, and when the bill comes, Carrie and Ted squabble good-naturedly over who gets to pay it. Carrie wins, but Ted insists on leaving the tip.

"A big one," says Charlotte.

"Oh, I know," he assures her. "I was raised to be an over-tipper, remember?"

"Waiting tables is hard work," Charlotte chides him, "and she might have a family to feed."

"She'll be happy with this, Gran, I promise."

None of them seem to want the lunch to end. When it does, Ted will drive them all back to Williams, where Carrie's car is. Carrie and Billie will return to Prescott, and Charlotte will go with Ted to Flagstaff. In a couple of days, she'll fly back to Boston.

The four of them linger over their coffee and tea, stretching their time together—Billie and Charlotte's last visit—as long as possible.

When they finally rise and start to make their way toward the lobby, Billie stops and looks back one last time. Leif is standing right there in his brimless white hat.

Goodbye for now, she thinks. *I'll be with you soon.*

———

"Why don't you two go and get the car," Charlotte says when they step out into the afternoon brightness of the porch. "Billie and I will wait here."

The two women sit in the rocking chairs they were never allowed to use as Harvey Girls.

"I don't think of it often," says Charlotte, "but when I do remember that day, all I can see is the horror on your face thinking you were about to watch me die."

"It was the scaredest I've ever been in my life."

"I'm sorry I put you through that."

"You didn't put me through anything, Charlotte. *He* did."

They haven't spoken his name aloud to each other since it happened. There's never been any need; that one pronoun said with contempt was always enough.

His body was never found. The rangers surmised it had fallen into some deep crevasse. As he had long been estranged from his family, and Charlotte was his next of kin, once the search was called off, no further action had been taken. No funeral or memorial. No words at all for a man who had loved words—mainly his own—more than anything.

"Have you heard from Henny recently?" Billie asks.

Charlotte doesn't answer for a moment, only lays her hand gently on Billie's arm. "She worked for the Red Cross during World War II. People weren't vacationing much during wartime, so business slowed here. She and Nora joined up together."

"Yes, of course." Billie shakes her head, frustrated for the umpteenth time with her faulty wiring. But what happened to them? She's too embarrassed to ask.

Charlotte doesn't wait for the question she knows is there. "They were in a clubmobile near the front line, serving food and bringing necessary items to soldiers. Their truck hit a land mine. They died together and are buried in France."

Perhaps it's not the fault of her failing memory; perhaps she had just wanted to forget. Billie sighs. "They were very close."

"Yes," says Charlotte. "They had each other."

Ted's car pulls up in front of El Tovar, and they can see their grandchildren talking animatedly, laughing at some shared joke.

"Is he married?" Billie asks.

"Divorced. What about her?"

"Single."

They grin at each other like schoolgirls. "Wouldn't it be something?" says Billie.

"It would be absolutely wonderful."

They stand—Charlotte needs a little help, and Billie gives her a hand—but before they reach the stairs, arms still hooked, Billie stops. She needs one more moment alone with her friend.

"You know my mind is going. They've got me in that place."

"Memory care. Yes, Carrie told me when she called."

"I just want you to know that no matter what, even when I don't know my own name, I will remember you, Charlotte."

"And I'll remember you, Billie. Deep in our hearts we're still those girls."

"Harvey Girls."

"Ready for anything," Charlotte says with a smile. "Come what may."

Author's Note

I first learned about the Harvey Girls and the vast hospitality empire they represented when I was researching transportation options for one of my previous novels, *City of Flickering Light.* It follows three burlesque performers who jump off an eastbound train in Flagstaff, Arizona, so they can try their luck in Hollywood as actors. They catch a westbound train to California, but as it was a long trip, I knew they'd have to eat. How did people traveling long distances by rail get a meal in 1921?

Well, if they were in the Southwest, they were in luck. There was an excellent and reasonably priced restaurant about every hundred miles or so run by a guy named Fred Harvey. As someone who wait-ressed through most of my twenties, the minute I learned about the Harvey Girls, I knew I wanted to write a novel about them.

One of the things that impressed me most about the Fred Harvey Company was that it was far ahead of its time in terms of valuing its female employees. Harvey Girls were well paid, and their contracts provided generous terms for travel (unless they married within the first year of service, and then they were out!).

Opportunity for advancement was also remarkable. Harvey Girls sometimes rose to the post of assistant manager or even man-ager, which was generally unheard of at the time. Alice Steele (the woman who hires Billie and Charlotte in Kansas City) began as a file clerk for the company in 1910 and worked her way up to head of personnel. Mary Jane Colter, a graduate of the California School of Design, was working as a high school industrial arts teacher when she landed a job as an interior designer for the Fred Harvey Company. Her artistic vision and work ethic so impressed Ford and Byron Harvey (Fred's sons, who took the helm upon their father's death in 1901) that she served as chief architect and decorator for the entire company from 1902 to 1948. These two were among the highest-ranking women in corporate America at the time, and they both worked for the same company.

If you'd like to learn more about the history of the Fred Harvey empire, *Appetite for America: Fred Harvey and the Business of Civilizing the Wild West—One Meal at a Time* by Stephen Fried is a comprehensive and truly enjoyable read.

The story of the railroads' western expansion is in and of itself a fascinating story. I was lucky enough to find a copy of *The Atchison, Topeka & Santa Fe Railway System Time Tables, November 1922* hundred-page booklet on eBay and snapped it right up. As a result, virtually all the train travel depicted in the story corresponds with the actual trains, routes, and schedules of the period. (This, by the way, is a prime example of how historical fiction authors spend way too much time and money nerding out on accuracy!)

The Harvey Girl phenomenon was known almost exclusively in the Southwest until *The Harvey Girls*, a musical starring Judy Garland, Angela Lansbury, and Ray Bolger, came out in 1946. It's simplistic and a bit silly, and real Harvey Girls felt it inaccurately portrayed their experiences. But they didn't mind when the song "On the Atchison, Topeka and the Santa Fe" became a huge hit; was covered by multiple artists, including Bing Crosby; and won the Oscar for best song.

Most Harvey Girls were trained in Topeka, so I knew Billie and Charlotte would start there, and it was fun to learn some history about a city that was new to me. Pablocito and his family live in a neighborhood called the Bottoms, which was home to a lively and tight-knit community of mostly Black and Brown people. It no longer exists, thanks to a program of "urban renewal" in the 1950s that razed homes and a nineteenth-century Black church in order to push through industrial parks, new developments, and an extension of I-70. Our Lady of Guadalupe parish, founded by Mexican Americans, does still exist, but the congregation soon outgrew the church on Branner Street that Billie attends with Pablocito, which was built in 1921. The current structure was built in 1947 and sits on NE Chandler.

I had a lot of choices as to where Charlotte and Billie would go next, and I chose El Tovar at the Grand Canyon because, with its awe-inspiring scenery and insular Harvey community, it offered a striking counterpoint to Topeka. (Also, my sister lives in Flagstaff, so it was easy for me to visit her and then pop up to do research. She and I actually spent a night in the El Tovar Suite, and watching the sun rise from the balcony was spectacular!)

I was fairly deep into Billie and Charlotte's first weeks there when I became aware of how the Grand Canyon's designation as a forest reserve in 1893 and then as a national park in 1919 wrought devastation for the Native tribes who had called it home for over a thousand years. The Havasupai, whose traditional lands included Grand Canyon Village where most of the novel takes place, were done incalculable harm by white environmentalists who wanted to "save" the area for use by white travelers.

In 1880, the tribe was confined to a 38,400-acre tract; this was further constricted in 1882 to 518 acres. In 1898 Forest Supervisor W. P. Hermann insisted that the Grand Canyon "should be preserved for the everlasting pleasure and instruction of our intelligent citizens as well as those of foreign countries. Henceforth, I deem it just and necessary to keep the wild and unappreciable Indian from off the Reserve . . ." The entire tribe was then confined to a tiny canyon-bottom reservation of less than one square mile in area.

I dove into learning as much as I could from books and articles on the impact of government policies on Native peoples, but I also needed to know what information would have been available to my characters in 1926. Thus I became an avid reader of George Wharton James, who wrote prolifically about his experiences and deep appreciation for the tribes he spent considerable time with in the early 1900s. He was one of their greatest supporters, vehemently insisting that they had been treated abominably. Yet some of his commentary is quite racist by today's standards.

Fred Harvey's children, particularly Ford and Minnie, were great admirers of Native artwork and each had extensive private collections. Minnie's husband, J. F. Huckel, was the head of the Fred Harvey Indian Department. I'm sure that, like George Wharton James, they felt they were a friend to the tribes in their desire to educate whites about Native American artists and provide a marketplace for their work. They helped to change the concept of the Native peoples from savage warriors to exotic craftsmen—better, but still fairly racist. And let's be honest, it was also a huge draw for Fred Harvey businesses.

I never found any suggestion by anyone that the company cheated or abused the artists, but they certainly fudged some things for publicity's sake. For instance, the daily five o'clock dance outside the Hopi House was performed by southwestern tribal dancers wearing the feather headdresses and fringed leather leggings of the Plains tribes. This was the image European Americans were used to from the movies, and the Fred Harvey Company felt no need to present a more accurate picture. And certainly the Indian Detours crossed the line from promoting tribal arts to intruding on Native culture.

There are few if any accounts of life in northern Arizona in the early 1900s written by Native people themselves without white assistance/intervention. Their languages were oral, not written, and though missionaries started creating phonetic word lists in the 1800s so they could communicate with—and convert—Native Americans, these were not generally used by the tribes themselves.

Hopi Summer, by Carolyn O'Bagy Davis, is based on a treasure trove of letters from Ethel Muchvo, a Hopi woman living in the village of Walpi, Arizona, on First Mesa, to Maud Melville in Massachusetts. They became friends when Maud visited the reservation in 1927, and they corresponded for over a decade. Only Ethel's letters survive, and they are in English. It is a captivating window into her world.

No Turning Back: A True Account of a Hopi Woman's Struggle to Live in Two Worlds by Polingaysi Qoyawayma as told to Vada F. Carlson was published in 1964 when the author was seventy-two. It was fascinating to read about the code-switching she had to do as she moved between the white world and that of her village of Oraibi, Arizona, on Third Mesa. One funny story she tells is about missionaries trying to teach Hopi children the song "Jesus Loves Me," the first line of which is "Jesus loves me, this I know." To them it sounded like "Deso lasmi, desi no," which in their language roughly translates to "The San Juan people are bringing burros," and it made the kids laugh.

Regarding the term Indian: In 1926 both whites and Native Americans communicating with whites used the word. It's a historical novel, so I chose to be historically accurate. By the way, in 2022 (nearly a century after the novel is set!) Indian Garden, where Billie and Robert see the man and woman hoeing and making a basket, was officially renamed Havasupai Gardens.

Astute readers might catch that the building next to El Tovar is called Bright Angel Hotel in the novel, not Lodge as it is now. That's because it was called a hotel from 1907 to 1934, at which point Mary Colter rebuilt and renamed it. The use of the term *hotel* was a stretch, as it mainly consisted of heated tent-cabins and eight guest rooms in the rustic main building. Meals were provided by Fred Harvey, but in a much less grand fashion.

I'm not sure whether Rudolph Valentino ever visited the Grand Canyon, but it's quite possible. It's always been considered a very chic (if you'll pardon the pun) place to go for all manner of famous people, from Einstein to Elvis, Paul McCartney to Beyoncé. Tragically, Valentino died of peritonitis from a ruptured ulcer on August 23, 1926, at the age of thirty-one, so I thought it would be nice to fictionally send him to a beautiful place in the last few months of his life.

If you've read my previous historical novels, you'll recognize Gert and Winnie Turner. (Winnie is Charlotte's friend from college.) The story of their meteoric rise as vaudeville acrobats is told in *The Tumbling Turner Sisters*. Gert then goes to Hollywood and is a secondary character in *City of Flickering Light*, where her marriage to costar Henry Weston is not all it seems . . .

I'll end with this quote about the Grand Canyon from the *Report upon the Colorado River of the West, Explored in 1857 and 1858* by First Lieutenant Joseph Christmas Ives of the US Army Corps of Topographical Engineers. It makes me chuckle every time I read it.

"The region is, of course, altogether valueless. It can be approached only from the south, and after entering it there is nothing to do but leave. Ours has been the first, and will doubtless be the last, party of whites to visit this profitless locality. It seems intended by nature that the Colorado river, along the greater portion of its lonely and majestic way, shall be forever unvisited and undisturbed."

Poor Lieutenant Ives sounds quite annoyed that he was forced to scout such a useless and uninteresting place. The almost five million people who now visit each year might beg to differ!

Acknowledgments

As with most historical fiction, this book took quite a bit of research. In addition to all the books, articles, pictures, visits, etc., there were several people who were truly invaluable in providing information I couldn't have found through the usual sources.

Sean Evans, archivist for the Special Collections and Archives at Cline Library, Northern Arizona University, not only helped me look through their extensive Fred Harvey holdings, but took me in the back room and showed me Mary Jane Colter's original architectural drawings for Bright Angel Lodge. It was so exciting!

When I reached out to Sharla Sitzman Cerra of the Table Rock Historical Society to ask a question about the location of the train depot, she responded with "Boy do I have stuff for you!" And boy, did she. Maryellen Fleming-Hoffman, director of retail at the Grand Canyon Railway & Hotel in Williams, Arizona, took me around the former Fray Marcos Hotel and chatted with me about how much things had changed. Mike Mayron, systems manager at Xanterra (the company that bought Fred Harvey), talked with me about the buildings at Grand Canyon Village, and other tidbits about what life would have been like in the 1920s.

My sister, Kristen Dacey Iwai, not only accompanied me on my main scouting trip to the canyon and stayed overnight with me in the El Tovar Suite, she also helped me track down people who could tell me more and listened to me rattle on endlessly about Fred Harvey minutiae.

Peter Bungart, an anthropologist/archaeologist based in Flagstaff, Arizona, has spent most of his forty-year career working for

Native American tribes in the Grand Canyon area. He was extremely helpful and generous in reading the story and giving me pointers for making it more authentic.

Charlene Bixler, president of the Waynoka Historical Society, which operates the Waynoka Air-Rail Museum and can be found at Waynoka.org, was kind enough to give me permission to use the wonderful picture of real Harvey Girls featured on the interior pages of the book. Though it was taken at the Harvey House in Waynoka, Oklahoma, that lovely curving lunch counter is similar to the one that was in Topeka. By the hairstyles, it looks like it was taken in the 1920s, too. I felt so lucky to find it!

My early readers, including my writing group, provided invaluable feedback on the first draft. Thank you, Cathy Toro-McCue, Megan Lucier, Kristen Iwai, Tom Fay, Randy Susan Meyers, Nichole Bernier, Kathy Crowley, and Liz Moore for all the ways you made the story—and every story—better.

My agent, Stephanie Abou, found the perfect home for this book alongside its "siblings," *The Tumbling Turner Sisters* and *City of Flickering Light* at Gallery Books. Many thanks to publisher Jen Bergstrom for welcoming *The Harvey Girls* back into the fold. Editor Abby Zidle gave thoughtful, probing advice about how to bring it to the next level. Her insights and suggestions really made it shine. (Also, she laughs at all the right places!) Ali Chesnick, Heather Waters, and Abby DeGasperis worked hard to steward this story out into the world. I'm so grateful to all of these smart women for helping Charlotte, Billie, and me put our best feet forward.

My deepest thanks go out to Paul Kuppinger, the father of a dear friend, who has long been a cheerleader of my historical fiction work. For years Paul took it upon himself to search out obscure photographs and articles that were a great help to me. Mostly, he gently urged me to continue working on *The Harvey Girls*, even when I had my doubts about whether I could do it justice. At one point I let it drop for a few years, thinking it would be one of those unfinished projects that writers often have languishing in a drawer or in a long-forgotten computer file. But Paul kept politely asking about it, and I felt I couldn't let him down. When I finally finished, I started reading it to him over the phone, because his vision isn't what it once was. His enthusiasm for the story was incredibly gratifying!

When I met Tom Fay, I was working as a waitress, and he knows better than anyone how I feel about this noble and often under-estimated profession. The man is an over-tipper from way back. He also worked in several restaurant kitchens in his youth, so you could say he was the Leif to my Billie (though we never worked together and are both brunettes of average height). I'm grateful for his life-long generosity of spirit, his delight in feeding people a good meal, and his love.